COSMIC FORCES:

THE PANDORANS

THE PANDORANS

BOOK THREE:
THE OMEGA SEQUENCE

(or
**Amethyst Pyne
In The Absence of Worry
- Brought About By The Belief -
That It All Makes Perfect Sense)**

THE OMEGA SEQUENCE

ALEX JAMES

Author's Note

Several plot elements in this novel rely upon prior knowledge of events in "The Pandorans - Book One: The Pandora Sequence", and "The Pandorans - Book Two: Pandora Inheritance".

Alex James
March 2020

The Pandorans
Book Three: The Omega Sequence

Cover Design and Illustration by Lily McDonnell

Book production by Ingram Spark.

First Paperback Edition 1.5

March 2020
(previously available in very limited edition demo run as second half of 'The Pandora Inheritance')

This book is dedicated to

Julian May

'Good night, Marc.'

THE OMEGA SEQUENCE

PART (.)

HEATHER

CHAPTER 1

The transparent helicopter flying west from Brisbane Airport across the Simpson Desert toward the Munga-Thirri National Park carried a married couple whose minds held the secrets to the existence of life on Earth.

The information that they, their friends, their families, and their company had guarded and studied over the past nine years offered nothing short of a radically altered perspective, perhaps even a new beginning for the human race. It would allow them to fully comprehend their past, to understand their present, and if all went well, place them among the stars.

Their names were Mitchell Pyne and Heather Everett, and despite all that knowledge, or perhaps because of it, they had decided to keep the reality of their situation to themselves.

At least, for the time being.

Until the world calmed down a bit.

You know how it is.

CHAPTER 2

Heather's phone rang.

She was surprised, for a second, to feel the Eve device vibrate in her pocket, but then caught herself; coverage was great everywhere now, even out here, on a helicopter in the middle of the desert. If she ever got bored with the view, which so far was highly unlikely, she was sure she could stream anything she wanted.

She smiled when she saw who was calling, and answered immediately.

'Hi Ames!'

Sitting directly across from her, Mitch sat up, surprised.

Heather smiled back at him knowingly.

Concern for his daughter, nine years now a Field Marshal in the Ymira Rebellion and the War of The Terrastral Territories, was never far beneath the surface for Mitch.

'Where are we?' Heather spoke aloud for Mitch's benefit. 'We're above the Simpson Desert in a see-through helicopter!' Heather's grin broadened. 'Yes, really!' A pause to listen, then: 'We don't really know! We just got to the reserved Cleverco bit of Brisbane Airport and there were fifty of them waiting there for us! Yes, really! Fifty see-through helicopters! Along with half of Cleverco! All these executives and department heads and CEO's and…'

Heather laughed at something her daughter-in-law said.

'Well, that's just it! They're all scared of us and we don't even know who half of them are or what they do! Cleverco might belong to me and your father but it's so enorm now that there's no way for either of us to keep track of everything that's going on, or who's doing it; even if we wanted to!'

Heather noticed something useful on the console beside her.

'Hang on a minute sweetheart…'

Within the small, sleek, insect-like craft, enough of its highly compact outer components were indeed of a high enough percentage of transparency to make all but the passenger-service insides seem completely invisible. Otherwise, just a few basic structural elements; the pilot's instruments and certain metallic parts of the dense engine machinery and rotors, throbbing softly over them, surprisingly small and very few, were plainly visible. Consequently, the ride gave them both a spectacular, near-spherical view of the vast desert as it flashed by below them; and the endless sky, expanding blue above; whilst also having a really good try at creating the fairly convincing illusion that they were genuinely, effortlessly levitating.

Within, Mitch and Heather sat facing each other in the transparent bubble-chairs, Heather with her back to the cockpit. Each had an Eve arm console, as would be expected on a Cleverco craft, and a minibar. Heather fumbled with the translucent slot, then dropped her Eve into the cradle and keyed in a few commands. Amethyst Pyne's face appeared holographically between them, mid-sentence.

' – don't know what press launch you're going to? When it's for your own company?'

Mitch laughed. 'Hi Amy!'

'Hi Dad! Can you see me? I can't see you!'

Heather smiled to herself. 'It's top secret sweetie; you can't see the insanity! We can see you though.'

Mitch grinned at his daughter's image. 'Hey Amy, you know what? It's like a merkabacopter…!'

Heather laughed and grinned her now world-famous smile. Rather than sit with her legs stretched out, as Mitch had, Heather had instantly crossed her legs into the near-invisible bucket seat, which had apparently reminded her husband of the few friends they had who were able to create what they called "merkaba light bodies", which they used to fly around all over the place, cross-legged, somehow wide-aware within deep-state mediation. While the two of them had some incredible metaphysical powers at their disposal, Heather had to confess, neither of them had had quite reached that stage; not yet anyway.

'You look beautiful!'

She knew that Ames never believed her when she told her that, but it was true.

'I just woke up!'

That was clearly true as well.

The head and shoulders of Amethyst Pyne were lying back, propped up on a mound of pillows not-quite the color of her name. Her lush locks of thick, blonde, bed-hair were spread out around her face and shoulders like some kind of indigenous Incan sun-symbol head-dress, and the quilt was tucked tightly under her slender but broad shoulders, with her arms poking out over the top.

Her elaborate, ornately patterned, sword-shaped tattoo, the origins of which remained shrouded in... well, perhaps not in complete mystery, but certainly an element of mysteriousness, was clearly visible down the centre of her right forearm.

Despite being a relatively recent addition to her physicality, the patterns within her body art looked timeless; at once as though they had been summoned from another, nameless era, perhaps from a country everybody had long ago forgotten ever existed, but still unconsciously recalled and loved; while also seeming as though peering into the intricate symbols might open some kind of bio or nano-technical vortex, which would connect you with a personal destiny that you, likewise, had forgotten you always knew, but had always been yours to head toward.

Heather blinked and looked away from the body art, back into Amy's eyes.

Wow; whatever it was, it was really something.

Amy harrumphed; it was something she did.

'Something the matter?' Mitch knew the cue.

Amy grumbled a bit. Even though she was staring into her Eve, right at them, with bleary, sleepy eyes, they were still utterly penetrating; teal-blue, crystal clear and diamond sharp, with the dark, arched eyebrows and long black lashes under her golden mane that apparently required no morning maintenance at all.

She would be twenty-seven soon...

(If she wasn't already, what with all her astral to-ing and fro-ing.)

But in short, even though Amethyst Pyne had just woken up, and had most likely just returned from, and slept off, some kind of intense astral battle, she still looked as though the quilt tucked under her arms was teh top of a strapless evening dress, and that she could quite simply, without any maintenance at all, roll out of bed, and be ready-made, all set to go wherever.

'I woke up and...' Amy yawned. 'Sorry...' She rolled her eyes. 'I had this... weird urge... to call you...?'

She shrugged a smile, quite sweetly, innocently and dreamily, into the phone.

When Amy returned to the Earth plane full-time, Heather knew, she was going to destroy the men of this world, possessing as she did the kind of unassuming beauty that accentuated the angel in angular. She could easily have been an actress, Heather kept telling her, but she had seen too much of how that had affected her limelight-loving mother, Janine, to consider it seriously.

Still... maybe.

Maybe, when things calmed down.

Heather had a feeling; a good feeling about that.

Something there...

But, not yet.

Not now; Amy did not want it now.

Besides, she was in the army, now.

And even though it was the astral army, and she was basically in charge of it all, it was still the army.

Nevertheless, once her business in the astral was over, Amy

would be able to do anything she wanted, and Heather knew that she would. They had spoken of it together at first, then planned it together, and were close to the point of execution now.

There was just one more thing that remained…

One missing element they needed to secure.

And that was almost done.

CHAPTER 3

Heather had watched Amy develop from an awkward, somewhat gangling but entirely adorkable older teen into a slender, almost feline young woman who projected a startling but unassuming confidence that she could now almost, but not quite yet, totally back up.

Although Heather suspected that Amy had yet to fully realise any of this herself, her demeanor contrasted a serious, almost inapproachable countenance with an unexpectedly devastating, disarming smile. Like all the best actresses, Heather had told her, she was mesmerizing when still, yet also highly expressive and delightful to behold when animated. After what they now referred to as her "growth spurt" at around twenty, she was also on the taller side of her gender, but having settled around twenty-two at six foot and one-half inch, on the shorter side of "very tall women".

Whether it all may or may not have had anything to do with the Pandora Sequence itself, or perhaps spending time out, on, over and within the astral plane, had once been hotly debated within their extended Pandoran family, but was now all-but forgotten (without, Bo Everett occasionally still insisted, adequate explanation).

But Amy's most remarked-upon quality, at least, most remarked upon by the few people who had actually met her in person during the past seven years, was something that Heather could see even now more than ever, watching just her head and shoulders on the monitor. You could see she radiated a kind of easygoing grace that was incredibly rare in the young women of her generation, of any generation, and it was something that was going to make her massively sought after when she finally returned to Earth for good (that was, assuming she was ever able).

For some people, a so-called 'normal life' was just not on the cards. So, Heather mused; say, as normal a life as a celebrity daughter of a trillionaire who was a secret astral semi-demi-goddess, or, agent of angels-of-sorts, could ever be expected to have.

Sure, things had been a little rough between herself and Amy at first, but as the years had passed, Heather had at various points graduated from initially being "*that woman*"; to gradually being "okay" after helping her with a dress at a film premiere, seven years ago; to then, after the still-quite-bizarre (to Heather, anyway) events following the near-fatal shooting of a Queen Elizabeth candygram (...) one day in an empty apartment block in Paramatta, four years ago, becoming "friends now"; to finally, solidly, not long after, having helped in an emergency situation, involving one with whom she had once shared mutual-animosity, but who now called Heather her 'unlikely human hot-friend', become the first person Ames called whenever she returned from the astral plane.

The person she now conspired with.

Heather was highly pleased with all that; and also with the fact that Mitch didn't seem to mind that he had been relegated to the second call.

Yes, in that respect, Heather Everett and "The Universe" had chosen her new family well.

'Amy...' Mitch smiled, and gave a little sigh. 'You know we hardly ever attend any of these things. There's too much other stuff to do, and it's always just another version of the Eve, or a new console or phone, or tablet or phablet, or fartlet or wearable whatever, and I barley know how to work the one I've got!'

That was another thing; Heather hadn't quite become accustomed to the fact that her formerly committed technophobe husband... of almost three years now!

Wow, how had that happened?

Three years?

Anyway... her lover of *almost nine years now...* (nine whole years since they had jumped off the end of the pier together, into the dinghy and... into the night!) not only had his own smartphone, but also knew how to use it. And not only that, he seemed to take it with him, almost every day.

Sometimes several times a day!

The fact that it was an Eve model three years out of date, and that he wasn't keeping up with his own company's annual models and semi-annual upgrades, was nothing at all when compared to the fact that Mitch Pyne, the former active luddite, was actually, almost, techno-proficient now.

'This whole company's run by cells of mad recluses, they say!' Heather exclaimed. 'Me and your father almost never go out, Oliver Hines has vanished and most people think Bo Everett is really dead this time, it's been so long since my uncle showed his face in public!'

'Not to mention you, my girl!' Mitch exclaimed proudly. 'Although your hiding away has actually worked out pretty well for the world, in a way.'

'What do you mean?'

'Well, when you first went off, you know we had to create a cover for you?'

'All those African crisis charities?'

'Well, as it happens, they're all doing very well.'

'Really?'

'Well...' Mitch shrugged '...why not?'

Amy grinned. 'It's good to hear your voices.'

Even though she couldn't see her, Heather and Mitch grinned back.

'It's good to actually *see* you, Amy.' Mitch sighed. 'I'm sorry you came back this time too late to join us, it's beautiful out here.'

Heather sometimes wondered if she and Mitch, and Amy, shouldn't show their faces more in public. But they had people now, who steered them toward the events that they were genuinely required, or needed to attend, for whatever Cleverco PR issue that demanded maintenance that week. Consequently, whenever they did appear at one of their company's sub-division launches in person, their constant surprise at what Cleverco was up to, or was coming up with, came paradoxically as no surprise.

Case in point; a fleet of fifty invisible helicopters.

'We tried to turn this one down,' Heather shrugged. 'But we got a message from Uncle Bo saying that we really should attend. It's Cleverco only; no outside press, so it must be something pretty impressive. They won't even tell us what it is they're unveiling, not until we get there; they want it to be a big surprise, apparently.'

'A personal recommendation from Bo Everett.' Amy smirked. She still looked lovely, even when she was smirking. 'When has that ever failed to surprise?'

'Now now,' Heather smirked back.

'How is he?' Amy asked her. 'Is he still playing around up in the *Lady Ann?* I went up and saw him a while back, and had dinner with him and Yelina. I didn't get the impression he was coming down any time soon; he has the spirits of too many old famous people to talk to, in that crazy hotel bar the ship recreated!'

Mitch smiled. 'He can almost get *Lady Ann* to go where he wants now, without skipping forward a month every time he starts it up!'

'He's doing very well,' Heather aired, only lightly defensive.

Mitch scoffed playfully. 'He says that on his next birthday he'll be fully two years younger than his official age with all the time skips he's had! He completely skipped the whole of the last World Series – and all he was trying to do was get there!'

'Yes, yes,' Heather smiled as Amy giggled. 'Well he's promised to leave her stationary over Machu Picchu for now. But he wants us all up there in a few months for our eight-year anniversary of saving the world.' Heather's eyes suddenly widened. 'Oh! And speaking of anniversaries! You'll never guess what I did this morning!'

'You... discovered someone had installed fifty invisible helipads in your back yard and wondered what you were going to do with them all?'

Heather rolled her eyes. 'No! I swallowed my engagement ring!'

Heather raised her hand and waved her ringless finger at Amy. 'See?'

'Well...' Amy took a pause. 'That *was* my next guess...'

'Oh...' Heather remembered. 'You can't see... but it's not there!'

'Let me tell you verbally what you are missing visually; she is waving her ringless finger at you,' Mitch reported glibly.

'It kept pinching my finger; I must have put on weight!'

In the short silence that followed, Heather swore that she could see Amy repress a doubtful frown.

She quickly kept talking.

'I couldn't get it off, so I put it in my mouth and tried to suck it off, and it just...' Heather raised her chin and made a loud, theatrical gulping sound.

'Seriously?' Amy gasped.

'Yeah, so... beat that! I can still feel where it scratched my gullet going down!

'Hear that Amy! She tried to suck off her ring and ended up going down instead!'

Amy couldn't help but laugh at the crude 'Dad joke', as Heather sighed helplessly.

'...well, some things never change...' Amy groaned.

Mitch seemed very pleased with that one.

'Listen you guys; speaking of time slips, how long has it been since my last visit? You know how time...?'

'...works differently in the astral!'

They all said it, simultaneously.

Amy nodded and sighed. 'I say that a lot, huh?'

'We all do,' Heather smiled.

'It's a thing,' Mitch shrugged.

'You and Uncle Bo are just as bad as each other with your hermit reps and temporal challenges!'

'It feels like it's been about a month for me, but when I look at the calendar in Harding's kitchen…'

'How is the old Ent?' Heather demanded.

'Say hi from me!' Mitch added.

'I will; I think he's out playing poker with those screenwriters from the valley. But has it been three weeks? A month?'

'It's been more like three months, sweetie,' Heather corrected. 'And that was just a pop back. It's probably been a year since you came back and properly hung out with us and stayed a while. But we'll be back some time tomorrow, although we'll probably be exhausted. How about we take you out for lunch the day after? How about that? Maybe see if we can't rope Trudy into dinner afterwards, as well? How's it all going anyway?'

Heather eyed Mitch. She knew he hated to think of his daughter at war, but at some point they had agreed, it was always better to know.

'Well, that's the thing I wanted to tell you; I think it's almost done.'

Mitch leaned forward. 'Really, sweetie?'

The relief in his voice surprised Heather; she'd underestimated the extent of the worry he'd been repressing.

'I really think so, Dad! The Draco agreed to a truce, a proper one this time, and so did the Cheneks. Which means all the other Anunnaki clans should back off as well. The Amethyst Palace and the Sea of Humanity are totally stable, and secure. And all the good energy from Cleverco is channeling up there, like a natural flow; like the path of least resistance. Like; the way it was always mean to be…!'

There was a pause.

They held their breath.

' – I really think it's going to work, Dad!'

Heather and Mitch exchanged glances.

'Are you sure sweetie?' Mitch asked. 'It all sounds a bit…'

'Too good to be true?' Amy smiled. 'Look, I know how it sounds. But remember; I've been here for nearly eight years. It's not just overnight. There's a lot I haven't told you. But there's one thing I don't get…'

'What's that Ames?' Heather asked.

'Well…' Amy huffed lightly. 'It's just that; I don't seem to remember anything. ' She paused and shrugged, smiling tightly. 'I mean; I remember all the… braid strokes stuff. Everything I just said. That the war's… over?' It was clear to Heather and Mitch that she was more than a little vague on the matter. 'But I don't seem to remember any… well; I guess - details? Like, actual facts? Just that there's a truce and a retreat. It's quite disconcerting, to be honest.'

Heather looked over at Mitch.

'Sweetie, that's just astral amnesia; you know…?'

'But Heather, I haven't had astral amnesia, not properly, like I used to, since that whole ambush thing in the Paramatta apartments. And when was that? Four years ago now; before you guys got married, even! Ever since then, I've established the connection; built my astral bridge; made the pattern like Suzie and Xylata taught me. I don't get astral amnesia anymore!'

Mitch looked back; he could see that her expression was slightly pained and apologetic.

'Ames, sweetheart… do you remember saying that to me before?'

Amy paused. She frowned deeply.

'No? What…?'

'Ames, do you remember saying to me that when you'd finished doing what you had to do, one day you would come home from the astral and tell us that the war was over; but that you wouldn't remember anything…?'

'What's going on?' Mitch asked, slightly concerned.

'Mitch; you have to trust me. She made me swear not to tell anyone else. It was part of it; she said the future of the human race was on the line.'

'She did?'

'I did?' Amethyst Pyne's pretty face was now screwed up in confusion. 'I…. what did I say; exactly?'

Heather looked over to Mitch, with another pained look.

'Ames, we shouldn't talk any more until we meet in person. We can't gap in public, so don't come out here, okay? There will be too much explaining. Just sit tight and wait for us to get back. We've been talking about this for five years; since Paramatta. You've sworn me to secrecy, even from your father. You made me swear on all our lives. We have a plan, but I need to remind you of what it is in person, and it should – if what you told me is right – make everything clear to you. Okay?'

'I… I guess?' Heather could tell that Amy didn't like it. 'When did you say you'll be back?'

'I don't know how long this Cleverco launch thing will go, but we'll call you, on your private Eve through *Lady Ann*; when we get in. Within twenty-four hours. Okay?'

'Okay…' The confusion remained on her face. 'Are you sure? I really said all that?'

'Many times; especially when it all started. I am fully briefed and prepared; I'll tell you everything you need to know. When we get back, okay? We should end the call now, sweetie. Okay?'

'Okay. I understand. Love you both.'

'You too darling,' Mitch smiled, a little tense.

'Bye now.'

Heather ended the call, and Amethyst Pyne's face vanished. Heather fell back into the chair.

'I didn't expect that today,' she sighed.

'No.'

'I hated lying to her.'

'And so now you have to do the thing.'

'The thing it all depends on. Not just yet. But soon.'

They stared at each other. Mitch shrugged.

'Can we do the other thing first?'

Heather shrugged. 'Sure. Why not?'

Mitch grinned.

This was his favourite thing, hers too.

'I would rather you told me, Hev. I just hope Amy knows

what she's doing.'

'She only told me not to tell you so you wouldn't worry. I mean; I haven't told you anything she told me about the plan. Just that there was one, and it was – good. Right? I mean; Mitch, I love you more than anything, but I couldn't tell you anything else, you know that. That would have been such a betrayal of trust, right at the turning point when me and Ames –'

'It's okay…' Mitch leaning toward her with a comforting smile. 'I understand. I trust you, and I trust Amy, more than anyone else in the entire world. You girls know what you're doing. More than anyone I've ever met, you two have your acts together. Whatever it is… I trust you completely.'

Heather sighed. She had a huge grin.

'That thing we were planning? If you're still up for it, now would be a great time.'

Suddenly the pilot's voice came through the speakers.

'Sorry to interrupt you Mr and Mrs Pyne, just letting you know we'll be touching down at Poeppel Corner in about thirty minutes… hope you've enjoyed the flight.'

Mitch and Heather stared at each other, agog.

'Thirty minutes?' Mitch exclaimed.

There was no response.

Heather raised her fist and rapped her knuckles on the transparent cabin wall behind her.

The pilot's voice came through again. 'Mrs Pyne?'

'It's Everett actually.'

'Please excuse me. I apologize. Mrs Everett, what can I do for you?'

'We kept our names.'

'Yes Mrs Everett, of course.'

'It wasn't my idea – Mitch insisted!'

'It didn't suit her!' Mitch called out. 'Heather Everett – how can you change that name!? It's such a great name! Heather Pyne sounds like a fragrance created by a focus group!'

There was a pause that was slightly too long to be read as

comfortable.

'Of course Mr Pyne.'

Mitch and Heather shrugged at each other.

It wasn't the first time.

Some pilots just didn't do banter.

'Did you say thirty minutes ETA?' Heather asked squarely.

'Yes Mrs Everett.'

Mitch guffawed. 'So we've come *how far* in one hour?'

'About twelve hundred kilometers, sir.'

'So this thing is *see-through*, and flies at *six hundred kpm?*'

'Yes Mr Pyne. I think it can go faster but I was instructed to stay at six.'

'Wow! What kind of chopper is this?!'

'With respect Mr Pyne, I'm not supposed to say.'

'You're not?'

'I think that's a part of it.'

'Part of what?'

'Part of… whatever this is, Mr Pyne. I don't really know. I signed a full disclosure agreement. And to be honest, I don't think I'm even supposed to tell you *that*.'

There was silence again for a few seconds.

'What do they call this place again?' Mitch asked.

'Poeppel Corner.'

'And it's the exact border of South Australia, Queensland and The Northern Territory?'

'Yes. I believe there's a plaque.'

'Okay. Thanks.'

'Not a problem Mister Pyne sir.'

They heard the comm cut out.

Alone again.

'So we … make these?' Mitch asked his wife. 'These… merkabacopters?'

'Merkopters?'

'Helikabas?'

Mitch and Heather looked at each other.

Heather shrugged again. 'You still wanna?'
'Sure. You?'
'Sure.'
Mitch raised his voice again.
'We were told this compartment is secure?'
The comm cut back in.
'That's right Mr Pyne.'
'And you can't see us?'
'No Mister Pyne.'
'Thanks, pilot. Give us a warning, five minutes before?'
'Understood Mr Pyne.'

CHAPTER 4

Heather saw her husband examine her for a second.

It was the dry season in Northern Australia and god damn hot. Or, *bloody hot*, she should say, but never did. Even though she had been attached to an Aussie for almost a decade now, and even had legit dual-nationality as an American-Australian, she could just not get used to saying *bloody*. Something about the American twang just made it sound wrong, particularly with the upper-middle Cali-drawl that emerged as her natural accent. She could still genuinely cringe over the one time she had heard herself attempt it in a television interview.

Still, it bloody was.

It was goddamned hot.

There was air-conditioning, and while the helicopter's minibars had been well-stocked with alcohol and sugar drinks, they were at least half filled with bottles of spring water. And while the plush seats were comfortable, there wasn't overly much to be done about the increasingly intensifying heat.

On the other hand, this worked okay for Heather, and she knew this about herself.

Complimenting her otherwise almost exclusively Celtic genetic heritage, her essentially pale Irish skin tone had a light Mediterranean edge from a lone maternal great-grandmother, which lent her complexion her a distinctive beauty and looked great in the sun, with a light sweat.

Also, while she and Mitch had met on the day that she had decided to shave her dreadlocks down to a number three cut, she had since decided to re-grow her straight, thick, dark chocolate brown hair down to chest-length. This also looked great on her.

For the Cleverco elite press launch she had chosen to wear

a light, calf-length sleeveless dress with a draping neckline, tied tightly at the waist, along with high-laced Romanesque sandals. Her dress was cotton; it was full and breathed, and was ochre-orange, almost the exact color of the desert below, and with the light layer of perspiration that had formed over her, popped to make her hair and skin impossibly radiant.

When they'd boarded the helicopter, Heather had also been wearing a complimentary dark-apricot underwear ensemble with her desert dress. But about three quarters of an hour into the flight she had slunk her arms back into the billowy cotton dress and removed the bra, then ten minutes later had stated 'fuck it' and snapped off the panties. The matching lingerie was now sitting on her apricot shoulder bag, under her seat, upon which she remained cross-legged, along with her wide brimmed apricot 'ladies day' hat.

Mitch too had disrobed for the heat.

Early on in his new life as a trillionaire executive, when he had realised that he would be forced to attend 'things', he had, as he'd put it, 'done an Einstein'. He had spent a week, on and off, thinking about which clothes he really liked, given that he was now immensely wealthy and could pretty much afford anything. He had then arranged some fittings, because as Heather told him 'you can do that when you're rich' at some of the swankier men's clothing providers in New York, to narrow down which of the sets and styles of men's clothing that he thought he genuinely liked, that actually looked good on him, that he thought he might buy. These selections were then narrowed down again, based on Heather's approval, as she was the one who would be seeing him the most.

In the end, it turned out that Mitch both liked, and looked good in, what he referred to as a 'Reservoir Dogs Suit'; albeit a very high and immaculately well-tailored version of such a thing. So Heather had bought Mitch three each of four versions of the suit, one for each season, along with matching longer jackets, coats and overcoats. She had also purchased white shirts and black ties to go with the suits, and corresponding black shoes, and black sneakers, for all occasions.

Mitch called this his costume, and since then had almost never been seen, even in private, wearing in anything else.

His decision had paid off; so far as Heather was concerned. He'd totally pulled off the look, and to his own satisfaction was forevermore in the public eye labeled and solidified as 'that person', which made managing his public profile a lot easier. He was even referred to by some of the tabloid publications as 'The Pyne Dog', which secretly pleased him to no end. To top it off, as was Einstein's original notion, he never again had to expend wasteful daily thoughts on what he was going to wear.

Whatever made him happy, Heather figured.

Accordingly, Mitch's black linen suit, number one in his suit rotation, had been broken out of storage given that Sydney was in midwinter, and now sat folded on his carry bag as he sweated it out, albeit lightly, in black boxer shorts and an unbuttoned white cotton shirt.

'So we're really going to do this?' Mitch asked.

Heather nodded to herself as she continued to stare out at the desert. 'I don't see why not, dearest; we said, if we could – flying above the Simpson. We haven't done that yet.' She hummed to herself. 'So, let's do it.'

The dress came off in one fluid movement and was on the floor at her feet before Mitch had his boxers off. She pushed his shirt back over his shoulders as he slid down the chair and she was on his lap so quickly and with such anxious momentum that their tongues slammed weirdly together as they went to kiss.

It was like a teenage dare, Heather thought, and her heart was racing.

Then, without trying and without shame, with a lot of energy and a surprising amount of space, they were having sex in a transparent helicopter, high above the Simpson Desert, well on their way to who knows where.

CHAPTER 5

Theirs had been the first of the transparent helicopters to take off from Brisbane, but they knew there were potentially dozens of other identical vehicles somewhere behind them; then again, given their odd transparency, they could really have been anywhere; even headed off in fifty completely different directions. They doubted that anyone had seen them and if they had, they didn't care.

After they'd done it, Heather sat back, feeling foolishly but wickedly naughty, happily contended and totally chilled out. She stared out again and found that she could barely break her gaze now. So totally captivated was she as they soared, impossibly smoothly, over the Simpson Desert, as the seemingly endless, massively intimidating expanse flowed past below in an almost uniform shade of deep and surprisingly bright orange-ochre, so much more vivid than the pictures she'd sourced to match her dress with, that time seemed almost not to exist. This was indeed a timeless landscape; one that was indisputably stunning and immediately mesmerizing, and although at first apparently stark, soon revealed itself to be decorated with the occasional, random sprouts of deep olive desert foliage, and punctuated by rising scar-tissued slashes of dark brown rock.

She quite consistently couldn't believe her eyes.

'I still can't believe I swallowed my engagement ring,' Heather heard herself utter.

'It's not lost forever…' Mitch smiled.

'Don't – even.'

She saw Mitch smile a little more, but only to himself.

It sometimes came as something of a surprise to her, how much she loved him.

Heather settled back again, and marveled again, both at the passing landscape at the speed the pilot had reported.

She'd flown on a number of helicopters before; she'd been an espionage agent for her uncle before he had bequeathed her his company, before she had fallen for and married Mitch, but never anything like this.

It was so quiet inside the compartment.

They'd barely needed to raise their voices to hear each other clearly all this time, so the noise reduction system was clearly first rate. And whatever the transparent walls were made of, they seemed to almost completely block the sound of the engine and rotors above them; plus, it was clearly one of those relatively recent jobs that had no tail rotor, which also cut down the noise. And the interior; just the two plush bucket passenger seats and the consoles, made the ride seem more like that of a first class airline than the rough flights aboard the few intolerably loud and cramped helicopters she'd previously endured.

Still, Mitch was a former film critic who still spent a lot of his leisure time sitting on a couch, feet up, and who generally enjoyed viewing marathons. He had therefore wriggled and smiled sarcastically as they'd first settled in.

'Leg room's amazing…!'

'Cleverco.' Heather had grinned, her best commercially appreciated grin. 'First world problems; are the first thing take care of.'

They'd laughed at that for quite some time.

CHAPTER 6

Mitch and Heather's company, which had been given to them as a wedding present, had at the time been called Lever, a portmanteau of two companies, one named Olivera, which had been owned by Oliver Hines, and another named Everco, which had been owned by Heather's uncle, Bo Everett.

But Lever had now, at the behest of first Amy, then Heather, had been renamed Cleverco.

Everybody seemed to like that name much better.

It was far less sinister, they all said.

Heather had heartily agreed.

Her life had changed radically since she had met and married Mitch, under the most extraordinary circumstances that probably most people could not even begin to imagine. And yet, somehow they had met, they had fallen in love, and they had married, under those incredible circumstances.

More than four years ago now, she and Mitch had quit drinking, and two years ago he had quit smoking. Now, looking at him, he was as fit and healthy a human specimen as any forty-two-year-old man with a healthy love of rich food and boutique soft drinks could be. He had also become almost as famous as his uncle-in-law, Bo Everett, who was pretty much, after the same series of extraordinary events, including being accused and quickly acquitted of faking his own death, now the most famous billionaire in the world.

And Heather loved Mitch more than any man she had ever loved; more than her first high school crush, more than Holland Pankhurst, more than anyone.

Heather was nine years younger than her husband and in much better shape; her espionage background had left her in good physical condition and since retiring from that world due to her newly acquired position in the public spotlight, she had worked hard not to lose her fitness, or figure.

Before they'd been formally introduced, Mitch had been a surveillance job for Heather, and she had fallen for him at first out of pity, as she had watched him drink himself to sleep every night, working a job he hated. When they had first met, Mitch had been infatuated by another woman, and had taken a few days to come round to the fact that he had stumbled into something rare and special. (His description, even if she did say so herself.) Things had developed, essentially in the 'happily ever after' mode, from there onwards, and basically, nine years later, Mitch and Heather were still fortunate enough to remain totally hot for each other.

Mitch and Heather usually made their "bonking dares" last quite a while; after all, why not? Both of them had little tricks and moves that they saved up and brought out at opportune times, erotic gestures that were afforded to them by their unique psychic states. So to compress all that down to under fifteen minutes, as they sometimes found themselves having to do on such dares, could be, if done right, at once exciting, challenging, demanding, and exhilarating.

They'd had sex in some odd places, Heather found herself briefly reminiscing as they changes positions around the five minute mark, but this one was pretty damn good.

One to freak the grandkids out with.

Heather looked across at him now and he looked back. She remained cross-legged but was now totally nude, and glowing, her breasts vibrating slightly to the blades of the craft, giving her an extra feeling of massage-like pleasure that added to her usual sense of post-orgasmic afterglow. They exchanged a quick look in which each told the other how totally naughty they thought they'd just been, then she once again resumed her vigil over the endless sands below.

This was supposed to be a posh do, after all.

'Five minutes,' said the pilot, not long after, and they quickly redressed.

Mitch had been very public, almost giddy, about informing the press that it had been Heather's unusual but gorgeous downward-pointing triangular smile that had first caught his attention. Heather had never given a moment's thought to the shape of her smile until then, but even now, well into her thirties, multi-million dollar offers to promote major cosmetics lines were still on the table, despite the fact that she was the face of Regene, their own genetic-cosmetics line. Heather had essentially seen no problem with embracing the idea that she had a world-class smile, given that she was indeed very happy most of the time, and had no problems using the smile every time the paparazzi were around. So far as she was concerned, if her genuine smile bought Cleverco lots of free press, and provided her company with a public face that, according to their marketing department, tested through the roof, then so be it.

And it had been that knowledge that had subsequently given her, and Amy, and their friend Xylata, the idea… the idea that was going to be executed, for real now.

She shivered a bit.

Was Amy really up to it?

Could they really go through with it?

CHAPTER 7

Retirement from being an active field agent in the industrial spy game had at first made Heather extremely restless. It had not been long however before she realised that she now had full access to almost unlimited wealth, and truly had no small amount of power and influence at her disposal. As she was not a psychopath, as were most of the people who were able to honestly state the same set of criteria about themselves, she realised that she should use that pent up energy to set to work and right the world's wrongs.

After some time attempting this, and with the cooperation of her husband, Heather had started to realise that corporate laws, in general, were made by psychopaths, for the use of psychopaths, to practice the art of psychopathery.

It was a good thing, they both realised fairly quickly after that, that the two of them were essentially super beings with spectacular metaphysical powers to match their wealth and influence.

Still, despite even that, and all the good, if somewhat clandestine work they had done throughout the second decade of the twenty-first century, and despite some of that good work being resisted or blocked or hampered or sometimes even reversed by what they and their company of friends would think of as 'the forces of darkness, if not outright evil', they still hadn't saved the world. They were, therefore, every now and obliged, if not forced, to do something normal; normal, in a normal fashion, to persuade people that they and Cleverco at large were in no way part of those aforementioned 'forces of evil', and were in fact...

...normal.

(Which they were not; they were not even remotely 'normal'.)

So now, here they were, landing in an invisible helicopter,

attending a large press junket for the high profile unveiling of a new technological breakthrough from a company they both owned, but felt unable, in the end, to keep track of.

All perfectly normal, move along now; nothing to see here.

CHAPTER 8

The sand wasn't as soft underfoot as it had looked from behind glass, but once you found a rhythm it was easy to get a foothold and walk around.

Also, the ground looked very different to the impression she'd gained from the air; it was anything but flat, with small rises and dips all around them, long, undulating sand-hills stretching away and across from their middle-ground, and wide sand-ridges extended out further – as far as they could see.

Of course, Heather realised, they were probably standing in one of those ridges right now, or they might look as though they were on a rise, if viewed from almost any other direction; that was just scale and perspective, just how things looked different from a distance versus up close. In some ways, she mused, it was like a giant ochre-orange ocean, frozen in time, and yet again, she knew it wasn't frozen, that all the sand was moving ever so slowly, crawling and weaving and encroaching with the wind.

Not that there was much of a breeze about now...

It was still, and dry, and yes; *god damn hot*.

There were more shrubs around than had been apparent from the air, and tufts of tough-looking weed and grass patched everywhere. Nearby stood a string of tight and gnarly trees that she wanted to call mallees, or maybe coolabah gums; maybe some of both, but she wasn't sure. There was a line of them across the nearest sandy ridge. Nearby that, a wooden walkway that led up to a small monument. In fact, there were three wood-slatted walkways leading up to the monument, one each, she assumed, along the separate border divisions of the two states and one territory.

Mitch and Heather walked, each via their own rhythm across

the sand, up to the edge of the nearest wooden walkway, then approached the monument across the groaning but sturdy-slatted path.

When they reached the monument, it turned out to be an iron disc, sitting flat upon an cylindrical concrete column about a meter high, with raised markings and writing indicating the three borders; South Australia on one half, and Queensland and the Northern Territory divided into equal quarters on the other.

'Well that's a sight to see,' Heather uttered. Then she looked around. 'What do we do now?'

Mitch sighed. 'If she's really back for good, maybe I should ask Amy to come along with us a bit more now? I really enjoy it when she's home. It's just, I…'

Heather looked at him.

She didn't often see him like this.

Not genuinely worried.

Hardly at all since their wedding day.

Mitch shrugged. 'I'm too scared of what she'll tell me. But I wish she would come and see us more often.'

Heather smiled. She understood. 'She spends time with us when she can. At least she hasn't disowned us like poor Jade.'

Mitch sighed and shrugged. 'Yes. But Jade will come round. I'm sure of it. She's different. She's…' He smiled, fondly but with visible concern. 'Jadey wears her passion like jewelry. It's not easy to see her like that, online and desperate for attention all the time, but as least I understand it. Amy is… she's a lot more sensitive than she's aware, but she buries it. And if what we've heard is true, she's had her heart broken more than once already…'

'Let's not go there again, baby. Huh? We don't know anything, not for sure. What Amy is doing, it's important. And look, maybe she's right – maybe it is all about to change?'

'The last time she told me what was happening in the clan wars…'

'Mitch, baby, really, she can handle herself, don't worry.'

'Can she?'

'She's the only human we know of who can fight off the Anunnaki at length, on their own turf, at their own game, at the same time wrangling all the other *humans* who've joined her, and the *Ymira Alliance* at the same time. And by all accounts, she's all but invincible. She's made it clear that she doesn't want us in there with her, or Uncle Bo. And you know that Suzie checks in with me, right?'

'Suzie Saturn?'

'No, Suzie Quatro; *of course Suzie Saturn!*'

'Oh…'

'…Trudy's out there with her, too; and our old pal Mendoza. Maybe even Pan himself…'

'Really?'

'Look, from what she's told me…'

Mitch threw her a look that said; be careful.

Heather knew; it was bad enough she'd told him there was something going on, after Amy had sworn her to secrecy.

'Mitch, it sounds as though the clans have finally figured out that they can't defeat them, or her, and they've all reached some kind of truce. That's what it sounds like to me. Okay?'

Mitch nodded to himself, but she could tell he didn't quite believe it as he looked out at the vast ochre expanse, hoping for something to take his mind off his astral warrior daughter.

'I don't like coming out here – it's Anunnaki Heaven.' He scowled childishly. 'There could be more of those massive dimensional gaps, like there were in the Mojave. How do we know we're not standing right on top of another clan treasure trove, or safe house? What if a thousand Chenek warriors come blasting through?'

Heather sighed. 'Mitch, that's not going to happen. Not in broad daylight. All that shit stays in fourth density; even they aren't bold enough to… why are we even talking about this out here?'

Mitch mumbled something.

Several more helicopters were coming in to land.

As helicopters went, they were fairly quiet, especially considering there were at least ten of them in the immediate vicinity. But they weren't truly invisible; from outside, the rotors looked larger, and the light caught the glass-like exterior at all angles.

'Bloody impressive though…' Mitch uttered to her.

A flash caught Heather's periphery and she looked up; out and across, past the rise. She thought she could see the glint of the sun on more of them, sparkling against the brilliant blue sky, coming in.

Then again, she also thought that she could see the same out on the horizon.

A flash of light.

Who knew what optical tricks the desert played?

'Did you see that?' Mitch asked.

Heather wondered if he'd meant the same thing; the glint on the horizon.

Odd. But she thought it better to be quiet, not to make his anxiety worse.

'I need to calm down,' Mitch sighed.

Heather laughed, lightly, and kissed him.

'You're a good father, Mitchell Pyne.'

'Cooh-eeh!'

The helicopters were doing their best to land at a fair distance from each other, sparing the people already on the ground the plumes of sand they generated as they came down. Nobody was getting out of their own until the rotors stopped spinning.

Out of the first helicopter that had landed stepped Shandi Strand, Cleverco's Public Relations Executive. Knowing Shandi, she had been the one to ensure that the precise landing distance between each chopper had been calculated to minimize the blowup. Sure enough, she headed straight toward them with an Eve tablet tucked securely under one arm, and her good shoes dangling from her other hand.

'Hello important celebrities!' Shandi cried out, waving her

shoes.

'I actually kind of like her,' Heather uttered.

'We both do,' Mitch smiled. 'That's why we hired her. And at least there will be someone here who isn't kissing our arses all day.'

Shandi reached them and huffed. She pulled a small bottle of water from the trouser pocket of her white linen pant suit and offered it to them before cracking the lid off and swigging.

'Stole it from inside the little insect. In case that Humphries woman screws up and leaves us all out here to dehydrate to death.'

She gulped and gasped.

'Do you know what's going on?' Heather asked.

'Don't you?' Shandi seemed surprised. 'Nice outfit by the way. Did you intend to put that underwear back on?'

Heather swore heavily.

'Don't worry sweetheart, we all did it.'

Mitch laughed. 'Bo told us to come. He didn't say what it was and there was nothing on the invite; just more marketing bullshit about Another Cleverco Game Changer.'

'Right. Well, whatever it is, this is all down to Humphries and her department; I thought it was those horrible little helicopters but apparently that's not the main show. Terrific for sightseeing and tourism though; they should walk off on their own. Or fly off, I should say. Up, up, ever up, just like Cleverco-Aero stock once we reveal them!'

The little glass helicopters were landing and depositing their passengers quite rapidly now; there were maybe seventy people standing out in the middle of the desert, if Mitch's quick head count was correct, like lost souls.

Some were clustering around the helicopters as they powered-down, but none were coming over.

'That's interesting,' Shandi said, looking across at the groups. 'She's invited Davinia Hines; she controls what was left of the Olivera hotel chain after the deal with your uncle. She's his step-sister, same father I think; they never got along but he kept all his hotels out of the deal and gave them to her, and now they're at least on speaking terms. Rumor has it she and Rio DeVora are a thing; Davinia Hines was there when that total uber-bitch Rio DeVora ambushed lovely Amethyst in that hotel room, in Paramatta of all places, and tried to get her to make an alliance with their new business cabal. I wonder if Humphries knows *that*…?'

Mitch and Heather exchanged glances.

'Ye-es; I'm afraid word got around about that…' Shandi uttered, still staring into the general distance. '…but not very far around. That *is* why you pay me, after all.'

'Do we pay you enough…?' Mitch smiled nervously.

'Since that day, Mister Everett and I have come to a very satisfactory arrangement, and besides…'

Shandi smiled at them both, beaming.

'It's all for the best cause; and we all like each other!'

Mitch and Heather could not help smile back.

'So…' Despite the mutual good vibes, Mitch tried to edge the topic away. 'By *thing*… you mean…?'

'By thing, I mean, a bi thing. Bee – eye. Davinia has three kids by three different fathers, all billionaires, but nothing of her own. Not like any of her contemporaries anyway. You know what they say about bloodlines and the wealthy.' She looked at Mitch and squeezed his arm. 'Always nice to get some new genes in!' She winked. 'Then again, that's what they said about Princess Diana!'

'Bloody hell Shandi!' Mitch half-laughed, half-gasped.

She waved her hand dismissively.

'Oh yes Mitch, we've brought the whole company out here to watch you being ritually sacrificed; Bohemian Grove was booked!'

Mitch's jaw dropped. 'Steady on!'

He was still laughing though.

Shandi released his arm with a huge grin.

'You're so easy, Mitchell Pyne!'

Heather had been listening, but she has also been watching Davinia Hines from a distance, like a desert coyote.

'We've never met,' Heather told her. 'By all accounts she had nothing to do with it... but still.'

'Do you want to?' Shandi asked. 'We might be out here a while. Might get awkward?'

Neither Mitch nor Heather had time to formulate a response. People were pointing at them now, as though they'd just figured out who they were. Or rather, Heather quickly reassessed, people were pointing in their general direction – to something behind them. They turned about to see that there was a wide arch above the closest major dune, like the entrance to some kind of theme park.

'Was that there before?' Heather asked.

'I...' Mitch stumbled. 'I don't know.'

Heather answered herself. 'I don't think that was there before...'

'Game changer...' Shandi uttered, sounding not entirely at ease.

'Better look like we were expecting it,' Mitch mumbled. Heather put on her wide-brimmed ladies-day sun-hat and mumbled at Shandi. 'When the hell am I going to put this underwear back on?'

Shandi shrugged. 'Everyone looks at your smile dear. Just keep smiling, and no-one will know.'

With that, the trio turned and departed, leading the way toward the top of the low rise, parallel to the tree line, heading as best they could for the strange monument.

One by one as the helicopters stopped, and the passengers disembarked, and they all vanished over the rise, toward the glowing arc, leaving the little plaque at Poeppel's Corner as quiet as it had been not an hour before.

It was a while though, before the screaming started.

THE OMEGA SEQUENCE

PART ONE

THYS

CHAPTER 9

Ritual.

They have to tell you what they're going to do.

They tell you within the cultural mosaic, and make it seem – through our heroes and fantasies – that the threat has been overcome.

But that is the fantasy.

The threat remains real.

CHAPTER 10

Thys Pyne lay back.

Back on the Earth Plane.

She'd stretched upon arrival.

Just those normal, unconscious unfoldings; the biological systems checks, wake-ups and restarts. But now she had finished the call with her Dad and Heather, she really stretched. Arms right out to the sides of the bed, tip toes to the bottom of the bed, back arched and neck stretching, and a noise like Miss Piggy.

'Heeeeiiiiiiiii – yuh!'

Then she snapped back to normal size, and huffed.

She blinked forcefully and assessed the dryness of her mouth.

There was an empty glass by her bed.

That was why she needed to pee so bad.

She thought of her friend, Suzie Saturn, who had laid back for years and years in a black starcophagus; a comatose rocker, until she had awoken to help Thys navigate her new life on the astral plane.

Back then, everyone had thought Suzie was dead.

Thys was that age now; twenty-seven. The age at which all the cool rock stars from the sixties and seventies had died.

Burned out, not faded away.

But, fuck all that; she had to get on with stuff.

And not that, she also needed coffee.

As she swung her long legs over the side of the huge bed, but still lay with the rest of her body flat out on the bed, she thought of her Aunt Saph, who still, after even more years now, slumbered beside her lover Holland Pankhurst in the second starcophagus.

She thought of going to visit them again, up in *Lady Ann*.

To also see Bo Everett and his honest-to-Gaia Earth Goddess

wife, Yelina.

Thys mused a second.

She could remember all that; her life, her crazy existence, back here in Third Density. Her ordinary human life on Planet Earth to almost everybody else.

But she could not remember...

Uh!

Astral amnesia.

She could not remember the war.

Or, well; that was not exactly true. She could remember there had been a war; she could remember all the business around the The Pandora Sequence that had started the war; she could remember The Intersection (she had been there a few times since that first time, when the Pandora Arcana had been stolen); she could remember all the business with Rio DeVora's conclave (trap) at Paramatta; that crazy-bastard demi-ego-god *Gordian* and the four elements who had pulled her apart...

...she remembered something very dark and else that was conversely electric and alive;

...she remembered The Realma...

but upon that...

most of all;

poor lonely Zyxzi did not dwell

– and The Amethyst Palace; The Sea of Humanity; *thesilverbluemoonroon*; and all of the battles she had fought with her loyal crew; Suzie Saturn and Field Marshall Xylata and their gang of Ymira.

So, she could remember, at least, everything up to...

Huh.

The last time she was attacked here, on the Earth Plane.

(Or... no; it had happened again since, hadn't it...?)

But... not the last chunk of time (which was always different) in the astral.

Remembering that the war was ended... but not how.

She probably just needed a break. It would all come back to

her once she... just jump-started her life here on the Earth Plane again.

The war was...

Her Eve beeped.

But her life was not.

The message had come through the app as soon as Thys had ended the call with Heather and Mitch.

Or was she Amy now, formally, back here?

On Earth…

…the Earth Plane.

…third density, 3D; the 'third dimension'.

Mystically speaking.

Mystically reading, she read the text again and sighed.

So he was still active, and the app was still working, still sending his fan club (or his fan base, or mailing list, or whatever he wanted to call them; 'followers', sometimes, or even worse, occasionally, 'friends') these random, mystical/conspiratorial reminders.

She wondered why the hell she had let herself download the Zaq Qwerty app in the first place, ignored it and pushed the extra pillows aside.

Then she lay back, remembering the recent conversation, and smiled at the realisation of how much she had come to love both Heather, whom she'd initially hated, and her once-estranged father, whom for many years she'd resented and ignored.

Wow.

Had she really been like that?

Even though she and Heather had experienced a somewhat and even literally rocky start, they loved each other now. Now, she wasn't so much a step-mother as a really-cool older-friend who just happened to be married-to-her-father.

When Thys had awoken to her first morning on the Earth plane in some time, she had found her Eve under her pillow, right where she'd left it, probably months ago now. The first thing she'd done, almost instantly, was to call Heather, and by proxy her Dad.

She hardly ever did that; she almost never looked at her phone that fast.

Some… urge.

She'd told them that, hadn't she?

She couldn't remember it that clearly now.

Whatever normal dream she'd had was slipping away, as dreams did on the Earth plane. Since she'd sorted her new life, her new sleeping pattern, years ago above an astral jungle with Suzie, she had spent almost every night since, most of her adult life, on the astral plane, dreaming properly. It was only when she'd a real break, a real gap in hostilities, that she liked, every now and then, to come back down to Earth and just… sleep, and dream, and forget.

…to dream on the plane on which she was born.

Like a normal person, a normal human.

And so, when she'd awoken this morning, naturally, after a natural dream that she had naturally soon forgotten, Thys had been pleased to find herself here, in what most people would consider 'the real world'.

Although, paradoxically, she had found herself waking in Hollywood.

That is, she had awoken in her bedroom at The Fork, also known cheekily now as "Harding's Hollywood Pad", on Mulholland Drive, above Los Angeles.

That was okay.

When she came home, still a bit groggy, and consequently wasn't quite ready to face actual home; not Mum and Saxe (did she still…? were they still…?); or Dad and Heather home, Harding's Pad was where she wanted to be. It was her home away from home…or, home between homes… or; something.

Wow, she was… pretty groggy…

The Fork had in fact been, up until about fifteen years ago, the home of an almost unbroken line of major producers for major movie studios, along with the odd name director, and even a bone fide movie star or two. But it was now owned by the

South African mercenary to whom her father owed his life, not to mention his sanity, and perhaps even his soul; and definitely those of his eldest daughter as well.

Mitch Pyne, via Cleverco, now paid Harding one hundred thousand dollars a month to act as a security consultant for his daughter, whenever she elected to reside in third density space.

Not that Thys Pyne needed it really; she was, after all, almost some kind of mystical superhero

(...which she would be pressed to admit, in her very-least-self-conscious moments).

But it made Mitch feel good, and it also gave her someone to hang out with, to whom no explanations were required, and who knew the score, absolutely.

In the past nine years, Thys had come and gone from third density to fourth, from the Earth plane to the astral plane and back again, with a kind of random regularity.

She had been making a bridge, making her path stable, creating a continuity between dimensions that would allow time, or at least her perception of time... or maybe, even, Time's percetion of Her, to flow in a more consistently navigable manner.

And it had worked.

Just as Suzie and Xylata had said it would.

Sometimes she had returned home for a few weeks, sometimes for a few days, but other times only half days, or occasionally just for a few hours at a time. Sometimes it had been mere minutes, panicked and desperate, searching for a solution, for advice, or just for normal human headspace; whatever, but the more she did it, the more it all started to make sense. To flow with a normal passge of events and immediate linear-conscious understanding of them.

And Harding had always come through for her in that regard. He had always been there. Harding had sworn to her that he would do it anyway, protect her wherever she went, regardless of the money her father paid. And now, somehow because of all that, they had become friends; she had her own room in his

Hollywood Pad, and her own key to the front door.

Not that she ever used or ever really needed one.

But it was a symbol, and she appreciated that.

Mi casa, es su casa.

Of course, she had her own place as well.

Secluded, "occulted" really, up within the Northern Beaches of Sydney.

Not to mention her own Pala... *place* in the astral.

But right from the start of the arrangement, which had been right at point when the war had really kicked in, whenever she had 'come back down' (as they had come to refer to it) from the astral to Earth, she had found herself arriving at Harding's Pad first.

Now, it felt like home base.

This bedroom, the room where she woke every time she came back down, was like an astral decompression chamber; a nice buffer between worlds, between Thys and Amy.

Furthermore, The Fork itself was like a debriefing station; once she woke and stretched and showered and dressed, the huge old house was somewhere she could wander around, reacclimatize, and nobody would bother her unless she wanted them to; although *really*, nobody but Harding ever knew she was there, unless she told them.

Which she never did.

Anyway, after that, after waking and debriefing and perhaps a stroll down Mulholland, wherever she went on Earth after that, Harding came too.

CHAPTER 11

It was just something that she couldn't help.

Whenever she returned, with her random regularity, from her escalating war...

She just didn't always want to see friends and family straight away. Nor did she always want to go straight back to Omega Cove, all alone with the ocean view. That was fine, that was what she wanted a lot of the time, to be alone, to decompress and unpack everything that had happened to her in the astral, to chill and watch movies and binge a few of those epic series people raved about.

Maybe even read a book!

At least a trade comic or two.

But not always straight away.

'Home base...'

Thys heard herself speak softly to herself.

'...then home.'

And Thys had especially not wanted to return home this time, not immediately, because...

She could hardly think it...

But, because...

...

...*thewarwasover.*

Uh!

She could hardly even think it!

...*over!*

At least, she kept telling herself, as though hedging her bets, as though not wanting to jinx it...

...he largest part of it was done.

Her war, at least.

The war in the astral dimension, in fourth density, to secure humanity its rightful turf there, was for the time being...

Done.

(Done?)

And that fact...

...needed time...

...to...

...sink in.

...yeah.

Indeed, that territory, the territory she and her allies had secured out there, also needed time.

Time also to sink in.

And so, while she could, she thought she just might.

Sink back in...

...herself.

Back into the bed, and…

Just…

CHAPTER 12

But she found now that she couldn't.

Her mind had passed the point.

It had been activated and wanted to think.

She sat up a bit more.

'Might as well let it…'

She felt resigned to that.

So.

When she'd told Heather about the war being over, she could tell that Heather didn't really believe her. Not fully. Mainly because, Thys had to admit…

'…I'm not sure I really believe it myself…'

She couldn't even really remember it herself, so how *could* she fully believe it?

And what had Heather meant?

'…a plan…?'

She sat up fully and pushed her hair back.

It was all-over.

She hadn't been drunk, but she had swigged back a couple of Ymira drinks. She hardly ever did that; but…

The end of the war and all that, she supposed…?

But the drinks had only made her exhausted, and so she hadn't tied her hair back before she'd slept.

So now it was everywhere, and tangled, with knots.

Like her mind; her mind grumbled.

There really was a plan?

She guessed she would find out soon enough, when Heather and Mitch got back; probably sometime this afternoon, USA time. But she didn't like that she couldn't remember.

Slowly though, she remembered more of the night before;

returning through the wardrobe into her room, undressing and collapsing on the bed, and before that... yes, celebrating with her friends in the astral.

There was probably opal everywhere by now, here in her Hollywood room.

Right throughout The Fork, no doubt.

But after that, not much else.

Now she was naked in the bed, and her clothes were in a pile on the floor, and she had to assume that she had something of a hangover.

Ymira shots were potent.

And blue.

In fact, they were *very potent,* and *very blue.*

They were... Bloop.

But... she hadn't had that much Bloop last night.

She might have mixed it with FzzLzzWzz...?

Maybe.

She didn't really drink anymore; so that didn't really make sense.

She thought again.

So far as she recalled now... the truce with the Draco and the Chenek clans had taken a long time to arrange. They had, in the end, played a long diplomatic game, with the final pieces falling either gently into place or peacefully off the side of the board over the past few... weeks, she supposed.

Time did, after all, work differently in the astral.

There had been no giant party, no astral VE-Day or anything amongst her friends, human or Anunnaki, forest chrome or desert chrome, in the Ymira clan's allied forces. She'd just had a drink with her fellow Field Marshall, and their trusted lieutenants... and come back down to third-density Earth.

Now where was *she?*

Where the hell was her fellow Field Marshall?

'Xylata!'

She sometimes came with her, went out and played poker with

Harding, or headed out to Los Angeles to see some old friends. Once time she had awoken to find her friend out on the balcony of her room, smoking a cigarette like some old Hollywood star, only to discover she had adopted the body of a nineteen-year-old Lauren Bacall.

'Xylata?'

Nothing.

'Harding!'

Neither of them.

The Fork was a big house with big rooms; a thirties house from the golden age of Hollywood, designed at once to impress and welcome guests; but also to instil a sense of comfort within the permanent residents, reminding them of their personal stature in an industry built on an enormous wealth of egos.

No other egos here, it seemed.

A slight echo, perhaps; then the house returned to silence for a second.

Then, beside the bed, the wardrobe creaked.

Still laying prone on the bed, Thys froze solid for a few seconds.

Then she ignored it.

Old houses.

Wooden furniture.

Hot weather.

She shook her head.

Anxiety was creeping in.

This didn't seem right; she felt groggier than she had ever felt.

Maybe she hadn't woken up properly, or hadn't slept properly, or hadn't slept as long and as well as she'd thought. She hadn't noted the time when she'd arrived, but she felt like she'd slept way past the standard seven or eight hours.

She sighed out loud.

'You just overslept, Amy-Thys.'

She lay back again, into the mass of pillows, and looked around the room.

'Or maybe…?'

She had been very, very tired.
That, she remembered.
'…I have slept exactly the right amount…?'
She smiled to herself, and sighed a little more sedately.
Surely, that was it.

CHAPTER 13

There had been a morning in Sydney, way back when.

After Paramatta, but before the first major Draco assault on The Palace.

It had been one of the first times that Thys had come to visit. Heather had been away, and her father had clearly been hoping to find something they could do together, to make use of the time with just the two of them, while they had it. But he had become caught up in sorting through the many boxes of undigitized documents that the Olivera people had ignored over the years, that had been found in several company-owned store facilities.

'There's a lot of stuff we own that's been forgotten by both Hines and Everett. Not that they ever actually knew that they owned these things. They were just packaged collateral in bigger deals; something to beef up the...' Mitch shrugged. '...I dunno. The balance sheet or spread sheets, or the corporate leger, or... you know. That sort of thing. Empty properties mostly. Must do something about it someday, I suppose...'

'Dad, you're just cribbing those terms from all the movies you've seen.'

'Oh Sweetie...' Mitch made a face. '...you know I do that with everything!'

They gazed over the boxes; they were all through the hall, and into the living room; all over the dining room table. You could easily tell the various groups apart, just from the age and colour of the cardboard.

'Still, if you ever need somewhere to stay...?'

Half an hour later, Thys had also become absorbed.

It was hard not to; she had gravitated to a group of five very solid-looking, deep-tan, tight-lidded, corrugated fibreboard boxes, and had found that each contained dozens of bright, yolk-yellow A3 envelopes, each in turn containing details of a property that she, technically, now, apparently, owned.

Sometimes she found that there were relatively recent updates within the folders; someone had cared, and kept the records, but most of paperwork, and the properties, had been either built or purchased by Hines's family in the first few decades of the twentieth century, and since barely remembered. There was a now-two hundred year old mansion in New Orleans that had been derelict since Katrina (that she almost gapped into straight away without thinking); a huge office block from the twenties in Burbank; office space in central London that was marked as recently as ten years ago as vacant; and a derelict castle somewhere in Wales, in a place whose name was about thirty letters long and unpronounceable even in her own head after trying three times.

'Dad…' She believed she had just found the perfect place for them all to picnic for the day.

Then, she heard her father whistle.

Low, and long.

Thys looked up; she knew what this meant.

This was something.

As she looked up, she realised that, at some point, apparently, Harding had joined them; she'd been so absorbed that she hadn't noticed. Neither had she noticed her father sorting through one of 'her' boxes, beside her.

'Hi Harding.'

'Good afternoon, Miss Amethyst.'

Mitch spoke deeply, enchantedly.

'Amy… look at this one; a converted three-to-four story apartment block – on Mulholland Drive!'

He pulled a yellow sticky note from the picture; Thys looked over.

It looked stunning. Thys took the note.

'Note says it's in need of repairs. Dated… wow. Ten years ago. That's pretty recent for this lot.'

Mitch stood bolt upright.

'Listen to this! It was commissioned in the late nineteen twenties by MGM, reputedly under the auspices the great wunderkind Irving Thalberg himself!'

'Wasn't he a big deal?' Thys tried to remember.

'Yes!' Mitch flicked her that 'what kind of daughter have I raised?' look, and she smiled as he continued. 'Ostensibly, it was a location where poached European talent could stay while they sorted out their movie contracts, and developed their first projects, but actually it was kind of a testing ground where they could have parties, and see who they were when they were drunk…!'

'And what their other vices were…' Harding offered. '…no doubt…'

Thys shook her head.

'Run by Mendoza's grand-dad no doubt!'

Mitch raised his eyebrow; like, *probably,* before returning to the text.

'…eventually it became one of the many getaway locales that stars used to hold parties in, and take secret meetings… names are here…; basically everyone from Mickey Rooney to Clarke Gable, from Judy Garland to Greta Garbo is rumoured to have stayed there at one time! Www….ow!'

Thys looked at Harding. 'Lunch in Beverly Hills, Mister Harding?'

Harding smiled. 'I would not say no, Mister Pyne.'

CHAPTER 14

Thys smiled as she lay back now in the gorgeous big bed, recalling her first memories, her first sight of the place.

She and Harding had followed her father's lead.

'Leave your Eves behind, they'll be safe back here, and we don't want to be tracked gapping.'

Mitch had then gapped them into an empty warehouse, somewhere in the Los Angeles Arts District. The space was huge, although the doorless room they'd arrived in had been built into just a tiny corner of it; two bare red-brick walls and an empty door fame under bare-bones timber rafters.

Mitch had gone to the cavity by the frame where a light switch once had been and stuck his hand down in the brick-dust to pull out a small plastic remote. He removed the back and slotted in a tiny silver battery coin he'd taken from the pocket of his his black suit-pants. He depressed the one button and they all heard a slight 'ka-chick' from the other wall.

Harding went immediately to the corner.

'I know this one...'

He pressed his hands against the closest bricks to the back concrete wall and found a hold in the mortar lines. Then he pulled the wall out. The whole thing swung away; a complete false wall. Behind it...

'Holy crap, Dad!'

'It's Heather's old L.A. stash from her spy days.'

The fake wall had a real brick veneer, but was completely hollow, with a real brick was facing them as it swung open. It was like a giant fridge door, with several rows of railed shelving, top to bottom, centrally divided by guns, lots of guns, hanging left to right in order of size. The top shelves were lined with lots of things that had been vacuum-sealed in plastic bags; half a row of cash bricks in various denominations, the other half all in US bills; three different sets of different hotel swipe cards, car keys, and passports; multiple Eve, i-Store, Galaxy and burner-brand devices; a proper Pleiadean Eve; underwear, tees, jeans, hoodies, still with the labels and price tags; boxes of sneakers, the same; a row also for Mitch, including, rolled up, a spare Res Dogs suit. Throwing knives and knuckle-dusters. Notepads and pens, sealed together. Then, under the guns, rows and rows of canned goods and long-lasting liquids. Bottle water and… basically three rows of survivalist gear.

Mitch took a cash brick, gave them both each one, then did the same with the burners.

'She doesn't use them any more, but they come in handly for travel.'

Harding nodded. 'No tracked gapping.'

'We're working on something a little more streamlined.'

'You are?'

'Sure sweetie; I'll tell you later.'

Thys looked at the phone.

'But these can be tracked of a cell tower, right?'

'Sure, but who would be looking?'

She felt a little bewildered. Mitch proceeded, with a loving smile.

'So we could just gap into this place, but who knows what we'll find?'

Harding nodded. 'Burner, cab, cash.'

'Exactly. And we can order some food if we get there, if we like the view.'

Before she knew it, they had walked out of a ground-level emergency exit onto a clean, nondescript street, lined with brick walls, solid grey veneers, and glass-fronted offices. The cab was just turning in, then they were off, heading through L.A. in mid-afternoon traffic.

Harding took the front and conversed in low tones with the

driver in a language Thys did not recognise. Beside her, Mitch was still engrossed in the file on the house, and she passed the time looking out of the window but not seeing anything as she thought back to the surreal warzone she had left behind.

'So it used to be called "The European Apartments"; although apparently nobody ever called it that. Quite early on…'

Mitch had still started reading aloud from the old manila folder, rustling the crinkly and faded-yellow notes.

Thys looked left and right.

She'd been on Mulholland before.

It had not ended… not; well.

Actually, it basically had *not ended.*

She was still *on that adventure.*

'Jeeez…' Thys whispered to herself. 'Yeah.'

'…the apartments were dubbed "The Fork".'

Thys took note. 'The Fork?'

'That's what it says here.'

'Surely we would have heard of that?'

Mitch shrugged, and kept reading.

Thys had initially been sceptical.

She had been able to find mention of the apartments online, but no recent pictures and only a few black and white snaps, all from the end of the drive, dating back to its glory days.

But now, as the cab started turned and started to go up, along Mulholland, she cheked her burner and found that it had wifi. When she'd googled "The Fork, Mulholland", uddenly there was a whole list. Not only was the apartment block infamous, at least amongst Old Hollywood buffs, and within nostalgia circles, but it was also very much lamented.

It turned out that during the slow decline of the once-majestic MGM in the last quarter of the twentieth century, the apartments had been sold off, by one of that sadly-fading studio's procession of uncaring new parent companies, then bought and resold so many times, in so many other real estate packages, that it had been allowed to languish, by all reports, quite badly.

Thys had read her research aloud, and by the time they had arrived, Harding had taken to looking through parts of the folder as well. He too was reading; even after he had peeled off a couple of notes from Heather's cash wad and paid the driver; even as they stepped out of the cab and started to walk up the very steep, very cracked concrete driveway; still, as they neared the top.

There were pine trees everywhere, and rocks, but they could see huge palms ahead of them, higher up.

'Extensive…' Harding began, thoughtfully.

Thys looked to him, reading the yellow papers as he strode upward.

'…history?'

'Yes, Miss Pyne.'

'Please, I told you before; it's Amy.'

'Very well. Miss Amy.'

Thys let out an annoyed sigh, but Harding winked at her.

Back then, he was still Mitch's bodyguard, but Thys knew that he used that title as much as an excuse to continue his strange but solid friendship with Mitch, for them to hang out together, as much as anything.

'For a while in the nineties during the film student craze, there was a tour; these are the notes. It is true. Many people stayed here; it says there were main apartments, for actors and directors and such, the ones at the front with the views, presumably; and some smaller ones for script doctors, or great technicians, for special requirements.'

When they reached the top of the drive, and the concrete flattened out into what must, at some point, have been a car parking space for about a dozen vehicles, they found more concrete; concrete steps led up from the concrete car park, to concrete paths all around the edges of the building. From the number of cracks, and weeds, they could tell immediately that the apartments had indeed been neglected for quite some time.

'Not unsalvageable…' Mitch had spoken, a little out of breath, but smiling. Then he looked around a bit more. 'Not great, though…'

The apartment block was impressive, there was no getting away from that. Big, and grand, and…

'Well…' Thys decided, optimistically. '…it must have been very lovely – once.'

That too was unmistakeable.

It was still quite a sight though.

The streamlined design flowed right across every surface; from the sharp, right-angle grooves that extended below the curved windows, to each of the fours floors being divided by the long, triple lines of (now, sadly-rusting) gutter and drain facades.

'Fixable…' Thys uttered.

The veneer of the apartments was still all white, but had last been replastered an eternity ago. Perhaps it had been repainted a little more recently since then, but not, in Thys' estimation, very recently, and certainly not so much as even touched-up since.

Not only were the gutters almost all completely rusted out, but she could see many sections where the exterior plaster had fallen away, or the paint was cracked and peeling. In some sections the peel was as long as the dead, black-brown palm fronds they were stepping over. In several places, the fronds had fallen onto the ground where the long droops of paint-peel had also fallen, revealing a long scar of plain, grey, roughness beneath the veneer, and creating a kind of dump of ugliness around the paths that would be enough to put many people off at first sight. That kind of mild but cosmetically ghastly damage was everywhere, Thys quickly realised; all along, the whole block was in desperate need of an all-over replaster and repaint.

No wonder the gardens close to the house were running wild; nobody had paid any true attention to this place in decades.

However.

Behind all of that…

Thys could see two long, three-floor apartment blocks, each flanking either side of the massively wide block. Both three-storey flanks were three very long rooms deep, with each floor surrounded by continuous balconies, wide with gracefully curved edges and rimmed by deep, covered patios, all lined with slim-framed, wide-rectangular windows. Consequently, the design afforded six very wide front rooms, each with a balcony view; three on either side.

'For the actors and directors...' Thys muttered.

Even from the outside you could see that each floor had the classic high ceilings of the art deco period that, along with the trademark curved windows, that made them look somehow huge; bursting at the seams from within. Thys could not help but see the two extending flanks as the long arms of the Sphinx, the curved and layered frontages its paws, and think of Leo, the MGM lion, who must have been at the heart of the architects imagination.

She assessed the flank, the 'paw', to her left.

The lowest section was a raised ground-floor apartment, fronted by a concrete patio and ledge which gave the impression, along with the second floor balcony that fully extended over and above it, of being extremely enclosed and secluded; an effect that was unintentionally enhanced by the wildly overgrown hedge and rose garden out front.

The second-floor balcony was set back a little, and book-ended by wide, rectangular, floor-to-ceiling corner windows; these were strangely enticing glass-framed cubicles, divided by glass balcony doors, and Thys immediately adored them.

The third floor, again set slightly further back for the layered, twenties cruise-ship effect (that had partially inspired the design art deco trend, Harding later informed her) again possessed a deep balcony, this time bookended by enormous curved windows on either corner, and graced by even wider, more elaborate, arched balcony doors; very apparently, even at first glance, pole movie-star positions on the top of either of Leo's paws.

Still higher, it looked as through the roof on each side was actually a patio, bordered by a simple, curved, single-railed steel fence, but it was impossible to see from the ground in front what else was actually up there, further back and deeper within.

Thys could only image the vibes from the parties, the wild twenties and thirties between-world-war debauchery, that must have penetrated those walls; and from what she also understood from the era and its talent, the loneliness and longing that must have been pressed into that glass.

She found herself walking toward it, keeping an eye on the rooms.

Watching for… she told herself squatters.

But she wasn't looking for squatters.

Her gaze couldn't help but flow along the balconies, exterior steps and balustrades, and become drawn into the building, between the flanks to the back of the block. There were central gardens, and a concrete drive leading to a heavily bolted garage, and above that a third block, right at the back.

Then Thys saw it; she got it.

That was it; where the apartment got its name.

The rear block was joined to each flank by a huge, curved, continuous wall; with the steps on each side leading up to a wide patio, currently almost completely obscured by an explosion of untrimmed palms, raging ferns, and at least three different types of ivy and creeper. The patio would catch the afternoon sun, and the sunsets, as would every western-facing front room in the block. That included the entrance lobby, the elaborately curved doors of which spanned the lower level of the curve itself. Only Heaven knew what lay beyond, she'd thought; but high steps and more glass, most likely.

But she saw it now; The Fork.

It was amusing really; it had been so-nicknamed because the whole building, while Sphinx-like with its higher rear block, was actually in the shape of a giant tuning fork.

'A tuning fork…' Mitch smiled, apparently catching onto the idea just as his daughter had. '…I get it. It's where Mayer's stars came to be reattuned to the MGM idyll, to be reincorporated into the MGM family.'

'It's a shame…' Thys shrugged. '…it really must have been very beautiful once. Still is, in its way.'

They moved up the concrete steps to the left; the ones that were least obstructed by fallen palm fronds and overgrown hedges.

'The window frames…' Thys noted.

'They've oxidized…' Mitch noted sadly. 'Green with… what is that? Green rust?'

'It is a patina…' Harding responded, his South-African accent never more pointed. 'The frames are copper. Somebody built this with the effect in mind; the colour is known as verdigris, the effect is well sought after.'

Mitch and Heather exchanged a look; impressed.

'It takes time for the copper to oxidize. Like their Statue of Liberty they have here; like the domes of all those Christian cathedrals in Europe.'

Thys saw Harding's gaze slide down this side, around the curve, and up to the other side of the inner Fork. He took it all in, with keen eyes and apparent understanding, very quickly so far as Thys could tell.

He turned to Mitch. 'How do we get in?'

Mitch held out his hand and upended the big yellow folder.

A normal bronze house key slid out and plopped on to his open palm.

'Thought I felt something…'

He grasped it, then held it out to Harding.

'Me first?' Harding smiled, and took it.

'Be my guest.'

CHAPTER 15

The wide, inward-curving glass frontage of the apartment lobby was centred by a large set of glass double-doors with long, elaborate metal handles, covered in peeling white paint, that squeaked when pushed down upon, still moved a bit, but had long-ago been tightly chain-locked to prevent access. However, the old-school steel padlock remained unresponsive to the one key.

Harding, however, had quickly located a thinly disguised and far-less grand side door, with a modest knob handle, camouflaged within the second-to-last, upright-rectangular glass panel from the left, where the key fit.

The door squeaked, then creaked heavily, but opened.

Within, the air was only slightly dank.

The lobby was plain, with no desk and just three large, wide wooden doors, evenly spaced. But it was strangely pleasing. The floor was a swirling salmon-pink and light-grey concrete mix, speckled with an opal-like finish, while the chamber's facing wall was another semi-circle of white veneer that reached the inward curving glass behind it, creating a crescent-moon effect that, as a space, felt special to Thys, even though it was completely empty.

Harding went up to the central door. While the outer key had been twentieth-century modern, this one looked less so. Harding crouched and assessed it.

'Needs a big key. Like a dungeon key from a fairy story. Big teeth, big latch.'

He looked around.

He assessed the door frame.

'Wood. But the rest is brick, with plaster veneer.'

He put his hand on the wall.

'Still solid.'

He looked around the curve again.

'No desk.'

He went around the wall, eying the surface carefully, then stopped. About halfway between the central door and the next door over, he pushed lightly against the middle of the wall. A small hatch spun open; a rotating slice of veneer over a gap in the bricks, centrally attached and dusty enough to have been reliably unused for many years.

Inside the secret hatch were three long metal keys.

CHAPTER 16

The main apartment in the rear block took up the higher three floors. The inward-curving, western-facing windows on the top floor, which ran along the inside of 'The Fork', were already catching the colours of the sunset over Los Angeles.

Thys, her father and his bodyguard walked up three flights of the central spiral staircases to this fourth floor, again noting that the rooms on each floor were mostly-all extremely spacious, some even stretching right back to the rear of the block; big enough for pool tables, banquet tables, dining tables, or four-poster beds; and enough room to entertain the inner circle of a movie star in what seemed like total seclusion.

Thys had seen and been in enough big wealthy houses by now, including Oliver Hines's accursed mansion (which, when she came to think on it, could not have been far from where they were) to know that the lifestyle was "always about upscaling". Bigger bedroom for bigger beds. Bigger display rooms for bigger collections. Bigger kitchens for bigger dinners, bigger rooms for bigger parties. More space to get lost in, the lonelier and more isolated you became. With this place the way it was now, that adage seemed especially true, because all the big spaces were completely empty.

After admiring the view, they moved back down; into the southern flank, then the northern. Eventually, Thys had started to notice that, whenever there was evidence of a leak in the ceiling, Harding would mumble something about the shameful neglect; how easy it would have been to fix the gutters before now, to paint the watermarks back; that it was shocking that this had not been done. Any room that smelled of mould, he would become extremely grumbly and walk away from them so that they would not have to endure his displeasure.

At the first of the big cracks that seemed more recent, he turned to Mitch.

'Miracle Quake, eh?'

Mitch smiled.

'Mmmm.'

Not long after that, working their way to the front, Harding looked up at another wish-bone crack above another big doorway.

'She breathes, this one…'

'Breathes?'

'Bricks breathe. Cracks are just personality. Smile lines.'

Thys had not been so impressed; not at first. It all smelled like mould after a while; and that had to come from somewhere. They had later located it in the ceilings; some kind of dirt-cheap insulation from years ago that had turned into a dark forest floor.

Also, Thys felt, the place had clearly been empty long enough to have that abandoned feel baked-in.

Some people liked that, Thys did not.

It made the place feel haunted; as though the energy of the people who'd died there, and whose spirits had remained somehow, now, outweighed the collective energy of all the people who had lived and loved there. There was something deeply sad about the fact that, despite having once been packed with demigods and kingmakers and artists, unparalleled in their time, they and this place were now closer to becoming all-but forgotten by almost everyone apart from buffs, like her Dad, than they were to that former practically-deified status. They were now like the lists of former royalty of European nations; curios to be dug up on Wikipedia.

But then, she saw the look in Harding's eye.

Something had him.

Some sort of historical inspiration; some kind of bricks and mortar romance. She nudged her father's arm with her elbow, flicked her eyes from his gaze, toward Harding, and raised her eyebrows.

'Huh?'

Harding was running his hand over the surface of a curved entrance to yet another cavernous, empty room, leading onward, into yet another.

'All this time, old girl. Just sitting up here in the sun. Bearing through the cold nights. Breathing. Patient.'

'You're going to need someone to fix this place up, aren't you Dad?'

'I am? I suppose I could put in a grant application to that organization that looks after old Hollywood – ?'

Thys nudged him harder. Arched her eyebrows and looked very, very hard at Harding.

'Oh!' Mitch coughed, fully comprehending now. 'Yes! That is, of course, unless… well; Amethyst…' Her father had smiled wickedly, right then. '…would you like to…?'

'I will help you.' Harding had spoken very quickly, very firmly. 'I will start tomorrow. You need do nothing, Miss Pyne; – *Amy*; I will make an assessment and report back to you, for the next time you return.'

'Okay.'

Thys had smiled broadly, but clandestinely at her father.

She felt weirdly as though she had just set up her widowed grandfather with his last chance at love. Then Harding had wandered away, opening a set of internal glass double doors, moving toward a giant, empty fireplace, and onward, into the labyrinth.

Thys remembered that night, how she and Mitch had grown hungry as Harding had walked the spacious rooms, assessing the state of the original timber floors, lingered in even more arched doorways, and high alcoves; peered out of the curved windows at the valley below. Then, long after sunset, as he had stood, seemingly as though he already owned the place, at the top of the left-side steps to the patio, awaiting delivery of the pizzas his friends had ordered. She had seen him trace his hands over the cracks in the paint on arched waves of concrete, along the exterior balustrades, as he'd walked down the old concrete path to the delivery car, to pay.

Mitch had transferred The European Apartments, which even they were now all calling The Fork, into Harding's name within a week. After that, it had been Mitch who had visited, and hung out with Harding, rather than vice versa.

'You are okay?' Harding had asked once, and only once. 'You have Byford and his men in Sydney?'

'All good,' Mitch had replied. 'I like coming here. I like this place.'

'Ah, it is not finished yet! I cannot say when! When is that daughter of yours coming back? I need someone to tell me how a woman would see things!'

CHAPTER 17

Thys had of course returned before too long, battered and bruised and finding it even more difficult to talk to her father and Heather about how dangerous things were getting; even when Xylata would sometimes accompany her for support.

And now Suzie was back and fully involved, she had lost her Astral Agony Aunt.

Somehow, that role, of confidante and advisor, of the 'been there done that' elder mentor, had gradually transferred over to Harding; her father's insistence that he be paid to accompany her while she was on Earth had actually made the transition strangely easier by making the beginning less awkward.

'You might know your way around the astral, but I'm not stupid, sweetie. The longer you're there, the less in touch you are with what's happening here.'

And this was *her father* saying this.

But of course, he wasn't stupid.

Thys had long suspected that he had known all along that Harding would become her perfect guardian. A few months later, when Thys had first asked Harding if she could stay at The Fork a while, rather than in Mitch and Heather's spare room in their central Sydney apartments, it had spurred Mitch on and he had formalized the arrangement.

Having taken the fourth-floor penthouse in the back section for himself (between the eyes of the Sphinx, Thys noted) Harding had offered Thys the biggest guest room he had; the top floor of the northern paw. The long rectangular room was the one she had assessed on that first day; surrounded with balcony, the front in particular offering an enviable view of Los Angeles. He'd purchased her an aptly named Californian King mattress with as close to an art deco four-poster bed as he could find (it was more Nouveau, Thys decided, but fitted the whole place, and the room itself, like a glove that had been on Leo's paw the whole time) which was almost too big for even this gigantic room. He had also installed an entertainment centre, mostly in the newly cleaned and insulated walls, that included a hanging widescreen, attached to a wrought iron medieval-style chandelier ring, that she could spin around the bed, psychically or remotely, to any angle she desired.

But also packed in there, along the side wall, again with barely enough room to fit, was Thys' pride and joy; her prized possession.

It was a wardrobe she'd seen, and told Harding about one time, walking around in the valley, that he'd remembered her liking and bought for her, without saying anything. Just, upon her next visit, the vastly wide and luxuriously deep four-door wardrobe had simply been there, installed within the giant bedroom, and that was all. She used it now as a symbol; as her entrance to, and exit from, the fantastic world of the astral; a terminus, a turnstile, an airlock, a bomb-bay door; and as soon as it had become her preferred mode of transport, from then on, this had genuinely become *her room*.

The wardrobe took up a whole half wall; from the end of her bed all along the right side, almost down to the balcony windows. Thys had gapped through it, into her bedroom from the astral, straight across the carpet, past the end-posts of her bed, through the central balcony doors, left and out along the balcony, left again and back in through the courtyard balcony doors, then right, straight into the kitchen, so many times now, that...

Right now, just thinking about it...

Made her hungry.

Thinking about breakfast (in the evening, she assumed?) Thys looked up at the earthquake tremor crack, the smile line, that ran along the cornices; the lines that showed where the house had breathed for almost a century now. There was a big wishbone one there, that came down the from the middle of the ceiling, that branched out in the middle to either edge of the door frame, that was a bit wider now.

It could look light lightning, too, and she liked it.

Thys turned out the bedside light again and lay in the darkness, staring out of the long, wide, art deco bedroom window, out of the balcony that overlooked the Los Angeles Basin, through its tall, rectangular, thin-copper frames; through the gossamer curtains that led out to the balcony.

She raised her hand and telekinetically separated the curtains.

They moved jerkily; she hadn't used her Pandora powers down on Earth yet, this time, and they could be a bit rusty at first.

Her stomach grumbled.

Now she could see clearly; over the balcony, out at the shining orange-white expanse that sometimes looked like an astral-neon brush fire, started by a blazing central crown, spread out down the central spine and out; framed in the sheer blackness of the night, with a sliver of stars above cloudless Californian early-summer night haze.

Her stomach grumbled again.

Had something creaked?

Was the house breathing again? The night getting cooler?

The number of stars that she could see beneath the ceiling were diminished by not just the city but the ambient streetlights of Mulholland, and the surrounding warren of roads, but they were still welcome, and still beautiful.

So, now; somewhere around three years later than the (she wanted to say... twenty-eighteen?) memories she had just drifted through, it was fully night here in Los Angeles.

June. Summer.

It felt like... before midnight.

Quiet.

Warm and snug.

Nobody needed her.

Gazing at beauty.

A few seconds of perfect peace.

She sniffed.

Her stomach grumbled a third time.

She needed a shower.

And there was still the pressing matter of that coffee.

Still, she paused.

Was she feeling a bit sensual?

Home, alone, on the Earth plane?

Earthy and fleshy and corporeal?

She wondered about it; about turning herself on.

But... she didn't know for sure that Xylata or Harding weren't here, and she never felt comfortable enough, doing that, unless she knew for sure she was alone. And besides, she didn't like having an orgasm on an empty stomach.

It made her feel brittle.

The wardrobe creaked again.

The door swung, a fraction.

It wasn't new.

But it kept happening.

There was a mirror on the inside of the wardrobe door.

That always happened, with every wardrobe she'd ever had that had an inside-mirror. She threw the giant quilt aside, rolled over and this time slid to a full sit on the side of the bed.

She huffed.

She couldn't just sit here, naked, not knowing if anyone was around. The night was indeed getting cooler, and the wood was indeed creaking.

Breezes?

She didn't feel any.

She couldn't remember if she had fresh clothes here or what? Maybe. Hadn't Heather sent her a box of samples from the new Cleverco casual wear line? Sports tops and jeans and stuff? Ages ago? Wasn't it around here somewhere?

She didn't want to gap into her Ymira uniform.

She couldn't even remember... had she worn that back?

Or changed, out there, before the Bloop?

And, even though she only really used the bedroom's massive wardrobe as a symbolic door to the astral, which was important in her line of work, hadn't she… at some point?

Put some…clothes?

In there?

Actual 3-D clothes in the actual third-density drawers?

Ugh.

She was so *groggy*.

She could barely summon the will to stand up.

She looked again at the beautiful, massive wardrobe.

It looked fantastic in the moonlight; basically the only thing in the room other than herself, the TV, and the bed.

It creaked again.

For no good reason she could see.

CHAPTER 18

Living in the astral with the Anunnaki was like living in another country, and every time she'd come back through the wardrobe doors she'd felt strange for a while, almost alien herself. It was to be expected, she had established that with Suzie, long ago.

Although, this time… it felt…

Weirder.

Every time.

It was always weirder.

She shook it off again, hoping that it would pass this time.

That Heather would call soon, and explain it all; why this time was different, why the end of the war should affect her like this.

'I might very well have actually been in Africa for all that time…'

Thys spoke to herself, noticing the edge in her voice.

'…working with my charities; no phone, no telly, no pop culture. Totally out of touch with what the western world at large is up to…'

She stood.

It did feel good though, being back on Earth.

Proper Earth as she thought of it, but (she had to admit) increasing less-so. It was all 'Earth' now; here and the astral, but, this physical part of it, where she had existed all through her childhood…

It was good to return, and be physical as she had always known physical to be, and stretch. She stretched out fully, her fingertips reaching for the high ceiling.

Then she let out a massive sigh.

She reached over to the TV, hanging from a massive wrought-iron ring that encircled the bed; Harding had taken note of the shape of the room and realised that, if the room were to be fully civilized, one must be able to watch television, and simultaneously admire the view.

'If the size of the bed and the shape of the room do not provide for both at once…' Thys spoke again, bringing in a mock-posh Hepburnian-American accent as she spun the huge television past the end of the bed, walking with it as she went, all the way to the other side, '…then the television should not have to be there, should it? In what, it has to be admitted, is its natural place, in the home of any modern twentieth century lady! Where? Well, where else? At the end of the bed, of course. But if it blocks the view? Why, if it blocks the view, then it should be able to move! It should – on wheels!'

Maybe both Audrey and Katherine Hepburn had walked around the bedroom like this, wheeling around a television, on actual wheels? The place had operated well into the fifties, after all.

She patted the enormous wrought iron ring, probably some kind of base left over from some kind of enormous lighting grid… or a Medieval-themed restaurant… or a sex dungeon? Or just a dungeon? Were there really any other kind? Anyway, just another of Harding's awesome finds from scavaging the stores and yard sales in the valley.

She didn't have the heart to tell him that, half the time, she just watched sitcoms on her laptop.

'News. No volume.'

The news appeared, and at first she ignored it and continued to try and place herself, and her mind, back in third density.

The astral was a real place, a real space, and the section of it where she'd spent all her time was a very real part of planet Earth. There were real territories, real borders there, even if they weren't quite the same as the countries and territories here in third density, even if sometimes the earth and the ocean were the same thing, and the sky and space could blend into one. Soldiers there, on her side, and their enemies, had fought just as hard, and died just as hard, as they would have in any of the many other wars fought on the physical soil of her home planet.

She stared at the news.

And then, whenever she came back…

'…every time, it's as though nothing has happened.'

The wardrobe door creaked again.

She turned and spoke to it.

'Nobody knows about my war, my battles, my commands and casualties.'

She gasped a little, took in a big breath.

Why was she…?

Was there…?

Something…?

On the floor in front of her was her black leather, crocodile-print jacket with the burnt-orange-chrome 'human designation' Field Marshall stipes and insignia.

When she did it up, it went down past here bum.

She lifted it from the floor where she apparently had dumped it last night.

'I mean, an entire clan of a whole other race…'

She pulled an arm through, pulled it over her shoulders, and pulled the other arm through, glancing at the wardrobe.

'…an alien race, who invaded the Earth's astral plane – *six thousand years ago!*'

She pulled it across and started buttoning, from the bottom.

'…a powerful race, too. A race who has bases *on other worlds*, who views the Earth, our home, merely as a multinational corporation would view a third world country ripe for exploitation…!'

She left the top two buttons open, like a big thick shirt.

She very much had the sense that she was not alone.

'…and a whole clan of them are fighting under *my command now*; a human!'

She stood up straight.

'For almost a decade now!'

Very straight.

'…a human, leading them against *many other clans* – of their own kind!'

She looked directly at the wardrobe.

'Can you believe that?'

The wardrobe creaked.

Something.

Or coincidence?

No coincidences.

Not for her.

Watching? Listening?

Understanding?

'You're not one of them, are you?'

She extended what psychic powers she had here on Earth and tried to gauge.

All that 'proper' Earth time later, she was still easily the Pandoran best at telekinesis, but the one worst at healing. She was good at spotting dimensional rifts, and getting out-of-body; but she didn't like it. Heather was great at that, and they were both very chatty when it came to telepathy. But her father was still the precision king of inter-Earth gapping, with virtually no temporal slides at all. The prediction thing; what the Pleiadeans called 'potency', and considered most important; that had been Aunt Saph's specialty. Thys was okay, but none of them had anywhere near the ability with prediction, with 'foresight', that Saph had had.

Poor Saph.

But that ability to determine; like the ability to determine whether there was something on the other side of a door you were about to gap through… Thys had started to think that that was really what the whole of foresight ability was about.

To see – potential, rather than just one 'set future'.

She sighed. And so, just as Saph had possessed that prescient ability in spades, so did she, Thys, ace the whole manifestation thing, on the astral, more than anyone else. The combination, somehow, of all those 'powers'.

That was how she had so impressed the Anunnaki.

They had never seen anyone like her.

'Right? The Ymira? Fighting for Earth, because they no longer believe that Earth should be secretly enslaved by their race. A race consisting *primarily of bloodthirsty, psychic, psychotic and psychopathic reptilians…!*'

Nope.

She got nothing.

No threat; at least, nothing along the vibe of Draco assassins or Chenek ninjas.

She shrugged.

It didn't mean she was out of the woods; she had almost said it to the wardrobe-ghost herself. The Anunnaki had fought; were still fighting, some of them, truth be told, some small groups of fanatics; for *all sorts of reasons.* Some spiritual, some pragmatic, some even economic and greed-driven, but regardless, some internally, against the way the Ymira clan had evolved, and was affecting others.

But…

…was it really over?

'Just because they signed a truce…' Thys looked at the wardrobe once again. '…doesn't mean they're not still out to kill you.'

She went to the balcony door and looked up at the big crack.

'So, yeah. Try telling that to your old school friends, when they asked where you'd been all this time, and what you'd been up to!'

Amethyst Pyne smirked to herself.

'Hey, that's not bad.'

The wardrobe creaked.

She looked over.

'No?'

CHAPTER 19

Thys walked out, onto the inner-balcony, and looked down into the courtyard. It was still a beautiful view of the city out here, out between the paws, down over the pine tree tops, over the rooftops.

Harding had long ago cleaned up the garden below; trimmed back the wild grass and creeping lawns to the edges of the concrete paths, cleared the drive up to the garage and repainted all the flowing art deco ledges and fences and facades... with a little help from Yelina, of course. Once she realised that he was serious.

In fact, the last time Thys had seen Yelina, she had been here, blessing the garden, and sunbaking on the now-pristine patio beneath the chin of the Sphinx, like Sophia Loren or Ava Gardner might have. Must have. Had, absolutely had.

Harding had left the picket fences white, but repainted the house black. She'd been shocked when she'd first heard; but totally amazed upon seeing the final effect, with the bright-verdigris edging on all the windows and door frames, and the polished brass fittings creating an astonishing, dimensional-depth effect.

'All that business with the black and white, before...' Harding had told her as they'd stood out the front, smoking cigars and drinking beers together. '...I got to thinking.'

Thys had found herself pleasantly surprised to find herself so pleased at his pride in the place. At that point, he'd done almost nothing else for six months. He'd even made friends with the neighbours; one one side a screenwriter who'd practically invented the comedy/buddy-cop formula in the mid-eighties, resulting in a long-running and lucrative franchise, and on the other side, a musical theatre producer who'd made a lavish movie of his biggest theatrical hit, and since retired with ten Oscars. Harding had started playing poker with them and a few other veterans from the neighbourhood, every second Friday night.

Remembering this, Thys realised that she had, once again, forgotten what day it was, what night.

Maybe that's where Harding was; up between the eyes of the Sphinx with his buddies.

Something drew her attention back to the courtyard.

There were three palm trees down each side, one at the border of each of the huge rooms, which were thriving. Out on the balcony she listened to them; on the third floor they were just nearby, and the high rustling of evening breezes moving through the fronds sounded like waves, crashing on a shore just outside. She could see them in the moonlight, waving and swirling, and with that, with her attention turning toward the aural, came the sounds of Los Angeles. The helicopters first, two… no three, thudding through the night air, and then the wail of police sirens in the distance. You tuned it out after a while; but then sometimes it came back, and you remembered how massive the sprawl of the city was down there. She could hear a song she recognized but couldn't place; played very loud but indoors. The houses to the north were more elevated and sometimes on the weekends there were three different songs echoing down, and Harding would put on some hihg-volume tunes of his own to counter them.

And so it went, all the way down to the suburbs.

Thys had seen things in the astral before she had departed. Perhaps because she was Australian herself, her attention had been taken by a group who had plugged into a temple, an old sound made new again, and were going to be, she could tell, The New Aussie Band; this generation's INXS, or ACDC… they were even going to have a four letter anagram as their name.

'Just because they sign a truce…'

However, more often than not, the differences between what she saw there and what actually manifested here were downright weird. This was because the reflection of all that; everything she'd known about, that had happened here on Earth during her time in the astral, had been filtered through the astral.

Through its *dreaming*, as the indigenous Australians might have put it.

She had spent so long in a land where imagination collected, where the responses to things down here, such as art, and narratives and ideas of all kinds, grew and took form. The astral was where dreams manifested, gestated and hatched, where they marinated and fermented. It was almost frightening, almost too real, to be back in the normal world, back to where those dreams had descended, solidified and were consumed; where they became shaped, moulded, engineered, constructed and erected, or were formalized in language or form – *form-alized* – in basic colours or tones, in the limited third density spectrum, their vibration inevitably lowered or constricted or made denser, cruder, harsher, or were somehow portrayed or enacted, then critiqued and destroyed or embraced and iconified.

'…just because they sign a truce, it doesn't mean…?'

After the dreamlike world of the astral, the return to the real could be, for a while anyway, almost too real.

While she had been away, each time she had known from afar what was going to happen, what was happening, or even had happened (or, depending on how long she'd been gone) *had been happening* here on Earth's material plane; in Los Angeles, in Hollywood, and back home on the opposite side of the world, in Australia, in Sydney, and just about everywhere else in the world for that matter.

It was, however, extremely strange to return and actually see it.

And to feel it; to sense physically that the dreams she had seen percolating in the astral had actually boiled over and here, on Earth.

'…doesn't mean they mean it?'

It was weird in this way, not only because by the time it manifested in third density reality, here, she had already seen it, (witnessed its reflection, and interpreted it through the lens of the dream world, there) within the abstract reality of the astral dimension, but it was weird also because, in coming back down, through or back into third density (she had never *really* gotten the hang of how she was supposed to say and refer to it) it just was never the same somehow, as it had been back 'up/out/in there'...

To see all that she'd seen in dream form become all that; all this; all that and more, back here in her reality of origin; it was simply too... she looked down.

Concrete.

But, she needed it to be that.

'Just because they signed a truce, doesn't mean they mean it.'

She needed it to be solid; needed, for want of a better term, a reality-check whenever she came here.

'Concrete reality.'

She laughed at herself.

'That's terrible. Not even remotely clever. Think again.'

Then she did.

'Or, maybe....? I dunno.'

She went back inside to check the television.

CHAPTER 20

Thys went along the balcony and into the middle room of what she supposed were her Hollywood apartments.

Her Prong of The Fork.

'I have a prong!'

Thys laughed as she opened the doors and entered.

Harding had installed a Cleverco entertainment core through the whole building; voice recognition and movement sensors ensured that whatever you were tuned into, it followed you from room to room, and synched with your Eve, until you told it not to.

'News, random.'

News was the best way of seeing what her enemy Anunnaki wanted humanity to see, and desired them to be feeling; she knew how they steered reality via perception from behind the scenes, employing the right kind of person here, the wrong kind of person there, to make things happen or make sure things didn't happen. In the end, she had learned over many years that with the Anunnaki clans working from their astral temples and influencing humans unconsciously, the Anunnaki version of the human race had been essentially running on autopilot for centuries now; pretty much since the invention of the printing press, if not radio, but certainly since cinema and definitely, definitely since television.

As for the Digital Age, well…

That was currently playing out… quite badly, she supposed, when she looked at the current, mean-spirited political trends.

They loved that, the old clans.

Fucking loved it.

There were protests all over every news service; everywhere

from Third World dictatorships to First World university campuses; including just a few streets from the Cleverco Castle (as it had come to be known) in Sydney, all approaching some kind of world riot.

Thys sighed.

For someone as mystically connected as she was, anything random that had enough complex variants could be used, fairly reliably, for divinatory purposes. Old school TV was great for that; songs on the radio, headlines on the internet; even trending.

And, although synchronicities weren't remotely unusual to Thys anymore, these days she was finding it hard to tell the difference between mystical coincidences and normality, given that, these days, a majority of news stories seemed even more relevant to her, just naturally, because she and her family were even more relevant to the world and things in general, now they were extremely wealthy and famous.

The Pynes and The Everetts were as much celebrities now as wealthy people *without* their own docudrama reality show could be. So, the things that the synchronicities were sometimes running through; was them.

That was strange, sure, but was it mystically strange?

Or was that just hard reality now, for Amethyst Pyne?

That had certainly been how they had achieved that accidental status in the first place, and it definitely was 'normal' strange; did that mean it was all to be categorized beneath that same magical umbrella?

And so, even though these synchronicities were, she supposed, to be doubly expected, they had become, consequently, twice as important to her.

That was what she was going with, anyway.

And so; she went with it.

Even if she did think it through again, every single time, every single morning she turned on the TV after returning.

This was her life now.

Life on The Northern Prong.

Instantly she saw what she always saw on the TV; that things hadn't changed since the last time she had taken a reading.

The protests in Sydney were taking place outside Styger Global and concerned the revelation that a covert government keyhole camera surveillance network had been planned for the majority of American cities, starting next year; the information had been whistle-blown by the notorious conspiracy activist Zaq Qwerty (he whose app sent her pithy little multiple, daily reminders that the world was not all it seemed) and now the conservatives were out for blood.

'Idiots.'

Generally speaking.

'*Idiots.*'

She moved across the apartment living room, past the long coffee table and between the huge cream couches and beige armchairs, and through the arched sliding doors and into the next room, where beside the small but well-designed open-plan kitchen, the TV was already on, just as the TV in the other room was already off.

She paused – to watch just a few seconds of Qwerty V Styger, she told herself.

Qwerty had recently outed Styger on a number of highly sensitive covert contracts for the US government, and it was now only a matter of who got to Qwerty first; the CIA, the FBI, the NSA, The Black Ops, et al, or even Old Man Styger himself.

'Fucking – idiots.'

Thys had known that the keyhole camera network, and worse, had already been operating for the best part of decade, and that, combined with everyone's smartphone trackers, and cameras, and addictive social media, there was no true privacy in the world anymore. As someone who secretly gapped, this was something that she and her fellow Pandorans found a constant bother.

'But who the fuck told Qwerty what Styger was up to?'

Thys wondered.

She put her hand on her chin and hummed out load, somewhat

theatrically.

'Hmmm....?'

Qwerty had also blown the whistle on Styger's secret installation in Alaska, where he was privately building the largest data storage centre the world had ever seen, large enough to rival even the US Government's own storage instillation in Utah. Although, one could not truly say 'the world has ever seen'… because nobody had yet been there, to seen it, and capture evidence.

The world had only Querty's word to go on.

Thys whispered to herself

'…well, I don't need to wonder about where he got *that* information…'

The summer-night wind blew in, whistling and wailing and very warm, and the lounge-room balcony door banged. That was odd. It was getting blustery out there, but the doors were on hydraulics and sealed magnetically unless otherwise ordered. And besides, she was sure she'd shut it.

'Harding?'

Nothing.

'Xylata?'

She went back in.

'Anyone?'

On the TV, she could see that the next story was about a fanatical Muslim terrorist who had been caught trying to suicide bomb a Regene clinic in New York, the fifth to attempt something like it within the month. This was despite the fact that Regene's medical and therapeutic treatments had been flourishing, and had saved many, many thousands of lives in the past eight years, post-Miracle.

So many people seemed to be benefiting; what a stupid response. Even the actual cosmetics line that they were probably still angry about, which, to be fair, had almost, quite truly, almost triggered the destruction of civilization, had slowly and responsibly been introduced across the world now. The corresponding legislation, to ensure that Regene was implemented under strict guidelines, had been overseen by former "mortal enemies" Oliver Hines and Mitch Pyne, her very own Dad, to generally pleasing effect.

Still, she only kept half an eye on this.

'Hello?'

Jesus, she was acting like a doomed damsel in some lame horror movie.

But there was a sense, one she had learned not to ignore, that the room had been inhabited. Was empty now; but… something had come in, after her, and gone out, when she'd called out.

'What is Regene really doing?'

Thys looked up at the TV.

The volume had come on without her asking.

'I mean, doesn't take much to see that the whole Regene gene therapy procedure has yet to come up with the promised 'cure-alls' that the Pyne takeover promised us!'

Thys ignored it, keeping her eye on the balcony door.

The curtains were blowing in.

The left-hand door was wide open.

The TV had randomly changed channel, as her voice command 'news, random' was programmed to do. Two people were arguing in front of a live audience, in the traditional chair-to-chair news forum style; suddenly the other woman responded and it was refreshingly, strikingly familiar.

'Cleverco promised nothing of the sort!'

Heather balked as Thys turned to look, giving her interrogator a flash of her eyes that suggested in no small way that she knew that her accuser was simply, outright, lying.

'What we did promise was that we would put the technology to –'

'A cure for cancer! A remedy for diabetes! A solution to dementia! When really, all you've done is to make these horrors *slightly* more manageable in the long run, while at the same time, charging people hundreds of thousands of dollars in *repeat business* –!'

'That's not true and you know it!' Heather was clearly filled with barely concealed contempt. 'What Cleverco offers has been proved as a radical improvement over all of those conditions compared to five years ago, and we do not charge –'

'*Where's the cures?*' The other woman demanded.

Then she looked directly into the camera, straight at the punters at home.

Feigning hardened heartbreak.

'Where's… the cures?!'

The channel switched again.

Thys was shocked.

So people were getting mileage out of how long it was taking to sort out the mess that Hines, in particular, and more specifically, Satanically-possessed-Hines, had left behind.

As things stood, people could change their look to resemble movie stars, but not look exactly like them. They could rejuvenate their own looks, their own bodies, even their health to a large extent; but it was still a matter of time, literally and physically, to see whether or not the treatments would last. Quite simply; in order to tell whether you could alter your genes to look different for fifty years, or look twenty-five for fifty years, or remain as healthy as a twenty-year-old for fifty years, you had to wait – fifty years – to see.

With some people the therapy seemed to take, with some it didn't.

The Regene promise was kept for some, not for others.

Some had to try again with a different sequence.

Some, again and again.

Regene remained, as humanity always seemed to, a work in progress.

It was like the old Anunnaki saying; *a lifetime guarantee means someone has to die.*

CHAPTER 21

Sigh.

Those Anunnaki knew a good 'old saying' when they made one up.

'Just because they signed a truce…'

There was a bathroom at this end; nothing could be done about the plumbing, in regard to getting an ensuite down at the end of the paw. The rooms that were all supposed to be the bedrooms, as opposed to the parlour with a view in which she was currently sleeping, were actually all down this end, facing out back into the lovely gardens and the view of the gorge that stretched past the long back yard.

'Shower, heat level seven.'

She unbuttoned and slipped off the Ymira jacket, hung it on the hook on the back of the door, and left it about half-ajar.

Harding had restored everything that required repair, but the original brass, the bone-porcelain and the white-enamel fittings had all remained in place, still in excellent condition. The huge, long bathtub hadn't been used in decades, but she had been determined to steal its born-again virginity at some point.

Not tonight, or this morning, however.

As she parted the new glass door to the relatively cramped shower cubicle, she heard shuffling. Like something big being dragged across the floor outside. It had been so clear, but so incongruous, that her mind had told her that it was the shower curtain – that didn't exist. She froze, one leg into the water stream, the spray on her face, neck and breasts. There was a weird clacking – or was it clicking? – that came with it.

She left the shower running and turned back, slowly.

She'd left the door open, and the fan off, so she could hear.

So she would know; there was something else in the apartment with her.

Although, she had gotten in.

Gotten undressed, turned on the water and – gotten in.

Half in, anyway.

Was she ignoring the fact that there was something else here?

Not ignoring, but…

It was just that… she didn't feel threatened.

Instinctively, she didn't feel…

No, she was imagining things.

She was back on Earth.

Things that go bump in the night; wind that raced down the balcony; Harding's home installations; wood that moved with the change in temperature; bricks that breathed!

A house like this could make all sorts of sounds!

As though corresponding with that thought, the TV in the bathroom came on.

'Quiet.'

It was Fox this time, and the steam was gathering.

Hopefully it would have changed by the time she got out.

Two things were on her mind now.

The fact that Heather had been fighting her own war, here, back at home, and hadn't said much about it.

And, the fact that she knew, from her time in the astral, that the Regene terrorist attacks were being supported by a dark cabal within the United States government who, with the help of the secretly-funded Black Ops NSA, who were so completely paranoid about the idea of people being able to fluidly look the way they chose to as opposed to the static way they were born, that they were trying desperately to destroy Regene by making it seem dangerous, and controversial again, by making people lose faith in it.

After all, that way was easier, and much, much less expensive, than keeping track of its use.

That was how they thought.

That was how they saw things; this was their world.

This was Old Earth, and deep down, even not so deep down these days, it had become clear that they were determined to keep it that way.

But there was a flipside of course; despite all best efforts, again as per usual, there was a burgeoning black market in identity theft. This was, of course and quite justifiably, really what the covert agencies were most concerned about; not only that criminals, activists and terrorists would learn how to employ those techniques faster than they did, but that ordinary people would as well. It was already happening with digital tech; and they had countered with CCTV, pinhole cameras, drones, facial recognition software, fingerprint ID's and retinal scans.

But what would happen when all of those things could be altered overnight with a tailor-made, designer-DNA pill?

Thinking about it almost made Thys laugh; that dark and psychopathically paranoid cabal would never survive in the true astral, where everything was fluid and nothing was ever as it first appeared.

Quite accordingly, the astral temple of the Black Ops NSA was a bleak and intimidating bunker, the kind of place that was fed by the deep ids of men who didn't even know they were fuelling the Anunnaki, and the snarling, open mouthed public ids of the dark masters who did indeed know, full well.

These places, these lightless compactions of the most psychopathic Anunnaki, sometimes erupted in the astral with acidic metals, and toxic silver-black lava, then cooled into massively dense, mountainous anti-cathedrals of matte-black steel, belching and billowing blood-black smoke, and bone-fragmented ashes; counterfeit constructions that were a cancer upon the astral plane, that poisoned human consciousness and promoted and rewarded nothing but the most self-interested and venal of human impulses and responses. In the very least, their auras blurred or blotted out all outside influence, like the blackened windows of a mega-casino; their frequencies were distracting, insulting, and depressing, like the most aggressive of commercial advertising; their vibrations deafening, and intimidating, like the crudest of baselines; the invasive tendrils of their ultra-dense foundations spread everywhere, an electronic infrastructure, humming and buzzing just under humanity's general awareness; and their toxic spores puffed out, covertly, like automatic air-fresheners, filled with weed-killer and fallout.

As for those who went to worship at these mountainous, bottomless ranges and pits… who could say?

Thys could not.

Why anyone would, what they found when they got there, what their reasons, their motivations, their rewards were…?

Only the bravest would even approach and negotiate.

She saw them, sometimes, watching the Dracopolis from the top of Port Ymira.

In the astral, these people, these dark minions, seemed to provide nothing but restriction; they provided to imagination what chronic arthritis did to sexual intercourse. And those whose influence fell under the long shadows that these temples of darkness cast seemed essentially to have even their basic morality confounded, their intrinsic access to natural law confused, and their ability to tell grace from harm massively corrupted.

And their one aim, in the end, was to infiltrate government.

To support the most powerful, whilst parasitically devouring it from within.

Until the host could not survive without it.

At worst?

Once one of these temples, and their acolytes and rulers took hold of a country… millions would die, openly rationalized, without remorse. They made no secret; they murdered plainly, and simply controlled everything – and it was said, openly walked the streets in reptilian form.

'When my people start killing your people out in the open, that is when they know they have created a realm on the Earth plane of pure chaos…' Xylata had once told her. '…where even if someone reported it and believed it, there would be nothing they could do. If you think about it along the lines of your chain of command, of animals; there are rules, natural laws. In different human societies, there are different animals that you may kill and eat, as opposed to those you treat like family, and for whom you will go to great lengths to spare pain. We have those rules as well; we may not kill humans. We may train humans to guard against other humans, to 'play roughly' with other humans; to frighten humans, when other humans get too close to us. If you fight each other, if you turn vicious, we stand back, and wait for you to kill each other. In the meantime, you do what we say, and your toxic love nourishes us. So, if you see one of my people willing to simply shoot a human, like Kyvza was prepared to do to you and your family in the Mojave vault that day; then you know, the trouble is starting. Great change will come; things will end; and people will die. And the trouble will be – grand scale trouble.'

And so, Thys had learned to avoid that darkness.

Learned to ignore it, and hope that, as her battles proceeded, that the Anunnaki astral temples in the darkest realms would slowly be drained by the natural, and slowly awakening, instincts of others to avoid them as well. It was just a matter of allowing people to see the alternatives, and to know they were there.

'Barcoda.'

The voice had come from the bathroom television.

'That's one of six. Six on a list.'

Thys froze.

She asked herself quietly, under the shower head.

'Did someone on TV just say...?'

She looked around, but the bathroom was filled with stream.

She could see that the TV was on, on the wall between the vanity mirror in the corner, and the sliding door to the toilet cubicle in the other corner.

She collected herself.

The shower had taken longer than she'd anticipated, as she'd let her mind wander into darkness. Showers tended to do that sometimes; especially at night, with the light off. The thoughts had triggered some anxiety, and her gut was a bit twisted now. She'd jumped a little when she'd heard that word.

'Nobody on TV should be able to…'

Barcoda was something that flickered around the edge of the dark astral realms like those falling green symbols in *The Matrix*. It was what remained of the idea that people should be marked; or chipped, an idea that had fallen out of favour, become obsolete, essentially, since the rise and exploitation of smart phones and social media.

'I know, ma'am…'

The oddly familiar man was looking out of the television, seeming to directly address her, through the steam, across the bathroom.

'…nobody should be using that word on television.'

Thys stared. The man spoke again.

'Ma'am? How about – Blackbrink?'

Thys knew that one too.

'That's the most dense of covert Black Ops…'

Thys spoke under her breath without thinking, as though this were some kind of test.

'…agents who had been deemed to have looked into the heart of evil and not gone over, remained sane, and maintained their covert skillset.'

She had seen the occasional albino bat, out upon the astral plane, way out beyond dreaming's normal processes, where some of the hardest-fought battles had gone down.

And down, and down.

When she saw these, Blackbrink was the name that always came to mind.

'Are you getting it yet, ma'am? Do you have any questions?'

Thys gulped.

Despite the hot water, she had goose bumps.

'I can't see you.' The man spoke calmly in an effort to reassure her. 'I waited for the steam before I patched in. This room is the most secure in this wing. Mister Harding has the place completely scrubbed, but there are still long-distance surveillance techniques –'

'How are you – ?'

'Fairly simple ma'am. Can I ask you another?'

She waited a few seconds, heard herself breathing, then heard herself speak. 'Okay.'

'Crossbreed.'

Thys responded straight away. 'Human chimeras. I've fought them; they're in direct...'

She pushed and received a good sense back that it was a young man about her own age; she pushed a little further.

He was telling the truth, she sensed.

No sansing, though; they would not see each other. At least, he had no desire to add an element of voyeurism into his mission.

His mission.

He actually... didn't like the fact that... that this was the only way.

'...direct philosophical opposition to Regene, at least as they see it. They have werewolves. Real ones.'

She listened to the hot water; and could feel he didn't like that. Not at all; that werewolves were real. Had been made real. He was a true believer; these things had to be stopped.

'Weathervane.'

'Climate mystics. They predict and exploit weather patterns; mostly science these days. Still, they used to do everything from making sure sad movies played on grey days, to movies about aspirant affluence playing in summer, so even The Sun and a blue sky seemed powerless to make you happy. This was back when network television was still useful to influence the masses; more difficult now with niche fracturing, but they can still make sure that the people they want to get rid of take a holiday in the path of a hurricane; or have one drink too many the night of a first snowfall. Or discover Leonard Cohen at exactly the right time. Am I telling you all this, or do you already know?'

'Ma'am; you are telling me that you already know?'

'That's your script talking.' He didn't respond. 'Why? There must be dozens of these old American B'Ops who are linked with the dark realms of the astral.'

'We know you go there. We know you're trying to do good. We won't get in your way. We just need confirmation for our own information.'

'So that you can cover your own arses by saying 'we thought she was one of us' if I go bat-shit mental, right?'

'It's your civic duty to cooperate, ma'am.'

'I don't think you can get in my way, agent. Other than allowing me to broil myself in here. So you're lucky I'm the good girl that I am. I need to get out. You need to fuck off.'

'I have two more names.'

'I know. Bloodroot, and Whitehole.'

The man vanished and was instantly replaced with an entertainment report.

' – that the long-anticipated new release from the eccentric but awards-friendly director, Adison Achilleos –'

'Off! Water off! Lock door! Fan on!'

There came a series of clicks and clunks; copper pipe and steel locks.

Jesus. An Achilleos report.

That was all she needed right now.

She breathed for a second, calmed down.

Could she get out of the cubicle?

Her sixth sense had given her no sense that the man to whom she'd spoken was a creep, necessarily, or a weirdo, or a perv.

But – *he had just hacked into her bathroom!*

If she gapped out; there could be no explanation, and they would potentially have it recorded. If she stepped out, she risked them having compromising video of her.

Only naked.

But still; naked!

And even stiller; no need to make it easy for them.

She breathed some more.

The steam was vanishing.

She took a risk and levitated the awaiting towel through a crack in the shower door. It was wrapped around her before anyone could possibly have seen or determined anything; although she was as certain as she could be that nobody was looking. She stepped out and grabbed a second towel and wrapped her hair in it, old-school bee-hive style, trying not to remind herself of Norions at the door in Paramatta.

Then she took the long, black Field Marshall jacket and put it on again.

She exited and went into the kitchen like nothing had happened.

'Bloodroot and Whitehole.'

He was on the TV out there.

His face and voice were digitally filtered with an excellent face-swapping program to look and sound like a very young Tom Hanks.

'Thought you seemed familiar...' Thys grumbled. 'Look, we all like Tom Hanks, but even him I don't trust him not to take a quick peek at me if he can.'

The man seemed a little put out by this.

'We're the legit arm. I've been told you have experience; that you're a grown up. They were his exact words.'

'Whose?'

'I've been told to tell you a password. I am recording audio only, so if I write it down, you'll know –'

'How do I know it's audio only?'

'Well, when I give you this password, you will know I can be trusted.'

'If you're over-riding basic cable with a signal that can't be detected, I assume you're somewhere close...?'

'Yes. But if you don't come looking...'

Tom Hanks held up a sheet of white paper on which he had written:

DELIGHTFUL SURPRISE

'…that would be much appreciated ma'am.'

It sunk in.

Thys relaxed a little more now.

Her senses had been correct.

'So, when you say legit arm, you mean of the CIA, and when you use that password, I am supposed be assured that you work with Bo Everett.'

'Yes ma'am.'

Thys considered again. Everett had once told her that if he ever needed to communicate with her through government agencies, in relation to anything that was occurring in the astral, he would use one of several two-word phrases from their first exchange, during the storm on his private yacht. He had done so once before, requesting her aide, using another phrase.

SOME SANDWICHES

He'd also insisted that if the phrases had been reused, they had been swapped from agent to agent, and were therefore, at teh very least, one degree less secure.

'Ma'am, I might very well be recording the video of this exchange, but I assure you, I am not. I might have tortured the man to whom Mister Everett gave this password in order to extract it, and am now using it against you under the guise of misrepresenting myself; but once again, I am not. Mister Everett informed me that if I told you this in earnest, that you were an extremely good judge of character, good enough to be able –'

'Bloody hell, agent; okay you've worn me down.'

She took a deep breath.

She was still hungry.

'So far as I can tell, Bloodroot's mission is to find the last survivors of dormant bloodlines that were once powerful. There are temples within the dark astral realms that have been sealed for hundreds, some of them thousands of years. It's believed that they can only be opened by their descendants; there's no historical records but we're talking things like… aaaah?'

She had to think; what would be the best example she'd seen?

'...like; the pure genetic lineage of the high priests who were sacrificing thousands of people a day on a production line slaughterhouse at the great descent of the Aztec empire; that kind of thing.'

'I see. And... Whitehole?'

Thys shrugged. 'Crazy. But they think on a huge scale. Whitehole is an organization that wants to harness some kind of many-worlds magic and bring in other timelines, to try and correct where things went wrong. There are lots of cults that want to try this; and there are alternate realities; there are windows to alternate realms, I've seen them.'

'Seriously, ,ma'am?'

'You've seen some of them. Filtered down, anyway.'

'I have?'

'Some of them have manifested here as TV series. Pretty accurate, too. But Whitehole is the organization that wants racial purity from the perspective of the white-European, psychopathic alpha-male paradigm. There are Japanese and Chinese and... well there are versions for just about any culture that has lost a major war or seen cultural erosion from a once-dominant paradigm. There are old foxholes everywhere, on an endless plane of astral purgatory, where people have curled up and plotted their vengeance for thousands of years... people who never gave up the war, who held onto the war for their parent or grandparents or...'

'I understand ma'am...'

'...they're just fishing holes for the Anunnaki clans who feed off xenophobia. Which is most of them. The foxhole planes remind me of those battered and scarred moons around Saturn...'

Tom Hanks was staring at her, half aghast, half in wonderment.

'It's... it's really all there? The dream world?'

'Ask Uncle Bo.'

'Uncle...?'

She shrugged. 'He feels like an uncle. Does that help him with whatever he's up to that he needs the CIA for?'

The agent nodded to himself, then spoke a little more candidly.

'Everett believes that all of them, all six, are in some way involved in direct attempts to destabilize Cleverco.'

Thys found that she was unconsciously fiddling with the towel around her hair. If she left it like this for too long, it would be a nightmare to manage.

'Agent, my people already know that there are myriad forces; terrestrial and asterrestrial, who use fanatical religious groups to destabilize Regene…'

'We're concerned with that as well.'

Thys nodded.

She didn't believe it.

Although, she believed that this guy might believe that's what his organization was concerned with, and be very real about what he thought was his place in the fight.

'Asterrestrial. Is that a real word, ma'am, or did you just make it up then?'

'I made it up. Not just then; a few years ago. It's a thing now.'

'If you say so ma'am.'

'Agent…' Thys considered carefully for a second. '…most religious protest groups have been coerced by Anunnaki clans who didn't care one jot what happens to them, or Regene, or Cleverco; just so long as the very idea of the existence of Regene and Cleverco continues to cause unrest within their ranks. There are several clans who exist by causing political shitstorms around badly-educated and ill-informed religious groups. These six cabals you just mentioned; they're all just pieces of shit, mixed up in the kaleidoscope of shit that makes up the larger, darker astral realm of mystical sewage they all come from. It's probably all guided by the same clan who festered the fear and ignorance that surrounded stem-cell research, as though it somehow involved killing babies, but set back medical research into terrible diseases by half a century. The suffering this clan causes is immeasurable. They keep to the darkest realms, and when they leave, all they spread is their shitty brand of toxic darkness; we've never been able to identify them or put a name to them. But they're there. Whichever of these six cabals is coming after Regine, we need to know which clan they're doing it for.'

'I don't know about that ma'am…' The agent cleared his throat. 'That's more your territory. I'm just on a fact-finding and surveillance mission, and I just happen to have a connection with Mister Everett from a few years ago.'

'Well, good for you. But thank you, and thank Mister Everett for me when you next see him.'

'I don't know when that will be ma'am. He's not exactly social these days. But ma'am; these… cabals. These six organizations? They're awfully good at it, wouldn't you say, ma'am?'

Thys sighed. 'We think it's all a smoke screen anyway, agent. We think they're actually the ones who do the worst of the Satanic shit; the ritual stuff, with kids… I feel sick. I don't even want to think about that, let alone… just talking about it makes me…'

Something shuffled, outside on the kitchen balcony.

'Is there anyone else here, agent?'

He looked slightly concerned. 'Not that we're aware…'

She turned back to the balcony doors.

'Are you sure? I thought you had someone in the house?'

'You thought… no!'

'Cut the connection, agent.'

She turned back to the TV.

'If I don't contact you in twenty-four hours, come find me.'

'Come…?'

'Now!'

He paused for the second, then the image cut out.

CHAPTER 22

Thys turned to the balcony.

There was a place in her brain; a physical place she was sure, that tingled when she was ready to use telekinesis.

Something electric.

It sounded clichéd, but it really was; static and electric in the air around her.

She parted the curtains and blew the doors open.

There was nothing there.

The lights were out in the courtyard.

The palms were crashing about like waves; it was humid and windy now. A tropical storm on the way perhaps. Something using the cover of the wind to sneak around…

Behind her the television suddenly caught her attention as it changed channels again.

'A few weeks ago, people woke to a new order in food management; a revolution in supermarket shopping called Phoodco.'

Thys turned fully and stared at the television.

It was Rio DeVora.

Since Paramatta, she had learned that DeVora's family owned and controlled DeVora Agricultural Systems, one of the world's biggest biotech corporations.

But she hadn't been anything like a big deal in her family back then.

Today, she was the tip of their spear.

Ever since Paramatta, since DeVora and Gordian, Thys had been further out of third density current events than usual, fighting hard to clear a space in the Terrastral Territories for humanity, using Port Ymira and the Amethyst Palace as bases of operations, as far from all of this awful politics as was humanly and reptilianly possible. During that time, Rio DeVora, once and also-ran, had emerged as her own force of nature, grown as a presence in the human collective consciousness, and been on her periphery of the battle in the astral as a constant potential threat, a constant lurking shadow, the whole time.

Thys respected her as an opponent, but she was evil.

She heard her phone ring from the next room.

She knew that if surveillance saw her in the bedroom without walking from one room to another, it would confirm all their worst fears. And they would have footage. If they didn't already.

On the other hand, it might have been her Dad, or Heather.

So she stepped out onto the balcony.

There was a weird smell.

And the concrete landing was… wet.

It hadn't rained.

Wet and… sticky as she turned right and walked back toward her bedroom, and re-entered.

The TV switched on.

Her phone was on the bed.

Unknown caller.

Nobody had this number other than people she knew and trusted.

'Hello?'

'You god damn bitch.'

'What?'

'Do you know what you just cost me?'

Thys hung up.

Wrong number or a prank; someone had gotten her number or called it randomly.

The report on the TV was going over the latest big business story; the creation of a massive new brand.

Thys half listened, half-remembered it happening; happening before it happened. Forming through the astral like a volcano suddenly erupting and creating a new Hawaiian island – the size of Australia. Just before the truce had been confirmed, it had been announced that Rio DeVora herself had shepherded a massive, world-shaking merger that consolidated several of the world's biggest multinational companies, including the world's third largest chemical giant, Wai, along with the medical supplies juggernaut Smith & Doublet, and the multinational energies and commodity traders Buch-Nadal. The new multinational giant, labelled the first truly, openly and actively aggressive globalist corporate power, was now the world's third largest publicly trading company, the largest based in the United States, and was to be known as:

Phoodco.

pHoodco.

Phoodco…

It sounded awful, Thys thought.

It had Draco written all over it.

To most of the world, however, it meant an overnight re-branding and consolidation of a number of famous consumer brands, supermarkets and retail chains under one name, and a steep reduction in price of a number of staple food and retail products.

How could that not be good?

Right?

Simpler was always better!

Right?

'We are pleased to announce that we have just finalized the purchase of Australia and Great Britain's second largest supermarket distributors, Shepwell's…'

A sinking feeling started to come over Thys as DeVora spoke.

'…which means that the Phoodco philosophy, of genetically-enhanced health products, and scientifically-organic foods, beverages and supplements, will now be supplied through Phoodco corner stores, supermarkets, megastores and gigamarkets…'

That voice.

'…immediately available to more than seventy percent of the western world's consumers, guaranteeing consistent, stable and reliable – genetically enhanced, or 'genhanced', and scientifically organic, or 'sciganic' health products – to the majority of health-loving humanity –'

Rio DeVora was an amazing looking woman, and you really wanted to be on her side when she smiled.

And smile she did.

' – forever!'

And her voice was rich and feminine; she ought to have been on TV.

It was a voice that resonated; a voice you did not forget.

And Thys had just heard it.

Her phone rang again.

Heard her voice for the second time; and now about to hear it for the third time.

The same number.

Thys picked up.

There were chuckles, and some genuine applause and cheers from the gathering at the press conference.

Rio DeVora smiled again.

Thys could sense her smiling on the other end of the phone.

'Forever, Amethyst. Powerful word.'

'So is Phoodco.'

'You just cost me – one point two million.'

Thys was starting to piece it together now.

The divinatory dip into the television was taking strong, bizarre turns because things were moving quickly.

She stepped back toward the balcony and realised that she had tracked blood onto the carpet. The wet stickiness all along the balcony was…

She went back out and looked over.

There was a body down there, with its guts ripped out.

Judging the distance that the poor ninja bastard had landed from the balcony, he had either jumped to get away from someone, or been thrown.

'I need you to explain yourself, child. Your violence. I need you to explain that to me – now.'

CHAPTER 23

Throughout the nineties, under the nom de plume Rio Violetta, Rio DeVora had almost become an American film star, coming up through the independent French cinema circuit, flirting with two famous Hollywood directors and making two critical and box-office bombs… and then she had quietly vanished.

Only a decade later, via the magic of the internet, and its Pied Piper whistle blowers, had it been publicly revealed that her parents were actually the trillionaire owners of the massive DeVora dynasty, and only then that she had been groomed to inherit the reigns.

Acting had been a game for her, a diversion.

But she'd possessed a strange quality, this so-called Rio Violetta; in Europe she'd been a critical favourite, a fashion darling, a politically incorrect sound-bite generator and an outrageous critic of her fellow world-stage celebrities.

The year she'd retired, despite or perhaps becasue of her US disappointments, she'd been a judge at Cannes.

Thys turned back to the TV, where her still image remained above the talking head newsreader, and considered her, far from the first time since Paramatta. Her mother had been one of the first black (half-black, anyway, which in America was all it took) supermodels, but her father had been a ruthless Gallic tycoon and almost, so long ago that everyone had almost forgotten, Prime Minister of France.

Even today he was hugely influential at the EU.

Suddenly there was another text.

Another pithy message from Qwerty.

From *him*.

They are changing the food so they can own its essence.

Through the food, they are changing people so they can own their essence.

They are reducing everything to chemicals with a dollar value.

Soon, they will own food.

Soon, their food will be the only food.

Soon, they will own you.

Thys shivered.
What the fuck?
Was Querty spying on her now?
'You are not explaining yourself very well, child.'
No; he was simply timing his texts extremely well.
DeVora, more likely, was spying on her.
Then DeVora was gone and the television news switched directly from that, as though it had not been about as worrisome a public announcement that had ever been made in peace-time, to something equally as bizarre, but almost totally benign; a Hollywood sex scandal.
'I think…' Thys whispered, carefully. '…that – you – explained yourself very well. To those who could hear.'
'Those mercenaries were extremely expensive.'
'You're blaming me for not letting them kill me?'
'You did not need to kill *them!*'
'I…'
Thys backed into the room, one eye on the wardrobe.
Then, as she looked at the bed, she saw it.

It was enormous.

It...

He.

He was curled into a ball, with his enormous eyes staring up at her.

He looked like he knew he might not be allowed on the bed, but he was going to try anyway, and see if he got kicked off.

Thys sansed, very easily, that his feeling was; he had been locked out, unfairly, and now he just wanted to be with her again.

With her again.

She caught her breath.

He had come from The Realma.

He had been hers.

He had been with her from a pup.

Outcasts, unwanted.

Bonded.

He had journeyed beside her, the whole time.

He had watched her go through the portal.

He had tried to follow.

She had wanted him to, but –

He had stayed to defend her passage instead.

He had tried to find her, when he could not follow.

He had seen her, through the grotto.

He had been unsure.

He had watched her from afar.

But now, somehow, because she had come back here; three, four...?

...years later; and decided that she was going to *stay;*

He had found a way through, finally, out of the wardrobe.

To protect her.

Like a good boy.

Jesus; he was half the size of the bed!

She felt tears down her face.

What were they going to feed him?

'Miss Pyne. I am going to give you another three seconds to

ans –'

'DeVora.'

Silence.

Thys held he breath. DeVora could not hear the tears. They were happy tears, but she would mistake them for fear. She released the breath as she spoke, steadily, low.

'I have just returned. Your emissaries have fallen victim to my security system. You wanted to test me? There you are.'

Breathing.

DeVora was speaking steadily as well.

'We have left you alone, Miss Pyne. We have stayed out of the way of your... paddle pool, and your fairy castle. The Draco use you as we would use a paint ball course. But now they are bored. I will not test you again; you seem to have power. I see that. Others may, but I give you this one warning. Stay out of our business. You know what it is. You were provided ritual. We told you, some time ago, the rules and the board, and we offered you a seat at the table. You refused to cooperate; what you did to Gordian was impressive, but unforgivable. You can never be trusted. In any regard; we know you will never join us, and so as a term of mutual respect; powerful woman to powerful woman, I repeat, just once. Stay –'

Thys hung up.

CHAPTER 24

Thys sat on the bed, beside Heff.

'What are you, anyway?'

She heard a thump - thump - thump as his pythonesque tail started wagging.

He was black, with a white chest, and red eyes.

He was a dog, the size of a small adult bear.

She had almost forgotten the books she had written; *The Chronicles of The Realma.*

What had he been in those?

Had he changed in third density, from second?

From the Inner Earth?

Never mind.

It would come back to her.

Just like Heff had.

She kept staring at him, scratching him behind his ear, which was a big as her hand.

He made a little half-sigh, half-moan.

Content, and apparently well-fed (she was still trying to ignore the blood, and... other stuff, everywhere) he closed his eyes and started to fall asleep.

Then, Thys cried.

She cried and cried.

Finally, Xyxzi and Heff had found their way home.

CHAPTER 25

Eventually, Thys got up and started thinking about cleaning the blood.

She looked at the TV.

They were still crapping on, replaying DeVora for the whole cycle most likely.

She sat back down.

'Well, I guess that's happening, then...' Thys uttered wryly, feeling somehow even more naked and alone, sitting wrapped in towels on the side of the bed, than actually being naked and alone made her feel.

Reality, she decided, sucked.

Then Heff moved and she remembered; she wasn't alone.

Harding would come back, once he realised what had happened. It was actually very strange that he had not.

Her father, and Heather, would be back tomorrow.

Xylata would turn up, sooner rather than later.

They would get together.

Suzie would show up.

Trudy as well.

Everett would come down, with Yelina.

They would sort it out.

She sighed.

The war was over; or at least, the truce was signed, but it was business as usual back on Earth.

Maybe she would have lunch with some old friends.

She would debrief with Harding.

He knew cleaners.

This would be okay.

She would ensure that he was okay to go, then they'd gap back to Omega Cove and take care of stuff at that end. She would contact her mother, the ridiculous Janine, and her sister, who had definitely settled on Saxe now, apparently. and let them know she was okay, she was back from Africa, her charity work was over for now, and by that time be ready to have dinner or lunch or breakfast with her father and Heather, and find out what the hell 'plan' Heather had been talking about.

She would try and do this without letting Janine know that she was not the first person she contacted now that she was back from…

She would probably need a sleep by then.

African charities.

Where was it that she was supposed to have been going all this time?

Her father had told them that they were real; had built wells and schools and hospitals and continued with good works to this day.

She had better bone up.

Thankfully all Janine ever asked was:

'Is it all going okay over there? Are you doing good things?'

Or something like that, to which she would respond:

'Yes, mother. It's all good, but… let's not talk about it. I'm here to see *you*.'

And that generally did the trick. She could have been in Africa or China or India, she could have been on The Moon after that; her mother never mentioned it again.

And Jade never even asked.

So she would do her duty as a good and loving first daughter, and responsible older sister, and that would all go fine, as usual.

Maybe this time, she could get Trudy alone.

If she could get her away from running all the protests, occupies, press conferences, covert missions and PR stunts The Pan was busy with, just for a few hours… maybe they could catch up in reality for once?

And then, the chance of catching up with Bo Everett and

Yelina.

And after all that, then…

Finally, there were…

The lovers.

She did not want to think about any of them, even though there were still three (and even a fourth, distantly, painfully) to think about…

But not yet.

Maybe not ever.

Maybe she was done; maybe it was time to call it quits, to be solitary and content.

Or find someone else.

Her guts twisted.

Too soon?

Okay.

Don't go there.

Don't think about them, any of them.

Talk to Heather again.

Heather was key to everything.

Yes. She would look forward to seeing all of the Pandorans, greatly she knew, seeing all of them properly, with time to relax without the pressure of going back, and that would suffice.

But even so, still; not just yet.

Heff grumbled, got up, turned around three times, then plonked down in a ball again.

Just like he used to, on her royal bed, back –

This time, she laughed.

Laughed and laughed.

What next?

She wondered.

What – next?!

CHAPTER 26

No sooner had she done this than she heard the text signal on her Eve go off again. She suddenly remembered that it had gone off 'last night' as well, when she had first stumbled sleepily through the wardrobe doors. It had shocked her then; she had essentially forgotten she had one, then the sonar ping sound she'd – apparently – set it on had gone off under her pillow in the middle of her sleep.

She had just turned it off.

This morning, there it had been again, fully recharged; natch.

The standard models had a lot more fancy reverse-engineered tech in them now, but they were still nothing on her fully tricked-out, souped-up Earthling-Pleiadean model.

So her phone was on-point, and fleek, but she was still dressed in towels.

She needed to get her shit together.

Crying, laughing, alone.

Jesus and Mary and Audrey Tautou!

Heff was asleep now.

Settled for the first time in...

She didn't want to think or she would cry again.

She touched his rump, affectionately, and he grumbled and shifted.

Yep, he was settled alright.

So she checked her Eve and saw that there were indeed a few new text messages she'd missed last night.

Jade: Are you back yet? Call me. Urgent.

Wasn't it always?

They'd catch up tomorrow, or later.

And one earlier, from Harding.

Harding: Came through and heard you snoring. Call your father and tell him you're back, otherwise I have to, it's my job. Back tonight. Dinner here at Fork or there at Omega?

Dinner.
Yes.
She needed to find clothes though, new clothes for her new, post-war phase. Again she thought; she was sure there were boxes of Cleverco-branded stuff all around the place, clothes and trinkets, both here at Harding's and at Omega, that Heather kept sending.

Heather designed at lot of the clothes herself, she was good at logos and branding, and had won some kind of award for it. She had designed the Cleverco logo too, based on Thys' idea; a stylish updating of the classic storybook crescent moon and star, with the crescent standing in for the C of Cleverco on the formal logo.

There were many variants but the principle palette was the navy, gold and silver one, the classic storybook-Nouveau, child's nursery tone.

She looked around.
Clothes.
The bed had been made, but the phone had been under the pillow where she had asked Harding to put it, if he ever found it laying about.

Her heart melted then, for just a tiny second.
That was something for an Old Dude.
He really remembered and looked out for her.
However...
He had not been expecting her.
Odd.
He usually knew.
But that meant he was on another assignment, or perhaps

wrapping up a poker game, or an affair with an actress, or a favour-job on the side. He was supposed to be retired now, and just minding her, but every now and then his past caught up. On those occasions, he generally asked some of his bodyguard friends, usually Byford and his men, to watch the house. But there hadn't been any - they would have reported in, before she slept.

She felt a bit sick.

Maybe...

She looked at Heff.

Could he tell the difference, if there had been both Byford's troops and assassins?

CHAPTER 27

Heather: (<u>12 hours ago</u>) Felt you pop in, assuming you're with The Ent. We're going to People Corner tomorrow. Let us know of you want to come. If you turn up in the desert out of nowhere it will need a lot of explaining. Dinner where?

That must have been last night, just after she'd fallen asleep.

What the hell time was it anyway?

Twelve hours ago?

Really?

Then, while she'd been in the shower, talking to the CIA:

Dad: Lovely seeing your face. Just a reminder: we're famous, so don't go out in public without Harding, and look out for the leprechauns!

Heather: (seconds later) He means those two redhead paparazzi, they've become quite aggressive lately.

Dad: Don't Google yourself. You know that never helps.

Heather: Okay, now you won't be able to help yourself. Try not to get mad. They don't know you. Only you do. See you soon. xxxxxxcetera.

Dad: Really, don't.

She wondered where the hell they were. She'd never heard of People Corner, or even People's Corner, if the auto-correct had jumped in. They must have been there by now. Still, it seemed like they were going to have a busy afternoon in the middle of the desert. In the desert, but somewhere public they couldn't gap in and out of…?

Regardless, they clearly had their hands full.

Had they been on a helicopter?

Is that what they'd said?

An invisible…?

Whatever.

She'd been half awake.

They could tell her tomorrow, or she would hear from them soon enough, no doubt, and she'd get the full story then, no doubt either.

Finally there was another stream of text exchanges between herself and three old school friends, whom she'd apparently arranged to meet in Sydney, that afternoon. She kind of remembered doing that last night, half-cut on creamy indigo astral chardonnay.

Oh.

Had she been drinking that as well…?

Chindigonnay?

Ewww…

Or, had she been?

She didn't really feel hungover, just…

Wait.

Hang on.

She had clearly been sleepy, and thought – this *next* Los Angeles morning – and now… where the hell was she supposed to be? And when?

With…?

Again: twelve hours ago?

Wow.

So the time here and the time there was… what?

Another text came in.

Brooke: Ems can make it too – 3.30 for drinks – and – whatever – at the usual café on George, evening free – see you there – looking forward!

Damn.

Drunk dialling, arranging dates…

She Googled: 'time in sydney'.

3.25

'Fuck.'

CHAPTER 28

As was now well-documented in Pandora lore, it had quickly emerged within their select group that there were precious few places left in the major cities where a borderline superhero could appear out of nowhere with her giant bodyguard and not be noticed by security cameras, secret government cameras, covert corporate cameras, or the cameras that everyone just carried around with them, which Thys was all-too aware, were as often as not all one and the same thing these days.

But she had her secret entrances into Sydney; abandoned buildings where they never checked the cameras (she knew, because she had disabled them and 'they' hadn't fixed them) or sometimes, the private residences of people who were influential enough never to have had them installed.

(But if they ever developed a program that determined whether or not the same people had entered and exited a building on the same day, she and her friends were all in trouble.

So far, so far as she knew, and she believed she did, that hadn't happened. Not as yet. Not if she had anything to do with it, anyway. Not that she or any of the fellow Pandorans would ever resort to sabotage in order to cover their tracks.

Perish the thought.)

Leaving Harding to his business, she was able to walk down the last few blocks of George Street in the knowledge that she was easily the least recognized member of her family, and that if she kept her head down she would probably be okay. In order to secure this, she had decided to avoid Google and just check her Wikipedia entry, regardless of her father's warning, to see what all the fuss was about, and what she might have to explain, should her friends ask.

She really wasn't used to this; she had getaways and haunts and men she saw sparingly for when she wasn't in the astral, but in general people weren't really her thing.

...maybe because of that?

Maybe... one fed the other?

But she suspected they never would be 'her thing', and even less so, now she was back.

Maybe even for good.

And if not for good, with the more recent fractions of 'here and away' proportionately reversed.

And relatively famous, apparently.

So, she called up and read her entry.

She hadn't read it in years.

After all, she was a big girl now.

She read it like the people she hated; head down, barely looking where she was going.

People.

She sighed.

I just have to deal with the fact that I am one of them.

CHAPTER 29

<u>Amethyst Pyne</u>

From Wikipedia, the free encyclopedia

Amethyst Sky Pyne (born 15th October, 1994) is the eldest daughter of <u>Mitchell Pyne</u> and <u>Janine Norway</u> and is the primary heiress to the so-called <u>Cleverco fortune</u>.

She is a notorious <u>recluse</u>,[1] working hands-on and anonymously within her various African-based <u>charitable foundations</u>, often in remote locations [2].

In direct contrast to her sister <u>Jade Saxe Pyne</u>, Amethyst has successfully avoided the media spotlight since her father's marriage to socialite <u>Heather Everett</u> [3] and the couple's subsequent receipt of ownership of <u>Cleverco</u> at the bequest <u>Bo Everett</u> and his fellow billionaire <u>Oliver Hines</u>, following the <u>Everco-Olivera controversy</u>.

Early life

Born in <u>Sydney, Australia</u>, [4] Amethyst Pyne has one sibling, her younger sister Jade Pyne (born 23rd November 1996). Both Amethyst and Jade were raised by their parents in the North Shore suburb of <u>Mosman</u> where they attended <u>Mosman High School</u> .[5]

Pyne scored high grades until the age of fifteen [6] when her parents divorced, after which Pyne's mother Janine received custody of both daughters [7] and subsequently moved them to <u>London </u>where she eventually married Pyne's step-father, <u>Jeremy David Vector</u>, a <u>BBC television presenter</u> and <u>documentary producer</u>.

Recruitment and Reconciliation

On her eighteenth birthday in London, Pyne is reported to have undergone a <u>spiritual epiphany</u>, [8] after which she immediately returned to Sydney. There she either actively sought out [9] or was actively recruited [10] by <u>The Pan</u> (at the time Pan's People) a spiritual activist movement started by Pyne's nominal godfather <u>Holland Pankhurst</u>, but at the time run by his sister, <u>Trudy Pankhurst</u>. Soon afterwards, Amethyst reconciled with her estranged father [11] and was later a bridesmaid at the his 2018 wedding to Heather Everett [12] .

According to several eye-witness reports, [13] she may have been present with her father at the time of the so-called <u>Los Angeles Miracle Quake</u>.

Career

Via her access to Cleverco, Pyne is a dedicated philanthropist [14] and charity organizer [15]. She is director of the <u>African Enlightenment Foundation</u>, the <u>Earth Solar Colonies Awareness Project</u> and the <u>Earth Wellness Epicenter</u> [16]. Spending most of her time in remote African locations, [17] she has only rarely been photographed [18] and has never been formally interviewed [19].

Media challenges

On the day of her twenty-third birthday, trillionaire media mogul <u>Wyatt Styger</u> offered ten million dollars for a video interview with Pyne, stipulating only that it needed to be clearly verifiable and of television broadcast quality [20], to which radio shock jock <u>Barbie Yeltsin</u> responded with a counter-offer of a million dollars for a <u>sex-tape</u> featuring Pyne that proved she had lost her virginity, stipulating that the tape needed only to be of internet quality [21]. Conspiracy theorist <u>Zaq Qwerty</u> then also offered a sum of money, ten thousand dollars, for proof that Pyne was still alive, and had not been sacrificed to the ancient Babylonian goddess <u>Semiramis</u> during the Los Angeles earthquake, in order for her father to make a <u>Faustian bargain</u> so he could become a billionaire [22]. At this time, none of the rewards have been claimed [23], and no response from Pyne, or any of her family members, has been forthcoming.

Personal Life

Comparatively few visual records of the adult Amethyst Pyne exist, nor many beyond her high school years; although she was extensively photographed at her father's wedding [24], given her long absence from the media spotlight, and lack of visual records in the period subsequent to her departure from London, and up to the present day, there remains an <u>internet conspiracy theory</u> as to whether the person photographed at the Pyne-Everett wedding, and at prior public engagements, was actually Amethyst Pyne, or an imposter [25].

Pyne is believed to own a home somewhere on Sydney's northern beaches [26], and to occasionally visit Australia [27], but is thought to reside primarily in various undisclosed abodes within several North African countries [26].

At the time of her eighteenth birthday she was in a long-term relationship with ex-classmate Nathan Juror, but that relationship terminated upon her return to Australia. [citation needed]

References...

Thys stopped there on the street and considered the entry.

She could see what they meant now.

She had turned twenty-three more than four years ago, but she hadn't checked her entry since then. The 'media challenges' section, and all the business about internet conspiracies, seemed new.

She was smart enough to remember what they'd said and realise that it was possible that her father had created some kind of elaborate cover story to obfuscate the fact that she had been in another dimension, thank you very much, fighting a war, almost single-handedly at times, that would secure the future of humanity.

But she still didn't like it.

Then again, reading between the lines, it did kind of make her seem like she might be some kind of a Cold War spy.

Either that, or a hapless patsy who has been sacrificed to a pagan Anunnaki god.

She wondered shortly if she should go on, but decided to proceed.

Google: **Amethyst Pyne**

Amethyst Sky Pyne - Wikipedia, the free encyclopedia
en.wikipedia.org/wiki/**Amethyst_Pyne**

Amethyst Pyne (born 15th October, 1998) is the eldest daughter of Mitchell Pyne and Janine Norway and an heiress to the so-called Cleverco fortune. She is a notorious recluse…

Early life - Recruitment and Reconciliation – Career – Media Challenges – Personal Life

News for **Amethyst Pyne**

Amethyst Pyne (RealAmyPyne) on Twitter
https://twitter.com/RealAmyPyne

Hi this is the real Amethyst Pyne – I am not active on twitter – do not believe anyone who says they are me!

The Official Website of **Amethyst Pyne**
www.amethystpyne.com

Under construction… please bookmark us and come back soon!
Amethyst Pyne | Facebook
Are you Amethyst Pyne? This Facebook page is…

African Enlightenment Foundation
www.africanenlightenmentfoundation.com

Earth Solar Colonies Awareness Project
Earth Solar Colonies Awareness Project

Earth Wellness Epicenter
Earth Wellness Epicenter

She didn't bother to check the charity pages; she'd seen them before, and while it pleased her that they were real, and doing whatever they were supposed to be doing, it irritated her that now she was back for a while, she would have to learn all about them with enough detail to fake her involvement.

She'd not considered that when she'd agreed to this, gapping out one Sunday afternoon when her father had quickly asked her permission, back to the astral war.

Hmmm.

Maybe that would be her next-next thing, after looking into Regene?

Charity work for real?

Maybe?

She'd have to bluff it with the girls this afternoon, like she did with her mother, but…

This would require some thought, and attention.

'Fantastic, sarcastic,' she uttered to herself.

CHAPTER 30

Thys walked on down George Street, under the shadow of several skyscrapers, toward the Bridge, trying just for today not to think about how her family owned that building there, and that one there; and of course the Cleverco Castle right over there.

But she was almost there now, at the cafe, and running late.

She had not been aware of any the weird offers, not from Wyatt Styger, Barbie Yeltsin, or Zaq Qwerty, and had no idea really how to feel about any of them.

Truth be told, the more she thought about them, the more she didn't like any of it very much, at all. But if she were to be honest, she was feeling sort of okay about being interesting, and mysterious enough to be the subject of her own proper internet conspiracy theory.

That was kind of cool.

She could probably use that to her advantage, or at least have some fun with it. Or, she could totally ignore them all, and go about her business of catching up with her friends…?

Yes.

That sounded good.

She was about to log off when she noticed some random text from one of the lower entries.

'…while her mother was very pretty, if not beautiful, her father's genes add something to Amethyst's makeup that make her sexy as well; genuinely sexy, the kind of sexy you achieve without trying, as opposed to the kind of 'Ice Queen Cool' pose her mother was so proficient in producing in her prime…'

Jesus.

In her prime?

Jesus Christ!

Had Janine *seen this*?

She must have... completely freaked out!

It effectively called Janine a... *a has been.*

Oh – God!

Thys was actually starting to sweat now.

In looks, Thys had taken after her mother, but since her odd growth spurt they had looked somewhat less alike than they had when she had been a teenager; still, over the years, and especially recently, many people had still told her that she was the spitting image of Janine... when she was the same age.

Thys knew very well that Janine had loved this kind of comparison; clearly she had produced two highly desirable and attractive daughters, one of whom was constantly compared to herself, the other who was also compared to herself, but who took more after Mitch. Janine had of course since remarried, but Thys knew that to be constantly reminded of her handsome first husband, without the burden of still being married to him, usually as she stood beside her equally, if not more handsome second husband, was also tremendously flattering. Janine was someone who attracted increasingly handsome husbands; for her third act, she would no doubt be the one who finally nailed George Clooney.

She laughed to herself.

That's if someone hadn't already!

Wait. Maybe someone had?

She quickly googled.

Damn!

Was she that far behind?

Gahd.

But still, it had been this kind of thing; her mother's open insecurity, of having to constantly and positively compare herself to her two teenage daughters, that had contributed to Thys fleeing from her London home all those years ago in the first place, and stumbling back to Sydney where she had eventually trained with the Pan, she now understood… just to get back at her.

And that fucking idiot she was married to.

Wow.

Wow.

Had she really just thought that?

That had just come up from *nowhere*.

She hadn't really thought about Jeremy, *Jeremy Vector*, for… well, years. He'd occasionally registered in the astral, mostly within the generally quite healthy masturbatory fantasies of middle-aged women who spent a lot of time in front of the television, but in truth she thought of him now more as someone akin to an average high school teacher she'd had to put up with for a while, rather than her actual stepfather of… *howevermany* years.

Still, him being a complete wanker had certainly contributed a few cobblestones to the path that had eventually led back to her father, and reconciliation, and… where she was now.

Hmmm.

A large drop of rain fell on the Eve screen, startling her.

Right now, she was…

Standing at the Bridge-end of George Street, about to get wet, reading what online critics thought of her mother.

She put the Eve back in her pocket.

It was time to get back to reality.

You're Amethyst Pyne, you've been doing charity work in Africa, and you're about… anywhere from five to three years behind on current third-density pop and political culture and reality, despite the fact that the fate of the western world resides squarely in your hands…

Or, dreams…

Or… something you can't remember.

She sighed, heavily and visibly, and reconfirmed.

This so-called reality really did not have as much going for it as one might think.

CHAPTER 31

When she had been dressing, very quickly, Thys had kept the news on.

What followed DeVora in the news headlines had been: something about exports being down, something about one of the wars in the Middle East going badly, something about the economy being in danger of underperforming, and reports that an athlete was in disgrace after being caught using performance enhancing drugs… these were all cyclic things.

Thys had seen them all percolating in the astral, but had been unable to effect directly them. They had all been designed to make people feel generally uneasy, dissatisfied, and betrayed. They were all stories that were essentially slight reinventions of the things she'd seen the last time she'd turned on a television in third density, many months ago now apparently, and the time before that, and the time before that, and so it went, on and on.

It had been one of the first things she had learned about humanity's dream-life and imaginative landscape; that it was incredibly difficult to change anything, or to effect anything that already existed. The Anunnaki had their stinking-evil astral temples that had roots so deeply embedded in third density that it would be impossible to destroy them, and even if she could, such an act would destroy the world as people knew it.

"Too deep to fail", she supposed.

She certainly had no desire to trigger Armageddon, or End Times, or whatever else you called it outside of Right Wing Christianity. Her family had been through enough of that!

Yet these Anunnaki temples were sapping away humanity's spirit, its independence as a race, and had contained humanity in order for their own race to feed from and exploit, like some ethereal combination of oxygen and nuclear fusion.

Thys and her Ymira allies had tried and failed to take control of some of those temples, after the Palace had first been attacked; and it had cost them dearly. Yet there were also platoons of Draco, and their allies, who had been killed during those first few failed attacks. Killed and incarnated into Earth's karmic system, a virtually unrecoverable disgrace by the standards of their race. There had been humans who had engaged in the battle, via their lucid dreams; some voluntarily, some not so much. Now many of them resided in third density psychiatric wards, or had been forced to take strong mood-altering medications, just to remain sane after what they had gone through with Thys and her troops, in that first year of the war-proper.

Eventually it had become clear that her task, their task, was as it had always been; not to destroy what was already there, but to clear out *new* territory in the astral.

So they had abandoned their futile and costly attacks on the Dracopolis, and retreated back to Port Ymira in The Sea of Humanity. That had always been an alternative space in fourth density; a place somewhere that something new and different and unrestrained could naturally and organically take form; something decidedly and wholly human, as opposed to resiliently reptilian.

Thys and her people had quickly begun to realise that once humans had a viable alternative to the psychological mazes and loops, and endless false- horizons offered by Anunnaki-influenced society as it stood, as designed and perfected by the Anunnaki over thousands of years of learning humanity's weaknesses, their glitches, and even breeding those exploitable traits into humanity more strongly, then they would gravitate to that alternative; that new place, very naturally. It would be a literal and figurative "dream destination" that was truly uninfected by the constant plagues of the Anunnaki anxiety viruses, and cancerous concerns.

Thys and her crew, her soldiers, her troops; her Anunnaki marines of the Ymira clan, had bet everything on this retreat.

On the Sea of Humanity, and the so-called (still against her will, but by that time, set in astral stone) Amethyst Palace.

Dreaming humanity would gravitate to these places, feed and be nourished; spiritually, intellectually and imaginatively from them, be inspired by and even co-create them, and would then thrive and prosper as something new, and better.

They *would*.

They *had to*.

Once that happened, that alternative would be further energized, and the source of anxiety would become de-energized and… well, that was basically how the astral worked.

'Give it time, Thystle…' Jason Axelrod had told her, after it had all been decided. '…give it time.'

CHAPTER 32

It was just that, before Pan and Suzie, and Thys and The Pandorans, only a small handful of others, a very few conscious humans, had managed to somehow gain unrestricted access to Earth's astral plane.

Although; that was not *strictly* true.

There had been those within the remaining indigenous people of the world, who had kept their ancient astral cultures alive.

But certainly, very few modern, westernized humans.

Not for… probably… well; thousands of years?

Thys had certainly not been the first of the modern, fully astral-empowered Earthlings, but she was unquestionably the strongest.

And now, she was back, and it was all very abstract.

Everything she'd done.

Very abstract indeed, now she'd come home, and slept on it, and thought about it again.

Almost like it had happened to someone else.

'Almost like a dream,' she said out loud, and laughed to herself.

Merrily, merrily… something echoed.

Only shortly, however.

Yet again, she hit the same speed bump.

The main problem was; even though she seemed to recall that the war was…

Over?

She couldn't remember…

Had their plan worked?

Had they succeeded?

She had fallen back onto the bed again, the side of her head bumping Heff.

'Rurr-rrrmmmmrurr.'

'Exactly.'

She supposed she would just have to wait and see what Heather had to say.

Wait.

Another day.

And put some shoes on.

CHAPTER 33

In other news, there had been a Bo Everett sighting, this time not in Peru, or Miami, but in New York, on the helicopter pad of the Cleverco offices there.

(That one might be real, she suspected… she would have to ask him, when she asked once again for permission to board *Lady Ann…*)

The last thing she found herself prepared to sit through as she dressed, without throwing a chair at the screen, was an entertainment report that had made the main news cycle; the announcement that there were still problems with the highly anticipated feature film, *The Law of Large Numbers*, starring Gabrielle Fenwick, Avery Messange, Krimson Azureus and Vance McLeod; an epic romance about the Los Angeles 'Miracle Quake' of twenty-twelve.

The movie had been scheduled to open the Cannes Film Festival in just a few days time, but apparently the notoriously temperamental director of the rumored four-hour film, Adison Achilleos, had been fighting with the heads of Olivera Studios, and their distribution partners, over the final cut and running time, and had less than a day to deliver in order to make the opening deadline.

Inside word was: the opening night film would have to be replaced, probably with rival director Parry Newsome's new drama *Spiritual*, another ensemble based on the Miracle Quake, although reportedly a very different take; this one based on stories of how people had coped with surviving, several years later.

That news in particular made her edgy. She sensed some new kind of trouble brewing in the creative ether, something she might have been able to predict or even correct if she'd been at home in The Palace.

But from here, she could only take a guess.

Thys liked Adison Achilleos.

After the premiere of *Umbrella Stand* all those years ago, she had gone back and watched *Little Pink*, and *In The Room*. They were beautiful films. *Umbrella Stand*, the last in the loosely-connected trilogy, had been an ensemble tour de force; a masterpiece, some claimed. Thys knew that *The Law of Large Numbers* was already a beautiful film. Possibly even a classic, maybe even another masterpiece. Certainly, a very strong contender for Best Picture at the Oscars (*Umbrella Stand*, her father's 'little engine that could', had gained eight nominations, but had only won one; Best Supporting Actor for Avery Messange).

Mitch had ensured that Achilleos had signed with Olivera Studios, and assured him of a healthy budget and full creative control of his next project. At the time, Mitch had been working under the assumption that he and Heather now owned the studio.

However a continued legal battle with Olivera Studios' current CEO, Ray Sachs, and his head of marketing and production, Anna Dryden, both protégés of "missing-presumed-murdered" ex-studio head Don Eissley (the Anunnaki-possessed psychopath who had tried to kill her, and everyone she loved) were making things maddeningly difficult for both Mitch, as he tried to wrest control of the studio from them, and the notorious visionary Achilleos, as he tried to retain creative control over his own masterwork.

How and why the – "still missing" – studio CEO's heirs and development slate were in control, still running nine years later, at a company that was technically owned by Cleverco, was a long and complicated story that involved intricate long-term contracts, iron-clad guarantee in profit participation percentages of net and gross profit-margins, and...

Thys could never quite understand.

To get rid of them, they would basically have to pay them so much that the whole studio would go under.

That was basically it.

And one that Thys…

Seemed to have forgotten to deal with.

Huh.

She could have done something about that, surely?

In the astral?

That was weird.

It had been such a long-time thorn in Mitch's side as well.

'We just can't get rid of them…!' Mitch had exclaimed, highly frustrated, more than once in front of his daughter. '…I finally own movie studio; and there's nothing I can do to stop their blockbusters being complete shit!'

And yet, she had not…

Maybe her lack of concern was because…?

Her father had already dealt with it?

Hmmm.

Mitch had indeed managed to start a small production company of his own, within Olivera Studios, but because of the iron-clad first-look and exclusivity clauses that applied to all of the production company contracts under Sachs and Dryden's reign, all the films produced under Mitch's new Cleverco Pictures shingle had to be distributed by Olivera, with final cut approval.

Given that Achilleos had never taken less than four years to make a new film, Mitch had felt certain that by the time Law of Large Numbers was compete, he would have long been rid of Olivera Studios altogether.

Now look where they were.

And on the flipside…

Thys entirely disliked Parry Newsome, and thought he was the least "spiritual" man she'd ever met, let alone someone to be making a film with that title.

Both 'Miracle Quake' films would no-doubt be filled with amazing special effects. However, Achilleos would use them in service to the plot, for awe and heart, while Newsome would use them to disguise the absence of those elements; she had learned that much from her ex-critic father.

Newsome's film, if he were true to form, would have several mean-spirited twists, designed to make people think as he did; that the world was awful, and cruel, and random, and that the idea of spirit itself was just a fantasy, a lame notion the weak-minded used to cope with their fear of death.

She sighed.

Christ, what an arsehole.

And the worst thing about it was; while Achilleos was still working for Sachs and Dryden, under studio philosophy of their mentor Don Eissley, Newsome had free reign under his own shingle at a major streaming service run by Cleverco's biggest new rival, Hypa.

Anyway, she was tempted to gap over there instantly and to talk to Adison, to impress upon him the urgency of finishing before Parry Newsome, but she knew, almost equally as instantly, that it would was a terrible idea. Adison Achilleos had enough to deal with; his muse, actress of the decade and long standing it-girl Krimson Azureus, having wrapped her shooting days for the film months ago, had once again and true to form vanished without trace, the modern day Garbo, they said.

Hardly.

Azureus was terrible.

But she was much-beloved, especially by Achilleos, so-hot -right-now; and right now, was total Oscar-bait.

According to the news story, she was rumored to be making an appearance on the red carpet at Cannes, but Thys thought it highly unlikely, given her previous track record. She didn't ponder the matter too long; she did not want to think about Krimson Azureus, or her over-exposed relationship with Achilleos, nor how it had supposedly ended. Nor about how massively over-rated this seriously untalented actress was, and the general public's inability to understand that she was nothing more than an appalling, third-rate ham.

CHAPTER 34

The story was running again on the TV in the cafe.

They made decent coffee here and not Thys, but Amethyst Pyne, as she was now required to think of herself once again, was enjoying hers.

Despite the TV, and the internet, it was a lazy Tuesday…

Or Wednesday?

…afternoon in the middle of May, in the really very cool-sounding year of twenty twenty-one, and even though it had rained all morning, apparently, and almost started again as she had made her way here, the sun had peeked out from behind the clouds just as she'd arrived.

Consequently, Amethyst Pyne and her three old school friends had been able to sit al fresco, along the drying pavement, outside the picture-post-card, almost-famous café, with the view looking up toward the southern end of the Sydney Harbour Bridge.

Amethyst Pyne stared out periodically at the visible arc of the giant, iconic structure as the afternoon settled in, the bridge's very presence seeming to loom, even from a relatively short distance away, over the ancient bars and shops along the low end of George Street.

It had seemed so long ago that she and her father had gazed down Pitt Street at the bridge, from a completely different aspect, upon the balcony of Pan's empty apartment... which was now Heather's private office.

She took a leisurely gulp of her double-shot full-cream latte as she finished telling her three old friends about her fake life as it stood, trying to remain true at least to the emotion of it, and it seemed to be working.

'So you live with your grandfather now?' Emily asked, not

quite getting the gist from when Thys had tried to explain it earlier. It was no wonder; she hadn't quite settled into the lie, and had almost stuffed it up, by trying to make it up as she went along, and being way too specific.

'No, I stay at his place when I'm in Los Angeles, which he keeps there, but while I'm in Sydney, he stays with me. I bought him an apartment here, under the one I bought for myself.'

'In the Cleverco building?' Emily asked. 'Cleverco Castle?'

They couldn't see the skyline from here, but the Cleverco building was dominant. She hadn't wanted to live there, even when Mitch had offered her one of the four – highly secure, hint-hint – penthouse apartments.

'Yes...' Amethyst lied. 'It's working out really well. I don't have anyone special right now, so me and grand-pop look after each other. But we never get in each other's way.'

Knowing that grand-pop was probably listening, somewhere within sniper-range, made her bite her tongue to stop herself giggling.

'No-one special?' Linh whined. 'It must be so hard, to tell who's genuine, and who's after the money...?'

'But it's very nice,' Brooke intercepted, 'to take care of your elderly relatives like that...'

Grand-pop would love that.

She could hear his grumbling and teeth grinding from here.

Thys smiled at Brooke then returned Linh the zinger she'd realised worked most of the time on people who passively-aggressively resented her being bizarre-stroke-of-luck wealthy.

She adopted a so-called "posh Australian accent".

'I don't know that I ever will trust another ordinary man, Linh. I suppose that's why billionaire heiresses tend to marry inside their same social circle; I'll just have to marry another billionaire. If he's got *his own* billions, then there's less of a concern that he's after mine.'

They were all stunned at the response, until Thys laughed.

Then they all did.

CHAPTER 35

Amy-not-Thys had been just about to ask them all for details; how were they doing? What were they doing? How was it all going? But then their pleasant enough, though slightly wary, initial catch-up was interrupted by a beautiful, dark haired, unmissable woman as she strode confidently past their al fresco table and called out cheerfully through a bright, full, rose-red smile that beamed directly and unmistakably at Amethyst Pyne, with the woman's huge, white, toothpaste-commercial-teeth glistening broadly, and her emerald stiletto heels clicking sharply past.

'Hi, Thys!'

She was medium build and curvaceous in a plunging, open-necked, bright Paris Green dress, tied tightly with a lime cord around her slim waist. Her thick, shoulder-length, jet-black hair flowed immaculately in her wake.

'Call me! We must catch up!'

The woman's brown eyes flashed and sparkled at Amethyst Pyne as she turned away to face the sidewalk. Then she waved again, absently over her shoulder, as she spun to turn a corner, singing out one last time.

'Don't become a lonely goddess!'

Amethyst Pyne's friends watched as the woman proceeded away, striding softly, shoes clacking with the confidence of a model in the last few seconds of a high-profile television spot for expensive shampoo.

Then she was gone.

Amethyst Pyne knew what they were all thinking; that they would never even *think* to dress like that on a day like today, even if they *could* pull it off; they had all dressed for a chill afternoon, and possibly evening, despite the late-emerging sun, and also, *how dare she.*

Collectively they turned back to face each other around the table again, both Brooke and Linh in turn shooting a disapproving look at Amethyst Pyne, having completely forgotten what they had been talking about.

'Was that Carla Gugino?' Emily exclaimed. 'The actress?'

'A *what* did she say?' Brooke frowned. 'Don't become a *what?*'

Emily shrugged. ' "Go pick up a lowly frog", I thought she said.'

'What?' Linh demanded. 'What does that even mean?'

'You know, like Prince Charming…' Emily remained star struck. 'Amy; how do you know Carla Gugino?'

Brooke rolled her eyes. 'Her father is friends with Bo Everett and Oliver Hines, Emily. Of course she knows celebrities!'

'That wasn't her,' Linh scowled. 'The actress you're thinking of is at least fifty. That woman was mid-twenties, if that.'

Emily huffed lightly at Linh. 'Regene, Linh!'

Linh shook her head and rolled her eyes across the table at Amethyst Pyne, as though she would somehow confirm Emily's stupidity. Amethyst Pyne did not respond appropriately, and that annoyed Linh.

'Look-alikes, Ems!'

Amethyst Pyne's three old school friends were all twenty-seven years old, as was she, all born in nineteen-ninety four (although Linh, the eldest, might have been twenty-eight by now). They were all pretty, but they were each in turn as different from each other as she was from them. Brooke was tall and muscular-thin; she tended to dress in pantsuits and long coats and scarves, as she had today, in an autumn brown leather coat and boots, with a tan and black ensemble. Linh was short and broad-shoulder-busty; she would display cleavage in the Arctic if given half the chance and always wore bright colors, immaculately matching from eye shadow to shoe. Today she was autumnal also, a lively tan coat with an orange shirt and white sweater. Emily was a natural blonde country girl; she always dressed nicely, and always seemed to look pretty without trying. Today she'd worn a black wool sweater with a matching skirt, and a long cardigan of swirling bright colors from her latest trip to India, alone. While Emily remained single, always complaining about it but never too much, Brooke and Linh had both married within the last year, tying the knot within six months of each other, as though it had been some kind of competition. But it had also been because, on the weird converse some women somehow maintained, they had wanted to share closely in each other's joy and the anticipation of preparation. If anticipation truly was nine tenths, then they had made it eighteen twentieths, if not twenty-seven thirtieths. Twenty-eight, even.

Amethyst Pyne smiled at the thought.

Then she frowned. Although the whole thing had seemed bizarre to her, and despite the fact that she had left far more immediately pressing duties at the time, in the astral, to attend both their weddings, she had wanted none of it for herself. But lately she had missed her friends and quite recently, since those pressing duties had begun to dissipate, and the…

Truce?

Ceasefire?

Why did it still seem so hazy?

…anyway, since then, she had found herself wondering about them more and more; how they were, how it had all worked out for them. She had made a commitment to herself not to pry on them from the dreamscape of the astral; that was never a good idea and she had, when she had first settled there, made some nasty habits for herself in the regard until…

Another thing she didn't like to think about.

She had even seriously contemplated maybe even sharing some of the more unusual elements of her extraordinary life with them. It had been more than seven years, nearly eight probably, since her father had tasked her with the duty of writing down the six people she trusted most in the world…

She'd done it without thinking.

But anyway...

Here she was.

Years later.

Without the excuse of a birthday, or a wedding...

Just... friends.

Chatting.

When they had done coffee regularly, all those years ago, usually on a Saturday morning, being out and about, they had all dressed in the regulation fashion-branded smart-sporty gear, to look as though they had either just been to the gym, or were on their way to the gym.

Which, of course, they hadn't been, and were absolutely not.

Generally, on a Saturday morning, they had all been way too hungover for anything remotely approaching exercise, let alone the gym, and had all been drinking espressos, or the latest healthy smoothie concoction, energy drink, or some other notorious hangover cure.

For Amethyst Pyne, after being away for so long, away from all this in particular, it had seemed strange, again, to give even a second's consideration to such a matter as what to wear, and yet, before departing, even though she had been appallingly short on time, she had.

There had been something even refreshingly normal about it, knowing that the safest play was to meet the old and the new half-way.

Heather had indeed dispatched a box of Cleverco-branded sports gear and casual wear to The Fork, all branded with Heather's cool-but-sweet-but-serious Cleverco moon and star logo, all stylish but firmly contained within the color variants of Thys' favourite Cleverco's pallete; combos of blue and purple, sky blue and violet, baby blue and lavender, navy blue and burgundy, contrasted with shades of grey, and black and white.

She had tripped over the box, trying to find it, shoved under the bedroom curtains at the edge of the massive wardrobe, but there was so much in there, just in that one box, that she had not been able to choose between tees, long-sleeved tees, round-neck sweaters, v-neck sweaters, various styles of jeans and track pants and trousers, scarves and runners... in all of those Cleverco colour palletes. By the time she had assessed them all it was too late to thrown something on; her mind was addled by too many choices.

She had found herself toying with the collar of her Field Marshall coat, which she was still wearing like a bath robe; and then realised. There was opal, all around the wardrobe. She summoned some and swirled it about her head and shoulders; this was her uniform, her costume, and it changed, when she applied astral energies to it, into what she needed.

The thing was; she had never done this before.

She had always changed clothes for Earth.

Never adapted, but remained... 'in character' she supposed, and laughed at herself. She did not know which was 'the character' any longer. Amy, or Thys. Neither.

She watched herself in the mirror as it happened; it was like fairy dust from a Disney movie, but it sparked and cracked with a real, and somewhat startling electrical charge. The miliray leather coat lengthened, softened, and came in at her waist. A hoodie appeared, burnt-orange, to match the coat's new copper belt buckle, and the new, more subtle epaulettes along the shoulder-line of the coat, also shining copper. Her regular black, Anunnaki-leather trousers softened as well, and tightened a bit; her military boots became more fashionable; she jolted as the high-heels extended, and were fronted with a row of straps with copper buckles.

She had been astonished; every piece of it somehow still reflected a part of her core-past, her history, but was now... literally "fashion conscious".

The girls, or 'women' now, she supposed, had all laughed when they had seen the branded scarf she had added to the outfit (she had tried on the a blue-burgundy one, just to see, and the opal had immediately changed the base colour to black, and the patterned, almost houndstooth Cleverco logos to ochre).

All in good spirits, of course... but; making her very glad that she had not appeared in the full company-branded ensemble.

Thys liked it though. She thought the scarf looked good and, truth be told, was proud of Cleverco.

(Of course, she didn't let them know that they she had been wearing a variation of the same outfit for... how many years now?)

'Black Irish,' Brooke shrugged.

'What?' Linh demanded.

'Black Irish; Irish descendants with Italian blood, it's a New York thing. They all look like that.'

'Like what?'

'Like her, or that other one…'

'What other one?'

'That other gorgeous actress with the beautiful face and hot curves who looks half-Irish and half-Italian, who all the nerds adore…'

Linh seemed appalled, then returned her attention to Emily.

'It can't be Regene, Emily,' she scolded, unwilling to let it go.

'I know that Linh.'

'Your father made sure of that, didn't he Amy?'

Yeah, thought Thys, or Amethyst Pyne, or Amy or Ames or...

She was Thys; she really was.

And Thys was not really listening, as she thought:

Maybe I have become something of a lonely goddess?

'You *know* that,' Linh continued to scald Emily. 'It's the law; you can't use Regene to radically alter your appearance without registration, and you can't alter your appearance to look *exactly* like anyone else, not just the famous people, but anyone; and you can't alter your appearance to change your age to the point of... what was it again?'

'You can't change your appearance,' Brooke spoke, trying to recall the common pseudo-legal phrasing, 'to the point of – is it *physiognomic disguise*? Isn't that what they call it now, Amy?'

Linh nodded. 'Physiognomic copyright and physiognomic identity theft are huge right now, isn't that right Amy?'

'I said *I know that* Linh,' Emily huffed. 'It means you can't legally change your appearance to the point of being unrecognizable. And you *know* that you can do anything you want with your face and your body if you have the money, and you *know* that if that *was* Carla Gugino, there is nothing to say she hasn't taken Regene to roll her body back twenty years or so; they do it all the time in Hollywood, and nobody says a thing.'

'You're such a smart arse, Emily. And, your face *is* part of your body, just so you know.'

Still, Thys barely heard them as they squabbled. She was vaguely aware of a digital bus-shelter advertisement across the street for an art exhibition called *Ashes to Glass*. She watched it scroll through some subtle animations of the sculptures on offer, most of which seemed to be of various celebrities in strange, Pompeii statue-like poses.

Suddenly she had an awful feeling.

Almost a premonition…

Although they'd just spoken, she hadn't actually seen her father, or Heather, or any of the others, not Everett and Yelina, not Trudy yet.

Not even poor Saph, still waiting… still sleeping her days away beside…

It was a spike.

She had not actually seen any of them for quite a while.

Suddenly, it was starting to get to her.

It had, in fact, been her father, Mitchell Pyne, who had made her a goddess in the first place. Had she ever thanked him? Properly?

Why did she suddenly feel like…

It might be too late?

She tried to snap herself out of it.

Okay, she thought, *back up.*

Goddess; strong word.

'Okay,' Brooke interjected, 'that's all very well – but back up ladies, back up – Amy?'

It so startled Amy-Thys/Amethyst Pyne that Brooke had so closely echoed her own internal monologue that she immediately started paying proper attention to the conversation again.

'*Thys?*' Brooke demanded. 'People call you *Thys* now?'

Uh-oh.

She could see it; they felt left out.

It was right there, in their faces.

A different name that they didn't know.

'Oh, no. Well, some.' The Ymira clan of the Anunnaki, for instance, she wanted to say. 'My parents – they still call me Amy...' Thys shrugged. 'Close friends still call me Amy...'

'And we still call you Amy!' Linh exclaimed, suddenly and shockingly; resentful. 'Who's *Thys?*'

Thys shrugged apologetically.

'It started a while back, guys. And sort of stuck.'

'So it's like amma-*thys?*' Emily ventured helpfully. 'Or is it Thys-t, like "fist"?'

'Like "this and that". No tee.'

Truth be told, Thys liked her name.

Another truth be told, it was hardly new.

People, people outside this peer group, aliens outside this dimension of reality (for fuck's sake!) had been calling her that for eight years now.

Again and again this was echoing in her mind.

Nine years since the Quake; four since Paramatta; three since the *real war*, the total astral shitstorm, had started...

Fuck!

She had been gone!

She was someone else now!

What was she *doing here?*

She was Thys now!

She didn't enjoy having to explain it, but she had realised for the first time now that it seemed to imply some kind of definite article, or presence, if not an action or even a performance; maybe even some kind of momentum.

Like, who's that?

Oh her? She's Thys.

This.

Then one would see immediately, oh yeah – *this* is what she is.

She's not that.

She's *Thys* kind of girl.

Whatever that was.

Now she was here with her old friends, Thys wasn't really sure anymore.

Maybe that was why she'd looked them up.

CHAPTER 36

Earlier, when Thys had arrived at the cafe a little late, she had quickly realised that the others had been late as well. The rain had dropped, then drizzled, but had stopped by the time she'd arrived, and she had optimistically taken a reserved sign and placed it on an al fresco table on the corner.

It hadn't been until she had entered the café to place an order that she'd realised how stylish her clothes were.

She hadn't really had time to assess, even just a quick-check in the full-length mirror in the corner. She'd been in such a hurry to gap there on time; really it had just been a second for a cursory swipe of eye-liner and lippie in the en suite mirror that told her the clothes were still on the right way round and had not reverted back to full-leather "astral commander".

'Do not leave this room until I come back!'

Heff had opened one crimson eye, looked at her, then closed it again.

Upon ordering, there had been three other women and two men in the queue, along with several waitresses bustling about in slowly crowding café, and Thys had found herself the equal tallest.

That was new.

Then she realised, as she'd caught her reflection in the café window, that the... were they actually black jeans? And the burnt-orange hoodie was fitted, and flattering; and white chest... exposing her throat... and was that...?

There was a necklace now.

Again; glistening copper, with a small but sparking amethyst crystal.

Where had that come from?

Her left hand involuntarily grasped at her right wrist.

The body art, up, under the sleeve.

There was opal coming from her fingertips; but it was not rainbow-coloured.

It was sparkling; gold and silver and bronze and... yes; copper.

It was not opal; at least, not the 'astral opal' she knew.

This was different.

Similar, but...

A different energy.

More... earthy?

Grounded?

More; oh... yes!

It was... fire. It burned.

It was –

I sense her! I sense her, she is there!
After all these years!
She is recalling her power!
Find the crack; find the pattern of her life...

There! She is there in the Earth Realm!
The power - the power at her fingertips!

Follow!
Follow the power and find the path to her reality...
...and drag - her - back - to - me - !
Exploit every vulnerability!
Play upon her every weakness!

Queen Zyxi is alive!
She must be made to pay for her crimes!

For it is I who command it – !

I, Supreme Lord Gorgian of the Realma – !

I who command that she is brought - to brutal justice!

She must be dragged to The Void - !

- and o-blit-er-a-ted!!!

Or, maybe the jeans were half a size too tight?

Actually... they were clinging to her slender frame under the long black coat, making her seem like some kind of fashion model, just casually out and about.

Or maybe? Not quite?

Wow.

Was that really what she looked like?

Actually, she looked more like an actress; someone good-looking who you usually see dressed up, or on television, or even in the movies, but today dressed normally, doing normal things, just trying to be normal – but patently not normal.

Heather would love that, with all her nonsense actress talk.

Or, maybe what she looked like was someone *trying* to look like an actress, looking like that, trying to nail that look, of being naturally fabulous, but slightly dressed down.

She had suddenly, momentarily, hated herself for seeing that, for knowing and assessing all those aspects of what she looked like; and that she had tried for none of it, made no effort for it, but that it had still... landed on her!

And then, that had been the moment when her three friends had arrived all at once.

CHAPTER 37

'So; who was she then?' Linh demanded.

Thys was just starting to realise how massively insecure Linh was. She was genuinely, irrationally angry that Thys now clearly had a life and friends apart from them.

'She's a friend of my Dad's,' Thys told them, semi-truthfully.

Linh rolled her eyes; *men*.

'No,' Thys corrected instantly. 'Mitch isn't like that. He loves Heather; Heather saved his life.'

'Last time I saw them, they did look really happy,' Emily confirmed helpfully.

Emily was the only one of the three that, Thys was realising, all very suddenly now, she still genuinely liked.

What did that imply?

That she really, kind of, didn't like… the other two anymore?

But even Emily was so hopelessly meek, and so keen to get along…

'They are…!' Thys smiled earnestly. 'They are happy! That woman is a business associate. She owns property, lots of –'

There hadn't been a lot of traffic this afternoon, not this end of town on a rainy day, but she noticed the black car with the tinted windows roll slowly past.

'Lots of what?' Emily asked.

The local CTV network had registered her presence and the local division of – probably ASIS? – had sent a car for visual confirmation. They'd have clocked her, affirmative ID, and would now be trying to figure out how she had come back into Sydney without them knowing, and from where – if indeed she had ever left. The Anunnaki and-or Sirian and-or Orion agents within ASIS would know she had gapped, would be intercepting, and reporting back.

Nothing would happen.

But now her radar had been triggered.

She had spiked.

She feared that she had more to be concerned about from the couple at the table inside the café who were surreptitiously trying to take pictures of her through the glass, on their phones.

iPhones, not Eves, she saw.

And in the cafe, just before her three old friends had arrived, she had heard someone.

She had ignored it or forgotten it; but it flicked back like a rubber band she had been stretching out ever since she had, indeed, heard:

'Is that Amethyst Pyne?'

'No.'

'I think it is. I think that's Amethyst Pyne!'

'Oh!' Emily gasped, as she realised. Thys was facing up the street, toward the bridge, but Emily had the best line of sight, directly into the café.

Brooke swung about and grimaced.

'Say cheese,' Thys shrugged.

Brooke sighed with disgust on her behalf, but Thys could tell she was excited. Nice of her to pretend though. She turned back.

'Do you look at that stuff? On the internet? They say that, after a while, famous people stop looking.'

'I'm not –' Thys began.

Linh laughed. 'Or get their people to do it for them, and only show them the good comments!'

'I don't have –'

But she stopped herself.

She did.

She did have people.

For a start, Harding was watching her right now, from

somewhere close.

'So you really don't know?' Emily was stunned.

'Oh, you have to show her!' Linh insisted.

'They even compare you to actresses and fashion models!' Brooke grinned. 'It's quite an honour, Ames!'

Emily had an Eve tablet she'd brought out from somewhere, and was scanning down a list. 'I bookmark all your fan sites, and profiles, just in case.' She shrugged. 'They say you know Gabrielle Fenwick, so you kind of started out with her look, then they say you're like a young Charlize Theron, but with bigger curves…'

'Curves? I'm gangly!'

They all laughed, explosively.

'Of course you are, Ames!' Linh mocked.

'They say Grace Kelly was five seven – and you're five eight.'

'Gangly like Grace Kelly!' Linh laughed again.

'But I'm…'

She was taller now.

Emily kept going. 'You're the same dimensions as Krimson Azureus, they say. The new Jennifer Hawkins!' Emily looked up and frowned. 'She's not curvy! Well, not that curvy!' She looked Thys up and down as she sat beside her. 'You're fairly curvy! But, not – big curves!' She flicked her eyes at Linh. 'These people don't know what they're talking about!'

Now Brooke was bringing out a tablet.

Emily continued.

'And as a family, you get compared to the Kardashians a lot. Not so much the Hiltons, they're played now anyway, but… your mum and Jade maybe – how is little Jadey? But it's Saxe now, isn't it? I still think of her as Little Jadey. She was so sweet!'

'I haven't seen her since –' Brooke stopped herself, remembering it was supposed to be their secret, that night with the drinking, and the eight thousand dollar set of seven coats.

'Not Little Jadey anymore, in some of these outfits,' Emily giggled, timidly.

Thys tried to look; DeVora's cabal had never used their

version the video, faked additions or otherwise. Cooler heads had prevailed all round, in fact, and Jade had decided not to release it.

But; had they now?

Emily was quickly distracted however, as she swiped away.

'...and they always seem to use the word 'estranged' when they talk about you and Jade and Janine.'

'Saxe,' Linh corrected, smiling tightly.

Brooke scowled as she scrolled through something Thys couldn't see from the other side of the table. 'You know your Mum and your sister are going to do some kind of kind of docudrama reality series?'

Oh.... *God.*

Thys felt instantly sick.

That was Janine's idea.

She'd been wanting to do it for years now.

Still coming up.

She could not be talked out of it.

Was that why Jade had called last night?

Was she calling to recruit her into stopping their insane mother's reality pantomime horror show, now that it was finally, apparently, an actual reality?

Or for her to come back from Africa and join in?

Emily and Brooke carried on.

At some point it started to become a blur.

Then, suddenly Thys was caught up in it, and taking it all aboard her battle-fatigued psyche. Quite abruptly, she felt that she no longer knew exactly who she was, or who her friends were, what she believed, or knew, or stood for. She had come back from fighting Anunnaki with her mental powers raised and sharpened to superhuman levels – *a Goddess* – only to discover a much harsher mental onslaught than any reptilian soldier could have managed; that of the *bloody* critical blogosphere and social media!

Which she wasn't even on!

'I love this one of you,' Emily angled her tablet toward her.

It's true; it was a beautiful shot of her.

Head and shoulders in an evening dress.

But did she really look like that?

'There aren't many pictures of you online, because you're always away with your charity work…' Brooke was still searching. 'I know the one I want…' She uttered under her breath. 'I just can't…'

Linh frowned at her, curious. Almost suspicious.

'Your photos always seem to be taken in one of three different places, or at least in one of three different outfits. We figured out it's because you've only ever been to three different red-carpet events.'

Thys recalled…

That was right.

She'd only ever attended three things with Heather and her father, at which there had been red carpets and flashes. There had been the *In The Room* premiere, of course, just after Paramatta. The black and the pearls.

Then the wedding, of course, at which she'd been seen in a flattering and tasteful but very sexy aquamarine bridesmaid's dress…

And then a charity dinner, for the Earth Epi-Wellness Being… Place… or whatever the hell it was she had supposed to have started for the environment – in a brilliant strapless cream creation, where she totally looked like a princess, with a diamond necklace and earrings that, if she recalled correctly, she still owned and were still stored somewhere in a wall-safe at Omega Cove; the location of which within said apartment she'd utterly forgotten.

Not to mention the combination!

That had been – a world ago!

On those three occasions, she recalled, during which she had gone places with her father or Heather, she had barely noticed the photographers; she had been doing her best to forget the war and ignore everything except being with her father, and Heather.

Emily handed her the tablet.

'Here.'

She'd entered her name in Google Images, and there she was; dozens and dozens of photos of her, on the red carpet, in so many different variations, but all from those three events.

'You take a look; you look so gorgeous in all of them!'

She knew that this was the case, because that was how people saw, and dreamed about her in the astral; in one of these three outfits.

And now here she was in third density, immortalized online.

'You'd better prepare yourself for some of this,' Linh warned. 'Don't read the comments on the fashion blogs, or look at the Twitterstorm about how these people aren't really you.'

'What?' Thys asked, somewhat meekly, feeling herself going into light shock. 'Why not?'

That was real?

That was still a thing?

How long ago had she been told about that?

How long did these ridiculous stories last?

Linh began, and Thys realised she had asked exactly the wrong question, in that Linh was totally prepared to tell her, and exactly the right question, for exactly the same reason; Linh had fed her the line, and she had responded exactly on cue.

Then the penny dropped.

Linh fucking hated her now.

'Some of them say your boobs are too big for someone who's only five seven or eight, and they have to be fake.'

'But how can they tell?'

Emily gasped. 'You mean they are!?'

'No! I mean; what does that even mean? You can't even see my boobs in any of these pictures! And don't they know about... well; bras?'

'Well, it's mostly men. A lot of this was pre-"me-too." Not that that matters; men are still pigs and incel trolls are still deplorables.'

'But what about... well, everything else?'

'That's what I said!' Emily expelled righteously.

'Said to who?' Thys demanded.

Brooke was virtually in a world of her own now, staring her own images, and across at Emily's tablet as well.

'You're wrong, you know; lots of women here as well, having a go at how you look. Having their say. Lots of people coming to your defence as well; don't let this put you off, lots of people adore you as well.' Her eyes bulged. 'Oooh! I love this pic, too!'

Thys was stunned; they were staring at her images online – but the real her, *the actual image source,* was right here in front of them!

'Sure, it's the only number that shows anything, and that's all neckline… I don't know what they're talking about, I don't think you've had breast enhancement.'

Jesus!

'I haven't!'

'There's this shrine, that's still operating, and goes back pre-Facebook…' Emily pointed at it for her. 'They have different statistics than most of the other sites, for your height and weight, and things like that, and your actual measurements. They say they know you. I don't know the name of the webmaster though.'

'How many different sites…?' Thys remained stunned.

'Oh, there are heaps, Ames. Dedicated sites, and some superfan or other always regurgitates your hottest images on the blogs and the tweets and the Facebook pages. There are like three people pretending to be your official rep on Instagram. You could sit here reading about yourself all day. I mean, I follow it because I know you, and I want to look out for you – but Linh knows more than anyone!'

Linh smiled over at her.

What had happened to her?

She'd changed.

She'd been – *waiting for this.*

Linh seemed to take a deep breath and proceeded as though she were some kind of half-baked celebrity reporter.

'Your statistics are reported differently, on an absolute *cavalcade* of celebrity sites that catalogue such things. Most fashion and celebrity bloggers agree that your bottom looks great, nice and round and just tight enough, but then a lot of them say that it's far too small for someone of your body type, and that you must have been *starving yourself*, like a bulimic or something, to stop your ass blowing out at the wedding. Did you have a growth spurt a few years ago?'

'I – well, yeah…?'

'Good, that's going to settle that one; no-one believes it but if you say you did, then that's going to settle that one.'

'With who?'

'The rich celebrity blogosphere, sweetie.' There was a slight edge of pity in her condescending tone. 'That also sparked the debate as to whether or not you'd had a boob job, because if you were bulimic, which I said you weren't, you should have been several cup sizes smaller, 'cause that's the way that happens with that. There *was* also an ongoing argument as to whether or not you'd had a nose job between the premiere and the wedding, but that just turned out to be different angles from different paps.'

'Paps?'

'Paparazzi. Lots of people thought that the nose job was your nineteenth birthday present from Regene, then lots more insisted you'd been completely made over for your twentieth birthday, and some went so far as to suggest that the treatment had all gone wrong, which is why you're hardly ever seen in public anymore. But it's generally agreed that you haven't had Regene yet, but you regularly Botox your forehead to compensate for the frown lines that have been left from the traumatizing divorce that Mitch and Janine put you through.'

'The… what?'

'There is further consensus as to your hair. I don't think this Ames, this is just so you know; so you can prepare yourself for the questions. They say that your hair is mostly extensions, because nobody has natural hair that long anymore.'

'Too much maintenance', Emily chimed in absently. 'Nobody would blame you Ames, it looks lovely today, really just natural and organic.'

Thys groaned deeply, inwardly. She tried to take a swig of coffee but put it down again; her throat had involuntarily constricted.

'My hair...' Thys cleared her throat harshly, then proceeded, 'it naturally gets more curly in the summer, when it's dry, then heavier and straighter in winter... it always has done. You all know that...?'

She was lying, just a bit; the astral...

It *had* changed her.

'You all – *told me* that, when we were growing up! That's how I know that – because you saw that – for real, in real time, as it happened, in reality, to me – to the real me!'

'And they say your hair can't possibly be actually this blonde, because your mother is a classic brunette, and your father and sister both have dark brown hair as well.'

'But... you all know – both my grandmothers were natural Aussie blondes.'

'But you have your father's blue eyes; that's obvious,' Linh smiled.

As though that were some kind of consolation.

'Look!' Emily pointed to another site on the tablet.

This one had before and after pictures of her posing cluelessly in her frumpy school uniform at fifteen (where the hell had they gotten them from?) compared to pictures of her on the red carpet in the princess dress for the charity dinner, probably... five years later? As good as five years ago! But; looking pretty damn gorgeous, even if she did say so herself, in that strapless cream number, with the way Heather had done her hair that afternoon, she remembered, up and Greekish with ringlets...

But –

Wait –

What –

'It's saying...' Thys scanned quickly. 'That I have a different body now! I was fifteen there – and this is me at twenty-two or something! Of course I have a different body!'

And sure, *sure* drinking Pan's potion at eighteen, almost nineteen, seemed to have spurred on a relatively late growth spurt a few months later, but who was to say that wouldn't have happened anyway?

Who?

These idiots?

And she had a very real and sneaking suspicion, ever since she'd seen herself today in the café mirror, that it hadn't actually stopped; that she had become… more.

More – Thys!

Somehow, ever since.

Had that been down to Pan?

Or the astral; the opal and the dreama?

Or was it just her?

Just Amethyst Sky Pyne?

Becoming who she was always meant to be?

But – the way Linh was talking…?

And, what the hell were they talking about anyway?

Puberty?

It was just normal for a girl, as she became a woman.

Wasn't it just hormones?

From the school photo at fifteen, to the red carpet in her early twenties, to who she was now…

At twenty-seven.

Jesus, was she really…?

Almost twenty-eight?

Almost thirty!

How had that happened?

And they were *all* that!

She had been whisked off into a whirlwind of adventure, of reconnecting with her father under bizarre circumstances, of coming out of training with the Pan and being shot at by monsters, then thrown into a war in another dimension that she, Amethyst Pyne, the tall, plain, clever girl, was winning on behalf of humanity…

And now she'd won it; humanity was making her feel like shit!

For being – *too gorgeous?*

But she wasn't even – a bit gorgeous!

And she had carved them out new territory!

She had opened up new territory, where humans could dream!

Without Anunnaki influence!

So that there could be more of them, so that when they arrived, they could direct their minds and make themselves more useful! Where powerful humans came now when they entered the astral, where one day she could meet them and explain to them what had happened, what was happening…!

Her eye caught another blog entry.

My Goddess…

The rudeness.

People who didn't even know, her calling her…

Such names!

She was reading the comments on Brooke's tablet now, scanning… scrolling down, down; deeper and darker and down…

Hateful people!

She was shocked, genuinely shocked, at some of the things they were saying.

Why?

Why?!

It was all passing in a blur now, and she was reading so quickly; she went to another tab and read the comments there.

Her heart was beating, pounding so fast.

'Ames…' She head Emily from far away, and ignored her.

'You shouldn't…' Brooke started.

'Let her,' Linh broke in harshly. 'It will be good for her. She needs to know.'

She was absorbing very quickly now; Brooke had all the tabs

open; fashion, celebrity, fan sites… all the old ones she knew, like Twitter, Facebook, Snapchat, Tumblr, Instagram, and other, massive social network sites that she didn't recognize, that had since emerged…

All the things that had destroyed her father's self-esteem…

Striking back at her, her media-cursed family – like an Orion Renegade!

Demolishing her soul!

Pages and pages… time was passing faster than it should, in her mind, in a blur, the way it could in the astral if you weren't paying attention, the way the hours did in third density when you were 'off somewhere', almost in the astral, and certainly when part of you was connected to it.

Finally, some impulse forced her, and she tore herself away and thrust the tablet back to Brooke.

'Enough!' she spat.

Weird sparks flew off ther tablet; gold and silver and bronze and copper.

'Jesus!' Brooke cried out. 'You didn't *fry it* did you?'

Her three friends were staring at her like she was crazy.

Like she'd just had some sort of fit.

But Brooke leaned down and looked at her hands; at her right hand.

'Oh my God, Amy, *have you got a tattoo?*'

Thys pushed the sleeve down.

The art on her arm felt like it was burning; like… had it… shown her part of her timeline?

The part, the perspective, that she had missed?

In four years, it had never done anything other than…

Be.

On her arm.

Just; body art.

But she never thought about it.

She never *really* thought about Paramatta, or the vortex.

Or

or

The Realma.

It was too much.
She held back tears.
The Realma; her other life that she had left behind.
Too much to think about; *too real.*
But now; Heff.
And – this.
She was gripping her right forearm with her left hand, too tight, and too weird.
She had become too weird.
'How can you read that fast?' Emily asked, almost frightened.
'I can speed-read,' Thys uttered angrily. 'You learn how when you need to sign contracts.'
That was total nonsense, but they decided to buy it.
What *had* happened?
She'd become obsessed, momentarily obsessed!
Obsessed!
Now the tablet was safely back in Brooke's hands, but she had so wanted the 'rich girl satisfaction' of breaking it. Of smacking it against the table, of smashing it into the pavement and crushing it under her huge, angry stomps.
She had been a millisecond away from letting that happen.
She gulped at her coffee.
Jesus.
How many times had Brooke googled her, to find all that stuff? And Emily with her bookmarks; all the same. All bookmarked, all catalogued and saved to "The Cloud".
Jesus.
How many different windows and tabs could you have open

at one time? There had been hundreds, and she had read them all, scrolled down them all, seen the comments, been in the pit, rolled in the dregs, taken the hits...

Then closed them all, and they had watched her do it.

Watched her do something… vaguely… supernatural, she supposed.

But that wasn't the only thing.

'There are people a lot more famous than me…' Thys spoke with deliberate calm.

'A lot!' Emily agreed, trying to help.

'How the fuck do they cope?' Thys demanded.

Her phone went off.

It was a message from Heather.

Heather: Anunnaki Gandhi

What the hell did that mean?

Then she caught sight of herself in the reflection of the phone's glass screen.

What kind of girl are you?

She didn't know any more.

But at that moment, she did know one thing.

She was lost.

'Spoiled trust fund bitch, one of the comments said,' Thys told them. 'Needs a good fucking. Needs a good slapping. Needs a real man. Dyke cunt-muncher. Reptilian bitch. Elite slag. Corporate cum sock. "Rape her with a machine gun".'

'Wow,' Brooke gasped, as if she didn't know.

'I don't even know what a trust fund is…' Thys shrugged. 'Something rich Americans use to pay their children allowances? I mean, that's something that only happens on television, right?'

She tried to laugh it off.

They all just stared at her.

She'd frightened them somehow.

She was alien now, on at least three different levels.

Three different kinds of 'other'.

Again she realised that, while she had tried to keep in touch with western television, and films, and books and comics and pop culture, because it had such an enormous impact on the astral, in reality she had only seen the creation and response, not the genuine article.

And now, she herself was no longer the genuine article.

Now, she had become part of it.

Someone the Americans and the blogosphere paid attention to.

She laughed to herself, glib, and once again tried to break the ice.

'Have I been referenced in a sitcom yet?'

Emily giggled nervously. 'Probably.'

Linh and Brooke were still wary of her.

'I heard Bo Everett referenced, before all this, before I met him and he became a real person to me.'

Real people.

Wow.

What did the internet care for real people?

Linh appeared to ignore what she had done, and proceeded as though the strangeness of her superfast browsing had never happened.

'What did Bo Everett care when people made fun of him? Who wouldn't be happy – with all that money? All the billions he left your father in his will?'

Thys sighed. She was getting sick of saying this.

'Bo Everett isn't dead. He just gave them the company as a wedding gift. He's off traveling.'

'Where?' Linh demanded, with a scoffing, humorless laugh. 'No-one's seem him in years.'

'I have,' Thys sighed absently. She became immediately aware of a sudden change around the table, an intensity, and realised that all three girls were staring back at her.

'*What?*'

'You've *seen him*?' Linh demanded.

Thys shrugged. 'He came to my twenty-first. He gave me a Pleiadean diamond... I see him every time I...'

'No he didn't! He didn't come to your twenty first! I was there!'

Again, Thys realised, they only heard what they wanted to hear.

'No,' Thys sighed. 'The other one – the family one.'

The three went silent.

'Still, Amy...' Brooke began. 'No-one has seen Bo Everett for – what? Six or seven years? No-one. Everyone thinks he's dead. And you're saying he came out of hiding to come to *your* twenty first? And you see him? Every time you...?'

Thys didn't like her tone.

It riled her.

'Yes. Bo Everett came to a small gathering at Hard – my grad-pop's place on Mulholland, and had dinner with me for my twenty first; along with about half a dozen other people.' She desperately wanted to add that she had seen him at least once every six months since then, on a spaceship she could probably see the corner of, right now, if she tried really hard; but obviously...

Then she heard herself keep talking.

'My Dad is married to his niece. Bo Everett's *niece*; Heather *Everett*, who Bo thinks of as his *daughter*, is my *step-mother*. I know it's true – I read it on the internet!'

Thys didn't like the way that had come out. It had sounded bitter. But, for some reason, Brooke and Linh and even Emily were all pissing her off.

'And *yes*, they own what used to be his company. It was a wedding gift from a man who didn't *want it* anymore, a man who *got* what he wanted and didn't *need* a giant company anymore. He still has money, Brooke. He still has more money than he knows what to do with. You don't know *what* I know about Bo Everett. You don't know what we've *been through*; not me and Bo, or me and my Dad, or Heather, or Uncle Pan or Aunt Saph or Aunt Trudes or anyone, not *any of you.*'

By the time she had realised that her voice had raised significantly, it had been too late to turn back. People from other tables were looking, but pretending not to. It was only a matter of time before some of the people who recognized her started recording and uploading, if they hadn't already.

'Who's *Uncle Pan*?' Linh demanded. 'You mean Holland Pankhurst? That man's a *freak*.'

Brooke chimed in. 'And who's *Aunt Saph*? Do we *know her*?'

'…don't forget Auntie Xy…' Thys muttered under her breath.

Emily was upset but covered it.

'Are you okay Amy? I mean, Thys?'

Linh stood suddenly. 'You think you're so great, don't you – *Thys*?' She accidentally bumped the table with her thigh. Brooke's latte spilled over, went everywhere. 'You vanish halfway through our first year at uni, even when we said we'd all stick together through thick and thin, then six months later you come back all aggressive and paramilitary, then you say you're going to LA. Then you vanish again, for almost *three years*! Three years *after* the Los Angeles earthquake – we thought you were *dead*, Amy! Who *cares* if you had Suzie Saturn stage her comeback at your twenty-first birthday! A few people did actually die in that earthquake you know, and we all thought you were one of them!'

Now the entire café was looking on; people outside, al fresco around them, and people looking out, though the glass. Even passing pedestrians were having a good look, and all of them, *all of them*, Thys could tell this without looking, were capturing it on their handhelds…

'Just because your *daddy* married Bo Everett's niece, and you've been living it up all around the world, don't expect us to –'

'I'm sorry!'

But Linh wasn't finished.

'– then after your twenty-first – nothing again! For *six more years*! Then you summon us all for *this* and act like it's *nothing*, like *six years* of barely seeing you is *nothing*, then tell us that you're the only person who's seen Bo Everett since he vanished!'

She scoffed with a kind of theatrical vitriol.

'Oh, and also, by the way, *I'm not Amy anymore!* Well guess what – *Thys* – I think we all figured that out – some time ago!'

Linh snatched up her bag, her sunglasses, and her Eve phone.

'You know most people think your *father* and his *trophy wife* had Bo Everett *killed* – don't you?'

Then she turned and stormed off, only pausing to turn and shout.

'Fuck you Amethyst Pyne! That money's turned you into a total bitch!'

Brooke was also collecting her things from the table; there were tears in her eyes that had formed as she had watched Linh.

She stood, then leaned in and hissed at her.

'If you're such a good friend, *Amy*, why don't you pay our *fucking mortgages?*'

Then she too stormed off after Linh, accidentally upturning a small bowl of complimentary Kool Mints off the table as she went; the little white balls fell everywhere, scattering as they bounced all down the sidewalk and into the rain-glistened gutter.

One of them fell in her lap.

She stared at it a few seconds, then picked it up and put it in her mouth, then crunched on it, mercilessly.

Everyone was watching now, filming; but Emily only watched as her friends departed, tears welling up in her eyes as well.

'Oh, Amy… we all used to be such good friends…'

Thys remained quiet. She was too tense to cry, too shocked, too hurt. And she would not give… the internet, she supposed, the satisfaction.

Far out.

That was the human race now.

They weren't called humans anymore. They weren't called Earthlings or Earthers or Terrans or even people.

They were 'the internet'.

Look at them.

(She was desperate not to; not to make eye contact with their desperate, cruel plastic lenses.)

Like she was some kind of fucking exhibit, or street fucking theater.

She stood.

Emily stood beside her, just as suddenly, out of an unconscious flight response, probably.

Both of them, bolt upright, facing their...

Audience?

Accusers?

Jury?

Or just... peers?

Just... dumb idiots.

Twenty-first century gawkers who didn't know better?

But then, something seemed to be going wrong. She was about to look; right at them.

About to tell them exactly what she thought of them.

Make a stand, right here and now.

But people in front, in her periphery, even as she looked right at them at last, were turning their phones back on themselves, as though...

They weren't working.

They'd stopped.

The internet had suddenly turned in on itself, and gazed at itself, its own screens, in an extremely sudden and weird way.

Then, the internet looked at each other.

'Yours too?'

'Yeah... it just –'

A few of the internet tapped their screens and looked blankly puzzled; then, the swearing started.

'What the fuck?'

'Bloody thing!'

'Where's my god-damn screen!?'

For some reason, people's devices weren't working.

Small mercies.

'What happened, Amy?' Emily asked, quietly.

Within seconds of being surrounded by what felt like an execution squad, they were instead given to watch an impotent arc of mindless strangers slowly dwindle away, grumbling. As though the 'kill switch' had been flipped to off, on a horde of mind-controlled zombies.

'Maybe... some kind of directed impulse? Maybe I do have some friends left...?' Thys turned to her, and realised what she'd actually meant. 'You know, Ems, you guys really are the last ones, apart from my family, who call me that.'

Emily shrugged. 'You'll always be Amy to me.'

Emily threw herself at her and they embraced tightly.

Nobody filmed it, nobody really paid attention, other than for the fact they they were pissed about missing filming it.

Then they cried, sniffling into each other's shoulders for a few minutes. The deactivated internet wandered even further away. Swearing and cursing and trying hopelessly to make calls out; tapping and even hitting their screens.

What good, Thys wondered, watching the internet dissipate, was a real, raw moment of celebrity emotion, if it could not be filmed?

By the time they'd let each other go, almost everyone was gone; they had all returned to their seats or just wandered off. Just two girls remained, watching... almost respectfully, Thys supposed, from a distance, themselves crying at the emotional truth and beauty of the moment. They might not even have known who Thys was.

Join the club, Thys thought.

Then the two last remaining watchers nodded at each other, held hands, and returned to their seats. Finally, one blew a kiss.

Thys smiled back.

It was over.

Then someone had gotten up from across the café and was coming out.

Thys intuited the word *autograph* from somewhere.

Then, like a virus, the idea was on everybody's mind.

They were up, they were coming.

Looking for pens, looking for paper.

All mobilizing with the same idea.

■ *Get her; she's rare – she might not come again* ■

'Ems; we need to...'

■ *Do not let her get away* ■

They would close in, on the table, on the corner; and this time they wouldn't need to maintain a physical distance for filmic perspective; they were coming right up, right into her space, and they would squeeze.

Push her back, into traffic.

Behind them, in that moment, just she could see that the impotent internet; the people, the mob-hunters, were falling back on the older ways of hounding, those that had been true and tested for many long decades before these new electronic ways, and that they were about to close in, all at once, with the hardcopy fallback weapons, Thys could also see, had also spotted a crop of fiery bright orange hair.

The red hair was running to get to them.

Down the sidewalk, toward them, from just a few shop fronts away.

The red-haired paparazzi; Mitch and Heather had warmed her.

The Leprechauns!

Raising something at her, metal and threatening.

And then they had to move, and move quickly.

CHAPTER 38

Thys dragged Emily by the hand around the corner and up the street, toward The Rocks. Then around another sudden corner, then up some old stone Colonial-era steps, towards the thin streets and steep, uphill, creviced stairways and alleys, through all that was left of Old Sydney.

After a few twists and turns;

'No, this way!' Emily had gasped, demandingly, at one point;

…and some clip-clopping work-outs up some more well-worn cobblestone stairways, Thys had slowed them.

Calmed down.

'We lost them.'

Emily smiled, but said nothing.

They had ended up on a long, thin street, with heritage-listed cottages on either side of them, with signs outside describing how they were being lovingly restored.

'It's like going back in time, when you walk through The Rocks.'

Thys smirked, still panting a bit. 'We didn't walk. I think we flew.'

Emily kept looking around.

The way she was panting, Thys suspected that she found it all very exciting, as though they might have been characters in some kind of Aussie action-thriller. Then she spoke, as she had for only a second or two that morning, quite candidly.

'For a while I was really interested in the Rocks. You know? In the history. I did all the tours. I even read a few books. And, it was so lovely…' She nodded at the old cottages. '…to see the way it was all being restored. But then, I realised…' She looked at Thys. '…it was horrible. Look it up yourself, some time. This place. The

Rocks. It was Hell. The whole of this city was, when they had convicts here. We romanticize it, but…' Emily looked around, as though searching for something. Then she let out a breath. 'Come on. My car's up here.'

Thys and Emily started walking.

CHAPTER 39

They walked like normal people, normal friends, back to her car, talking about their old teachers, about other people they had gone to school with, Emily telling her the most sad or amusing or unexpected fates of their old classmates. Emily led them to a carpark, and into an elevator, going several floors up, with Thys still checking behind them every now and then.

The mop of bright orange may or may not have been one of the leprechaun paparazzi her father and Heather had warned her about, and the threatening metal thing might just have been a camera, and not a gun; but there had been no point in hanging around to find out.

Finally they walked a long row, and reached Emily's car, right up the end.

Emily looked at her through the huge blue eyes which, at least for many of the quieter boys at their high school, had made her the most attractive of their quartet. Back then, the four of them had comprised the cute-but-clever-girl clique; not the hot girls, not the cool girls, not the geek girls, but the clever girls. They had been separated when Thys' mother had moved to London, when Thys had been fifteen, but her mother had always returned to Sydney during the major holidays to see her family, and so the four girls had maintained contact. When Thys had later returned to Australia independently, to attend university with her friends as they had always sworn to do, they had all gone together, all arts degree girls at the same campus. But then Thys had discovered her Uncle Pan's podcasts and YouTube channel and everything had changed.

She had begun to think that maybe she had a new quest now; well, an old quest that she needed to re-energize, one bestowed upon her father way back then, that she was doing her best to see through.

But… why had it gone so wrong?

Had she approached the wrong people?

Or had she gone about it all wrong?

Had she thought about it too much?

Or – was it just too late?

It was quite simply much, much harder than she'd thought it was going to be. But, she supposed; how she'd first thought it was going to be, had… not involved a lot of thought, really.

'What are you thinking about?' Emily asked.

'Oh, the distant past.'

'We're only in our mid-twenties and we're brooding on the past…' Emily smiled. 'I had barely started my life, and I was obsessed with what it would have been like to live two-hundred years ago.'

'Hell?'

Emily smiled, tightly. 'They're saying there's no such thing a midlife crisis anymore. That we're all so over-informed and hyper-analytical and self-involved and compassion-fatigued that we all have post-traumatic stress disorder to competing degrees, and all we can expect is a whole series of mini-breakdowns every five or ten years, until something gives.'

'Great.' Thys smiled back. 'Who gives? Them or us?'

Emily's car keys jingled as she fondled them nervously.

'I think eventually we all just give up.'

Thys nodded and shrugged. 'I'm kind of hoping it's them who give up.'

They both looked at each other, wondering if they were talking about the same thing.

'We lost touch,' Emily sighed, as though it were somehow something serene and romantic. 'Your life's different now. It happens. At least, it seems like it does. It seems like this is what would happen if we were in one of those independent movies, where you don't know any of the actors, so it seems more real;

and the people in it are really honest with each other. We'd just be kind of be… done. Move on. And then, cut to ten years later when we meet on the street, and exchange polite pleasantries. Roll end credits, that's just how life is.'

Again, Thys almost cried, but managed not to.

'Ems…' she began. 'The way it all happened, with Bo Everett and with Cleverco… it happened in a way that… it's difficult to bring anyone else in.'

'You've been with The Pan all this time, haven't you?'

'Kind of…'

'It's okay Ames. I know you're not a terrorist.'

Thys laughed softly to herself. 'No. Well, I'm kind of an insurgent, if you really want a definition. But − for humanity, Ems.'

Emily smiled and shrugged. 'Okay.'

Clearly she didn't understand, and didn't care that she didn't, and it was all way above her pay grade anyway. All she wanted was to write essays about Bella Swan and Katniss Everdeen, and how they compared to the heroines of Jane Austen, finish her Master's Degree in Modern English and find her Edward Cullen − but really find a Mister D'Arcy.

'Let me ask you something Ems…?'

'Okay.'

'If you could be a superhero, with any power you wanted, what would it be?'

Suddenly, a tear rolled down each of Emily's cheeks, and she laughed.

'A what? I don't know…'

'Let me start you off. What if you could *read* people?'

'Read their minds?' Emily shook her head. 'No. I don't want to know what other people are thinking. Most of the time I don't even like what they say out loud…'

'No, not exactly that − like, if you could know how they're feeling, for real. If they're lying or scared or… happy?'

'I think that would be cheating.'

Thys sighed and nodded. 'I do too.'

Even now, Thys could have just…

But, Emily was her friend, and that would have been a violation of her personal code. She hadn't done that on any of her friends, not ever.

'Well, how about if you could see the future?'

'What, like – all of it? Who I'm going to marry and how many kids, and when I die and all of that?'

'Sort of… more like – impressions. Suggestions. As though the future had a plan, but there was a fair bit of wriggle room?'

'I think that would be cheating too. If I wanted that I'd be one of those stupid women who go and get their Tarot cards read every week.'

Thys nodded to herself.

Emily sniffled.

Thys was just beginning to become aware that it was the last time they would see each other; Emily seemed all too aware.

'What about if you could go anywhere – instantly?'

'Like – back to India again? Or Bali?'

'Click of your fingers, you're there.'

'Can I take my friends?'

Thys paused for a second. She swallowed.

'Not really. You can't really tell anyone about these superpowers. Just three or four other people who might have the same powers. Although… everyone seems to have the powers differently.'

Emily's face went blank and she stared at Thys for a second.

In that second, Thys knew. Emily had realised.

Thys was talking about herself; what she could do.

Then her blank expression broke and she shrugged.

'That would be okay – like, tennis-portation, or whatever they call it, but, just to get away. If I was going somewhere, I'd want to go with Linh and Brooke, or with – you know,' she rolled her eyes, 'a boyfriend or something.'

'Well, they both have husbands now.'

'Yeah…'

Thys caught the edge of something then, a psychic impression she thought instinctively that she ought to…

'They both seem so unhappy, Ems. You're not unhappy are you?'

Emily looked at her seriously for a second. In all the years she had known her, Thys had never seen Emily's serious face.

'I don't think they should have gotten married to those guys.'

Thys hadn't expected that. 'Well… sometimes it works out…?'

'No, Ames… I mean – I think *they* should have gotten married. Just – not to those men. I don't think it's fair on them. The men, that is.'

Thys looked at her unfamiliar expression for a few seconds, her serious face, until the penny dropped.

'Oh…!' Thys aired.

Emily nodded.

'Ohhhhhh…' Thys added, as it sunk in. She wondered why she hadn't seen it years ago. All those sleepovers. And still with the *Xena* binges, after all this time.

And now they were married… with mortgages.

'Why did they do it?' Thys asked.

'Their families. Very traditional. Very, *very*.'

'Man, are they gonna regret that!'

Emily nodded. 'I think they already do. Big time. I mean, what if they have kids? I'm sure, despite everything, they're really *doing it* with those guys.'

Thys thought for a second. 'In this day and age…?'

'Traditions hold on.'

Thys shrugged it off. She had to – after all, what could she do about it, really?

'But – what do *you* want Emily?'

Emily shrugged back. 'Love. Someone who loves me. Who I love.'

And what could she do about that, really?

She didn't have those higher plains powers; to find the blue-yellow to her red-green, or whatever.

'You don't want me to pay your mortgage?'

Emily giggled. More like the old Emily now. Less serious.

'I'm still renting! And even if I did meet the right guy, I'd never get married so young, or so soon!'

They smiled at each other, a little sadly now.

'Look; there's more.'

'More what?'

'Well, more options, for superpowers.'

Emily laughed. 'Ames, I have to go. I'm having dinner at my mother's, and you know what that means.'

Thys smiled. 'You do the cooking!'

'Exactly! So I have to start now!'

Thys knew she was lying; they have all freed up the evening. But it was okay.

'You're sure? You don't want to be empathic, or clairvoyant, you don't want transportation? What about hands-on healing? Or astral travel? Or – what about telekinesis?'

'What's that one again?'

Thys sighed. But she was smiling, despite herself.

Emily smiled. 'Why don't you marry Ice Styger? I mean, if you have to marry another billionaire? He's so cute. He's like, *really* cute.'

'I couldn't stand his father, for a start!'

She rolled her eyes. 'Yeah, there is that!'

Thys smiled. She hugged Emily again, then she unlocked her car and got in. Thys stood there as she started the engine and the window slid down. Emily looked up at her.

'All that magic stuff. You can do all that. Can't you?'

Thys didn't know what to say.

'I won't tell. No-one would believe me.'

'Yeah I can.'

Thys' heart skipped a beat as she heard her own confession.

It felt great.

Liberating.

'Keep doing what you're doing, Thys. That Regene thing, it's better now. The way they started, if what the news said about that was true, it would have been *really* bad. It would have ruined everyone and everything. Everyone knew that, but no-one could resist it. What your Dad and Heather and Oliver Hines did to make sure it wasn't that… toxic? You just keep going with all that.'

Thys nodded.

'Okay.'

'You keep fighting for us, Amethyst Pyne.'

'I will. See you Ems.'

Emily smiled, a sad but satisfied smile, exactly the kind of bittersweet finale smile she would have wanted from her indie movie, and drove away forever.

CHAPTER 40

Thys stood in the car park crying until a large, scarred and deeply tanned hand came down on her shoulder from behind. It rested there a few seconds, then she spun about and buried her head in the enormous, muscular chest of the man who had broken cover to comfort her.

'That was harsh, girl,' Harding uttered.

'No...'

'Yes it was child. But pay it no mind. You can never go back. But sometimes you have to go back, in order to find that out.'

Her Grand-pops hugged her tight.

'How do you know...?'

'You've been nine tours away in a war, little girl. Nine tours, nine years. You're one of us now; you have been, a long while.'

Although the lifelong mercenary's words made her feel a bit better, Thys doubled-down and kept crying.

CHAPTER 41

Thys gapped herself and Harding back from the car park, directly to the main second-floor living room in The Fork, with the view between the prongs over Mulholland and into the valley. There they sat together, as they sometimes did, on his enormous leather couch, him sitting slightly away from her, she leaning forward over the California King-sized coffee table and alternately crying, drying her eyes, blowing her nose, and spilling her guts while she ate Tim Tams and drank hot chocolate.

'A long time ago, Dad asked me to do something,' Thys sniffed.

'The list?'

'I've told you?'

'A few times...'

'Well, I never really had the chance to actually think about it, not seriously. I just scribbled it down. But I knew it wasn't right. I had things to tell him... I didn't have time to think it through, let alone do anything about it, until now. I... I've mused over it, over the years. Thought about it, when I could...'

Harding uttered. 'Over the years...?'

She gave him a terse look.

'And what did you find, Amy Pyne?'

She let it go, sighed and shrugged. 'After today? That if you have an important gift to give to your friends, it's best if you have friends to give it to...'

Harding gave her a sympathetic smile.

'I know that one, little girl.'

It wasn't creepy when Harding called her that, in his odd South African accent. 'Liddle gell'. It was purely affectionate, kind of ironic-sarcastic-dry, with just the right amount of his own wise-reflective sorrow edged in there.

She wondered aloud. 'What kind of a girl am I?'

Harding smiled.

He was a handsome man, tanned and scarred and probably somewhere well-over sixty years of age now, with a grey buzz cut and clear, pale-blue eyes. Although she had tried to get him to wear some clothes of a less inherently aggressive design, she had not been able to persuade him to wear anything other than his black and khaki paramilitary gear (although he had seemed, at least at times, to have compromised by switching to dark green and brown colored hiking clothes, which in some Los Angeles circles were still considered fashionable, or at least cool).

Today he had dressed for Sydney winter in shoes, shirt, trousers and sports jacket, in four totally different shades of olive, somehow coordinated, she was sure accidentally, that he had thrown on just before they'd left. Like her, he'd had only minutes to prepare when he'd synchronistically returned to The Fork, just in time, but still he looked good. He was fit; lifetime fit and he would basically look good in anything.

Harding considered.

His eyes fell upon their coats, thrown over the back of the couch. Back on Mulholland, it was summer again, and they had both, almost instantly, abandoned their coats and jackets upon reemerging here.

'We are used to it, the quick change, the summer-to-winter gapping.'

'Huh?'

'What kind of girl? You are Amethyst Pyne; sometimes Amy, sometimes Ames, mostly Thys now, and there is no-one else like you. Therefore you are no kind of girl, you are unique.'

That just made her cry even more.

She really bawled it out for a full minute after he said that.

Harding had frown-lines and smile-lines and a few old scars dashed across his leathery cheeks, and a huge vein down the center of his forehead. Thys thought now that she knew every one of those lines, from studying his face over and over as she'd watched him, sometimes perhaps even unknowingly, as he considered the advice was giving her. For years this had happened; she had watched him as he had advised her as to how to fight a war he had never participated in, and had barely even seen, that was an entire dimensional level of existence away from him.

'War is war...'

Harding had told her that, the first time she had sought him out for advice, and asked whether or not it was okay.

'...wherever it is.'

And he had told her this again, many times since.

'I know war, little girl. I will advise you, and we shall see.'

Now, he smiled again, and nodded at her.

'You are not even a girl now. A woman. That is for sure.'

'A woman...' Thys heard herself echo.

They heard a coyote howl, outside in the hills somewhere, but not too far away for them to be able to hear it indoors. It caught their attention, then they smiled at each other, recognizing between them their mutual, battle-ready alertness.

Then Harding continued.

'Technically, definitively, pretty much in any culture, you are no longer a girl but a woman; twenty-seven? Well-past twenty-one years of age, and that is pretty much the universally agreed absolute maximum limit for being a "girl". From then on, if you are still a little girl, it is only because you are *choosing* to act like one.'

Thys nodded. 'When I knew that the war was over... well, that it had stopped, anyway... it seemed like a chance to get back to normal.'

Harding chuckled. 'Neither of those things ever happens. Time marches on, things change, but the war marches on with it. It just changes location. And normal – there is only the veneer, and pretense. Underneath, everyone is different. There is no normal.'

'Don't I know it...'

'You think it will start again? This fourth density astral plane war?'

'I don't... I don't want to talk about that.'

'I understand.'

'To be honest, Harding, it's all still a bit hazy.'

'I understand.'

'But... I have a list now, of six things, six things that add up to more of the sum of their parts, that I can do, and I've been able to do for years now, that made me able to go and fight that war. And I got very good at those things. So good... that I used those abilities, the whole of which makes me who I am now... to hold back...'

Harding studied her, then looked away.

'...to hold *them* back.'

Harding looked to her again. He didn't like to see her in pain, to see her struggle psychologically like this.

'I understand,' he repeated simply.

'And there are the others, who are the same as me... not just the other Pandorans who Uncle Pan chose, but others in the astral. But it's like, I know them when I'm there, but when I'm *here*, I forget who they are.'

'Last time we spoke of this, you said you thought that was for a reason; that the two worlds were separate to protect you all, not just from your enemies, but for your sanity. Do you no longer believe that?'

Thys shrugged. She wasn't really listening.

Harding was accustomed to this. He had learned a lot about women, just through his friendship with Thys. He let her talk, and listened.

'Sometimes when I see them, it's like... like none of that other stuff ever happened. Suzie and me, we fight together in the war, in the astral, but here...' Thys sighed. 'We see each other according to her tour schedule.'

'Some see it as a privilege when a famous rock star makes time for them. There are many demands on people of that level of celebrity.'

Thys stared at him. He was being serious, but he was also being facetious. She tried to hold the gaze, but a smile broke through and she nodded.

'It's nice, nice to see her, here in reality, if only for a night here and there. It's nice that she played a few sets at my birthday, that she felt like doing that to get herself back in the public groove. But what we do together in the astral… we never talk about it. I mean, we do, but not for long. We never properly… debrief? And anyway, I came to *that* party late, the whole Suzie Saturn party. The ship into the void. What happened with Suzie and Vance. Petitioning the Elohim. I didn't go right up to the end with Dad and Heather… I stayed in the astral and got caught up in this fucking war…'

Harding grumbled. 'They all have their own lives, child. It is hard for a returned veteran. Time passing. Things only you have seen.'

'Is that what I am now? A vet?'

'That's what it sounds like to me. Like you have a kind of post-war stress. It sounds like you need to debrief with your Anunnaki comrades. Purge some of your tension.'

'I'm sure I do, I mean, I'm sure I did. I may, or may not have gotten completely plastered on that blue Anunnaki wine last night – so, that's there. And when you drink *there*, it makes it even harder to remember when you wake up *here*. That's, when I am here. But when I am here, I just don't know who to talk to…'

She smiled, helplessly.

'…like I said, there were other humans in the astral, but… some of them were anonymous, and most of them… even if I could track them down, they're not *friends* exactly. More – associates. Anyway, mostly there's no way to tell who they were, or are, in this dimension. I'm the only *known* human being on our side to participate in that war who isn't an actual celebrity, back here…'

She could tell Harding didn't believe her. She didn't believe herself. Maybe she didn't want to see them. Maybe she didn't want to remember.

She didn't know.

She needed time to figure that out.

'So don't speak to humans.'

'But I…' she sighed.

'But what?'

'I need *human company*, Harding. These past few years, I don't know what I would have done without you. But I need…'

Harding leaned backwards in his chair. 'I understand.'

She smiled warmly at him. 'All the things I can do, all the things I have done, I have to keep it all secret. I can't share anything with anyone else. And yet, it's all such a large part of my life that it means I can't really ever be close to anyone else. Not for long. And when I say close, I mean *close*, as in, *physically close*.'

She had never seen Harding actually blush, but this was the closest she had come.

'Yes,' he nodded. 'Yes indeed girl. You are a woman now, yes. I understand.'

'I have lovers, Harding.'

'I know. I do not judge.'

'I think I still have two, or three, who would see me. See me tonight, just a phone call. But it's getting to the point where I might have to choose, and… how can I do that without telling them about the Pandora Sequence?'

The coyote howled again. It startled Thys this time, but naturally Harding seemed not to have noticed. That made it seem worse somehow, his pretending. Like he was trying not to worry her. This one had sounded closer to the house. Harding shook his head.

'Girl, if you need to choose, if you are hesitating, maybe none of them are right?'

'I know, I know. But I can't keep leading them on, letting them think we're going to – end up together. But I still need…' She sighed. 'I still need someone, Harding.'

Harding tried to speak again, but she could see the words get lost in his tree-trunk of a throat. But she needed to say this out loud, to an adult; an adult human, who could understand.

'There was a time, a phase, one time when I got back, I just did – *that*. But then I got myself into knots, and there was a time when I couldn't even do *that*. I didn't think I could be intimate, not even casually, without wondering if this was someone I could share the Pandora with. I mean, I got sick of the – I didn't want to – but I couldn't figure out…' She looked at him. 'Am I making sense?'

'No, but I think I know what you mean.'

Thys laughed, and blew her nose.

'I just wanted to be honest with them. But it's such a huge gift…'

'A huge responsibility girl, a huge burden.'

'I felt I couldn't even sleep with anyone, without…'

Harding shrugged, as though to say, *anything you say is fine with me.*

'I kind of started… spying.'

'Spying?'

'Watching.'

'Watching?'

'Like Heather used to watch Dad. It started out as checking, to see if they were good people. I can… get into places. Be invisible. I started doing it, with the people I was attracted to. Then it became…'

Harding shrugged again, the same way.

'It sort of became exciting. In that way. And I was doing a lot of it.'

'I see.'

She checked his expression. He was trying to remain blank, but neutral and receptive. He was doing pretty well under the circumstances.

'I kind of justified it by saying… well, if Heather fell for Dad that way, maybe…' Thys squirmed a little. 'A friend kind of… pulled me out of it. But it was becoming… addictive.'

Harding cleared his throat. 'I understand. You felt that you could not risk connecting with anyone… without knowing who they were first. You had the means, and so you became voyeuristic. It was… porno.'

'Harding!'

'I am sorry, but that is how is sounds, child!'

'I –'

'But – where you can meet them, afterwards, if you like them. Like strippers. So I hear. In certain kinds of clubs…'

Thys could feel herself blushing now.

'Jesus!' she squealed.

'Girl, you see what I mean? No-one is normal. We all have different aspects, do we not? Some of the views those aspects offer begin at the top of a slippery slope. Is that not true? But you see; you did have a friend, to take your hand, and pull you back up.'

She knew exactly what he meant and she smiled, wide and warm.

They were silent a little while.

'It all started very innocently Harding, I promise!'

Harding laughed suddenly. 'If that is all you have to answer for at the Pearly Gates, my dear little girl, then…'

She looked up, staring at him with pleading, little girl eyes.

'Girl, most people with your abilities would not stop short at a little voyeurism. They would be robbing banks and becoming zillionaires. They would be disposing of people they did not like! You are an angel, just watching!'

He laughed then, heartily, and she felt herself relax.

'What about the proper stuff?' Harding asked. 'When your friend pulled you off the ledge of voyeurism, you returned to participation?'

'Like I said…' Thys shrugged. 'I've had… three. On and off. All different. None… the one.'

She was becoming a bit sheepish now.

Harding shrugged. 'Had?'

She let out a heavy sigh.

'I don't know, really! I don't know how much I should want them, or if I want them, or which one to go to now, even if I want that tonight, or if I'm using them or they're using me or if I even really *actually like* any of them – or they like me!'

The coyote howled again, and this time was joined by two more. There was no question now; they were closer to the house. It had sounded as though they were just outside.

Harding cleared his throat and grinned.

'Have you played the trifecta?'

'What, like – a three-way? No!'

'No, no; have you fallen in love, had you heart broken, then fallen in love again?'

She scowled. 'No. Just the first two.'

'I see. Your heart was broken.'

'Once.'

'Have you ever broken a heart?'

'Probably. I don't know. There was someone... I think. It wasn't...'

'You have broken hearts, you just don't know it. A girl with your looks; you are... you will have done, believe me. But it is different for girls, no? Excuse me – for women? For some, but not for others – and then again, maybe for everyone, at times? And don't worry about the coyote howls, they are just looking for trash.'

Thys shrugged.

That seemed to fit the conversation somehow.

'But in some ways it is the same – for men and women, isn't it? It depends on how your brain is made, how your body responds. Your...' He quickly patted his chest. 'Your ticker? And what your guts tells you; if it twists? And your senses – never forget looks, and smells, and taste. How they sound, how they dress, what those things reminds us of, consciously, and unconsciously, within the unregistered realms of our psyche. Scents we don't know we are taking in. We know it is worse not to respond to all that, when we feel it, no? To – repress, you see? That is bad. You are woman enough – you are strong enough, with your list of things you can do, to control the situation. But if a situation feels wrong, why do it? But then again, if it feels right to challenge those feelings, to just go out and fuck – oh, I am sorry, that was indelicate –'

'No, Harding, really, I need to have an honest conversation!'

'Well – if it feels right to do wrong, to do bad things – not that they *are* actually wrong or bad – I mean, we men, some men, call it... "sport fucking" – ? Women – "friend sex"? Is that what they call it now? And you can handle yourself... it is like war, sometimes. You know; working the angles, going on instinct. The war of the sexes. Many women I have worked with, fighting women, covert women, they have done this, sporting, to work it out. Better than the alternative; a woman who develops too many muscles, like Jo Sara. In my opinion anyway. But you can handle yourself. In any situation, I would think. Am I wrong?'

Wow, she thought to herself. The machismo perspective.

But it felt great, hearing that, from a man's man.

And it was thrilling, almost, to hear an honest perspective from a friend, no matter what that perspective was.

Her friend, Harding.

'But then; to me it sounds like you have had enough sport. Enough – maybe it is "fuck buddies"? Is that the term? Never mind. But if I were you – and you and I know that the universe is listening – I would stop. You want to find a serious partner, tell the universe; here, I will stop with the sport and the buddies, send me something I can share my gifts with. Demand it! You have done enough for the universe, let the damn universe do something for you!'

Her jaw had dropped.

'Really?'

'Yes girl! Really!'

She watched as Harding's eyes suddenly strayed, darting away from her, and narrowed slightly. She knew he had surveillance monitors everywhere, and alert signals scattered throughout the house that only he could see; the house was as secure as any military safe-house, so he'd said.

And, she knew that he also monitored a second house.

Well; maybe not *house* so much...

The old Hines mansion, now derelict, only a few miles up the road.

'There's activity...' Harding uttered the declaration as though it were part of a second, ongoing sub-conversation between them. 'Probably kids.'

'At the Hines House? You're sure?'

'It's on the Haunted Hollywood tours now, on the star maps. Kids take dares. But sometimes it's occultists; I call Byford and his men, and have the kids... persuaded not to return. For their own good.'

She smiled, then returned to the previous subject. 'No.' Then she sighed. 'Physically, there's nothing I can't handle. Not with what I can do. But – emotionally?'

Something vibrated in Harding's pocket.

Thys knew him well enough to know that if he had left a phone on while he was talking to her, when it rang he needed to take it. He lifted the phone to his giant head without pause.

'Go.'

Thys watched. Harding's face was amazing. It gave nothing away as he listened, and his mind, so far as she could pick up without trying, was essentially unreadable.

'Tell her yes. Yes to all three.'

Harding ended the call.

'Everything okay?' Thys asked, knowing it couldn't possibly be.

'That explains the coyotes.'

Thys gulped. 'It's the house, isn't it? Something's happening up at the old Oliver Hines place?'

'Yes. Lavé wants to meet us there.'

Her heart skipped a beat.

'Tarni Lavé? She's there?'

'Yes. I think she's on to us.'

Thys smirked. 'She's been on to us from the...'

Harding smiled at her, smug.

'It had been some time since you have seen her. Did you have a falling out? I thought that after –'

'No – I – it's fine.'

Harding nodded.

He could tell, she knew, without the slightest effort, that she way lying.

'What does Tarni want to meet us *there* for?' Thys wondered aloud.

Her look said to Harding; *do not say anything else about Tarni Lavé.*

'…at *that* horrible place?'

'I am sure we will find out soon enough, but, look…' Harding leaned over the couch, toward her, earnestly. 'Once, many years ago, your father offered you something. It was the same offer your father had been made, essentially, by the person who trusted him the most, and who had started all this.'

'Good old Uncle Pan. And look where it got him. Almost a decade in a black Sirian coffin, on a broken Pleiadean spaceship.'

'True, but your father gave you the same offer because he loves you; and because you need to share these gifts with other people – of your generation. Your father does the best with it he can; he bends the minds of business psychopaths so that they make decisions that don't threaten the human race. He buys farmland. He has poisonous growth and fertilizer chemicals outlawed. He tries to prove that certain electrical frequencies are harmful. That, sometimes, emotions matter in the world of science. But you need to have a say as well, here on the third density, the third plane, on Earth. You need to start building. Is that not what Xylata and Suzie taught you? You have your bridge. You no longer lose time and your astral amnesia is getting shorter and less stressful, exponentially each time you return. Build something here. That you can use. If everything you've told me is true, yours might be the first generation in six thousand years who can actually control their own destiny. Why not act as though you have one?'

Thys nodded, and she believed it.

She knew that was true; she knew that this was what she had been doing it for; forging a new astral frontier for the human race…

'I know that Harding, and I appreciate it, more than anything, that you understand my situation, and me, and can tell me that. But, of the nine, the nine people who are already enhanced with the Pandora Sequence, it's ended well for some of them; Bo has his the *Lady Ann*, and Yelina; Dad has Heather, and they have Cleverco; and that's doing, as you say, good work. Suzie got her career back, her life and her timeline back, and apart from having two sets of memories, she's back on track and doing fine. But Vance doesn't remember anything. He doesn't even seem to have his powers still…'

'He has three Oscar nominations.'

'Harding, he was possessed by Lucifer! That can't be good! But Dad says we should just let him be!'

'Mitch says he is bound to win an Oscar this time round; for playing a Derek Nurding 'type' in this Achilleos film, this *Law of Large Numbers*. I put ten thousand dollars on him at two hundred to one, six months ago. Now he is six to one.'

'Harding; he was *there*, all the way through to the end! And he doesn't remember! And possessed by Lucifer? If something like that happened to someone I trust, or even love, just because they trust or even love me…?' She threw her hands up. 'You see?'

Harding grinned. 'It's good that you care so much; think so much. Mitch knew what he was doing. He's a good man, your father.'

'I know, I know. But look; Pan himself is still in that starcophagus, Bo says that Saph is still sleeping next to him, and has been *all this time*, without so much as a *conversation*. Trudy can't come out in public without the risk of assassination; I mean, from what I know, nobody knows where she is half the time! For her own security! And I'm more at home in The Terrastral Territories than I am on Terra Firma! Being enhanced with the

Pandora Sequence is not all it's cracked up to be – most of the time it's a target on your back…!'

'Amethyst – Thys; listen to me. You finished your war three days ago. You celebrated one and came back here and slept for two –'

'Two?'

'Close enough to; then you called your friends you hadn't seen for all that time you'd been away and discovered they had changed. That they were pissed at you for growing, and leaving them behind. Who knows? Maybe you're not really friends anymore? It happens. You still have to be careful, yes, but things have calmed down now; you have what you wanted.'

'Do I?'

'Have you contacted The Pan? You had friends there – those three nice girls who were on the helicopter with you – Lorena, and Capri, and April. You all lost friends that day. Have you seen them lately?'

'No. I saw Lorena at Paramatta but she thought I was Christ Returned.'

Harding's eyes narrowed.

'The one in the lift with us?'

'Yes.'

'I see. But still; Trudy will know. She loves you like an aunt; she wants to speak to you, whether she is in hiding or not. And don't you think after spending so long in fourth density space that Bo Everett would not desire your opinion on his ever-humanesque ship? You have spent more conscious time in that other dimension than any other living human! Call him up; this time, I will come with you! All this time and I still haven't seen the damn thing!'

Thys sighed. 'I don't know. I feel… anxious about seeing them all.'

'Amy-Thys, you have friends. Real friends. None you can make love to…'

'Well –'

'None you can admit to?'

'I suppose – ?'

'But that is how you meet people you can make love to; by socializing – hanging out – with the friends you *do have*.'

'Do you have someone Harding?'

'Just like you, I have several. For different moods. And now I live here, I meet actresses who grew up watching Eastwood and Arnie and think I am the next best thing – even though I am the real thing. Years ago that would have appalled me, now I find it amusing. Maybe I *have* been here too long?'

Thys found this highly amusing and blew her nose heavily as she laughed along with her cool Hollywood Grand-Pop.

'So you feel better?'

'I don't know Harding. Pan, Saph, Vance, Trudy…'

'So far as missions into oblivion go, they are all still alive, are they not? That is not a bad result. Room for improvement, yes. Tragedy? We shall see.'

He smiled warmly. Thys removed her Eve from her pocket.

'Aha,' Harding grinned. 'Taking action. This is real soldiering.'

Thys dialed.

'I'm calling Mirabelle.'

Harding was impressed.

Mirabelle Contrelle was now Cleverco's private security and surveillance head, and as it turned out, genuinely one of Heather's oldest friends; not to mention the Pyne's nominal personal assistant. And, she was currently in charge of EverSky One.

Thys shrugged. 'Heather trusts her. Almost as much as Dad trusts Tarni Lavé.'

'I am aware of this. Mirabelle did not lie to us in Paramatta; she used to work the second shift when Heather was on surveillance. They ran covert missions together.'

Thys nodded. 'She was spying on my Dad too, before he and Heather fell in love. Heather says Mirabelle knows too much about him to let her go. She said, she's seen him in the shower.'

'And she's definitely seen what you can do.'

'Mmmm.'

She returned her attention to her phone, making a gagging sound with her tongue out.

'I vetted her,' Harding shrugged. 'She vetted fine.'

Thys' eyes bulged. 'Is that a double entendre?'

Harding didn't answer.

'Contrelle Travel, how many I direct you call?'

'Hi Mirabelle. It's me. I need some surveillance details.'

'Civilian, or other?'

'Just civilian, so far as I know.'

'Name?'

'There's three.'

Harding checked his security feeds while Thys described what she needed, then had the details sent to her Eve.

'There's one more thing,' Mirabelle offered. 'Is Harding with you?'

'Yeah.'

'Can you put me on speaker?'

'Sure.'

She did, and Harding made a face, as though he had no clue what it could be about.

'Hello Harding.'

'Miss Mirabelle.'

'I thought you both should know; there is something odd happening with all the satellite services, and the cell phone towers. It's global, all satellites, all towers; the whole global digital network. Some of our people think there's been some kind of massive, coordinated attack, and the whole thing is about to go down; like, cascade exponentially. Personally, I think it's some kind of game-changing virus. But there are also signs of strange activity on some of the moons of the planet Saturn, on Pandora and Prometheus, possibly about the Saturnalian rings, so there are also theories that it may be something celestial, atmospheric. Basically, nobody knows. Harding, I know you keep a hardcore landline fixed wherever you are based, but it might be wise to maintain a landline internet connection as well?'

'Who could do that?' Thys asked, horrified. 'Bring down the whole of Earth's satellite communication system?'

'I haven't the faintest idea. Maybe you should ask some of your friends. Your *other* friends?'

There was a pause as Thys took in what had just been said. 'Understood.'

'I've sent that other information to your Eve. I suggest you back it, and everything else, up. Is there anything else?'

'Keep us informed,' Harding ordered. 'Landline if required.'

'Of course. Good night Harding, Amy.'

'Thanks, Mirabelle.'

Thys ended the call and checked her phone.

'Saturn has a moon called Pandora...' Harding hummed. 'This I did not know. Surely, in your world, that must have some significance? Some relevance in the synchronicity?'

The information Thys had requested was there...

And – curious.

There was also another text.

From – him.

From Qwerty again.

The Romans re-branded as Christians and used their war machine to absorb or destroy everything else.

Christianity is now a corporate brand.

Corporations are temples for psychopaths.

Psychopaths gravitate to the corporate structure.

Corporations are legally treated as people.

Many believe the model for the Old Testament Christian God is psychopathic.

Humanity serves a series of psychopathic temples and gods.

Thys sighed.

She would have to read that one again.

What the hell was his game now?

'Okay,' Thys nodded at Harding, her eyes now long-free of tears. 'I'm human again, grounded in high emotional release; I'm good to go.'

'Very well. Let's go and face the ghosts of the past.'

'And Tarni Lavé?'

'Girl, that's what I meant.'

THE OMEGA SEQUENCE

PART

NOWHERE

CHAPTER 42

Since DeVora's ambush, and Gordian's assassination attempt at Paramatta, what Thys now assumed (hoped, desperately) to be the final three years of the "The War of the Terrastral Territories" had been very bad.

The fluid dream world scenarios had, in fact, at times, been utterly terrifying, beyond anything young Amy Pyne could ever have coped with. Additionally, almost ironically, the fighting had become more "human" as the war had gone on; more savage and bloody and ruthless, aimed at inflicting greater pain for greater numbers; dragging in more human imagery, and hardware, and skill.

Being an astral war, the battle scenarios within those last years had begun to cross both temporal and psychological boundaries too, eventually cracking open vortexes into the physical plane, and crossing into real life, as it had that day in Paramatta, and even merging, or gapping, into real, physical, human wars on the Earth plane.

Nothing like this had ever happened before.

Thys had been to some places; she had completely lost perspective a couple of times; she had nearly lost her sanity twice and her life, her actual life, given that she was in a seemingly endless situation that involved constant danger...

Well, she thought... maybe, very close three actual times.

There were times when she had been forced to send Xylata away, and take over herself. And there had been times when Xylata had sent her away, and taken charge.

There had been times when they had both been burned out, but there was nobody else, and they had kept each other going.

Because of all of these times, they now trusted each other

completely.

Thys did not know where Xylata went when she sent her away; but she always came back replenished, refocussed and re-strategized. Thys knew though; more than just sleeping soundly, for sanity, in her *silverbluemoonroom* (which nobody could find but everyone assumed was in the middle of the Amethyst Palace) these were the times that Thys needed to vanish.

She had tried isolation within her own, private astral bedroom (truth be told, although she could always, instantly get there, not even she really knew where it was) but it had been woefully inedequate; the sense was ever-present that she was still there, still on the astral plane; she could still feel the enemy simmering, the enemy raging, the next battle starting to boil; still feel all the people looking for her, waiting for her, needing her to come back.

But she had to come back *strong*.

Thys found herself again thinking of Suzie Saturn's imagined, magical bar, *Jeers*.

❲ *Where nobody knows your name?* ❳

Suzie had stared her straight in the eyes.

♪ *Kid; where nobody gives a shit.* ♪

Thys had thought long and hard.

Where... nobody.

Nobody.

And so, what had eventually become known as the Nobody Places had begun to emerge.

CHAPTER 43

When Thys had first realised that she could gap, the discovery had been very exciting. But still, the practice had been a little frightening. When she had returned from her first astral battle, over the Sea of Humanity, using Everett's boat to fight off hoards of Anunnaki, employing the craft eventually as some kind of silver-"surfer-bitch"-mecha-board, she had been somewhat shell-shocked.

Or, hell-shocked?

(Actually, it had been more like heaven than hell, truth be told.)

Xylata had been so satisfactorily stunned at her success that she had come 'back down' to Earth to seek her out, and from there, a great military partnership had been born.

But regardless of how she felt about the subsequent experiences, Thys had been so drained by the events at Paramatta that she had forced herself to remain in third density for several weeks before going back, just to wrap her head around all that had happened; the atoms, and The Realma; her new tattoo and her new outfit...

...and to ensure that she would be able, if she did go back and proceed with the war, as she had outlined it to Heather and Xylata, that she would be able to proceed and maintain her sanity.

After she had been reunited with her father and Heather, who seemed then to be the only members of their original party who would be returning to third density any time soon, it had become clear that Thys needed time alone.

And so, after a while, she had been happily left to her own devices to test her new powers.

The first thing she had done initially upon realising that she could use telepathy was find a way to control her telepathic and empathic reception centres; to shut down the mental noise of all the people within her vicinity.

It was easy, once you got the knack; it pretty much had to be, otherwise any kind of consciously sympathetic telepathic or empathic ability was going to be useless, by way of driving her insane with the endless useless internal chatter, or the constant white-noise barrage of all the high and conflicting emotions of all the other people in the world.

(Who were, she quickly realised, in one way or another, and quite frequently in an ever-shifting kaleidoscope of many and varied ways, all completely mad.)

When she had learned to turn the volume down on the psychic kaleidoscope, Thys had turned her attention to the other powers she had been given.

The most obvious was the so-called "out of body" power.

She and the other Pandorans had been the first humans not only to consciously traverse the astral, but also to have the ability, which was innate but terribly repressed in human beings anyway, to take their physical form into the astral with them. Not; fall asleep and them meet somewhere in a kind of virtual, spiritual otherworld, but to actually, physically, go there; through portals and gaps, and such.

The Anunnaki had possessed the ability to do this for twenty thousand years, apparently, and had never looked back. But she and her human friends had seemed to possess the added benefit of being able to easily, and physically, traverse the "higher realms" of fifth and even sixth densities as well.

Maybe even beyond that; none of them were even now totally sure where they had been, what "the void" had been, where Suzie and Lucifer had plunged to their fates.

Still, back then, in the early days, she had figured, with the fact that she had naturally been able to jump her spirit from her body (like a ghost) when she'd been shot by Eissley, and that she had been able to come and go from the astral regularly and easily, that she pretty much had that one down too.

It was the teleportation thing that initially gave her the heebie jeebies.

While gapping from third to fourth density seemed second nature to Thys, paradoxically, gapping from one third density location to another was, somehow, somewhat more nerve wracking.

Gapping into the astral was like diving into water; there was initial anxiety, then the sudden body shock, but once you were in, you were in. Most likely wondering what all the fuss had been about in the first place; rushing from exhilaration and adrenalin, then turning around and manically encouraging everyone else on the shore.

"Come on in! The astral's fine!"

Gapping location-to-location within third density, within what most people would consider the real, physical world; the everyday Earth as everyone knew it, had seemed, at least at first, like learning to jump off a trampoline, or vault a gym horse. If you weren't a natural, you had to find your own balance, your own centre of gravity, your own coordination, and then trust yourself.

Easier said than done, as any awkward adolescent would no doubt quite readily attest.

When she'd first returned, Thys had stayed secretly in her Uncle Pan's old storage apartment, where her father had been living as a borderline alcoholic for almost a year, where Heather had first found him and decided to rescue him, and where years later Heather was destined to set up office.

Thys, still Amy even to herself back then, had taken the guest room because the main room had smelled like her father, and that had made her feel ill, because when he had stayed there, he had smelled like stale beer, sweat and cigarettes. She didn't even want to think about all the skanks and wanks he'd had on that bed. Euch!

So she had taken the spare room, cleaned the main room, washed all the sheets three times, aired then flipped the mattress, left all the windows and the balcony doors open for a week, then eventually settled everything back down again. By that time, she had realised that the spare room and the main room were exactly the same size, as were the beds in them, and that therefore, the spare room was now the main room. Which was which, it appeared, was only a matter of where the primary householder slept and kept their stuff.

During that time, she had gapped in and out of the room, and into the corridor, and into the spare room, and all over the apartment as required.

There was just one thing that stood in her way.

Doors.

She had found herself quite irrationally afraid of gapping and getting stuck in the door. She had told herself that this was impossible, that everyone else did it all the time, but then she couldn't get the thought out of her head. Then she began to think; if that thought was lodged in her head as an irrational fear, then she might very well end up doing that to herself unconsciously. Like when driving instructors tell you not to look at the thing you're afraid of hitting, because the direction you fixate upon is the location you'll end up.

But of course, when she finally raised the courage to close the bedroom door and stand right next to it, an inch away, then gap anxiously into the corridor outside, she had succeeded without incident.

And had wondered what all the fuss was about.

It was nothing!

She'd immediately gapped through the closed door into the refreshed now-spare room, then ping-ponged back and forth, bedroom to bedroom, laughing hysterically as she gapped through door after door, then back into the living room. Then she gapped back and forth between more complex barriers; the giant racks of bookshelves where Pan kept his anthropological, philosophical and occult tomes. Then, after checking it was empty, she had gapped from between the shelves to the apartment block corridor outside.

Then, checking again, to the elevator.

For a second she had felt a childlike frisson of naughtiness doing this, which was something she adored feeling. That was closely followed by a powerfully adult charge of devilish but entirely pleasurable anxiety. Somehow, in a way she had yet to process, a whole new world had opened up to her that was conversely, bizarrely, utterly normal. It was new, but not like the dreamlike co-reality of the astral. It was new *here,* in third density reality, at home.

Then, in a sudden panic, she had gapped to the security room and stolen the hard drive that stored the corridor and elevator security footage while the doorman had remained predictably asleep.

CHAPTER 44

Although she didn't like to entertain the thought, Thys had been well aware that, upon her return from the astral, Heather and her father had been having some sort of epic sex marathon. But during the intervals, when they had been around, and doing normal things like having dinner, Heather had thrown Thys all sorts of advice from all quarters, about all sorts of things.

Because they had been 'busy' since the earthquake, mostly with the transfer of Cleverco (then still Everco and Olivera, merging as Lever) and with the many business and legal and corporate distractions this entailed...

(...*and fucking, mostly fucking...*)

...they hadn't really managed to sort out too much to do with their abilities themselves. But one of the things Heather had tossed out at her had been this:

'Photos are useful, but be careful where your mind wanders; your unconscious will protect you from killing yourself but our egos get in the way of not being seen. Our egos want us to pop up in front of everyone and go *hey look what I can do!*'

Thys thought about this as she sat on the balcony of Pan's 'antique occult bookstore', staring out at the okay view of Sydney Harbour, and ran the angles.

Right. Security cameras were everywhere, so you had to find the dead spots. Thankfully, she also knew where the secret cameras were. People were in most places, so you had to go where there wasn't anyone, or at least *appear* where no-one would see you arrive – or, where your arrival would allow you to hide in plain sight; like, in a throng, at rush hour, or where there were lots of people internalizing, paying no attention.

She had also started to realise, as had all the other Pandorans, that something was blocking their long-term foresight. There was something in the future that they couldn't see past, that was not allowing them to get a large impression of their immediate future, as Saph once had. So, she had downloaded some podcasts about remote viewing and heard some of the most famous practitioners claim that there were some things 'the universe'…

(…whatever that meant. 'The universe'? She still wasn't sure – did people just mean 'God' when they said that? But not wanting to be lumped in with all the Christians and the Abrahamic religions, with all those conservative and repressive connotations…? Or did they mean it like her father did, convinced that the universe itself was some kind of massive conscious entity of which we were all, at the very least, an expression…?)

…anyway – many remote-viewers and clairvoyants were claiming these days that there were some things 'the universe' didn't want humanity to know, events that were coming, and that one of these things in particular was not so far down the track.

Regardless, Thys had found herself moving along pretty fast with all this, and she hadn't paused then, or even since, very much, to consider what it might be. She later looked back on it as one of her less-than-wise "whatever happens, happens" phases.

But as for the matter at hand; this strange kind of immediate foresight seemed to work in tandem, as a short term function, with the gapping.

It seemed to Thys that to work like this; if you tried to gap into a room you couldn't see inside, you just had to imagine the reality that the door had another side and that the floor you could see going under the door continued on.

It kind of worked on trust, or even faith.

Reason, even.

The floor on the other side was there, and would be there in another second when you gapped onto it. It was done on faith, but with the odds solidly stacked in your favour. However, if the room was, unbeknownst to the gapper, filled with crates or boxes or guard dogs or crocodiles, or; well, whatever would make a potential emergency scene out of a girl gapping into it on faith, and spontaneously appearing beside it, you would get a strong feedback push to say 'space not available.' If you then pursued that thought – questioned the thought – more often than not you would receive a strong impression of, say, sharp teeth, or 'Chinese vitamins', or even on one occasion, something she later learned was called 'a glory hole'.

This was, she learned years later, what the Pleiadeans referred to as 'potency'. And gradually, through that, Thys had begun to experience what Heather had warned her about; but it had taken until several years later, in the wake of Paramatta, where she had in fact heard that term for the first time in relation to gapping, for it to really mess with her head.

CHAPTER 45

She was almost ready to go back.

She could not comprehend the atomic adventure she'd had in first density, and she had resolved that within herself now; what she remembered, or more accurately, what remained, was somehow summed up for her in the simple 'ohm' chant when she meditated, in a super-early childhood memory of street lights, and in a song she could never quite remember, but could always, almost hum to herself when she heard bits of it in other songs; but never the actual one, exactly.

The Realms she had pounded out, into her laptop, as an epic fantasy novel.

It was rough, but it would do until she had the time to sit again and clean it up.

Kind of long, too.

Maybe it was a trilogy?

Anyway, she had promised herself that, one day, she would.

One time, as she was writing the acknowledgements at the end, she had drifted off. Dozing and daydreaming, her hand had slipped on a key. A webpage hand sprung up, and in her hypnogogic, suggestible state of consciousness she had fallen upon a typical clichéd coffee advertisement of a beautiful, young, iconographic Italian woman, sitting in a piazza café, somewhere stereotypically "Italian", with an espresso cup before her, looking out; all wistful and romantic.

And before she had known it, half-awake, Thys had wished herself there.

But she had ended up floating in the astral.

The model in the picture had been there alright, but it had been some kind of idealized, astral version of herself; one part of the model's compartmentalized psyche that existed in the astral, and fuelled her ego with the energies of all kinds of admiration, generated from the many public images of herself that abounded throughout western culture.

Thys recognized the situation instantly; it was actually quite a common thing, if not essential, for models and certain kinds of actors.

Through all the attention the ad generated, the model was essentially being worshipped. In the astral, as she slept, which presumably she was doing now, she could feel it, and now, during slumber, she was writhing in ecstasy, receiving all the erotic energy of the sexual daydreaming that her café-girl image had created.

All the men who looked at the picture and fantasized about, say, picking her up at the café, taking her to a hotel… she being his mistress, his girlfriend, his partner, his wife. All the women who fantasized that they were that woman, vacationing in some idealized Shirley Valentinesque escape, thinking back wistfully on the night before… to the tall, handsome stranger who had appeared out of nowhere…; he being any one of a million variants.

Variation after variation, and all of them, this model in some way felt.

Thys could tell, and she was good at telling; this model would soon start to feel it within her ordinary, waking life. The campaign must have been successful. She must have been getting a lot of exposure; soon, that DNA would be activated; soon, someone would want to know… what's she like with dialogue?

And then, the fault line would breath in, and try to claim her.

They were so good at this.

Somewhere in the back of her mind, Thys knew; that was the kind of basic fantasy she too had desired to enact. Or at least, these were the kinds of thoughts, desires, fantasies and idealized reminiscences that the advertisement had been designed to trigger; scenarios that had been skilfully implanted by other forms of archetypal fantasy, reinforcing and complimenting each other over the years, since childhood, ad infinitum.

Somewhere in the back of this woman's mind (the actual real woman who had modelled for the advertisement) there was a store of sexual confidence; within her spirit, the potential for projected desirability. And now, in addition to that, there was a rising reservoir of immense and powerful energy, technically at her complete disposal, should she choose to access it, to use it, and learn how to wield it.

But this was the problem with third density; the model, whoever she was, might not know that, and probably didn't. The Anunnaki would be siphoning that energy off from her, from this astral collection point, and channelling it off to their own ends – *probably to sell more coffee.*

Thys had sighed and gapped back to her laptop.

CHAPTER 46

Curious now, and weirdly pissed off, Thys became strangely determined to make something out of this situation.

However, when she tried again to redirect herself to gap to the real piazza, back down to Earth, to somewhere "more authentic", she had reappeared indoors, at a photo shoot. The model in question, a naturally blonde, Polish seventeen-year-old named Magdalena Pacula, who with jet-black hair and the right makeup looked like a gorgously archetypal Italian signorina, was there this time, real and in the flesh, sitting at the same table, looking beautiful and wistful, just as she had, or did…

…or would?

…in the photo.

Just before her first, pre-orgasmic sip of espresso…

But behind her was a giant green screen.

'What the hell are you again?'

He had spoken in a hushed voice, barely above a whisper.

All eyes were on the photo shoot; the flashing of the photography and the occasional shouted direction from the photographer, so that no-one had seen her gap in. But a man with a high-end Eve tucked over his arm, pointing out at her as though demanding to see her papers, had immediately approached. Thys had sensed that he was somehow in charge of the space, of the studio; it was his task to create a space within the space where the artist could work unhindered, undisturbed, and he had quite rightly and with extreme perception sensed a subtle shift within it, probably even before she had gapped in, before she had even realised herself that she was there. He had turned around immediately, instinctively, to pinpoint where the shift had occurred.

To her.

'Amy.' She had responded quickly, instinctively, in a similar hushed tone.

He tapped and swiped the tablet screen a few times.

'Amy?' He sounded very frustrated.

'From the agency.' Thys remembered this kind of thing going on with her father's magazine, when she had been a child. She knew how it went. 'They told me to come down right away.'

The man had looked her in the eye then, through his fashionable black-rimmed hipster glasses.

'Who did?'

'Upstairs,' Thys kept going. 'They told me to come down and see what the fuss was about.'

'Fuss? There's no fuss?'

'They said the background image was some main-drag piazza in Rome. It's not supposed to be.'

The man sounded massively affronted. 'Rome? It's not Rome! It's Tuscany – we sent Robby and Roberto there and they said it was not only outside of the main drag but utterly-totally out of the way and *maximum* non-touristy. They just sent these background shots in this morning!'

'Robby and Roberto are in Rome? They're supposed to be – ! Oh, never mind. When did they go?'

'No, no, not Rome!'

'Then what's the name of the town?'

Thys could not believe she was trying to pull this off.

She had never been possessed of more contained excitement, outside of the astral war.

Wave, wave, tap – tap.

'Viniziarra!'

The man had looked up from his Eve.

All Thys heard was a dimensional echo.

'What! *Amy?* Where did you go?'

CHAPTER 47

So, she'd googled it, and found a picture of the village, which had looked empty. Then another, then several others, then nothing more. There seemed to be less than a dozen photos of Viniziarra. It seemed that the little town, or village, or whatever it was, might not only have been small, and off the main drag, but quite possibly completely deserted as well. And, if it were not, then it was certainly sparsely populated enough to clear out when a photographic crew came through for an advertising assignment.

So she had taken a calculated risk and simply gapped into the most remote-looking street, as seen in one of the few pictures of the village she could find.

The first thing that struck her was the heat.

Then she had immediately lost her footing on the stone-cobbled street. She had of course witnessed people as they arrived through a gap and all anyone would have seen, had there been anyone about…

Silence.

…at least; the way the brain translated what had happened, seemed generally to be; a person stepping out of nowhere with a light behind them. Not particularly bright, not heavenly or angelic or anything, just; kind of mildly back-lit.

But there was no-one around.

Regardless, she had gapped into Viniziarra directly from Pan's old barely air-conditioned apartment in the middle of the transition between a Sydney winter and a Sydney spring, where it had still been quite mild. This had been like stepping directly into an industrial kiln.

Thys wandered a bit down the curved, stone street.

It looked exactly like all the little streets in small and remote

Italian villages that she'd ever seen in the movies, in all the ads, in all the…

But this was real.

She was here.

The modest old wood-panel doors, the cracking white-painted walls, and the sturdy but ancient-looking bricks and stonework.

Everything weatherworn beyond measure.

The thin street opened into a central courtyard; she could tell immediately that the village was high on a hill somewhere, and which one of all the centrally collected streets led out of the village. She could see from here; the road out even ran down through an olive grove. There was a well in the middle of the courtyard with a small statue of Saint Barbara (a worn plaque read) the patron saint of artillerymen, that had been erected at the end of the First World War. But what most caught her interest was a small store that had signs, mostly in Italian, stuck to the shutters of its closed double-windows. One or two though were universal; in fourth density, she'd seen their astral cathedrals. There was Coke, and Heineken, and Visa. And beside them, another, hand-written in bold caps, carefully laminated.

WI-FI – BAD.

She smiled to herself.

She was going to like it here.

CHAPTER 48

It seemed like a dream but it was definitely the café from the ad; she recognized the wrought-iron hooks of the hanging basket plants, and the swirling etchings carved around the edge of the door frame. But without the additional, corny flourishes that the ad agency art and set designers had deemed appropriate, it was somewhat more plain. However, it was also a lot more – dare she think? – *genuinely* rustic and charming.

Although the door to the store was open, the village seemed deserted and the store looked pitch dark within, despite the stark sunshine. The ad had given the romantic impression that the café was small but thriving; outside in the central village courtyard there were only two tables, one on either side of the store's blackhole entrance, with three wrought iron but thickly cushioned seats at each.

There seemed to be absolutely nobody around.

Still, if they really did serve coffee here, she liked it even more.

Suddenly a middle-aged man stepped out and stared down the road, out of the village, as though waiting for someone who was late. Then he turned, like the man with the tablet at the photo shoot, as though unconsciously sensing a new presence in his sacred space, and saw her standing at the entrance to the courtyard, assessing the store.

She heard her own heartbeat once, very heavily, up into her throat, and pulse out of her ears.

The man spread his arms in a highly welcoming manner.

'Isadora!'

Thys was stunned.

'*Isadora!*'

'I'm...'

'You are like Isis! You must be from Isis!'

'I...'

She stopped herself. He wouldn't understand what she was saying.

'I'm Australian – I'm sorry, I only speak English.'

He looked at her, suddenly filled with concern, and ushered her fully to his side, then to one of the table settings. She felt as though she were twice his height.

'Here, here, you sit, you sit down!'

'Espresso?' she asked.

'Yes, yes of course! I'll get you a water first though – okay?'

She sat.

The cushion's plastic cover squeaked, but the ancient iron chair was well designed and embraced her with a surprising comfort-level.

Without waiting for her response, the man rushed inside.

He returned within seconds holding a tall glass of clear, chilled water.

She accepted and sipped.

'Drink up,' he insisted. 'You're very warm!'

There was genuine concern on his wide features as he brushed back his long fringe of thinning black hair, so she sipped again. Only after she'd gulped half the glass down, cold-scalding her throat in the process, did he seem satisfied. Then he nodded happily and went back inside.

She sat there for a few minutes and felt a rush of exhilaration.

She'd done it.

She was halfway across the world in the middle of nowhere... about to have a perfect coffee.

The man poked his head back out.

'Americano?'

'No,' she smiled. 'Australian.'

'No, no, I mean, would you like Americano? I add a little water and some milk – you'll like it, I think. We had photographers here last year, Australian – they pretend to like espresso but when

I switched on the second day and gave them all Americanos they all smiled and nobody complained.'

'Whatever you think,' she smiled gratefully.

She did prefer Americano, or at least a lungo or latte, to espresso – but she hadn't wanted to feel… inauthentic, she supposed.

How stupid.

She leaned back and crossed one leg over the other, and stretched her arms high.

One minute she'd been sitting on her Dad's old couch, thinking about who to thank for inspiring her magnum opus, wondering if she should watch a box set of some old BBC costume drama she'd found under the sofa, the next minute she'd been dozily looking at a half-familiar ad on some regular website she'd barely known she'd opened, and now, after a bizarre couple of detours, here she was.

Then she saw her sneakers.

They were almost new, and way too cheerful; white with pink flourishes and grey piping. Clearly, they hadn't been used to hike up or down here from anywhere. And she wasn't sweating, like she'd been walking a long way. *And* - and, even though that was a big presumption (as she had no idea where, or how far away, the nearest anything actually was from here) she was betting herself that on a day like today, a walk to the next village or town, or anything anywhere, would raise *at least* a slight sweat.

She'd done very little that day and her hair was still clean and relatively freshly styled, at least to the small extent that she even went to make her long, thick mane do anything but simply *be*. Her makeup was still at least visibly half-present from her morning meeting with a man from Cleverco about the ridiculous monthly allowance her father had insisted on paying into a bank account, that after years she'd only just formally signed for, then and there, under mild duress. When she'd gotten back to the apartment, she'd changed out of her "good impression" clothes and into comfortable home clothes, intended for indoors during a late Sydney winter; the sneakers, grey sweat pants, a dull pink tee and a matching dark grey and pink-piped zip-front hoodie. It all matched and was off the rack from a novelty clothes store; one of those perky ones that sold mostly Japanese pop-culture items. She'd seen it in a display window and it had stuck in her mind for three days; she'd returned and bought it for that very reason, and because she had nothing to sit around watching telly in, and wanted something that required minimal effort. She'd simply gone into the store and told the girl; 'everything on that mannequin please'.

Thys was mannequin sized; tall and slender, with a nice bust and bum, and since her "growth spurt", ordering off a mannequin had usually worked.

But the upshot was; here in Viniziarra, she looked wrong.

She would instantly have registered *wrong* on this man's radar, at the very least unconsciously.

If he became consciously suspicious, there would be some explaining.

But then again, maybe it wouldn't be that way?

Maybe…?

The man came out of the café with her Americano in a tall wide mug, along with one for himself, and another tall glass of iced water. He smiled gently as he sat down beside her, offering the water. She returned the smile as she drank it down, feigning relief.

'Thank you so much!'

He kept smiling.

'So, you only speak English, is what you said?'

'Yes, I'm sorry, I must seem like such a touris –'

The penny dropped, hard.

She was speaking Italian.

She was speaking Italian and she didn't know how.

'Did you become lost? Are you a student? The heat, on a day like today, it can creep up on you, you don't see it coming and suddenly – bang – you don't quite know where you are, or who you are, or what you were doing any more.'

She sipped the Americano. It was delicious. Truly.

Then she saw him look down at her virtually new, certainly un-hiked-in sneakers. Then the winter pants and the hoodie with the *Earthen Hype* insignia over her left breast. She unzipped the hoodie and took it off, faking a reaction to the heat. She hadn't even actually had time yet, to get genuinely hot.

Then she remembered; she wasn't wearing a bra.

He seemed to register this, but not necessarily in a creepy way. More in a; that's okay, that's nice, whatever passes through, kind of way.

Then he smiled at her, uncertain.

Screw it, she thought.

Do it.

Go for it.

Be that girl.

'Thank you for the coffee…?'

Searchingly… confident.

'Tutto. My name is Tutto. My store; Tutto's.'

'I might like to come here, Tutto, every now and then, out of the blue, and just sit for a while, and have a nice coffee. I need somewhere where I can come and do that. Would that be okay?'

He assessed her for a second, and for that second his eyes, which were grey, seemed devoid of all the implied mirth they had so innocently projected just a second before.

Then his smile burst forth again, warm and kind.

It was genuine; she felt it.

'Isadora…!'

Still smiling, he lifted the mug and clinked it lightly to her own.

'Anything for you!'

CHAPTER 49

And so, every time she vanished to her Nobody Places, she started with a morning coffee at Tutto's, whether it was morning or not.

'Tutto...?' He had told her one time. 'It means 'everything', 'anything'. They call me that; they mean my store, it has it all; everything and everything.'

She didn't know whether his mind had filled in the gaps about her sudden appearance and inappropriate dress, and that he had decided not to ask questions and let that be. Or, whether her sudden burst of confidence during their first conversation had suggested to him in an almost unconscious manner that something *other* was occurring; that he was perhaps playing some small role in a larger metaphysical drama, and he had perhaps gone with that?

Either way, he had gone with *something*, and she had gone back many times since, and they were firm friends now.

Two other things had emerged out of that day.

The first was that her unconscious mind had translated a foreign language for her.

Pondering this, she realised:

I speak to Anunnaki.

They are not only foreign, they are alien.

Of course my mind does that.

The second was that in order to have seen the photo in the ad, then to have gapped to where it was being taken, she would have to have travelled backwards in time.

Certainly months, maybe even years.

Backwards, into her own pat; into the reality of events which had already gone by.

That was not supposed to be possible.

...surely?

But.... just as with the foresight-barrier; the thing that none of her fellow Pandorans could not see past when they looked into the long-range future (or the "potency wall", as she had begun to think of it)... the thing that all The Pandorans knew was there, and was potentially coming...

She decided not to think about these things, and to just push on with the matters at hand.

"Whatever happens", she decided…

CHAPTER 50

It turned out that Viniziarra was populated mostly with older folk, who made the majority of their annual living by renting empty houses to seasonal workers who passed though. Tutto's store serviced several of the other, surrounding villages and was something of a hub for them all. The villagers were generally present at twilight, both sunrise and sunset, when they would shoot the breeze twice a day for an hour or two, then retire back to their own respective homes or businesses, indoors.

Thys had since snapped a selfie on her Eve in front of a tight group of stone pines that were clustered on a small rise, and backed by a short, sheer rock wall, located a good, steep, three-minute hike above the village. Before doing this, she had scoped the surrounding area and decided that, unless you were absolutely focused on that point, and actually waiting for someone to appear, you would never see anyone gap into the forest edge and walk down the hard rocky slope, that was in some seasons deceptively covered in soft amber pine needles, down the hill to the Viniziarra.

The idea that this would be the starting point of a regular circuit did not emerge fully-formed from her mind, not until she had returned to Viniziarra a few more times. One time, during the second pause in astral hostilities, she had again brought her Eve with her. She had simply rolled out of her bed at Harding's place after a night out, drinking with her old school-friend Brooke, and her sister Jade, or Saxe, or whatever she was calling herself when she was drunk, thrown on a coat and some sneakers, and gapped straight there.

It hadn't been her exact intention, but it had just… happened.

It was where she had imagined.

Where she had wanted most to be.
And something in her mind had gone…
…why not?
Hadn't she told Tutto she would be back every now and then?
And hadn't he always been fine with it?
And, my God, she needed a decent coffee.
Now.

CHAPTER 51

Things always seemed exactly the same in Viniziarra; this time was slightly cooler maybe. The air was always fresh and clean and she realised instantly that she had been sweating under her quilt all night and stank severely of alcohol.

Then she had a moment's panic.

Pulling on the coat that she had staggered home in last night, over her pyjama sweat-pants and tee, like a dressing gown, to go downstairs and a make a hangover coffee in front of Harding might have been okay… but haphazardly gapping to a remote Italian village to buy a coffee, like this, in front of an old barista she'd only bought coffee from maybe half-a-dozen times?

Worse; she had gapped right into the village courtyard.

She found her sunglasses and her Eve in her coat pocket, and her purse in another.

Standing there, she quickly tried to put the pieces of her hungover mind together. She recalled that it had been three months since she'd last been back in the world. She had secured what had seemed like a whole sea within the astral ocean, where her fight had started, and then even taken some astral 'beach'. Then the Cheneks had stopped coming. Xylata had negotiated a temporary cease fire, and the two of them had returned to third density.

In the meantime, the massive structure that the Ymira Clan were calling the Amethyst Palace was staring to take shape… and Thys had recently learned that Xylata's clan had started to use accelerated clone-bodies that had been enhanced with stolen Regene technology, as per her request that they no longer 'possess' unwilling humans, in battle also.

So, she had spent the night drinking into the impossibly

beautiful face of Jane Fonda, age; Barbarella.

She'd gone to see her father and Heather that night, a Friday, and while she was there Jade/Saxe had called (to ask for money, Heather had quietly opined) which had turned out to be true (don't ask, don't get, Heather had further opined, sympathetically though philosophically) and the Pyne sisters had, through that conversation with her father, arranged to meet the following Monday afternoon.

Thys had a previous engagement that Monday evening, which was to catch up with Brooke for dinner, but without the other two girls in their regular clique, Linh and Emily.

They liked to do that sometimes.

(Shhh!)

But Thys had been sure she'd be done with Jade by dinner. She'd gone to see Harding next, on the Saturday night, and they had sat at his bar at The Fork and for the first time he had offered her a regular bed and permanent berth in his giant, essentially empty Hollywood abode.

Then Sunday night she'd seen Trudy, and caught up on all the gossip within The Pan, the subjects pertaining to which, she barely remembered anything about anymore, other than Trudy's continuing narrative.

So, in effect, she had been drunk all three nights in a row.

Maybe… it had been her birthday?

Mid-October?

That would explain it.

She might have been… twenty-five now?

Ugh.

One thing she *did* recall was that, for some reason that she *couldn't* recall, Heather and her father were about to quit drinking.

For good… or something.

She had seen no indication of any such thing that night.

Something about lime green houses, or… something?

Whatever, anyway…

Thys had decided not to drink on the fifth night of her astral shore leave, and had gone to see her sister that Monday afternoon with the solid intention of having a coffee or two, catching up, and leaving early.

But two coffees had turned into one coffee followed by a hair-of-the-dog Russian coffee, followed by just one glass of wine as the evening had fallen, to another glass, then calling Brooke to tell her to come and meet them *here* instead, wherever *here* had been, and Jade and Brooke getting along famously, as she'd forgotten they always did, because after all, Brooke had known Jade by proxy, and seen her grow up and become a woman, and had known her as long as she had known Thys. There had been another bottle as night had set in, then finding a bar where they could order some nibbles, and then ordering cocktails, and then they had raged onwards into a full boar girls-night-out binge that may or may not have involved dancing with strange boys.

Thys didn't recognize the coat she was now wearing.

She was sure though, that she had worn the coat home last night…

Then she remembered that none of them had left home that afternoon prepared for an eventually chilly night out, in a late Sydney springtime, and that she had bought the coat from a high-end fashion store that had, for some reason, remained open in the city very late on a weekday evening.

Or, had they seen someone inside the store and demanded to be let in?

There had been thumping on glass and shouting, she recalled, and the waving of a gold credit card and offers of bribery.

Presumably that approach had succeeded.

Standing now outside Tutto's, contemplating her fragmented memory, Thys realised that her tongue had stuck to the roof of her mouth while she had reminisced. Forcing it to peel off with buds that tasted bitter and rancid, she thought that she had, in the process, perhaps lost a layer of skin from either her tongue or her palette, or both. Her lips felt like scar tissue and she wondered whether or not, if she were simply to gap back home, just that second, anyone would see her.

She put on her sunglasses and opened her purse.

Inside there were many receipts, the top one jammed in so clumsily that it fell out at the first opportunity. She snatched it from the air somehow, mid-swirl, and read the sharply printed text through dry, practically un-blinkable eyes.

She had purchased *seven* wool Earthen Hype ladies frock coats from the Earthen Hype Boutique; one burnt-sunshine -orange, one ocean-navy-blue, one crystal-cabernet-crimson, one indigo-aubergine-amethyst…

She looked down.

She was wearing, she assumed, the burnt sunshine orange one.

Why wasn't she wearing the ameth…?

She sighed. Never-mind.

…one lemon-delicious-yellow, one emerald-ever-green, and one violently-virulent-violet.

Her eyes scanned down.

Each worth seven thousand, nine hundred and ninety-nine dollars.

'Holy,' she had said aloud, '…fucking – shit!'

She looked at the line of figures again.

$7,999.

Each!

She looked down at the coat she was wearing.

There was no way to tell.

She looked down at the total at the bottom of the receipt.

Five – five – nine – nine – three – dot – zero – zero.

She couldn't fathom it.

It didn't compute.

She kind of remembered buying them…

Earthen Hype Boutique, the receipt said.

She looked down again at the coat.

It was a burnt-sunshine, orange-wool frock coat alright.

The material was a beautiful, deep, tiger-fur orange, dark and smooth. The pattern contained a slight echo of that big cat's stripes, with its jagged black-lined patterns, and white stitching along the lapel. All the buttons were black, and, she focused very deliberately to make this out; the pattern also contained what might have been a tip of the hat to bright auburn autumn leaves, weaved into the subtle, tiger-like design. Looking more closely, almost transfixed now, she saw that there were swirling lines of deep tangerine richness through the pattern as well, with deeply stitched ripples of dark auburn, like wood grain, contrasted again with a deeper, vibrant, solar-rays amber.

God.

No wonder she bought seven.

The material was *stunning*.

The cut was difficult to tell; but it was a frock coat.

How could you go wrong?

She could see that the length was past her knees, the mid gathered at her waist; kind of French Revolution, kind of American chic, but…

Her mind flipped again.

Was it *that* beautiful?

Eight grand beautiful?

It certainly didn't particularly suit the warm weather here.

Thys had no idea.

Was it morning or evening in Viniziarra right now?

The sun was behind the mountains, which were behind the hills that were behind the village, but she had no idea which direction the village faced. Either way, there was no way that anyone but the most dedicated Goth would consider it frock coat weather.

She tried to put the receipt back in her purse, but about a dozen more fell out and became caught in a light breeze, fluttering onto the cobbles and flitting about the fountain. Saint Barbara ignored her as she scooped them all up, snatching at them like a child chasing butterflies. As she shoved them all back into the receipt slot of her hitherto immaculately sorted private contents, she saw a few more of them.

They also had lines of numbers on them.

Totalling thousands of dollars.

Again – each!

All of them five digits long!

And, some of the five-digit-figures started… not with a one, but with a two!

Santa Barbara!

All from Earthen Hype.

Boots, shirts, blouses, skirts, dresses, lingerie…

She didn't want to know!

What has she *done?*

She slammed the purse back into the side pocket of her new 'burnt sunshine orange' frock coat and went and collapsed into one of the chairs outside Tutto's.

She'd spent – it must have been – more than a hundred grand!

A hundred grand!

On an entirely new wardrobe!

On clothes!

Fucking clothes!

She'd *promised herself* she'd never do anything *like that!*

Earthen Hype….

She remembered… arguing with Brooke and Jade?

That she didn't like Krimson Azureus.

She preferred GG; Gabby Fenwick.

They'd gone ballistic.

Jade had even stormed off.

And the woman in the shop had been horrified for some reason…

…

Ewwww…

…

This was baaaaaad…

…

This was bad, wasn't it?

…

Thys sat there for a few minutes, stunned at her own super-brat behaviour, even though she essentially could not recall any of it. Finally, Tutto emerged from his store. He saw her immediately and smiled.

'The usual, Miss Isadora?'

'Long black please Tutto,' she croaked. 'No milk.'

She sat there and drank the coffee, and several tall glasses of iced water, without him saying anything. When she had finished the first coffee, he brought her another without her asking. Then he sat with her, and looked at her across the table, with an earnest expression.

'Are you taking care of yourself Miss Isadora?'

Christ, did she look that bad?

She smiled. 'I think it was my birthday. I had been away from home a long time, so before I left there to come back home, I had drinks with... someone I work with there. Then, when I returned home, drinks with my father, then the next night with my grandfather, then with my sister and a friend. This morning I woke and... I had to get out, so I came here.'

'You came here quickly?'

'Very quickly.'

He nodded. 'I'll make you breakfast.'

'No, I –'

'Tut!'

He vanished inside.

The smell of the eggs and bacon from within the store had at first made her feel ill, then hungry, then ravenous. By the time he had brought them out to her she had been ready to devour them like an animal, and had shown actual restraint for the first few bites before hoeing in like the runt of the litter.

'It's good to see you eat!' Tutto laughed.

After that, she drank more water and had a third coffee.

Then some freshly squeezed orange juice.

Tutto retired inside to serve the increasing parade of villagers who were coming in and out of the shop. It had taken her way too long to realise; they had not only come to see her, the mysterious Isadora appearing once more, but also; the girl in her pyjamas and an eight thousand dollar orange and black frock coat, just to have a look, then move on.

Then, as the food digested, her brain started to kick in.

She recalled that the previous four nights had all been happy ones, and for that she was grateful. She had good people. When she finally found the courage to sort through her purse properly, she found a few other receipts from last night; two separate cafes, a bar and a night club, but nothing like the cost of even one item of her new wardrobe.

Looking around with a clearer head and tidier purse, she had decided that it was morning, and sure enough the sun had started to rise over the distant mountains, behind the hills, behind the ancient array of white and brown houses. The black and orange coat was on the chair beside her and she decided that it was indeed a fine garment. The wool felt like mink and the cut was very stylish, with a big collar and cuffs, and ornate buttons, but not so arch as to go out of style any time soon. It was classic, timeless, yet unique. The auburn and sunshine suited her, she knew, as did the length for her lanky but busty – no, she was supposed to say 'curvy but slender' – frame.

As drunken, eccentric clothing purchases went, she could have made a lot worse.

For a start, she could have done it online!

She laughed at the thought.

There, she was laughing.

How bad could it be?

Now her inner monologue sounded like Tutto, she realised.

She checked her phone and saw that it was tomorrow in Sydney; she had wanted to be here in Viniziarra, in the morning, and had jumped forward half a day. She remembered what Mitch had told her about such events; that she should remember that she hadn't aged, so she hadn't lost half a day but gained it.

At this point, she didn't really care.

All she knew was that she needed a shower.

She thought about gapping back to Harding's, or to her father's, or even to Omega Cove, but then again, looking at the coat, she thought; why not just keep going?

She had the money to go wherever she wanted, and nowhere to be, and no-one to be there with. She hadn't felt sad about that; in fact, it had been quite liberating. If she could come to a remote little Italian town for a decent coffee, where could she go for a shower?

Well, a waterfall, obviously.

CHAPTER 52

Obviously!

Yes!

One of those waterfalls on a tropical island, on one of those little islands in Thailand, or wherever. She took out her Eve and typed 'tropical island waterfall' into Google images and it came up with exactly the sort of dreamy vision she had imagined, or that, she realised very quickly, her culture, or even the Anunnaki, which were essentially one and the same, had programmed her to imagine.

Still.

A nice idea, within anyone's matrix of reference.

But she still didn't know what to do about Tutto; she'd really blown it this time.

She had an unpaid tab.

He never asked for money, but what if he'd grown suspicious?

She'd always come spontaneously; always intended to bring Italian currency, but somehow never had. If she offered a credit card, he would know who she was; and if she offered cash, he would know where she'd come from.

But did he know already?

When he spoke to her, she heard an Italian accent. But he was speaking Italian, and her mind was translating it, and also allowing her to speak Italian back without trying. Therefore, it was only her perception that was supplying the accent, because she expected it.

If there were any logic to this situation...

...which quite frankly at this point she couldn't care much less about let alone have any confidence in her ability to divine, but anyway...

...if there was? It would suggest that he also heard an accent. And that accent would be Australian. So, he would have gathered the same...? Or, perhaps he had expected her to be American? And so he heard... New York? Or, generic American? Neutral mid-Atlantic, like on television? Or local Italian?

But hadn't she told him, ages ago, that she was Australian?

Although, hadn't he seemed incredulous?

Still, to fork out Australian notes, as though she really had just been parachuted in, might still rouse suspicion.

Tutto stepped out. She smiled up at him.

'Was that passing parade all for me?'

Tutto smiled back. 'They heard us talking; vibrations of any kind carry all over this place, any frequency. They didn't recognize your voice. It's like a deer in a forest when their ears prick up, even though they haven't seen the hunter; they just know something has changed, something is different.'

Thys nodded to herself.

'So where do you go now?'

Thus shrugged. 'I was just wondering that.'

'You're on holidays?'

'Yes.'

'Alone?'

She hesitated a second. 'Yes...'

'Then go where the wind takes you! Where the tide carries!'

'I think I will. How far does your wireless access go?'

'Everywhere; there is a special tower over that hill.'

'But the sign says...?'

'Tourists. If they stop here they never leave.'

She laughed. 'Then what am I?'

'You are something else, Isadora.'

Now that was charming.

'Tutto my friend, can I buy some soap please? Only; I will have to pay you for everything next time – is that okay?'

Tutto smiled warmly.

'I will keep a tally.'

CHAPTER 53

Thys walked out of the village and down the road, through the olive grove and saw nobody. Then she sat and drank some of the bottled water Tutto had given her while she searched the images again for something suitable. Some of the waterfalls clearly had tourist shacks nearby, others were so tall that to bathe under them would have surely crushed her under their sheer volume of water. There were a couple of forest-looking waterfalls that looked low, and quiet and deserted, but which upon further investigation it turned out were, of course, parts of exclusive resorts. Finally though, she found one with a kind of gentle-looking fall, and a wide spray that looked like something one could bathe beneath without being pummelled and drowned. There was no indication of where it was, however; the photographer had taken several shots for an online stock library, but they had guarded the secret of the waterfall's location so as to, presumably, maintain the exclusivity of their images.

She thought briefly, decided not to think, and to heed Tutto's advice.

So she wandered into the olive grove as far as she could, and then gapped into the picture.

CHAPTER 54

Thys was totally startled when she gapped straight onto a high ledge in bright sunlight, with the gush of a strong wind whipping about her face and ears. She was standing on rocks, surrounded by bright-green foliage, but...

Stable, despite the fact that she was now trembling a bit, a little shocked.

'...woah!'

But she was, perhaps not quite as she had hoped, faced directly with a view that exactly mirrored the photo; she had transported herself to the very spot where the photographer had snapped the picture of the waterfall.

She calmed a bit.

The breeze wasn't strong, she realised, it had just been present, just sudden. The sun was very bright though, and the sky as clear, and as shockingly sky-blue as any sky she could recall.

She stared down again, comparing the tablet image with the actual reality one last time. The photo had been taken with a long and powerful zoom from the outcrop upon which she stood, looking down at roughly forty-five degrees. The giant, mossy arch upon which the water did indeed fall, was, she estimated, fifty meters down and several hundred away.

Behind the waterfall there appeared to be a huge, dark grotto, which had not been so apparent in the long-distance details. From this height, at this distance, it looked to be about maybe two or three metres high and about six or seven meters wide; about the width of the waterfall itself when it cascaded into the deep ledge above the grotto.

The waterfall she'd wanted was there though, real as anything.

It spurt forth from the middle of the rocky tan and chocolate-striped crater wall about twenty meters up, and cascaded down to hit an outcrop, below which it sprayed out to perhaps twice its original radius before the grotto, down into a large, crystal clear, aquamarine pond, unsettling only a small portion of its otherwise glassy surface. The aqua pool itself, not quite big enough to be called a lake, covered almost the whole of the crater floor, other than a section of shallow, and a short shore, beside the grotto entrance, from which extended a long bed of big mossy rocks.

Looking around, it would seem almost impossible to climb down there without mounting some kind of at least moderate-level operation, given that the crater walls were all inwardly concave and pocketed with outgrowths of brightly-leaved but gnarly-shaped tree trunks and branches, wildly growing shrubs of all colours, huge drooping vines that presumably hid quite a lot of whatever else grew out of, or perhaps lived within the crater walls, and layers of sharp escarpments that definitely looked potentially deadly should one fall or swing against them.

Basically, it would be impossible to access the pool without carefully abseiling or being lowered in by helicopter. As it was, the photographer must have climbed down a precarious ledge or two, down from the rim, just to get this shot, from this vantage.

No wonder he wanted to guard the location.

Where the hell was she?

Pacific Ocean? Indian? Atlantic?

Who knew?

Then she remembered; again, it was an echo of what Suzy had told her to find!

A place of her own!

But; had she found it?

Another one?

An ensuite to her secret astral bed?

An after-Americano shower?

A place she could come to, but that she didn't know the location of?

She would see.

She would see!

Thys thought about holding her breath and just gapping over the water, right above the surface of the pool, but then again; not with a brand new eight-thousand-dollar wool coat on. If she took it off, which she was wont to do in the heat of whatever locale she'd gapped into, she might not be able to find it again, gapping or no gapping, because the waterfall and pool seemed to be located on the floor of a crater of some kind, which was perhaps two or three hundred meters wide, that the pictures hadn't shown.

She stared out with what felt like midday sun glaring down on the whole scene under an impossibly electric blue sky, and wondered again, with a renewed urge to get down there, if there was actually any place to safely set foot out of nowhere. But surely the details in the zoom shot had to be real also; just because she couldn't clearly see the small stretch of 'lake shore' from up here, other than as a short pale strip in front of the grotto, it had definitely been present in the photos, right? In them, it had looked perhaps to be composed of sand and pebble. Assuming the photos hadn't been faked or digitally doctored, as many of the other googled waterfall photos obviously had been, she should be okay, she reasoned. She would just gap right there; right into the short stretch of probably-sand that had made the photo, and this angle, look so damn picturesque in the first place. In fact, it was about as picturesque as anything she'd ever seen in this reality.

She wondered.

Was it wise?

Maybe no-one else had ever bothered to try and get down there?

Maybe she would be the first?

But get *where*?

She looked up behind her, but she couldn't see past the rim of the crater, nor any easy way to climb up. She probed with her mind, but got the push-back. It wasn't safe. A drop, she sensed. She listened. She could hear the ocean. Waves crashing. Was this a desert island?

Part of one of those... what were they called?

Island chains.

Archipelagos!

One of them?

Was the waterfall fresh water or sea water?

It had to come from somewhere, but she couldn't see behind it from here, over the opposite rim of the crater.

Sea water was no good for bathing, really.

'Hello!'

Her voice echoed back. A few birds shot out from the crater rim, but otherwise nothing.

What the hell.

She gapped.

CHAPTER 55

The grotto was about twice her height and became pitch black about ten meters in; it clearly went back somewhat further. The beach wasn't so much a beach as a shallow mud bank the colour of sand, mottled with pebbles mostly too big to walk on. But the mud supported her weight and was easy to traverse. Better for her cleanliness, if she intended to bathe, were a series of flat, dry, and amazingly smooth granite rocks to the right of the grotto, away from the waterfall spray, where she could easily remain dry and even sun bake, if she so chose. She removed her coat and lay it carefully on the granite sun bed, then slipped off her sneakers and socks.

Then she looked around.

Technically, theoretically…

…there could have been anyone or anything watching from just about anywhere. She looked up and assessed the walls in a full three-sixty circle from her new vantage. There were shady sections along the inside the crater, even with the noonday sun belting down directly into the centre. The rays on the crystal pool created a shimmering glare that could, if she wasn't careful, become annoying; from certain angles it was like a sharply mirrored glare. With their shadowy recesses, the crater walls could easily have had all number of cave or tunnel exits that led directly back to a resort. She had seen such things on travel shows. Even the darkness of the grotto might have led back to the pool and bar for a hotel complex, or simply to the view from an exclusive resort.

But somehow, here, she thought, and *sansed* – this was not the case. Nobody had set foot down here, perhaps not ever; but at least for a very long time.

Still, she rolled up her track pants and walked back around the mud bank, where she squatted down and splashed the water a bit.

It was warm.

She licked her hand.

It was fresh water.

She'd done it!

First time!

Slowly, she waded in.

She made slow steps, carefully planting her feet, one before the other and repeat.

She was on rock; very solid rock.

Looking down she saw the surface was tan-coloured underneath the aquamarine. It was slightly slimy, but not slippery. She advanced, a few more steps; seven, eight, up to her knees now, about five meters in. Instinct stopped her and she stretched her toe forward. There was nothing. She drew it back and felt the edge of the nothing, where the stone beneath her feet vanished. She stared into the crystal water and could see; yes, there was a drop. A shift in water colour; the tan shade was gone. Carefully she lowered herself and sat on the edge. She was up to her shoulders now, with her feet dangling over the edge.

She almost couldn't stand it.

But nothing touched her feet.

Nothing nibbled at her toes.

No sharks of course; but no snakes either.

No fish…

No teeth bit off her foot, and no tentacle dragged her down.

A bird squawked, way up high, like a parakeet.

She withdrew her legs and stood again with a light splash.

Tutto had given her a commercial soap brand in a package.

It felt wrong, as wrong as it would have been to bring in the kind of perfumed commercial detergent they called shampoo these days.

The least she could do was –

Gap.

Her favourite health store, back in L.A.

The rack of organic soaps; glycerine and essential oils, handmade by the owner.

She grabbed one quickly, a lime green one, and –

Gapped back.

Yes.

She had gapped back, exactly.

Just by remembering what it was like to stand there and hear the hiss of the waterfall to her left, staring into the blackness at the end of the grotto, she had gapped back.

She would never forget that, never.

She would always, always, be able to come back here.

Then she remembered; all she needed was the picture.

She slapped her head.

When would it sink in?

When would it become second nature?

Then she laughed.

'Who cares!'

The echo came back and she laughed at it.

That was why she had come here in the first place, to calm down and stop thinking like that, stop critiquing herself, second guessing herself, berating herself.

She moved toward the waterfall, feeling the edge of its spray on her face.

The end of her hair became wet, and pressed onto her long-sleeved tee to cover her chest, and suddenly her clothes felt very heavy and burdensome.

She looked around.

She was *sure* she was alone.

Still, she couldn't quite *believe* it.

But she could remove the track pants, surely. She still had knickers on, and besides, the wet tee would stretch down to cover them.

And anyway, that was just like a bikini bottom.

But…

What if there was a photographer?

Just; what if, somehow?

She sighed.

Who cares? Right?

She pushed the saturated track pants down to the tan rock under her feet, stepped out of them and lifted the saggy duds out of the water. They were incredibly heavy and wakward as she went to throw them up onto the sun bed with her coat, then was worried about getting that wet, and threw the track pants instead onto the mud. What the hell; she would wash them later anyway.

Then she remembered; and again she kicked herself.

It really, still, was not second nature.

Not here in 3D – none of it was.

She focused a second and raised the track pants telekinetically.

People thought this was to do with somehow applying pressure at a distance through mental will, but she had never found any such thing. It had always seemed to her like a cross between pushing and asking; an essentially passive task. It was just a matter of whether you could do it, or could not.

She submerged the trackies in the water again. Some dirt dispersed from them, then she floated them through the air to land gently on the flat granite, near the coat, but not disturbing or wetting it.

(Or, she cringed, diminishing its value.)

That done, she pushed her hair back. It was so thick, and the waterfall spray had made it thoroughly wet now. She saw that her nipples were sticking out under the tee. She didn't care. Or, maybe she did. She didn't think about it. Instead, she slinked forward, one foot at a time, as she had before in the other direction, with her toes searching each time for the edge of the drop.

There wasn't one.

She was a meter into the spray now, and it was glorious. Colder than the pool temperature but wonderful and exhilarating.

There was no drop here; she could do it.

She could stand under the water and:

Suddenly she was ripping off her tee and tearing down her knickers, throwing them telekinetically over with the track pants, holding her face up to the spray and scrubbing her hair with the homemade soap, scrubbing it across her breasts and under her arms and over her tummy and between her legs and it was glorious; glorious – glorious – *glorious!*

She stepped further in and let the pressured edge of the waterfall-proper douse the soap from her hair, then she scrubbed it some more and doused it again. She held her face up and drank the water from the fall; she could taste the edge of *stone.*

She spread her legs wide and scrubbed the soap there, then up her bottom, then she doused her torso again, feeling a momentary erotic charge, then she stood straight and let it just fall directly upon her, all over for a while.

Then she stepped out, feeling high, and went to find the drop again.

Finding it, about twenty paces into the pool, past the edge of the waterfall, she traced the edge right around with her foot; it seemed to stretch from just before the granite sun bed, and extend right across to the other side of the fall, essentially a curved lip, about half a meter deep, across the edge of the... what the hell; she was going to call it a lake. The rim dipped there, on the other side where it connected with the rocky crater-wall, and she allowed the water level to rise to her chin before stopping. But it seemed to rise again, further out, to where it connected again with the edge of the crater, toward the back. There, a high craggy arc began; a dark and steeply, inwardly-curved wall perhaps five meters high. The pool ran along the edge of the crater there, but further around, under the edge of the big arc, the rock floor of the pool rose sharply. She assumed that was where the underwater escarpment ended, and if she chose to swim over there, she could easily have walked around as she did on this side; it did look awfully slippery and craggy though.

Another time, perhaps.

Out there, before her, on the far bank, the whole edge of perhaps three quarters of the pool was covered in flora; reeds and maybe lilies growing up, vines slinking down and in, trees and shrubs of all varieties, snaking and twisting out of the crater edge. Seeds from all over the world, she assumed, or at least from all over wherever in the world she was, could be dropped down here in the bird poo; she could see several extended, eternal blotches of the guano, smeared down in timeless deltas from various nests above. Clearly, transported seeds easily took root here and thrived, if the variety of flora was anything to go by.

So, there was soil somewhere beneath…?

And under that?

Where did the fresh water come from?

Where did it go?

How deep was the underwater drop?

An abyss?

Could she swim down, and find out?

Maybe – gap here with scuba gear?

That was, assuming she could get someone to teach her how, and raise her ability to some level of proficiency where she'd be happy to come here alone and essentially seek to *pothole dive, alone…*

Or just; hold her breath and see?

She stood on the edge of the escarpment, neck deep in the pool with her hair floating in the water around her, and thought about just dipping down and seeing how deep it was. She was sure she could see under the water; it was so clear; it was just the glare of the sun that prevented it being totally transparent.

Or she could just… hold her breath and… gap?

Underwater gapping?

She felt no push back from the idea, even when she imagined dropping the to the depth of a diving tank.

But she hadn't, that first time.

Instead she had washed the clothes she'd slept in with the soap and, as they dried on the sun bed, she had laid beside them.

Up there, she had thought she'd heard the ocean. Or had it been the echo of the waterfall?

She wondered where she would go next, and what she would have for lunch.

Was she in Thailand?

The Caribbean?

Somewhere in Indonesia?

What was good to eat in those places?

She giggled to herself.

Starting to relax for the first time in…

Who cares?

She was… relaxed.

It would need to be something, anyway (she decided, now that she knew, for the first time that this was going to be the formation of a progressive ritual) that she could eat every time.

Something reliable, like Tutto's coffee.

The sun had beamed down, onto the sun bed.

The stone was so warm and smooth.

She reached over with her eyes closed, and grabbed her knickers, and put them under her head.

There.

That… was nice… and warm… and

CHAPTER 56

'It all used to be like this.'

The voice was old.

'You would call this a sacred site now, but when everything was sacred, nothing was.'

'Really?' Thys asked, dreamily.

The old woman was sitting cross-legged behind her, massaging her temples as she lay on her back, on the rock, in the sun.

Thys was looking down at herself from outside and above, shielding herself from the sun, from being burned where she had fallen asleep. The old woman was so brown it was impossible to tell if she had burned in the sun, or would ever, or ever could. It looked as though she had spent her whole life outdoors. Her face was wide and her smile enormous, her long teeth and curly hair bright white, like pearl. Her brown eyes widened as she grinned up at Thys, as Thys floated in the air, as though they shared a hilarious secret from the other Thys, the flesh Thys who lay on the rock, talking. The old woman's eyes seemed like two suns, dark and amber-brown, with pupils like bottomless pits that led to the centre of the Earth.

'Then nothing was sacred?'

'And everything. The concept was redundant. We lived and came and went, on the land, and through what you call the astral, through the densities...'

She laughed, a kind of comforting cackle.

Thys laughed too.

'...densities. How funny. How funny you new people are.'

'New people?'

'Yes; you think you have been here a long time but you haven't. You think we were here, roaming like savages and eking out an existence from the dirt, before you came. But no; that was after you came. You measure time like you measure the land, and say two-thousand years, and six-thousand years, and forty-thousand years and so on. But that was not what it was. There was time, but it was not dense. You did not wade through it like treacle, like mud. It was not dense.'

Thys sighed.

She was listening, but she was sleepy.

'Do I know you? Were you here before?'

'I am always here. You don't know me, not until now, but you know my five times great granddaughter, and my fifteen times great granddaughter. Or you will. I forget. Treacle time. It bogs everything down.'

'Treacle time…' Thys laughed, dreamily.

'Everything changed when he went mad.'

'Who?'

'The construction boss. Mad as a cut snake.'

'Really?'

'I'll tell you a story.'

'A bedtime story?'

'A dreamtime story.'

'Okay.' She yawned.

'Once upon a dream, there was an Emperor and an Empress. Far away.'

'Far, far away.'

'Don't fall asleep yet. You need to hear this.'

'Okay.'

'Child!'

'Okay…!'

She smiled, warmly. 'Okay then. They ruled all the land, the Emperor and Empress, and sky, and the stars and all there ever was or is or ever will be, but it was all empty. So they decided that they liked to create. To design and build. They decided to build everywhere, so they would have places to be and see and understand, and they sent mighty Kings and Queens, their offspring, out to build things, and to guide and support the things; those entities that had emerged there, with mercy and wisdom. And the Kings and Queens could build whatever they liked, because they were so close to the Emperor and Empress, as to still be part of them but separate, and they knew that what they liked would suit, and be almost the same. And there was just enough variation between them all, and so very many things to be built, that each one would be unique, but still come from the hearts and minds and loins and strengths of the Emperor and the Empress. So wherever they built, the Kings and Queens of the Emperor and Empress had children too, and they were the Princes and Princesses who would be in charge of making everything else, all the detail and variety, and making sure it all went to plan, and that it was all good.'

'Wow.'

'That's right. And everywhere they built, which *was* everywhere, planets formed. And out of the planets, people grew.'

'They grew?'

'Yes. They grew, grew and grew. Wherever you build planets, there are souls. Souls come from the centre, from the energy at the centre of the galaxy, which is in turn powered by the energy at the centre of the galactic cluster, and so on and so forth, right back to the centre of the universe, where the Emperor and Empress still live. Souls are attracted to planets, and that's why, wherever planets grow, souls come through them; and the people grow to house the souls.'

'That sounds nice.'

'It was. For… ever. For so long, it seemed like forever.'

Thys took a guess.

'But, was there one planet, where something bad happened?'

'Bad?'

'Bad. An accident maybe?'

'Maybe?'

'No?'

The woman smiled, and caressed her temples. 'Nobody knows.

You see, the King and Queen of each new planet lived at the top of the world. And one day, nobody knows why, or how, the King of this planet just looked at himself and said 'I am at the top of the world, therefore there is no further to go; I must be The Emperor!' He simply forgot who he was. And then, to make matters worse, he started to think he could behave like the Emperor.'

'No!'

'Oh yes.'

'So what happened?'

'Well his Queen started telling him; no, you're not the Emperor. That is a very bad mistake to make! You are deluded! But the Mad King wouldn't believe her. In fact, it made him so angry, he tried to have her killed. Then he killed anyone else who ever mentioned her again.'

'Really?' Thys was shocked.

'Oh yes. And things were never the same after that. The balance was never restored.'

'What happened to all the people?'

'The Mad King lied to them all. Remember, he didn't really know he was lying, he thought he *was* the Emperor. But because he was filled with doubt, and pain, and was broken, he became meaner, and more brutal. He thought his Queen was evil, and that she, and her memory, had to be wiped out forever. But without The Queen, the people went mad, and their city went crazy, and then, one by one, all the people in all the cities followed suit. It was like a virus. Only, none of them knew it, none of them knew the truth; at least, hardly any. Because the Mad King was so powerful, and still held great sway.'

'Didn't someone try to stop him? What about the Princes and Princesses? His children, who helped build the city?'

'To the worker, the foreman has all the power. If the foreman never tells the workers that there is an architect, or a company, or Heaven Forbid, even a purpose and a design, then, what hope do they have?'

'So did they try?'

'Some of the Princes tried to stop him peacefully. And when they failed, and the Mad King punished them, some of the others tried to depose him, then even assassinate him. But some of them just couldn't do that, couldn't join in; he might have been mad, and cruel, but he was their father. They had to protect him. There was a huge fight, a great battle, but the Mad King stayed in power.'

'How?'

'Chaos has a way of favouring the mad. The rebel Princes and Princesses were trapped at the top of the city. They tried to tell the workers what was happening. But the Mad King was a tyrant now. And because his rebel sons and daughters had gone down to the lower levels of the city, and spread out through the other cities in disguise, to gain power down below, and try to rebel again, he felt that he couldn't trust anyone anymore; he did not know who, down below, would be plotting against him, or whose hearts and minds had been infected by his rebellious offspring. So he became jealous, and paranoid, and eventually, completely insane. He tried to kill them, he tried to wipe them all out. All the people and all the cities. He told himself he had. But he couldn't. The planet kept re-peopling. When he realised that he couldn't wipe them out forever, that made him even more insane. If he was the Emperor, he thought, why couldn't he kill them all for good? So he started making up excuses. Filling everyone's heads with lies. Lies he even believed himself.'

'That is so sad. The poor King. The poor planet.'

'Yes.'

'When did this happen?'

'Many thousands of years ago, in treacle time.'

'And what happened in the end?'

'The Princes and Princesses who remained on the lower levels of the city, and in the other, lesser cities, started making their own kingdoms and queendoms, and fought amongst themselves. They too went insane. There were more battles, over hundreds of years, as all the people in all the cities slowly all went insane as well; insane in so many different ways that sometimes it is – was, hard to count. But the Mad King still held his grudge. Sometimes he would team up with some of the Mad Princes, who had forgotten that he was their father by now, to vanquish the power of the Mad Queens. Time and again, this happened… until almost all the power of the Mad Queens was gone, and only the Masculine Insanity remained. And, yes, prevailed.'

'That's not the end is it?'

'It might have been child. But you see; every city had a heart, which is also the heart of the Empress, and every city had a mind, which is the mind of the Emperor, and all of this, to them, happened… in the space of an afternoon.'

'An afternoon off.'

The old woman laughed. 'Maybe.'

'How can they be in two places at once? Their hearts and minds?'

'Child, you must not make the mistake your scientists make, of thinking that just because things are one way here on this planet, from your perspective, that this is the only way they can be, or are, everywhere else – that is neurotic, and will feed the power of the Mad King.'

'Okay. But – what happened?'

'The Emperor and Empress sent another King. To correct the mistake of the Mad King. But the damage was done.'

'There was no hope?'

'The Mad King vanished. Nobody knows where. And the Second King died, from despair, at what he saw. Then, even that story became corrupted by the Mad Princes, and the truth became hidden all over again. Now all the people live in broken cities, ruled by insane Princes, and the few who have the truth are unsure.'

'Now?'

'Yes child. Now.'

'What was the name of the planet in the story?'

'Some call it Urantia, some Terra, but most would call it Earth.'

'And what will happen to it?'

The old woman laughed.

'The Mad King has left traps behind. He could not understand, if he were the Emperor, how the people he had grown from the Earth could begin to understand what the Mad Princes showed them; how they could start to rise up, and construct, to create as he had. To rival him. So whenever they came close to that, he struck back, and wiped them out. It was as though… maybe that, maybe something along those lines, was the thing that had driven him mad, made him forget in the first place.'

'What traps?'

'Child, there is a technology being created on your world as you lay here in my arms, that the Mad King would have destroyed the Earth for. It is still far from the power of creation of the Emperor and Empress, but it begins the path to creation itself. All the peoples of all the planets reach this point, and many pass it responsibly, but on this planet, when the Mad King vanished, he left his… programs. Still running. Do you understand the analogy child? Have I chosen the right words from the right time?'

'Yes my Queen.'

'Traps, I said, didn't I? It is as though he left his traps running, so he could not be followed to wherever he went. But they will assess the new technology and they will act. And when they act…'

They heard a rumble in the distance.

A heat.

'…it will be the end, this time, I fear, for the Earth. The children of the Mad Princes know this is happening, and they are preparing.'

'I am scared, Empress. I am scared of the Mad King's traps, I am scared of the Mad Princes and their children… and I am scared that when I wake, I will not remember this story.'

'You may not, but, fear not. You will remember its essence, when you need to.'

'Who are these children, Empress? Where are the Mad Princes? Why are you telling me this?'

'Because you must stop them, child. Why else?'

'Why me?'–

'Why anyone?'

'How will I know what to do?'

'Child; the present incarnations of the people of this tragic world talk of the Dreamtime, of the Songlines, as though they were oral history, and myths made up to explain the landscape. It was not like that. Inner, Earth and Astral were one. The Mad King broke that, and the Anunnaki came and exploited the division, but it was not their design, and he did not remain to see their conquest play out. The Second King was killed, or surrendered, although part of him remains. But child; despite what you hear, there is no King, and no Queen ruling this planet; he is long gone, and she is nowhere to be found. Chaos is coming, and what did I say about chaos?'

'It favours the insane.'

'Close enough. But the planet can be made sane again. At least, a start can be made. The division can be healed. The Rainbow Serpent, child. When it wakes, you must be the one.'

'The one to what?'

'You must stop them child, or the Planet of the Mad King will burn.'

'Stop who?'

'All of them, child.'

'All of who?'

'Oh, my poor child… you are not listening. You must stop them – *all*.'

A tear rolled down each of the old woman's cheeks.

'One at a time, if you must. And in the here, in the now, and in the chaos to come, there are so many different ones… so many, so many… *somanymadmenandwomen*.'

CHAPTER 57

She woke with a start, on the rock with her knickers under her head, startled and disorientated. She must have been laying there a while in the midday sun, but she was not burned.

As she considered this, she heard something growl.

There was something in the grotto, down the back, in the dark.

It was moving.

Waking.

Her heart skipped a beat.

How long had it…?

It?

What was it?

She heard something sniff, and snort, then shuffle around, then, quite distinctly, turn around and retreat further back into the grotto.

'Heff?'

She asked softly, trying to make herself believe it was all a joke.

'Is that you?'

Strangely though, she wasn't afraid.

But she didn't want to push her luck.

She quickly put her shoes back on over the clean feet that she had dangled in the water, slipped her knickers up, then gathered the rest of her things in the pockets of the orange coat, threw that on and gapped out.

Just as she did, high above, something bright reflected at the top of the crater's edge; a trick of the light, or the gap, she decided, and didn't think of it again.

At least, not for quite some time.

THE PANDORA INHERITANCE

PART TWO (or so)

TARNI

CHAPTER 58

'The story of Thys Pyne and Tarni Lavé was, in a way, the story of real estate; of how Thys had ended up with an exclusive apartment on an exclusive beach. But it was also the start of another story, a more grand story of land, and landscapes, and towers and monuments, a more lofty and altogether more terrifying story that began with Thys Pyne coming to the start of a realisation of how crafty her father and her older, sometimes much older, friends were.'

Thys heard these words echo in her mind somehow, as though relayed back through the astral, in a waking dream.

That happened in Los Angeles, where the focus was so much on narrative, and plot, and forward momentum; just out of the blue a lot of the time.

Narration, drifting up from the San Andreas fault line; stories that had caused the Miracle Quake, bankrupted the city and almost destroyed the American economy.

Even now, nobody was sure what the long-term damage was; on the country, its psyche, on the world, but there had seemed to be some kind of restoration of spirit, of liberty and pioneering, of industry and can-do, in the reparations.

However it certainly, if the seemingly unkillable Eissley-incarnation of Olivera Studios was any indication, had not made the movies any better.

CHAPTER 59

Thys hadn't seen Tarni Lavé for three years now, but for a short, intense time she had felt closer to Tarni than anyone she had ever known.

For a while after Tarni had found her the apartment, and what had happened there, she had been reluctant to return.

But in the end, she realised that she was always extremely glad to have it.

Thys caught herself; that *had* sounded spoiled, even in her own head. A three hundred square, seventh floor apartment in an extremely private cove, with ocean views, and she was 'glad to have it there'.

She couldn't believe that she had, once upon a time, allowed herself to think that way.

Now it was her Fortress of Solitude.

She hadn't asked for it though, and back then hadn't thought that she would ever really need a place of her own.

The ambush at the Paramatta apartments had been a thing.

So much of her life since then had been framed by the phrase; "since Paramatta".

It was just the way things had gone.

Shock can change your direction; it can define all that follows.

So, this was a time, just after Paramatta, after the first series of the truly grueling astral battles when she and her troops had foolishly tried to lay siege to those particularly evil, black-matte, bile-spewing Anunnaki temples in the Dracopolis, when she had come back to third density totally drained.

She had been back and forth, sometimes seeing her family, sometimes keeping to herself, almost always checking in with Harding at The Fork, building the bridge as Suzie and Xylata had taught her, but she had never really settled.

She had never really been settled in third density, as such, she had realised.

Eventually.

Not since she had been a child in Mosman, if ever.

As a teenager she had been back and forth from Sydney to London, always shifting, her life and friends and opinions and perspectives… and then there had been The Pan, and The Pandora Sequence, and The War.

It had been then, during the first major period of the astral war, every now and then, that she had first begun to return to the Earth plane without letting anyone know, and venturing out on her own, without telling anyone.

It hadn't been mean-spirited.

During that time, Mitch had been terrific with her, as had Heather. They were both good listeners, and when they hadn't been listening they had talked again of how their part of the story had climaxed. She had again spoken of how their victory had demoralized the enemy Anunnaki, and how it had therefore spurred on her own series of campaigns, and a subsequent series of small victories, and then she had told them of the campaigns since. Mitch had reflected proudly as to how her victories in the astral were in turn being reflected back on Earth; and of how, when people joined The Pan, they would often speak of waking from their sleep as though suddenly aware, suddenly free, suddenly unbound.

"Literal awakenings", he'd joked.

Thys had been overjoyed; proud of herself, and energized from the pride she saw that her father had in her.

But she'd kept her stories clean; she had not spoken of the defeats, and she got the feeling her father didn't like hearing about how mean and dirty it could become, when the astral fighting got real. The kinds of nightmare horrors they sent against her, the blissful dreamscapes they tempted her with; the times she had given in, all but to the last minute; and the times when she had questioned her sanity, to the last second; or gotten so deep into levels of active creativity and fantasy that she didn't know any longer what was real, or if she'd ever know, or find home, ever again.

It had also been around that time that several other revelations hit her.

One was that it wasn't really fair of her to stay with her father every time she returned; to visit a while, sure, but not to stay. Not for Mitch to see her every newly processed post-traumatic emotion unfold in slow motion before him, even as she witnessed it also through her reveries.

The second revelation was Harding; that her friendship had really kicked in. They were more than mates now. They were family.

And finally, perhaps even most importantly, given what came after, it was also around this time she came to understand that her father, and by proxy herself, were now people who had people.

CHAPTER 60

That was what happened when you were wealthy, Thys now knew; you employed people to be your people, and then you asked those people when you wanted something done.

The night she had discovered this they had been reminiscing about Mitch and Heather's wedding, how nice it had been to see her sister Jade-Saxe… okay, *Saxe,* if that was what she wanted, despite the fact that she had never returned from London to see them again as she'd promised, and how silly Mitch's ex-wife Janine had been to do a no-show at the last minute.

Still, that was her mother, Thys knew; that was Janine. She was an actress now, on television, like she'd always wanted, and she knew drama; she knew that sometimes not showing up made a more powerful statement than making a scene.

But if her mother could not, or as Thys suspected, would not, any longer choose to divide fantasy from reality, then so be it.

By then, Mitch Pyne and Heather Everett had become the Cleverco celebrity versions of themselves, as properly famous as wealthy business people could be, because while Mitch was good looking, Heather was especially so, and together they were being as altruistic with their fortune as any obscenely wealthy couple ever had been. But they had also attracted fame because a celebrity wedding, of any kind, was always a media circus, and this total media-celebrity package had attracted attention from just about everywhere.

After that, each time Thys had returned from the astral war, her family's celebrity had only increased. In fact, the entire extended family, including her sister and her mother, had become celebrities now too.

And didn't Janine know it.

Didn't *they* know it.

And, the fact that this new and ever-escalating situation had created quite a unique problem for both Mitch and Heather had, in fact, led to Thys owning her own apartment.

Mitch had told it roughly this way.

CHAPTER 61

By using the powers that had been bequeathed to them, Mitch and Heather were capable of instantaneous personal transport, just as Thys was also capable, from one place to another via gaps between the Earth and astral dimensions, between third and fourth density, whenever they liked. It cost them nothing; there was no expenditure of any kind for them to do this. Essentially, they just had to think it, to visualize where they wanted to go, a gap opened, and it happened.

Thus, they had come to call it 'gapping'.

And, as Thys well knew, as well as anyone living, the process expended even less effort than opening a traditional hinged and handled door, and walking through.

It was the astral, and it worked.

The trouble was, and had been for some time now, that as internationally recognized celebrities who had made names for themselves as high-achieving charitable crusaders, Mitch and Heather could not readily appear anywhere without being spotted and identified, and consequently recorded by all forms of social media. As a further consequence, especially after their radically escalated post-wedding celebrity, their days of thoughtless, carefree day-tripping through dimensional gaps were now limited to non-public places.

For this purpose, Mitch had some time ago secretly purchased a series of what he called "gap houses"; the fruition of the idea he had first "floated the idea of floating" to Everett, just before the Kamikaze Anunnaki attack on Cleverco, and which had crystalized after he had begun using Heather's secret stash network to get about the world more quietly.

In short, Mitch had come to the conclusion that it would be

a good idea if he and Heather could arrange to own one "secret home" in each of the world's cities, so that they, and everyone else in their extended family, could gap around secretly, as they pleased, and would always have safe haven when they did.

He had moved to establish this personal travel network early on, and it had been one of his first and most startling wake-up calls as to the extent of the empire he now controlled, and the power he now commanded... (not to mention his own ignorance).

One night Mitch and Heather had been out to dinner when, having been harangued by not only The Leprechauns but the general paparazzi at large, all evening, en masse, and after having a few drinks, they had struck upon the idea of what they now called the GAN, or, The Gap Apartment Network.

'How many cities can there be in the world?' Mitch remembered asking Heather, quite drunkenly as it happened. 'I mean, real cities? A few hundred?'

Upon arriving home he had absently sent a text to find out who it was that handled acquisitions or purchased property for Cleverco, and had asked to see them. Before long, at nearly midnight, a woman had arrived on the doorstep of their large and well-appointed Sydney home, declaring herself to be one Tarni Lavé, and believing herself to be the person Mitch had asked to see.

'Good evening Mister Pyne. I am sorry to bother you but Yelina sent me? If you remember, I looked after her properties when I worked for Bo Everett. I still do, but now I work for Cleverco?'

Still quite drunk, and with a classic, drunken, laissez-faire attitude, Mitch had stated very clearly and confidently that if she were a friend of Yelina's, she was a friend of Mitch and Heather's.

Tarni had felt it necessarily polite to informed Mitch that they had actually met before, several times, as she was reporting directly to him now, and had done so as recently as three months ago.

Mitch had ignored that, asked her in, poured her a drink, and proceeded to tell her exactly what he wanted.

'Hi Tarni!' Heather had called from another room.

Mitch had ignored that too; it was all too confusing, who knew whom and worked for whoever from when and where.

He was just laser-focussed on his current project.

Mitch asked Tarni to purchase a nondescript house in every major city in the world, and in each house to have an active but totally secure workstation. The name of the city the house was in was to be painted in bold lime green letters on the main wall of the main room, and there also had to be a functioning kitchen and a king sized bed. That way, he informed Heather (but not Tarni) all they would have to do would be to think of the name of the city, in bold lime green letters, and they would instantly gap there – into a fully equipped, totally secure apartment.

It was genius.

Total genius!

Tarni Lavé had ignored the apparent insanity of the request, and only asked two discrete questions.

'Mister Pyne, what would be your definition of a major city sir?'

Mitch had shrugged and drunkenly called over his shoulder. 'Heather!'

Heather had been changing a few rooms away, ready for bed. She too had had a fair bit to drink.

'Yeah?'

'How big is a city!?'

'A city!? I don't know – ten-kilometer radius? Twenty?'

'No – people! How many people!?'

'Hundred kay!?'

Mitch had turned back to Tarni.

Her blank expression had given nothing away.

'Sound about right? A hundred thousand?'

'Very well sir. And one more thing; it's possible we may have office space going unused in various cities of that size. Would a conversion, if less expensive, be preferable to a purchase?'

Mitch had shrugged. 'Sure; don't buy anything if we don't have to…'

'Very well sir.'

'And one more thing.'

'Sir?'

'Don't tell anyone. Only you can know. Okay?'

'Yes sir.'

'I mean it; *no-one.*'

'Of course, Mister Pyne.'

This had seemed not to surprise her at all.

'Thanks, Miss Lavé! Let me know!'

CHAPTER 62

Three weeks later, Tarni had returned and reported to Mitch.

Mitch had almost forgotten, and being reminded of that night, slowly, had filled him with an awful, creeping dread.

Pretending not to notice this, Tarni Lavé had proceeded with her report, regardless.

The process had been interesting, Tarni had stated.

'It has quite accidentally, or even serendipitously, drawn attention to the many now-redundant, unoccupied, disused or derelict business properties that, between them, Mister Olivera and Mister Everett have owned, that have now passed ownership to Cleverco.'

'I think... I got wind of that. I think... that started this. The Fork? Mister Harding's place, in Los Angeles...?'

'Indeed.'

She had informed Mitch that, according to his and Heather's recommended definition, there were a great many cities in the world with a population of more than one hundred thousand, and by taking the liberty of raising the definition to one hundred and fifty thousand people, a more widely recognized definition of a city in any case, the number of properties to be included had been brought down to a more reasonable three thousand.

'Jesus Christ!'

'Sir?'

'I thought there would be no more than three *hundred*! Maybe less!'

'Oh, no sir.'

'No?'

'Don't concern yourself sir. By using available properties, I was able to bring the number of purchases down to just over two thousand.'

'So you've bought two thousand properties… and done what I asked with them?'

'Yes sir.'

'And – no-one else knows?'

Tarni smiled reassuringly.

'I used a different name in each location sir, and a different shelf account. A different decorator was hired in each city. None of them could possibly know about each other. I did use some of the other people from the property department to source one or two of the purchases, but in the end they were all directly purchased by me, using unique and secure aliases, filed under faked or non-existent projects, and all the orders as to the specifics were given only by me, to people only I spoke to, using many different disposable "burner phones", that have since been all but vaporized, Mister Pyne.'

'And… what did it cost?'

'The total cost, including the requested décor and amenities, was just below three hundred and seventy million dollars, sir.'

The look on Mitch's face at that point was priceless.

'I took the liberty of setting a maximum property purchase at two hundred thousand and most of the time the property purchases came in well below that.'

Mitch felt ill.

'Three hundred…'

'If I might say so sir, I assumed the matter was urgent. I worked very hard on it. All the properties are bargain properties in good neighborhoods – most have a view. Also, many of the preexisting properties, most of which were the aforementioned business locations, are warehouse loft conversions that are extremely well situated. And with the resources we have at Cleverco, I was able to source many bargains. It's amazing what can be found, with the right people and the right resources. Basic maintenance on the properties will cost roughly half a million per year; with your blessing Mister Pyne, I intend to employ ten people to travel full time to inspect and clean the properties while they are dormant. Even with those added costs, and general maintenance and amenities, I can estimate that the investment will double its value within ten years. I admit sir, I did speculate as the purpose of the endeavor, but whatever it was, I can assure you it was a good fiscal move on your part.'

Mitch considered the situation very carefully.

'Miss Lavé?'

'Call me Tarni, sir. Please.'

'Send an encrypted email to my daughter, and to Mister Harding, and to Trudy Pankhurst, and to Bo Everett… and if you can, get a message to Suzie Saturn.'

'The rock star, sir?'

'Yes. Tell them, and only them, what you've done. And don't worry about the maintenance crew; we'll sort something else. Only you can know.'

'Yes sir.' She had suddenly, for the first time Mitch had seen, seemed very unsure about it all. 'But, sir..?'

'Yes?'

'I don't know how to encrypt a message sir. Not secure on that level sir. Not if it's for the Mister Harding I think it's for. Sir?'

'Tarni?'

'Yes sir?'

'I just decided to create one of those things… one of those… "people around you all the time" things…'

'An entourage sir?'

'No – the other one. The formal one.'

'A personal staff, sir?'

'Yes, Tarni. One of those. You're on it.'

'I am sir?'

'Yes Tarni.'

'I am now a member of your personal staff, sir?'

'As of this moment, Tarni, you and you alone *are* my personal staff.'

Tarni Lavé hadn't known quite what to make of that.

'And triple your salary.'
She smiled.
But what else could he do?
She knew too much.

CHAPTER 63

As Mitch and Heather had told the story at length to Thys, she had thought about how she loved them both dearly, and had found it wryly amusing.

'I quit drinking the next day,' Mitch had shrugged.

'Me too,' Heather had shrugged also.

The two of them had sworn an oath between them to take, from then on, their responsibilities and most particularly their money more seriously. General ignorance, broadly defined drunken requests, and the resulting total shock aside, Mitch and Heather had apparently used the gap houses regularly since then to travel the world on their own secret and presumably sometimes personal business.

They had also learned, through using a glamour, to briefly disguise or obfuscate their appearance; although, they had discovered quickly that even as a short-term disguise, a glamour was a difficult thing to maintain, for people as confident and grounded in their own identities as they were. Frustratingly, their unconscious egos simply prevented the trick from working for any useful length of time past which their concentration had been broken. In short, it turned out that they each required a level of commitment to their performance that they both generally found too much of a reach, and quite exhausting.

Before they'd gotten the hang of using the GAN however, some journalists and, more dangerously, some paparazzi photographers had become suspicious. For example, how could "hot, newly married mega-rich couple" Mitchell Pyne and Heather Everett be in Rome at seven in the morning, then Sydney at half seven, then Tokyo two hours later? It simply wasn't possible, and yet; here were the photos?

'What did you do?' Thys asked earnestly.

Heather explained. 'After some fast talking and liquid lunches and simple financial favors, most of it went away.'

'You bribed them?'

'Bribed and lied. After a while people make up their own realities, find their own reasons, then they lose interest. You'll see. Journalists are mostly rationalists and once they start carving up the facts with Occam's Razor, who knows what they can convince themselves is true? Remember; most people think it's that "the simplest explanation is always right", but what it actually is, is that the line of reasoning with the least assumptions should be favored, or is *often* right. Which is essentially meaningless. But when it's used by a certain kind of serious-minded, neurotic rationalist, it generally gets equated to 'at the end of the day, whatever I think is right is always right'. But I digress; we haven't done a lot of lying and bribing to prevent our powers being discovered, but that time – we absolutely did. Lied our asses off and spent a small fortune to make it go away. We didn't have a choice, we had to. And despite the odd, online conspiracy theory –'

'About, I'd say, half of which...' Mitch made his confession face. '...were pretty much about half accurate...'

' – it pretty much stayed away.'

Thys laughed.

'Since then there have been two paparazzi photographers who have just been totally pig-headed and unswervable. They chase us everywhere we go.'

'We've met a few other people like us...'

'Rich celebrities...' Heather shrugged, fessing up.

'...and they assure us it's perfectly normal to have your own twenty-four seven paparazzi tag-team. It's a badge of honor. It means you've made it.'

Mitch and Heather's paparazzi tag team, it turned out, according to Harding's research, were a brother and sister team named Pearle Horne and Shaun Peeler, two highly visible orange-haired former stunt motorcyclists who had gradually made the transition from touring the nation as lower-billed performers on the carnival circuit, to risk-accepting moped-style celebrity photography, when the latter had started to bring in a lot more cash than the former.

'They're persistent little clowns...' Heather had smirked. 'Purists, too. Won't even think about the new drone-camera thingies, apparently.'

It had taken a few months after Mitch and Heather had first hit the scene for the fire-haired siblings to appear, and persist full time, but eventually they had all formed an unspoken truce and established some unspoken boundaries. Now it seemed almost odd to Mitch and Heather, to leave the apartment without at least one of the two, Sean or Pearle, being there, snapping away, shouting for a smile or cheekily demanding to know if they were in a good mood, or post-coital, or what they expected to do that day.

Regardless, Mitch and Heather now had to be extremely careful when out in public, and were forced to plan their every gapping-move with great attention to foresight, even with the GAN, lest their secrets become exposed.

'Here's at least one thing you can do, when it happens to you,' Heather had told Thys.

'But it won't happen to me.'

Heather had smiled.

Ever so slightly condescendingly.

'Amethyst, one day that war you're fighting will be over, and you will come home for good. We all have the gift of foresight, to various extents, thanks to Pan, and although none of us have practiced enough with it, we can all see that, soon enough, there will be massive changes. A whole change of direction.'

'There's something in the astral,' Thys had muttered. 'Xylata sees it too. Something is blocking the potency, past a certain time; some say months, some say years, but never very many. Something won't let us see past it.'

Heather smiled proudly. 'And I'm sure that sometime in the

next year or two, you will find out what that is, and deal with it, just like you've dealt with everything else that has blocked Cleverco's path.'

'Huh. We'll see. It's getting rougher.'

'Regardless. One day, when that happens, and your work in the astral is done, on that day, you will be the very tall and slender and willowy beauty who is the daughter of one of the richest men in the world, who has a strong inner-confidence, but a coy outer-sexuality, both of which are easily read and utterly adorable, and a little bit adorkable too; who has an impossibly thick and luscious lioness mane of blonde hair that flows like a rainforest waterfall…'

'Lionesses don't have –'

'Hush now, I am telling you how the world will see you through the Media Gaze!'

'Oh.'

'…and; a great many of the women on the planet will want to know your every move like a soap opera, and what you want to wear, and where and what you eat, and where you go, and who with, so that they can compare their own lives and loves and likes against yours.'

'Oh, yes. I have seen this…'

'…and; a great many of their husbands, bosses, brothers and lovers are going to want to either see you on the cover of a magazine in a bikini, or topless on a yacht, or better yet, looking stunningly confident and beautiful on all kinds of red carpets around the world, in figure-hugging or figure-enhancing evening dresses, or beautifully photographed in someone beautiful's beautifully photographed movie, beautifully lit, in or out of a bikini, or in lingerie, or even showing some boob if that makes you feel good, or 'if the role calls for it and the scene is justified within the context of the script', or, 'if the money's right' – which you'll never have to worry about –'

'Heather; *why would I be in movies?*'

'Oh, you've got it, Ames. Just like you mother did.'

'*Did?* Bloody hell, wicked step-Mum! Don't let Janine hear you say that!'

'That was a bit – I didn't mean that. Damn; don't tell her I said that, will you?'

They laughed.

' – and; where was I? Media gaze? Male gaze? Female gaze? Gay gaze? Anyway; I can see, Ames, that you're puzzled, and you don't know it yet, even though you exist for the most part in the world where all this *starts*, but unbeknownst to you, my darling stepdaughter, you are at the age where it doesn't appeal to a serious-minded, beautiful young woman to be noticed, even though, if you play your cards right, it is all going to happen for you anyway, so that when the astral war does end, and you do get back, there with be nothing, absolutely nothing, you can do about the fact that what I just described is what people will want from you.'

Heather couldn't have loved Amy any more than when she had responded with a question.

'Where do people think I am now?'

'They think you're building schools for poor children in Africa somewhere. We actually have people doing that anyway, but obviously, you are not part of it.'

'But can't they see that?'

'No. Nobody's ever tried. It seems, not even the paparazzi want pictures of you doing that.'

Thys had huffed.

And then, she had accidentally picked up something from Heather.

She would never do it deliberately, but it was such a startling thought for Heather that it had come though quickly; strong and clear.

Heather had wondered then, quite secretly but with absolute honesty within her private self, whether or not Amethyst Pyne ever really wanted her war to end.

CHAPTER 64

There was an echo there, too, now she thought about it.

Not of that night; but something Heather had said about it, later, another night.

When they had been planning something even more important.

Even more… daring.

And vital.

'That was the first time I truly saw you…'

Thys heard Heather saying, in the echoes of memory.

In a castle, at a table, with a big fire and a phantom dog, after a long, long day.

'…as a symbol for something.'

CHAPTER 65

Amethyst and Jade Pyne had been the only children of Mitch's marriage to Janine Norway; two daughters, born in quick succession; one tall, blonde and intense, the other short, brunette and frivolous.

Although there remained little love lost between her parents, especially after Janine's sudden decision to divorce had resulted in a downward spiral into near-alcoholism for Mitch, her father had by all accounts found it difficult to hold a grudge.

After all, that dark and grim path had fortunately only amounted to the first steps toward a much deeper and wider terrain; along the road that led toward the ultimate heights of his life's actual goal: finding Heather.

And so, as he had told his daughter Amethyst that night, Mitch had for a time tried to keep the London-based Janine and Jade out of the limelight, to protect them.

That was, until he realised, quite quickly, that neither of them actually desired his protection.

Quite the reverse, as it happened.

With the allowance Mitch now gave them (and every other member of his even distant family) Janine had quickly used the money to support, and inevitably resume her long dormant acting career, much to the apparent chagrin of her academic second husband, the celebrated BBC presenter Jeremy Vector.

Janine had quickly accepting a stunt-casting stint on the long running British soap opera *Coronation Street*, essentially playing herself. A steady stream of television roles had followed, including a respectable fourth place on a recent season of *Strictly Come Dancing*. Still very healthy and attractive in her "early-mid forties", Janine's position as a UK-based Australian media celebrity now seemed assured for many years to come.

His second daughter Jade was another story, and was no longer speaking with her father, despite her continued allowance. Together, however, Janine and Jade, reinvented at some point as Saxe, had proceeded to accentuate the notoriety of the Pyne name throughout the United Kingdom, accentuating the fame levels and celebrity expectations of not only themselves, but Mitch and Heather, and inevitably Thys, 'the boring one', in the process.

'You have previous form, of course…' Heather had tried to explain. '…with the fact that you are a former member of the – how to the media put it, Mitch?'

'Errr; metaphysical activist and paramilitary group.'

'That's right – the metaphysical activist and paramilitary group, The Pan. So, when Amethyst Pyne does finally return from 'Africa' and show her face, the press will most definitely want to know; have you been secretly working for The Pan? Have you come back to work for The Pan again? Are you the secret leader of The Pan?'

'But Trudy's the leader of The Pan.'

Heather had just smiled. 'So, the thing you can do? We always *seem* to go by private plane; the plane has to be seen to travel, so unfortunately we leave a carbon footprint. We can't help that, but with any luck the work we do will mean that won't matter soon. So anyway, you get on the plane, then, during the flight, you can gap it somewhere else on the GAN network, hang there while the plane travels, and you don't have to sit on the plane for hours. Then, before the plane lands, you gap it back on board. Works with any form of conventional private transport, and the paps and the security footage-finders are satisfied. We also have several *sail-powered* yachts navigating the globe at any given time. Remember Captain Mason? He coordinates it all. It helps if we're ever caught out being where we're not supposed to be. Make sense? Okay?'

'Okay.'

CHAPTER 66

The conversation she'd had with Mitch and Heather that night, maybe three years ago now, however strange, might have left her head spinning, but it had also brought Thys' attention to Tarni Lavé, and prompted Thys to call her.

Given that she had decided not to stay the entire length of her breaks from the astral war with them, an apartment now seemed an obvious solution.

Thys had begun sheepishly with Tarni.

'Something with a harbor view...? Would that be... too much?'

'I assume you mean Sydney Harbour?'

'Is that okay?'

Tarni had paused for a few seconds.

'Miss Pyne...'

'Amy.'

'Thankyou. I wasn't sure, given...'

There had been only a very slight awkward pause.

'...Amy; you and your family are celebrities now...'

Thys could tell that Tarni was speaking carefully. She wished she had used a web cam, because it would have been easier to read her intent if she could have seen her face.

'...and, we both know Mister Harding, who works for you father?'

Thys smiled to herself. 'I believe I recall a Mister Harding.'

'I can ask Mister Harding if he can select something for you – a list of secure premises he's happy with that you can select something from. I know there are several... nondescript but well-appointed apartment blocks in decent areas that will match your description, and requirements, that are specifically designed for those with your specific security concerns.'

Thys had thought for all of a second.

'That sounds just the thing.'

'Well. Okay then.'

After a few hours, Tarni Lavé called back.

She had sounded nicer than before, more mellow, and Thys was happy to hear from her.

'Amy, I have been informed by several people close to you that there may be certain… added areas of security that are relevant to you?'

Thys had hummed. 'Okay.'

'Mister Harding seemed very adamant that he attend all of the inspections with you.'

'That's fine, I'd expect that.'

'Fine? Terrific. So; you're aware of an associate of you father's named Yelina?'

Thys was confused; just for a second.

But then she realised; Tarni was being careful.

'Yelina?'

'Yes. I have done some work for her. You might recall hearing her name? She is very interested in property. She's given me a list that she says you should look at first; just you and Mister Harding. Once you've narrowed it down, you call me back. Is that okay with you?'

'Me? Is that okay with you?'

She could tell from Tarni Lavé's voice that she was smiling.

'If Mister Harding and Yelina are in agreement upon how something should be done, I don't think either of us would be wise to argue, would we Amy?'

Amy smiled too, back down the phone.

CHAPTER 67

Late the next afternoon, Thys and Harding had met at one of their favorite nondescript Thai places in a Sydney backstreet, for pre-ordered takeout that came in the kind of tall, cardboard containers that were easy to carry around and eat from.

They were early, or their order was late, and so they sat at a little white table that almost but not quite made Harding look like he was an adult sitting with a child on a play set.

It amused Thys every time and he knew it, but said nothing.

'I approve of three of the five she has sent.'

'Have you been to them yet?'

'No. That part is strange; I wanted to talk to you about that before we go.'

Thys nodded. 'I wondered about this when Yelina's name was mentioned. They're not, like, gaping holes in the ground that lead to a well-appointed but slightly damp cave in the Inner Earth are they?'

'No. But that would not shock me, either. I think, after Paramatta, this Lavé woman, she may have an inkling as to who you really are.'

Thys smiled. 'Who I really are?'

'She has not given me addresses; she has given me pictures.'

Thys narrowed her eyes. 'Pictures?'

'Yes.'

'Only pictures?'

'Yes.'

'So – how are we supposed to get there?'

'Yes.'

They sat in silence a few seconds. Thys's stomach growled.

'Someone knows I can gap.'

'Yes.'

'Yelina knows I can gap.'

'Yes.'

'So – does Tarni know I can gap?'

The attendant called out behind them.

'Order for Harding.'

'Yes!'

Harding paid and Thys pondered, then opened the door for him as they both exited onto the street.

'If it's Yelina, it's not a trap, right?'

'I assume. Tarni Lavé was there; after the hole closed. She worked magic, you said? Cast a spell on the door?'

'She drew symbols and threw some dried herbs around.'

'She saw the portal?'

'There was nothing to see. A shimmering hole in the roof. Vandalism. A trick of the light.'

'She knows we behave as though it is all real; the other Realms, alternate dimensions and such? The astral plane? She works for Yelina; she is related, perhaps?'

'I think so.'

'And if I recall, she was there when Doctor Tzaebi arrived.'

'Yes.'

'So, she saw you gap; out of the car park with Xylata.'

'Yes.'

His Eve went off.

He checked it.

'Everything else checks out okay.'

'Then – show me one of the pictures and let's go have dinner and a view.'

'Yes.'

CHAPTER 68

Thys had led Harding through a gap to each apartment.

They had gone through quickly at first, without eating, just to see.

The first one had been a high rise, somewhere in the middle of the city, with such a complete and stunning view of Sydney Harbour that Thys would not have thought it physically impossible.

And yet; here it was.

She was starting to learn what money could buy.

The second one had been a view from the North Shore, looking west toward the famous Harbour. Again, the views, unobstructed by the expected land masses or angles she had seen herself, when exploring the area, which she knew, or thought she had known well from growing up there, were incredible. A private and very exclusive residence, no doubt, into which photographers had never been allowed. Old money; snobby.

The third had been a smaller apartment block, much further out, away from the Harbour, up in the Northern Beaches.

'Here,' Thys had been immediately taken. 'This is where we eat.'

Harding had called Tarni, who had been expecting their call.

'The northern one. Hedging her bets.'

'There in thirty.'

She had taken thirty-five, but by that time they had treated themselves to a good look around.

CHAPTER 69

Tarni Lavé had stepped out of the elevator, smiling as though she had no idea what to expect. Likewise, she was much younger than Thys had remembered; and she guessed that they were around the same age.

'So!' Tarni had looked at Harding, then Thys, and spread her arms. 'What are we thinking?'

This Tarni seemed completely different somehow.

The tour had begun quickly, and as Thys listened to her voice, which was deep but quite lovely, she thought she had detected the edge of a non-Australian accent that Tarni was either covering very deliberately, had become accustomed to hiding so that it was just under the surface naturally, or that she had been correcting, or just living in Australia, long enough for it to have altered unconsciously.

It was odd, Thys considered, that she couldn't tell, and in fact she got very few clear psychic impressions from Tarni at all. Maybe that's what had bothered her the last time. Or maybe it was because she had been going through one of the longest and most insanely stressful days of her life?

Who knew?

Regardless, it seemed that Tarni Lavé was a person who both presented and organized herself immaculately, with a clipped voice and a no-nonsense approach.

She also possessed an arresting, even starling exotic beauty that had completely slipped by Thys at every other encounter.

'You've probably noticed that all of the outer walls are glass. All the surround-windows are made with the same technology they use to make the transparent surfaces they rely upon to keep people safe in space; current generation. They are coated with an adjustable nano-polymer that, at the high-end, makes it nonreflective, and impossible to see in. It can be adjusted like so…'

She pointed a remote at the glass and a tint appeared.

'You can make it go up and down, like a blind, or dim all the panels, or just one, by percentage. You can adjust transparency from the inside to any degree, also.'

'Cool!'

She smiled, and Thys saw that Tarni's huge, angular eyes had enormous whites and extraordinary dark brown pupils, which brightened to an amazing gold in and around her irises; the same gold-streaked, deep-brown that seemed to flow throughout her thick, curly, but tightly-bunned hair.

'Useful,' Tarni responded.

She also had huge, radiantly white teeth and a broad mouth with full brown lips that made her precise pronunciation a double-treat to behold; not only was her voice evenly feminine and mellifluous, but watching her lips speak those words was akin to some masterful act of command within itself, almost that of a gifted puppeteer.

'Now here's something else you probably didn't notice.'

Whenever she spoke, it made Thys shameful of the lazy Australian drawl she had allowed within her speech, and caught herself offering up, all too often. And, despite her professional tension, Tarni quite often smiled, sometimes to herself, sometimes in response to a remark but, Thys was beginning to notice, never at her own wry remarks.

'We were really caught by the sunset; over the bluff behind us.'

Tarni Lavé was almost totally deadpan.

'That's how they get you.'

She hit another remote. They were standing in front of the elevator now, which opened into a large central vestibule that extended right up to the main windows. Right in front of them, a whole floor-to-ceiling panel, probably three meters across, slid aside.

Thys was stunned; there had been no indication that there had been an opening there – that appeared, at first, to open right out… into nothing! A cool breeze swirled through and for a second Thys thought; *what an insanely dangerous design!* Then she realised; beyond the sliding door was an almost invisible glass balcony.

'As with the adjustable windows, the balcony encircles the entire floor.'

They moved through and stepped out.

'The balcony glass; all dimmable, as well.'

'Bullet proof?' Harding asked.

'I think you know that it is, Mister Harding.'

'Just Harding.' He nodded and smiled. 'Probably withstand a missile from a rocket launcher.'

Thys glanced at him. 'Let's not tempt fate.'

Tarni looked over to them. 'I don't judge, but if you're bringing a drug war to Omega Cove, the asking price just radically escalated.'

When Tarni did smile, she had such highly-apparent cheek bones, centered by a wide, gently tapering nose, and a chin and jaw line that curved with such angular grace, that Thys could almost not stop looking at her, so unique, so startling was her attractiveness.

'No...' Thys smiled. 'No wars will find me here.' She glanced at Harding. 'That's the point, right?'

They walked around the balcony. Tarni was almost as tall as Thys, and at first appeared heroin-chic thin. But then Thys saw that the well-fitted black business suit, and stylish white business shirt, virtually the same as she had worn before, and what Thys would soon learn to be her own Einsteinian outfit, allowed for her high, perky bust and tight, tiny bottom to suggest that beneath the suit was a lean frame that was well-worked upon; fed by a healthy, respectful diet; exercised by a will and method as neat and compact as every other aspect of her apparent persona; and basically, extremely tight.

'Now, you've probably had a good look. Let me give you the lay of the land, and show you the things only I can show you.'

Thys felt suddenly a little but thrilled.

'Okay.'

CHAPTER 70

Tarni hit the dimmer again and the balcony rail darkened from full, transparent glass to a more steely ice-blue. The rail was more than a meter high, with a flat shelf and drop-shield. The wind blew across, through Thys' hair, tossing the long curls back over her right shoulder, caressing her ears and neck.

Suddenly, in place of the cove, she could see the whole of Sydney Harbour, as good an exclusive and unobstructed view as she had ever seen; as good as any of the other choices available on her exclusive real estate shopping list.

She wondered, not for the first time, where they were exactly. And, given this clear example of superior, probably alien tech; how much Tarni knew.

'As I said...' Tarni switched the view back to what Thys assumed was real-time. '...they call this place Omega Cove.'

She pushed the remote again, and the true view returned.

'Not hard to work out; it's a pretty much circular cove, divided by a very narrow outlet. This exclusive, executive apartment block is located at the opposite end of the outlet; looks straight out to sea, if you look down to the beach, past the lawn and garden down there directly below, you can see the central pier, which is lined up, dead centre.'

'It's lovely.'

'The other apartment blocks, on either side of the cove, are also privately owned; but not by us.' She smiled at Thys. 'Not by Cleverco.'

'By who?' Harding demanded.

'Whom by?' Tarni returned. 'The one on the right, the southern tower, belongs to The Sirians, I believe.'

Tarni looked from one to the other.

Harding and Thys exchanged glances, as Tarni looked away again.

'All three are the same size, and basically the same design, from what I can tell. Built by human architects; plain steel and concrete, brick and glass, but commandeered and modded by aliens. I've never been over there, by the way.'

'And the other?'

Tarni nodded. 'Yelina in her present form has been on the planet for some forty years. Until the *Lady Ann*, this one to the left, the northern tower, is as close to a home of her own as she has ever had in this time, within this... do we say dimension?'

'We can.'

Tarni nodded. 'I've only been to Omega Cove once before; we had a family occasion over there for the weekend. It's just like this, but the central security is; different. Yelina says that there's almost never anyone in this or the Sirian blocks; but they are leased from time to time to special clients.'

'Such as?'

'As you can see, each block is seven floors high, American standard counting ground floor as the first floor. The first four floors of the southern Sirian tower are, according to my research, apparently, permanently leased by a shelf company that's owned by one of the major talent management agencies, from back when they had more of an interest in our cultural direction.'

'The eighties.'

'So I believe. It means that, when there is someone else in the cove, you never know who it might be; depending on what production is shooting out here, or which music star is in detox, or what housewife is in scandal mode. It is, as you will soon understand, always somebody who does not want the press, or anybody, to know where they are staying while they are here, or be able to find them.'

They stared at the Sirian block, off to their right, for a few seconds, looking for movement and, although they would never admit it to each other, a possible celebrity spotting.

There were neither of those things of course; it was too dark, and in the darkness it looked utterly abandoned.

Still, the two uninhabited companion towers, unlit, facing outward, and as good a distance down each side of the cove as to almost become invisible at night, did nevertheless suggest a small community... in a strange way.

Harding stared out to the sea.

'Pretty hard for the paparazzi to get out here too, I would imagine? The water's apparently pretty choppy out there on the other side of the inlet.'

Thys sighed. 'Just, remember they not only have increasingly amazing, digital telephoto lenses at their disposal these days, but also that they are attached to drones now. Heather was saying that whatever place we take; remember that.'

Tarni waved the remote at them.

'Remember this. Dimmable. Black-outable. However...'

She paused as she noticed that Thys was smiling, and looking down to the water.

The Moon was out, and near-full.

You could see the shore below; you could hear it from up here, seven floors up, clearly, lapping against the shore, and you could smell the salt water. You could hear light splashes, and wildlife moving around in the trees. There would be possums and bats and koalas. Owls, ravens and magpies. All sorts.

'...there will be no paparazzi.'

Thys frowned. 'How? Surely...?'

She hit the remote. Suddenly, just as with the transmitted view of Sydney, they were faced with an astonishingly realistic depiction of the cove in daylight.

'Recorded today. Three in the afternoon. You can see; the inlet might be narrow but the cove is actually pretty big.'

'And where are we again?'

'The Northern Beaches. Palm Beach, where they film *Home and Away,* is further north. Manly further south. We're at one of the ones in between.'

'Omega Cove?'

'Yes. There's a decent curve of beach on each side; a little down from the pier. The northern stretch is better, but it's difficult to access when the tide is up.'

She manipulated the controls, moving 360.

'All around is basically an amphitheater, big rocky walls, crags all along, gums and shrubs hanging on for dear life, all the way up.'

They could see it; see it all.

'Of course, you would have had a decent view on the way in, but you can't see past the trees in some parts. I know the road is steep and bendy, but… did that bother you at all? You get used to it, I'm sure. Where did you park by the way?'

Harding was prompt. 'Oh, we parked back along the road up there; we wanted to walk down and have a good look. I like to get my bearings; for security.'

Tarni nodded and smiled. 'Well, that must have been a decent hike?'

'Downhill…' Thys shrugged. 'Easy.'

Tarni kept smiling, then shrugged.

'Dimensions?' Harding asked.

Tarni looked at him strangely. 'Dimensions?'

Harding looked her straight in the eye.

'Rock face, distance across?'

Tarni didn't miss a beat. 'I think the drop is about one hundred feet back behind us; it comes down to about fifty behind the northern and southern towers; the access road starts from behind Yelina's, and winds up the side, up to the turn-off, off of…?'

'Pittwater?' Harding suggested. 'Or, was it Barrenjoey?'

'We were admiring the view!' Thys covered.

Tarni stared at them for a second, almost amused.

Then she pointed behind him at the elevator.

'That's technically the front, because you enter from the lobby on that side, as you know, because, that's how you came in.'

She smiled tightly.

'I think the main beach on the Yelina side is about four hundred meters long, the cove itself is about a kilometer wide, and again that deep; there's a lot of bushland back there, on all sides. Lucky, very early on, someone managed to get local council approval to dig out a private road, otherwise there would have been no access, and no apartments.'

She smiled, again tightly.

'There were beach shacks here, for a long time, I'm told, but they were sold and vacated in the early eighties. It was the original, non-Indigenous owners who split the land into thirds, built these and sold them off. The pier has, apparently, been there forever. There's a dirt road behind this block, it splits and leads back to either of the other blocks, then continues on as the road up to the rest of the world. All been the same since anyone can recall.'

Thys nodded. 'But, how have they kept is so secluded? I've been all up and down; all though the coast, there is not a section of coast anywhere in Sydney where the walls of the shoreline like this are not plastered with houses; houses upon houses; architectural feats! But this? Omega Cove? Comparatively untouched!'

Tarni looked at her.

The moonlight was beginning to turn the whole cove a soft white, and it was catching the gold in her irises.

'It might be luck, and money.' Tarni ginned. 'It's about all you ever need, really. But in this case; no. And you can stop lying. I know you – gapped? In here. I arranged the GAN Network for you father, I work for Yelina; she is my great grandmother, and she has trained me in Inner Earth energy manipulation.'

Again, Thys and Harding exchanged looks.

'We weren't sure; sometimes people wig out, and don't remember. Can't remember. Or, don't want to.'

'I remember everything.'

She nodded sharply at Thys.

'Everything.'

CHAPTER 71

'So though here…'

Tarni led them back to the vestibule, in front of the elevator.

'The apartment is a single floor, but if you want, I suppose you could live on every floor. One for every day, I suppose, if you count the lobby. Cook out and sleep on the beach on Sunday.'

'Just one will do, to begin with.' Harding grumbled.

Tarni cast him a glance. 'Spoil sport.'

Thys laughed, despite herself.

'So, if you do come in normally, ever; you enter though the elevator; it's like your front door. The vestibule is central and comes through to here; this space, where we have the open, invisible balcony door. It's left empty, but you could have anything here. A beach-facing couch, a dining table, anything. Okay, off and around to the right; kitchen bench, very well-appointed kitchen, views again as you can see, from the bench either side; and we walk through here to get to the north-western corner; enormous eight-seater couch; home entertainment wall; there's a giant TV that slides out of the wall there and practically divides the room again; balconies on all sides, the pier down there and through there to the bushlands, we can see moonlight hitting the top of the back wall of the cove; all yours if you want to climb it, from this side of the cove of course; and now continuing around; elevated dining in the central section; as I said, the entertainment wall slides out and divides it off, if you like; past the end of the table and through here; a spa in the north-western corner, looking down across the – did I mention the invisible balcony on all sides? – treetops and bushlands and the cliff walls again; talk to the koalas while you relax in luxury; and through here, we're at the front now; looking directly at the cliff-face, down over the carport which I hazard a guess you will never use; through the laundry and there's my car parked under the triple veranda carport, which again, you will never use; the pantry through there leads back to the kitchen, but through here and; here we are back at the elevator, and the vestibule; doorway here to the stairwell; runs down side by side with the elevator to the lobby; across past the elevator again; other doorway through here; storage, looking out down over the front of the house again; lots of lovely cupboard space; basically a corridor through to; south-eastern corner, bedroom; don't be disappointed it's just the spare room but access to the bathroom; still basically looking out over the cove though, with the views; have guests and impress them while they fall asleep; around here and through to bathroom; enormous shower; lovely, white and clean, heated tiles of course, huge mirror, basically the whole wall; and through here; long, long walk in wardrobe, lovely, lovely, lots of clothes space; that separates the bathroom from…'

Thys was impressed. 'Wow.'

'…master bedroom. Best view along with the vestibule; right out over the cove and everything. One sixth of the total floor space; you can have a workspace in here as well if you like. And then, back out there is the empty space AKA the vestibule; and back to the kitchen.'

'Wow.'

'Loos over there, connected the bathroom. See how I took you right around the ring of the house, and ended up here? Impressive, hey? Every room is fully air-conditioned, but you can just turn it all off if you like and open the windows during the hot summer nights and sleep like a baby up here in the cool evening breeze. Or, close it all and blast the fake cool, whatever your pleasure. It's not just the bathroom, all the floors are all heated slate for winter, the kitchen is all stainless steel, lovely looking but a bitch to keep polished, but still; lovely. Change any of the décor you like, if you want to claim it, it's yours.'

Harding chimed in. 'I would like a doorman from my trusted pool stationed somewhere at all times.'

'Of course. You saw the lobby when you came in. After walking down the hill, didn't you Mister Harding?'

'Just Harding.'

'That should be no trouble, then?'

Thys walked to the view again.

Tarni came up behind her.

'I know it feels like I am selling you something you already own, but this is one of just a few places all three people; your father, Harding here, and Yelina, all agree you should be safe in.'

She handed Thys the remote.

'Speak into the top like a handheld mic. Say open bedroom bay-window.'

'Open bedroom bay-window.'

Another invisible door opened, clicking almost soundlessly out of place and gliding across, leading out onto the balcony again.

'There's one in every room.'

Thys stepped out.

The moonlit view really was tremendous.

From this corner you could see clearly that, from the curved, rocky face at the back of the cove, the decline was low to begin with, then dropped more steeply behind the opposing apartments before coming right down to meet with the edge of the beach. With all the surrounding gums, and the two beaches either side, the aspect was tremendously pleasing.

Further out, on each side, the rocky walls continued from the end of the beaches, past outcrops of jagged rocks, and out into the larger bay. There they formed the inlet as twin, low, pincer-like escarpments, each with rocky edges, topped by impenetrable-looking, tightly-shrubbed and thickly-treed bushland; the classic east-coast edging. The cove entrance itself was indeed tight, and presumably hard to spot from open water.

'Very secluded.'

Tarni nodded. 'That's the appeal, of course. I'll tell you now; if you don't like the sun waking you up, black out the windows now.

It's like a golden spotlight from God. You won't sleep through it; nobody can.'

Thys wasn't so sure about that.

However...

'Perhaps that's the appeal as well...?' Thys hummed. 'You're locked into the natural order.'

Tarni nodded. 'Nice thought. And, as you no doubt saw, you will get the patterns of the sunsets, right across the sky from behind us. And as you know, Sydney-coast sunsets are spectacular.'

Thys nodded and walked further down the balcony to the corner.

'Just... again? Where are we exactly?'

She turned around, but realised that Tarni hadn't followed her.

Harding seemed to be quizzing Tarni about the height of the cliffs again.

Probably just giving her a moment to herself.

It didn't matter.

She looked down at the water, over the top of a giant eucalyptus ghost gum, within which, to her utter delight, she could see a koala, fast asleep, almost right in front of her. They were somewhere secret, and secluded, toward Avalon, perhaps somewhere past Dee Why... she supposed. But... within some small part of that exclusive, wealthy-weekender area that somebody smart had held onto forever, then somebody obscenely wealthy, probably someone like Rio DeVora or Oliver Hines, had managed to convince their heirs to part with.

And now, it was hers, if she wanted it.

She looked out at the view again.

Yes... once your eyes adjusted, she told herself, once you made sense of what it was you were seeing, the cove was actually quite wide.

Wider than she'd first thought.

She could see a trail of street lights now, snaking away there along a chunk of jutting coast, left and right in different patterns; trails of white lights just past each pincer-like edge of the inlet, and then, gazing even further out, and somehow to the sides simultaneously, even further inland; maybe not so far away, the lights of private homes, the ones she would actually expect to be here; packed in and clinging close to the shore, along the cliffs and rises; and the views it, they, offered; then back; more densely packed… roads and roads and glass; windows everywhere; light coming on as the darkness…

Closer in now; coming back toward the cove; a road, as though a beaded string of white fairy lights; the extension of the main local road that ran along the top of the cove?

Then the pattern widened again; even more, as though she could… around the edges of the inlet; *see* behind her as well.

A suggested hidden suburbia, distant yet all around her; and all around, the expanse of moonlit treetops…

And back, pull back, returning to her cove again; glistening now; looking occultish, the colors of the moonlight blending with the gossamer reflections off the water; like something she would see at the edges of an astral border.

Then she realised; it basically was.

What she was seeing now, around the pier lights on the water, further out but allowed in, somehow, by the moonlight on the foliage, was a glittering web of a neon metropolis, and suburbia, and street-patterns, which were curving in, across the outside of the walls of rock before the ocean.

It was impossible.

But; she was open to it.

The remains of the light of the sunset, the golden and pink light, captured somehow. The telescopic, almost kaleidoscopic effect of the light, and her vision, being focused upon the tight lens of the Omega inlet; she was probably at least one third directly accessing the astral, the so-called other dimensions, melding over into visions of fourth density, with an edge of the light-powered geometry of the Sirian-dominated sixth density spreading out like a web from the city, radiating its power as a major human hub.

For a moment her mind, her powers, had allowed her to bend the light, to see the whole surrounds of not just the cove, but the entire eastern coast; and the city, down in Port Jackson, from which it all spread.

Jesus.

This was it.

This place, it had been made for her.

'Yes…'

Harding sighed, suddenly right behind her, looking out, then looking back at his ward, so in tune with her that he had nailed the very moment when she had made her decision.

'I thought you'd choose this one.'

CHAPTER 72

She still felt strange about the money; guilty somehow.

'So if I take it, how much will this cost the company?'

Tarni was beside Harding, and she shrugged. 'Don't ask me. But if I had to guess, I'd say that, seeing as this particular building is already owned by Cleverco, it would technically cost you nothing. But we will have to turn down other clients who want to stay here; if you want to make this your actual home, and be free of people. However, if you start your own company, and rent out the other floors – not that you would want to, just saying; apparently that is good all round for tax deductions.'

Harding spoke softly. 'I suspect, Miss Lavé, that somewhere within the internal cogs of Cleverco, that wheel is already starting to turn?'

'You did not,' Tarni growled, equally as soft, 'hear that from me. But you must hear this; I must call you out. I need to know the reality of who you are and...'

'That's okay...' Thys agreed. 'Allow me. We didn't drive here or walk here. We haven't set foot in the elevator. I can gap, at will. We gapped here. Nobody knows this place exists because it has been sealed off by the Sirians. Since the eighties? Although these feel like they were built in the seventies, and renovated. They do that. They've seen the monstrous greed exhibited on the other beaches; they wanted this one kept. They kept it for themselves, or for agents of theirs who need recovering. There was an Inner Earth portal here, as there... are? Or were? In all the other coves, right back along, right into Port Jackson and back; all the way, everywhere along. But this one remains untouched, and protected by Yelina. You can't stop progress, or greed, or money, or appalling taste, or aspirant, affluent, arrogance; but you can seal off one niche, and keep them away, by surrounding it in a Sirian web, and never letting anyone else know it's here.'

Tarni was smiling, tightly, wry.

'So, given all that, you'll take it?'

'I will.'

'Good.' Trano smiled, comfortably. 'That's good.'

Harding was relieved as he turned to Tarni.

'I'll take the floor below.'

CHAPTER 73

This time around, Thys had almost immediately liked Tarni Lavé, and had hoped to spend more time with her after she and Harding had effectively taken the building. Despite this, and while she was sure, or at least she felt quite strongly, that they had gotten along well during the arrangements, for a time after that they had met only in a professional capacity, such as matters to do with the apartment's security; random things Thys would never have considered, like making sure Harding had access to all the security passwords, installing a landline connection at his insistence, and making sure the apartment had both a dummy safe, and a real one.

'It has been sealed by Sirian security technicians. People will drive past the main road and not see the road that comes down here. Nobody remembers it any more; it was sealed in nineteen eighty-one. You cannot access the road by car unless you have a Sirian key. But you can never be too sure. A dummy safe is always pertinent for important people.'

Given her personal code of psychic conduct, Thys had never tried to read Tarni to see what might be in the way of their potential friendship. She did not get the sense that their past encounters, or their past behaviours, or attitudes towards each other would count against her. Nor had Thys empathically tried to feel what might have been wrong, even though she sensed, quite normally, that there was more to know; and that both of them would like Thys to know what it was.

A month later, after the security arrangements had all been finalized to Harding's satisfaction; after the official Cleverco paperwork and government tax work had been signed (although for what specific tax department, Thys could not imagine) and the keys had been handed over; after Tarni had dropped around once more to inspect the final touches on the newly decorated living room and refitted kitchen; after Thys had shaken her hand, and she had departed having dispatched her final professional obligation to her, to Harding, and to her father and to Cleverco (which was the recoding, using a light device that recorded one's holographic image, of the Sirian crystal key) Thys had been pleasantly surprised when Tarni had called her again.

Might she be up for opening a bottle of wine, to commemorate the fact that it was, in fact, all done? And, of course, that the exact, correct shade of slate-brown couch leather had finally been narrowed down, selected, purchased, custom-made and installed?

Thys had quickly found that pleasant surprise had turned to curiosity. Although she would have welcomed such an advance, there had been no previous sign that something like this would happen, and it was clearly beyond the bounds of professional courtesy.

Curiosity had quickly turned to excitement.

CHAPTER 74

Tarni drove out from the city one evening on a hot and humid summer night, after work. She turned up at the apartment exactly on time, the Sirian key's manifest still encoded to her body print, with a bottle of red wine and a bottle of white, and a still-hot but quickly cooling pizza from a place about five minutes down the coast that she had remembered Thys liked.

When she arrived, Thys was surprised to see that she hadn't dressed in her usual business costume of black pantsuit and white shirt. Instead, given the increasingly oppressive heat, she wore a long, loose, ankle-length dress that swept down her height from a central halter strap, exposing her lean shoulders, toned forearms, and the tight, smooth skin of her upper back, while also displaying her pronounced shoulder blades above a tight bow that gathered the flowing garment loosely about her ribs, but obscured the rest of her slim physique almost entirely in a red, yellow, white and black, spiral Indigenous Australian pattern.

The day had been warm and Thys had been sitting on the bed, online almost all afternoon, trying to catch up with the world, with the balcony windows open and a high, light breeze coming through the apartment. Although she'd been nervous about sharing an informal evening with Tarni for the first time, she was so unaccustomed to socializing that by the time she realised that she should probably dress for company, she'd only had time for a quick shower and to discover that the Cleverco box Heather had sent here had effectively been hidden somewhere in one of the efficiently concealed built-ins during the move-in.

But now, moments later as she answered the door, with Tarni punctual as ever, she was dressed in the same outfit she'd been in all day; white cotton pajamas that could only just slide by as a legitimate summer outfit, with no bra.

Tarni gaped. 'Oh my God you look beautiful!'

Thys gasped and told her the same thing, simultaneous enough so that it did not sound girlish or insincere. In fact, neither had lied and both had been startled at how much they hadn't lied.

They had immediately taken position at the kitchen bench, with both sets of windows open, and the evening breezes coming in over a magnificent sunset. They ate the pizza hungrily out of the box, each with a giant glass of red wine. They talked about the apartment, then the area, then the local flora and fauna, about which Tarni seemed to be particularly well informed. Then, Tarni asked Thys a few questions about Africa, which clearly caught her off guard, and she quickly dropped the subject.

'So is Yelina really...?' Thys asked in response, just as quickly, the first thing that came to mind.

'My great-grandmother?' Tarni shrugged. 'Sort of.'

'Oh.'

This was an odd conjunction, Thys knew, with both of them knowing they were lying to each other for the first time, and neither of them wanting to.

'Look...' Tarni shrugged her bare shoulders again, awkward but somehow simultaneously loose, and spread her hands helplessly, casually waving half a piece of pizza. 'You've clearly never been to Africa. Right? Is it okay if I say that?'

Thys gulped and nearly choked on her pizza.

Before she could respond, Tarni continued.

'I know Mirabelle Contrelle. She used to work with Heather; I know they were both spies for Bo Everett. I know that when Heather was active she worked corporate espionage in the field, and Mirabelle ran the covert side of EverSky One. I think she still does. Has Heather trained you to replace her? Is that why you come and go and no-one knows where or how? You can use gapping to spy, right? I won't say anything, it's just that – it's not difficult to notice these things, being your Dad's personal assistant. I mean – we're kind of friends now. Aren't we?'

Thys stared at her and nodded once, sharply.

It was all she could manage.

'I haven't cleared it with your Dad, but I can be professional. That's what all those apartments were for, right? Gapping in, and spying? I – regardless, I just want *you* to know that Mirabelle knows, and I know, but no-one else knows because – we won't talk. I don't know her that well, but Heather trusts her. She's basically Heather's right hand now. We believe in Cleverco. Yelina is like family to Mitch and Heather, and Yelina *actually is* family to me. She sent me to him, when your father needed property management. Is this okay? You look worried.'

'No,' Thys had almost choked again. 'Go on…'

She took a quick swig of wine.

She hadn't been sure what they would talk about, whether or not they would truly get along; but she had not been expecting this.

'If you're a spy, for Cleverco, I want to help.'

'I'm –' Thys wasn't sure. 'I – no, that's not what I am. Is it okay if I don't tell you what I am?'

'Sure.' Tarni smiled. She was disappointed, but not offended. 'Look, I understand. I really do. I mean…' She twirled the stem of her wine glass. '…all that business in Paramatta; that woman who was shot, who looked like… well, you remember. Although; I'm not sure, exactly… how well I remember it? Exactly? In all the emotion and excitement. You know? I know I said I remember everything. But it might just be – my version, maybe?'

'We can… compare, if you like?'

'I mean; you know how it is. With parents. Family. I was trying to do well by Yelina; she taught me spells and told me what to expect. Lock the door, cast the spell, let nothing out. I didn't know as much back then. But; that was my forst portal.'

Tarni was containing herself, but even so, she was as excited as Thys had ever seen her, even at the slightest hint that, as she well suspected, Thys was not all that she seemed.

'And by the way, you're not the only one. I mean – I'm… I'm

not just your father's PA either.'

'You're not?'

'I mean, there's others, besides me, on his personal staff. But Mitch knows who I am. He knows I'm related to Yelina. You might say – when there's work that needs doing; when what Yelina wants, and what Mitch wants; when those things overlap, that's what I do.'

Thys was surprised, but not shocked. 'Like; eco-stuff? Like; the symbol and the spell you made on the door that day?'

'Yeah. I mean…' Tarni made air quotes. '…"property management". You know?'

Thys wasn't quite sure she did.

'Like…' Tarni looked her right in the eyes. 'Cleverco is trying to buy back properties that bio-engineering companies and people like DeVora have purchased, or leveraged, from farmers, to try and prevent them from monopolizing the multinational food markets with genetically modified crops. Do you know about all that?'

'Some,' Thys frowned.

She did of course.

'A lot of these companies, DeVora most of all, have an occult element embedded in them. You know about that?'

Thys was silent.

'I'll talk to your Dad tomorrow. Maybe that's all I can say. I'm sure he'll be okay, but – when there's something that needs doing in that regard, I'm one of the people he, and Yelina, send in to get it done.'

'Oh…' Thys said.

She really didn't know what to make of that.

CHAPTER 75

Things were subsequently a little tense.

'I've freaked you out, haven't I?' Tarni had broken off some small-talk, mid-round, and blurted that out.

'No! I just – I'm away so much – I'm not used to – no, really!'

But once they realised that they'd been in London at the same time, years ago now, without knowing it of course, things changed again, and they forgot all about their previous uneasiness. They chatted comfortably again for a while, until Thys yawned involuntarily.

'I'm keeping you up!' Tarni spoke earnestly.

'I'm sorry! No; I've been online all day. Where I've been, I get a kind of news, but I need to try and keep up with what's happening here; so I can compare it to what it looks like… over there. Before I have to go back.'

'No, no, I get it. Sure. Let's hook up later in the week? When do you have to go back?'

'Umm, okay; I'm not real keen on going out in public just yet though. Do you mind coming back here? My shout this time? I never know when they'll need me back again, but it won't be for at least another week.'

'Great! I'll bring the wine again,' Tarni smiled.

Thys walked her to the elevator, and they kissed politely on the cheek.

'We're exactly the same height,' Tarni smiled.

Thys lightly touched Tarni's upper arm with the tips of her fingers, gently pressing the strong, tight muscle there. She surprised herself; she wasn't, generally, an informally tactile person.

'Different builds,' Thys smiled back.

Tarni kept smiling and stepped back as the elevator doors closed.

'I've never gone out with someone the same height as me.'

She smiled, very widely, her hands behind her back, her thick lips and white teeth as devilishly attractive as Thys had ever seen them, as the elevator doors closed between them; good night.

CHAPTER 76

Thys had barely slept that night, her stomach in knots.

Had she been joking?

What had she meant?

Why would she say something like that?

She had slept though, at some point.

When she had awoken, she remembered a dream of the apartment gardens, such as they were.

In the dream, the apartments had remained unchanged from everyday reality. In the past few weeks, Thys had familiarized herself as best she could with her new home, while she could, and now, in the dream, she was doing it again.

She walked into the ground floor of her apartments, as she'd come to think of the building, into the wide, dissecting central corridor. Upon entering from the carport through wide, sliding glass doors, one was faced with a central elevator pillar with huge, mirrored doors. There was also a security desk to her left, and a fire-door, which opened into the emergency stairwell, to her right.

The glass doors closed behind her with a polite hum.

As they did, she saw in the reflection that, behind her dream body, there were people outside. They were standing there; they had not followed her in but they had walked behind her and watched her enter.

Is it her?

Had she heard someone ask that?

She turned back to the glass but they weren't there any more.

Just the dark, empty carport, and the dirt road leading away.

She looked back to the elevator, and the mirrored doors.

They were still there, behind her in the reflection, only they had retreated to the shadows.

She could still see their silhouettes.

Still watching.

Earthlings, conscious, but not human.

She moved on, taking no notice of the thin, bearded man in the suit, at the desk.

'Show's begun. You're about to make your entrance.'

Past the elevator, there were two surfer cabins on the right, with bunk beds and mattresses and bare bones amenities. To the left, maintenance, electronics, and caretaker rooms, then another set of doors, also sliding glass, leading outside.

According to Tarni, the whole floor had been 'flood proofed' several years ago, after a huge coastal storm had drenched the entire level, burned out everything, and taken three weeks to repair.

'Once every twenty years, something blasts through...' Tarni had told her. '...but the tech in this place; if it fell over, the whole building would probably float on its side.'

Each of the three Omega Cove apartments were set back from the beach about fifty metres, erected upon a deep bedrock rise that ringed almost the entire cove.

She could feel it, under her feet; a huge curved ledge of ancient rock, ringed right around.

Because the dirt access road ran along the back of the cove and into the carport of each building, it was the rear of each apartment that faced the beaches, and out to the ocean; three rectangular blocks of almost purely reflective glass; practically camouflaged.

She could feel them, too.

A warm hearth on the north curve, a cool channel on the southern. Her; facing east, walking outside.

Out the back there was a modest patio, then a large, square patch of cooch lawn that had once been surrounded by an obligatory English rose-hedge, the somewhat imperious intent of which had been long ago eclipsed by the wild native shrubs and bushes that surrounded it. The effect now, decades later, was as though someone had spread a quaint picnic rug in the middle of a savage jungle, and the picnic rug had gone native; the bright red roses had become wild, and huge now, tall and expansive with flowers the size of breakfast bowls, reaching within and intertwining through the yakkas and banksias and beyond.

She felt something in her heart, felt as though she had fallen a few inches as the ground had given out slightly. Then she saw that there was a man, dressed in a Sunday-best suit, with a straw boater and a big moustache, and he *was actually laying down a picnic rug on a lawn*, a lawn he had carved from the undergrowth and sewn himself, twenty feet by twenty feet; a woman passed by, also dressed in Sunday best, holding a picnic basket which she lay down on the rug.

She saw, sansed, that he had come to survey.

He knew of this place because that was his job; he had come out here, erected a surveyor's hut... it was standing behind her. Small, two sections, bedroom and office, all made of wood. He was that kind of man; he could cut down trees and build this on his own home as part of his job, then return to the city and be a gentleman.

He was probably the reason she knew that her beach was six hundred metres long.

They were married. The wise woman at the end of George Street had told her that if she wanted a child, she should go to the open air, go to the ocean, and try to concieve there – in the open air. He had thought of his old hut, still up there, and brought her here, all the way up. Brought everything he could think of to make her comfortable on the big cart.

He was thirty-five and she was twenty-three. He had a serious face that had a certain appeal, but he planned ahead in his mind and often did not speak for long periods. She was pretty but had a tendency to imagine the worst. His penis had larger-then-average girth; she was concerned it would hurt. Her breasts were large; he worried that she would be ashamed. They needed to speak to each other about things

There was a rough path to the beach that extended directly from the middle of Thys' back door, directly to the start of the pier at the dead-centre of the cove. The path extended from the far edge of the lawn through a gap in the wild roses and descended comfortably but steeply for about twenty metres with coastal bushes and shrubs and grass bordering either side; effectively a tall, natural hedge of wild foliage which grew around the massive, smooth, wind-twisted rocks that were all through the bushland that surrounded the block.

The path ended at the edge of the bedrock, meeting with the end of the pier about three metres before the one-metre-drop down into the sand on either side.

She did not know what had happened to the surveyor and his wife.

The ancient wooden pier had been well-crafted.

Perhaps they had worked it out, perhaps he had built this, too?

The dark-brown planks had greyed, but were still thick and solid. The fourteen pillars, which looked to have been taken from the trunks of surrounding gums, stood like rock. Thys estimated that they were about three metres apart, with flat rails extended between each, most of them still quite even and level, so the pier was about twenty metres long, bedrock to jumping-off point.

She could hear the water lapping against them, even in the dream.

The cove looked enormous from here, the curved walls high and distant, the three glass blocks twinkling but insignificant.

The Milk Way was astonishing; so full, so bright.

The earth shook.

Thys looked behind her.

It kept shaking and she could hardly keep her balance.

At the top of the pier, at the end of the path, there were four people;

a white man and a white woman, and an Indigenous man and an Indigenous woman.

They were facing a crystal woman, and a tree woman.

And, a star man, and a sea man, standing further back.

Thys knew... some of them, somehow, in some way.

There were two teenagers.

They both had brown skin, lighter than the Indigenous couple.

There was a lot of embracing, a lot of crying between everyone. One of the teens went with the star man and the crystal woman, the other teen went with the tree woman and the sea man.

There were many forms of consciousness, from in and around the cove mostly, standing along the beach, watching.

There had been some effort to provide some rock steps on either side of the pier, and there were the remains of some salt-decayed railway sleepers there, but the two short paths to the two short jumps to either side of the walkway were essentially desire-lines that had been created over decades by people who lacked the patience for either of the 'proper paths' down to the sand.

In the dream however, Thys found herself on one of the second paths, the 'proper paths', down to the sand, following the original designer's intent.

The proper path went off to the right, starting from the end of the short back-patio and heading off through the surrounding bush, under the shadow on the cliff, parallel to the beach, through a wide crop of sharp yackas, bitou bush, tangled undergrowth, rocky ground, and long-ago fallen trunks, before it curved sharply back toward the sand and came out about twenty metres past the first few pillars of the pier.

Thys could see from here that there was another, similar path, even further along and around, leading up to the Sirianapartments. And yes; there was another, on the other side, that led to Yelina's building.

Nobody ever used these meandering paths anymore, including Thys.

They were there, they were real, but...
Nobody used them.

She walked along the path and heard a repetitive slapping sound, like one person clapping very hard for someone. But it was sex; a young man with a blonde beard really going for it from behind, while the young woman, with her legs spread very wide, leaned into a tree branch, hanging from both hands with her boobs bouncing in circles.

He was looking down, through the trees, over her shoulder, at a bunch of surfers in wetsuits, way out in the cove, waiting for a wave to come.

The guy out there was the fucking the leader of the tribe, the tribe they had all started up here, in the weird little cove, where nobody knew, nobody had found, nobody had fucked up yet; and by fucking the girl he was cheating on his boy, who was out there on the water with the leader. He didn't give a fuck anymore; they were always out there together. He loved his boy, but he had told this girl that he loved her too. You couldn't help who wanted to fuck who; not out here, not in this day and age; that had been the point. But the leader – he wanted to tell everyone. First pick and then divide up the sloppy seconds. Well, now he was fucking the leader's main girl; fucking her while he watched him out there, watched them, so buddy-buddy. Telling his cult – that's what it was now, a cult – who could fuck who, while he fucked everyone! Well he was going to fuck her and fuck off. Leave a message by fucking her, leave straight away, leave the cove, leave the tribe; it was all for shit, anyway. Free love was fine if you were the alpha dog; but he was a lone wolf and he needed to run. And the leader really was turning their whole scene, that had started so well, with magic in the water at night, and asking the local spirits for permisssion to start a tribe here; all that for shit, for a fucking cult, just like those fucking Manson freaks from last year...

Thys moved on from the angry man. Traditionally, she didn't like sunbaking on beaches; her skin was too pale for prolonged exposure to Australian sunlight, and she didn't like the way the sand got everywhere. She would not have made a good hippie, or surfie. But she liked walking along beaches, and the sound of the wind and the waves, the clarity and density of the stars at night, and the general, allover beauty of them.

Omega Cove was brilliant for that, for just zenning-out, because there was never anyone there. Not while she'd been there anyway. And, even at high-tide, the water never came up so far that she couldn't take an easy stroll along 'her beach'; being, she considered, the sand about fifty meters to either side of the pier and back.

Sometimes she would go further.

Take a walk past the Sirianapartments, or Yelina's place.

You could tell, somehow, where the territory overlapped. You knew when you had crossed over, and were now walking on Sirian crystals, or the coast of the Inner Earth.

But at night, you could not walk further than the far side of each of the other blocks. On the Sirian side, the main beach ended a little further down from the apartment, where the ocean's constant pounding had created a massive outcrop of coastal boulders, above which the cove arose to greet the outer-ocean with a jagged cliff wall. In the day, you could walk a short way across there, and there were tidal pools. But there was no getting all the way around at any time of day, to where the curve of the omega symbol came tightly back around, and pointed back out to the greater Pacific.

The beach on Yelina's side of the cove was the same.

Just down from her apartments, a high and jagged outcrop of dark rock rose dramatically out of the bedrock, deep-brown and patterned in stark, linear, strata-like shards. Thys suspected that there was a tidal pool in there, too, but there was no way in. The outcrop had been eroded by the ocean at an angle too high, been sheared by the sand and wind too sharply. Even in low tide, Thys had to walk around it to access the beach on the other side. But at night, you would not dream of even trying to swim around it.

Something growled.
The pool was deep and molten.
Many voices; far away.
In pain, crying for release.
Others, eager...

There was another path through, if you knew it.

Although it was complicated enough to be treacherous, even in twilight, there was a second path that divided from the first. This diversion from the other 'proper path', from the left side of ther lawn, was hidden by a group of rocks that you swerved to avoid about a quarter of the way along, and so, like magical misdirection, your eyes never fell upon the secret that was passing right before you.

Once she had found it, she had gone up to the bedroom to try and see it better. She quickly understood why the secret path to Yelina's night-beach seemed hidden; the path passed immediately under the huge lemon-scented, white-barked eucalyptus gum that stood outside, and reached up to just below the main bedroom.

The beautiful tree was fully six floors high, with branches that spread as wide as the breadth of the building, and one third down to shore. The branches were populated by a colony of possums, who also occasionally ran through the ceiling, and was also regularly traversed by one of several koalas on their trundling evening food marathons. Sometimes one would sleep there.

The long, secret path would be hidden by the tree from anyone looking out, on any floor other than this one. But here, on the highest, seventh floor, she could see over the tree and beyond. She could see how the secret path ran parallel with the driveway for a while (hidden again by a row of stringy gums and many metres of dense bush) then veered up, toward the ocean, but passed over a rocky ridge that lined with even more thin stringy barks. Here, the path circumvented the huge, circular stack of jutting crags.

But Thys could still not see in.

Not even in the dream flying.

Not even then.

From there, the secret path curved back down, the gradient a little less concerning, until it exited onto the second stretch of Yelina's beach through a hedge-like wall of high grass and tight bush, as though it had been designed that way.

Once Thys had discovered it, the new path had become an easy and picturesque stroll during the day, a mildly perilous venture when the moon was out, but a potentially dangerous rocky walk on a moonless night, to be addressed with all due caution.

But it was worth the walk, when she felt like it; when a stroll and a think on the end of the pier felt somehow too exposed, even here. The beach was a glorious stretch which curved inward, almost right down to the start of the inlet. From there you could see, up close, the larger, more concave, more ocean and storm-pummelled cove wall, even access the bedrock if the tide was low and the weather good. She had found signs of fishermen having beeen there, perhaps recently, amid the potholes and rocky tide-pools.

Perhaps there was a gap beneath the Sirian fence?

Perhaps some of the locals knew well enough to keep quiet?

Perhaps.

The young man was running, but stumbling. He had left his message, but he had not left in time. The tribe leader had found out and run after him. They had run and run; now the young man had fallen at the top of the rocky ridge and busted open his knee. He had taken a terribly wrong turn, in a place, at a time, when that was all it took to be judged. They had all been judged; they just didn't know it. The (cult) leader (...for now, in the end, that is what he had becoome...) chased him into the water, but held back. The girl who had been the weapon ran straight past the tribe leader to the man with the bleeding knee who was calf-deep in the water, and the sharks took them both very suddenly. The tribe leader found his greater spirit again, at the last, tried to save the girl, but stomped directly into the start of a feeding

In the dream, she had also taken the long path to the beach on
the Sirian side. All along the path, and in deep the bushland all
around and through the cove, were dreaming spirits. They were
everywhere; in the big gums and the stringy gums, in the sharp
yakkas, in the grass and in the fallen trunks; and when she got to
the pier again she saw them there, too. They were jumping in and
out of the water from the end of the pier like children, and there
were things, coming up from the deep, arcing on the surface and
diving again, creating beautiful patterns in the water itself.

At the end of the pier she saw that there were spirits along
the shore and even on the roof of the apartment block. They
were all different, and while some were deeply connected to the
Inner Earth, others were humanoid, more dense, and might have
been called sprites, or nymphs, or even elven. Some seemed to be
echoing the Indigenous Aboriginal People in form; others not.

Thys played and sang and swam with them in the astral that
night, not as a frontier astral warrior, but as a normal psychic,
dreaming in a place that was legitimately magical, and they had
wanted her to be there.

They had wanted Tarni to come back, too.

All the while, other beings, more conscious and alert, watched
passively. Thys was aware that if she made a wrong move somehow,
they would deal with her. Somehow. But she hadn't; had known
she wouldn't.

She had woken tired, and restless, but conversely with the rare
pleasure of having had a normal dream, something she was rarely

afforded these days, what with her thoroughly lucid, genuinely physical, unique astral existence.

She had texted Tarni immediately, without thinking, to ask when she was free for dinner again.

Tarni had responded politely, positively, but with no textual excitement.

Thys had not known what to think.

She had decided to take a morning stroll on the beach and contemplate her new friendship, and why she had suddenly become so anxious for Tarni to like her, to think she was cool, and okay, and worth her time; why her feelings were so acute.

She had walked out and taken the left-hand path down to the secret beach, and had arrived there just as she had realised…

She had not known that the path had existed.

She had never walked under the lemon-scented gum, over the rocky ridge, around the back of the jutting crown, and down the easy slope to the secret shore.

She had learned about it… in the dream.

In the dream, it had seemed as though she had always known.

And now; she had always known.

Except…

Huh.

Thys had smiled, and been ever-so pleased about that.

She had even sunbaked, for just a few minutes.

CHAPTER 77

That afternoon, as Thys was reading about the further expansion of "Hell on Earth" that was being enabled in the Middle East over oil exploitation, and the extortion of Health care in the United States and elsewhere by, essentially, demonic entities, her father had called.

She was relieved to stop her research.

The world needed so much help.

'Hey Dad.'

'Amy, what did you say to Tarni Lavé? Have you two been swapping notes?'

'What?'

Thys was startled beyond coherent speech.

'She – I didn't –'

He hadn't sounded this angry with her since she'd been a kid.

'She is my personal assistant, Amethyst. Do you know what that means?'

'I'm sorry, Dad, I didn't think it would be –'

'Didn't think it would be a problem?'

'I just didn't –'

'Didn't think? No, neither did I. That's why I told her that you've been out there on your own all week. I think you two should know each other; she's Yelina's contact with Cleverco. I thought you'd get along. If you won't go out and meet boys, at least you should have a girlfriend who isn't a reptilian alien.'

Thys sighed.

'You can be a *real bastard* sometimes Mitchell Pyne.'

Mitch laughed, in the way fathers do when they've teased their daughters into a tizzy, until she had hung up on him.

Heather rang back about ten minutes afterwards.

'I know!' Heather stated immediately. 'You know what he's like! He still thinks it's funny!'

'Well, it's not. I like her.'

'Well, to his credit, your father thought you would.'

Thys grumbled. 'What about you? Do you like her?'

'Do I?'

Heather clearly thought it was an odd question.

And Thys knew that it was.

She wished she hadn't asked it.

What did it matter?

'Sorry Heather, it doesn't – '

'She's a handful. But; you're more alike, I think, than… different. Is there… something you want to tell me?'

Thys wasn't sure what she meant.

This was the weirdest vibe she'd had with Heather for…

Years!

'Tell you? No. I mean, I like her. There's… energy here. Yelina stays here, I think. There's Earth Energy. Second density stuff. Inner Earth.'

'Are you okay?'

'Well, yes. It feels like home. But…'

'So you're… *really* okay?'

She seemed to be insinuating something.

'I… I think the apartment likes her, you know? Because of all that. And because, you know, I was there once. I think Dad was at least partially right; I need a friend who isn't… who's human, I guess, but who gets what's going on.'

She immediately felt like she'd betrayed Xylata, and Vlynk and Tzaebi, and Gexvi and Lyveq… but then she remembered.

They had all told her, at one time or another, exactly the same thing.

There was a pause.

She could tell Heather was smiling.

CHAPTER 78

Tarni had returned the next night, with all their correspondence achieved simply, via text.

Thys had ordered delivery from an Indian restaurant in a small "holiday hamlet" further up the coast that was only open a few nights a week, and overpriced, but only just; just enough for wealthy people to think it made it special.

She had been receiving the order in the lobby, and was handing over the naan bread and rice and butter chicken she had ordered for Zeke the doorman (who would never buy it for himself, even though Harding paid him very well) when Tarni had pulled up in her sleek, dark blue car.

They had ended up eating in the lobby with Zeke, and talking about movies, and, once they started being honest, how awful the movies from Olivera Studios had been, and couldn't Thys have had a word to her father, or someone at least, to do something about it?

Thys had said she would put it on her list, the list of things that now, even all this time after the Cleverco merge, she still wanted and even needed to change about what had been the Olivera half of her father's relatively new company, and they had left the subject at that.

Zeke told them about his divorce, and his two daughters, and his gay nephew who had been disowned by his father and had come to his uncle for support, and how he had taken a while to get used to the idea. And, how his new girlfriend, who he was going to ask to marry him on the weekend, had made him see that it was okay, and was helping him to try and get through to his homophobic brother, who was worried more than anything that his son would never have a son of his own.

'For every Zeke, there's a Zeke's brother,' Tarni uttered, after dinner, as the elevator door closed.

Thys sighed. 'I don't think any of the work you do, or I do, is going to change that. People are people.'

'Do you really think that?'

'I know that. Where I've been… there are layers and aspects to people, you wouldn't dream of it, seriously; layers deep, generations and reincarnations deep. Who we are, here and now; we forget all that.'

The elevator pinged, and opened into the vestibule of Thys' apartment.

Thys gulped; Christ, what had she just said?

Without thinking!

It sounded bat-shit crazy!

She stepped out, but Tarni remained inside a few seconds.

I guess this is where Tarni gets off, Thys sighed to herself.

Then, she was very glad she had not said *that* out loud, as she turned to see that Tarni was just standing there, again, with her hands behind her back...

As though, Thys thought, she were trying to echo… when she'd said what she'd said.

Last time.

Thys managed to speak.

'I'm sorry I didn't walk you out to the lobby the other night; I only thought of it afterwards. I… well, you know I don't have visitors. And I've certainly never lived anywhere with my own private elevator, and little vestibule lobby, like this before. I only just realised I'm supposed to close it off. I remember you telling me that, but… I like it, just there, all open.'

Tarni nodded, and smiled tightly. The weather was still hot, and she was wearing another long, cool dress, the same basic design, from the same line, Thys supposed, that was black with brown and ochre and red waves on it, like Dreamtime snakes; another beautiful Indigenous art design.

'So, we have your father's approval?'

'I guess,' Thys laughed. 'He was a bit of bastard about it though.'

'Do you think he knows?'

Tarni stepped out of the elevator.

As she did, the doors closed behind her.

CHAPTER 79

'Knows what?' Thys asked.

She heard a tension in her voice.

She hadn't been aware that she was holding it.

Tarni looked at her, curiously.

Sagely, almost.

Thys shrugged and laughed shortly. She had a bottle in each hand that Tarni had once again bought; red and white again. Tarni had also brought a four pack of locally brewed beer.

She found herself hoping that Tarni found her look pleasing; she'd remembered to wear underwear this time, and for some reason had put on her best. It was still hot and she hadn't closed the windows in three days, even keeping them open overnight as she'd slept on the giant bed. Harding would have been furious, but he was in Canada, doing a favor for Heather, so what he didn't know...

She had assured him that she would be okay, that she would not stay here alone.

She'd lied, and he'd known it.

At least, she'd thought she'd been lying.

And she'd thought he'd known it.

Her pale yellow dress was low cut, with shoulder straps over the white bra straps, and knee-length; still, almost a negligee, her father would have told her, and complained about the habit of the current generation of wearing pajamas and negligees as everyday attire. But it was perfectly acceptable in this heat, and she noticed that Tarni had kicked off her sandals as she'd walked in, so they were both now in bare feet.

'Is that beer still cold?' Thys asked.

Tarni followed her through to the kitchen. She opened the

fridge and placed the beers inside, then took two out and handed one to Thys. They were still chilled enough for a hot night, so they cracked them and clicked bottle necks, sharing smiles.

'So, do you have a boyfriend?' Tarni asked. 'We didn't talk boys last time. You seem kind of a loner, if you don't mind me saying.'

Thys made a face; she twisted her mouth and crinkled her nose.

Tarni laughed.

'I am seeing a guy…' Thys began carefully. '…who is very, very good at what he does, when I need him to be.'

Tarni smiled. 'I see. I've known men like that. Had their numbers.'

Thys laughed. 'Oh, I think we've all got their numbers; at least, past a certain age. But… I am also seeing a guy, for a very different reason, and for a very different outcome. They're both…'

Thys sighed, and frowned.

'I suppose; one's a buddy, and, one's… an arrangement?'

Tarni frowned. 'Oh-kay…'

'And I am refusing the advances of a third guy, who most women in my position, with my… ambition… would see me as crazy for not leaping into bed with straight away, only – I like him, and letting him sleep with me would be the absolute worst thing I could do to him. But I think it's going to drive him crazy either way.'

'And which way is it looking?'

'He needs to finish something he's working on first. I'll let you know.'

Tarni swigged her beer. 'Uh-huh.'

'I've…' Thys started.

Tarni stared at her with her huge brown and gold-centered irises; they were on fire.

She kept talking.

'…been out with – men – as tall as me. Taller, usually. I kind of like that. But it's not a deal killer.'

Tarni kept staring.

'But I've never been out with a woman, as tall as me.'

'Is that a deal killer?'

Thys gulped. 'I don't really know what the deal is… there.'

'There?'

'In that… department.'

'And what department is that?'

Tarni smiled, again somewhat wicked, but now thoroughly suggestive.

'What department is it we're on, up here? On the seventh floor?'

CHAPTER 80

It was frustrating, Thys thought, thinking back on that time, how people came and went, how relationships sometimes suffered, or ended, or were put on hiatus or hold or on long distance or went at kangaroo hops, at the expense of higher responsibilities.

But Tarni hadn't been that.

Tarni had been…

Thys felt her stomach knot.

That hadn't happened regularly in a while, but it was happening again.

Harding lifted himself from the couch and went to the mini-bar.

Thys stood as well. 'You think you need a drink to face the haunted house?'

'Need – no,' Harding smiled warmly. 'But I think you'd be okay with one. Just this once.'

Too right, Thys gulped.

The Hines House had become something of a Hollywood attraction now; left derelict for years at Yelina's request.

Legend had it that the house had turned on its owner, and attacked various celebrities at one of his notorious charity galas. Most of those present seemed to corroborate the story that someone had spiked the punch with psychotropic hallucinogens.

Thys walked to the bar as Harding slid her drink across. He knew what she liked; they had shared many discussions at Harding's Hollywood Bar, and even though she hardly ever did drink any more… there had been times.

'And not just to face the house.'

Thys smirked. He didn't know what he knew; the business with Tarni had happened just before he'd formally moved into the sixth floor.

But she knew that he knew… something.

'Most of my friendships…' Thys spoke quietly, almost to herself. '…my relationships with people my own age, are lost to the winds…' She felt suddenly, genuinely, wistful. '…to eight years' worth of war, and to the alienating effect of…'

'Wistful doesn't suit you, girl.' Harding smiled and raised an eyebrow. 'The alienating effect of secret superpowers, maybe?'

'Thank you, Alfred.'

Harding chuckled, threw back a shot, then poured another. Thys swirled her drink and took a sip.

'It's like,' she mused, 'I don't really have anything to compare my life to in this density, other than pop culture, because I haven't *had* a life in this density…'

'Pop culture's not so bad.'

'It's about as reliable an educated guess. Brooke and Linh and Emily today… I had nothing. Nothing, Harding.'

'Maybe. Maybe so, maybe not. Reconnecting, sometimes, takes time…'

'I thought me and Tarni were going to be… best friends. Maybe more.'

'I did too.'

'I moved into that apartment… how many years ago? And we haven't spoken since.'

'Since…?'

'Yes, Harding. Since.'

Harding hummed. '…I do not know what happened between you. I did not pry. You elected not to tell me when whatever happened, happened, and you dealt with it alone. From that moment on, I have essentially never left your side. But I never asked; was it anything to do with her – business? Should I have been watching out for her all this time? I don't know if you are aware; she still works for your father occasionally, but she hasn't been on his full-time personal staff since – maybe three months after whatever happened between you. I would not ask, but it seems that she has reemerged, in tune with the Hines House arcing up…'

She *hadn't*?

Then – where had she *been*?

'…no, there's nothing there. She's with us. I know that. With us, with Cleverco, via Yelina.'

Harding nodded, satisfied, and picked up the previous thread.

'Your pop culture cues. People write those things, those songs and shows. Those films about life and romance. They base them on their own lives.'

'You learn this from playing poker with people who haven't sold a screenplay since the eighties.'

'I learn it from people who sold screenplays in the eighties because they knew what people wanted from their fantasies. What truths they were ready to face about their culture, and what lies they were prepared to invent. The stories of any cultural age exaggerate, but unless they are fully fascist, usually only by degrees. And there are a great, great many of them; a great number of teachable moments, illustrated. A lot of life lessons demonstrated. And since the internet, since culture has fractured so radically, there are more than enough teachable moments and life lessons for everyone, from all walks of life. Otherwise people, their audiences, would not respond as they do. Otherwise all the niches would collapse and evaporate.'

'You really have spent too long in Hollywood, Harding.'

Harding laughed. 'It's true I play poker with some writers. They like my stories. There is one who won an Oscar in the seventies. There is another who won an Emmy last year. There is one who helps my ideas find their way into Jason Statham movies.'

She laughed. 'Harding, I do like a man who can make me laugh.'

He smiled at her.

'Amethyst, I am at a time of life…' Harding shrugged, almost awkward. '…you are too young for me to find attractive in that way.'

'What?!'

'I just don't feel it. Say what you like.'

'But – you know I would *never* –'

'Oh yes you would. I am very good at that game. I have charm. But I am not interested. I am your Grand-Pop, am I not? Your cool grandfather? We are family.'

'Yes!'

Harding smiled weirdly at her, deliberately, she knew.

'What?' Thys demanded, matter-of-factly. 'You don't think I'm attractive?'

'You have filled out nicely. Let's talk about something else. I am starting to feel nauseous.'

'Thank – you!'

The inflection was totally *fuck – you*!

Thys stood tensely now, with her hands on her hips.

'Are you okay to gap?'

Harding sighed. 'I didn't mean –'

'Yes or no?'

Harding put his drink on the bar, reached under and pulled out two pistols, both pre-clipped into a double shoulder holster. Then, a compact military utility belt. He removed his leather jacket, adorned himself with the guns, then replaced his jacket faster than she had ever seen even a fashion model change dresses between catwalks.

'What?' Harding shrugged, clipping on the belt with a whip-like snap.

'Nothing. I remember there's a driveway fountain out front. Is that okay to gap to – Tex?'

CHAPTER 81

Thys gapped them straight to the fountain at the top of the long, forty-five-degree incline that centered the patio outside the mansion. Even in the dark they could tell that the place was a total wreck, an overgrown ruin, and that it was totally, utterly, "Haunted As Hell".

There were several warning signs, placed both by the local government and by Harding himself, ordering people not to enter.

'Are you okay?' Harding asked.

'I'll let you know.'

'I mean…' Harding spoke quietly. 'Did you feel that? The gap – you have piggy-backed me through many times. That time felt different. As though…'

Thys frowned. 'Yes. Like I had to – push?'

'Hmmm.'

'Forget it. I'm just in a mood.' She looked around. 'Have you been back here since?'

There was no moon out, but the starlight seemed to allow them enough vision once their eyes adjusted.

'Yes. I come back regularly to check on the water feature.'

She knew what he meant; the four Orion Renegade Agents, and the wannabe film producer, Don Eissley, who had been trapped in a crystal prison, in the downstairs bathroom, after a failed attempt to kill them all. Eissley had claimed at the time to have been agreeably possessed by a powerful Anunnaki warlord, Vgyrl, who had since gone missing from the astral plane.

Presumably, he was still trapped in there, within Eissley, as well.

'All this time…' Harding grunted, rummaging in his backpack,

'...they have not moved one inch. Like a pre-climate change glacier.'

'Good. They can fucking stay there, for as long as a fucking Ice Age, for all I fucking care.'

Harding chuckled. 'There are two things right now I have always wanted to ask you, my cool granddaughter, that I believe I might.'

Thys sighed, frustrated and a little frightened.

She did not like being here. Eissley had shot her in that bathroom. For real; shot her with a bullet from a gun in order to end her life.

And she had nearly died.

She tried to take her mind off it.

It had been just minutes after that, after Trudy had healed her, that her father had offered her...

She gulped.

Being quiet, here, was the wrong choice; Harding's stupid questions were better than the eerie silence.

'Okay. What?'

'Why have you and your father let Don Eissley's slate of terrible movies go on for this long? I know they make money. But they are – very, very bad movies.'

Thys went to answer. Zeke the doorman had asked her the same thing, ages ago, as had... many others, now she thought about it, across the years.

And yet...

The answer was at the front of her brain, on the tip of her tongue. It was an answer she couldn't tell very many people, but she could tell Harding.

It was, in fact, way overdue to tell Harding.

'I...' Thys felt her mind lock down. '...I can't remember!'

'Truly girl?'

'Harding, I... since I got back this time, there's quite a lot I can't remember.'

'It's always like that, isn't it? You always say that. That your memory vanishes like a dream, and takes a day or two to return. An astral adjustment period, no?'

'But this time...' Thys sounded genuinely concerned. 'It's different. It's really like – I'm blocked. Like the memories...'

Harding handed her a small flashlight. She switched it on. It was shockingly powerful, like holding a light saber.

'Jesus!'

'Military search and rescue,' Harding nodded.

Thys just kept talking. 'It's like the way I fleshed out after the Pandora Sequence. I don't remember that happening, either.'

'Don't worry so much. It will come back to you.'

'Heather says she knows why it's happening. And she'll tell me – or fix it – when she gets back. I wish they would hurry up and get back. What time is it here? The sun must nearly be up? It must be evening by now in Australia?'

Harding ignored her concern, and changed the subject back.

'How do you know the growth spurt wasn't just natural? You were barely nineteen. That happens. I have seen it many times.'

Thys sighed. 'I went up a size all over, Harding, maybe more, even my shoes – six to seven. I actually got a few inches or so taller, too. I was five eight. I'm six and one half now! And my eyes have turned a sort of *teal*; they were standard blue before.'

'I noticed.'

'You did?'

He didn't reply.

'Hardly anybody said anything. The internet and my shitty frenemies think I took industrial doses of Regene.'

She ran the beam over the front of the house. The Tuscan arch and patio, which led to the covered landing and the front door, were now matted in long, draping strands of dense, dark ivy.

'And I never used to enjoy ice cream. Used to be; I could take it or leave it. Now I crave it. But I hate fish.'

'And you want me to take this crazy potion too?'

'I never asked.'

Harding hummed doubtfully.

'Your father asked.'

He shone his beam straight through the front door; the insides seemed to swallow the light, like a rod down a drainpipe, revealing just a square hole where the huge double doors once had been.

'I know. He told me.'

'And Everett,' Harding aired. 'He almost fired me for not taking it.'

'No he didn't.'

'He was very cross. He let me come and work full-time for your father. Ten years I worked exclusively for that man.'

Thys couldn't tell if he was joking or not.

They heard a car begin the ascent from the bottom of the drive, then saw the headlights break the decline at the end of the drive at forty-five degrees.

The knot in her gut got tighter.

She tried to ignore it, but her body was flooding with anxiety.

'Why can't Bo just tell people he's alive?' Thys grumbled, a bit louder as the car approached. 'It's ridiculous.'

'The way your friends reacted… I'm not sure he can anymore.'

'My friends! I was going to offer them Pandora!'

'Those three? *They* are the people you trust most in the world?'

'They *were*. Now it's you.'

Harding nodded. 'As you should.'

'I don't mean professionally, Harding, I mean –'

'I know girl.'

'Good.'

Harding grumbled again. 'I still won't take it.'

'I know, Harding. Jesus! I just got through telling you I know! But – I can't seem to trust anyone else. Not that far. Not somebody *new*.'

'Miss Lavé is not new.'

Thys ground her teeth. 'What was the other thing you wanted to ask?'

'Well,' Harding smiled broadly. 'I had no idea you were so

keen on Miss Lavé. Does this mean we can talk women? I mean, do you like your women to have breasts that are big and bouncy? Or low and pendulous? Or just the small, fit ones, like Miss Lavé?'

She bent down and scooped up a handful of gravel, and threw it at him, immediately wishing she hadn't as it clattered and echoed all around the rotten crumbling courtyard.

'You're a bloody pig Harding!'

The car pulled up, over the driveway rim and into the circle, drowning out Harding's evil chuckles.

Tarni politely switched off the headlights as she turned, to avoid hitting them full in the face, parked with little ceremony, and immediately opened the door. Harding lit her path across the forecourt to them with his flashlight, then she switched on one of her own.

'Thank you, Mister Harding.' She nodded, then turned to Thys. 'Very good to see you again, Amy. Although; it's Thys now?'

'Yes. That's what some people call me.'

'I like it.' She smiled politely at her, then looked up at the crumbling mansion and spoke almost absently. 'It's a pity we can never sell this place. It's always going to be a damn nuisance. Four o'clock on a Tuesday morning.'

Tuesday evening in Sydney, Thys thought. On Tuesday afternoon, her woefully ill-equipped best friends had called her a bitch. She had once thought Tarni was going to be her best friend, she had told Harding. More. Now she was acting like a company consultant. Still; she wondered what Tarni had meant, that they could never sell it. Of course, by now Tarni must have known what had really happened here. Given the rumors, and what had happened between them…

Of course she did.

But Christ, had it really been that long?

Four years?

She didn't look any different, but she was acting like nothing had…

But what had happened, had proved beyond a shadow that

Tarni was totally aware of the reality of…

'Did you get the message from Contrelle?'

'What message?' Thys snapped, unintentionally. 'I'm sorry,' she sighed, quickly pulling herself together. 'It's this place. I spoke to Mirabelle just twenty minutes ago – ?'

Tarni's expression gave nothing away.

It accentuated her beauty, but in a way that was cold.

Runway cold.

'She's sent a voice message to all your father's personal staff. She expects that the digital network will collapse within the next few hours. Satellites, towers, everything.'

'What!?' Thys exclaimed.

'That will not be good,' Harding growled his understatement -of-the-century dryly. 'Does she know who's done this?'

'No idea, apparently. She rang me personally to say that it means they've lost contact with Mitch and Heather. They were at some press junket in the outback somewhere, maybe with some other Cleverco people.'

'I know,' Thys frowned.

'My main concern is that their return journey may in some way involve Sat Nav and GPS – almost everything does these days. Airports are closing as we speak. Flights are being canceled, planes grounded. But Contrelle says that the United Nations don't expect food riots, at least not on a large scale, until the whole power grid goes down. And that isn't going to happen. Not yet, anyway.'

'She said that?' Thys gasped. 'Not *yet*?'

'No,' Tarni aired. 'That's just me. Sorry.'

'You can see her point thought,' Harding spoke darkly.

Tarni swung her torch wide, around the overgrown garden that encircled, and in many places encroached upon, and even within, the wrecked building.

'We could put up a fence…' Tarni observed wryly, walking up to the fountain, her other hand in her pocket. It was a warm night in Los Angeles, and although she wore her trademark white shirt and black business suit, she had left her jacket in the car.

Thys eyed her up and down; she might have been mistaken in the moonlight, beside the old fountain, for some kind of chic Creole Vampira.

'…but the fucking occult-*tits* would just tear it down.' She angled her voice toward Thys, wry again, keeping her gaze on the mansion. 'Or it would just become some kind of symbol for them, something they could use. Keep their magic contained. You know how ritual magic works; second density energy into the third through sixth density symbolism, all that jazz.'

She removed her other hand from her pocket and produced a set of keys. She dangled them like a cat would dangle a dead rodent.

'Probably don't need these.' She re-pocketed them. 'We'd better go in. You'll both need to see this.'

Harding led the way.

'Follow me.'

Tarni turned to Thys.

Her face was hard, reflecting nothing of what had passed between them.

'I meant it. It is good to see you again. Is it Thys? Or Amy?'

'Thys. You can call me Thys.'

Tarni smiled tightly.

Then she followed Harding as he walked toward the shattered entrance.

CHAPTER 82

Thys had genuinely thought that she would never return to this place, even though it had been just a few k's down the road from The Fork all this time.

Some kind of essentially nameless, but certainly "Satanic-esque" entity, "The Dark Thing", had psychically manifested here, coming from the void between the higher and middle dimensions, to keep Oliver Hines prisoner for years, and force him to act out his darkest business impulses, as though he were the worst of planet Earth's many psychopaths.

Then Yelina had half-demolished the house by accelerating the growth of its local flora, and opened a portal through which her father, Heather Everett and Suzie Saturn had continued right up to The Abyss, to face off with Lucifer himself (who it turned out, in true Luciferian style, had been traveling with them the whole time). Then, to top it off, some of the most evil artifacts in occult history had apparently been atomized in what had remained of the garden.

So, as symbols went, not a particularly –

'I don't particularly want to be here either,' Tarni muttered.

Thys didn't respond. She didn't like it that this cool, exotic, born-with-her-shit-together woman she'd once hoped to be her BFF, who had ended up, for a time, becoming – she had to face it – meaning much more than she'd expected her to, was now giving her the creeps.

The mansion interior, if you could call it that, was just as Thys had expected. Although the ceiling had been smashed outward by Yelina's accelerating Earth magic, and parts of it were still scattered about the driveway, the trees and vines had closed over in the ensuing nine years to create a new, thick, natural canopy.

So it was pitch black inside.

The classic double staircase, curving in on both sides, that had once wrapped up to a beautiful mezzanine balcony, was barely recognizable now; parts of the mezzanine still jutted out above them, but the staircase on the left was totally shattered, and the one on the right went half way before vanishing into blackness.

Beneath, there had once been several doorways leading to different parts of the house, but all that remained beyond a cursory, ivy-covered frame was what looked like a long, dark tunnel that seemed way too thirsty for their torchlight, leading into an apparent abyss; all that remained of the mansion's main ground-floor corridor.

'Are there supposed to be people here?'

They saw a ghostly light down the end of the tunnel, and for a second it was illuminated with weird, overly contorted roots and vines.

A figure appeared.

A woman.

'Did we all just see that?' Harding asked.

They all shone their torches down the tunnel; the woman was certainly approaching, walking toward them, slowly at first, then with almost instant confidence.

'Anyone know her?' Tarni asked. 'Because, if not... I don't think she's a ghost.' The woman was wearing a summer dress, striding down at them with even greater confidence now, even under Harding's insanely powerful flashlight beam.

'...I think I should warn you,' Tarni added, 'she is undoubtedly an alien reptilian. An Anunnaki possessing a human body.'

The woman continued to stalk toward them fiercely, until she suddenly jerked, having lost balance on one foot, and stopped still.

'Mother – *fucker*!'

Thys grimaced warily. 'I think it's okay.'

The woman yelled. 'Turn off that *fucking torch*, Harding!'

Harding obeyed, although Tarni kept hers firmly on her target.

Thys sighed, but smiled, directing her comments to Tarni.

'You... *have* actually met her before. Along with this big lug, she's basically the best friend I have in the world; both the astral world and this one, it seems. And, how come you can suddenly sense Anunnaki?'

'I've learned a lot of things...'Tarni spoke softly, without taking her eyes off the woman, who was now aggressively slipping off her stilettos. 'Or don't you remember?'

In the darkness, Thys blushed.

The woman in green was very vocal.

'If I have broken a *fucking heel again...*'

'She's not dangerous?'Tarni asked, puzzled.

'Oh no. She's highly dangerous. And she's much older than she looks.'

The woman replaced her high heels and continued her approach, regaining her composure; her cool instantly restored. For the second time that day, Thys was greeted by the spitting genetic image of the young Carla Gugino, glowingly-beautiful in the haunting torchlight as it caught her Paris Green dress.

She stared Thys down with angry, hazel-brown eyes.

'I can't believe you made me come and get you! And here, of all places!'

Close up, the Black Irish Anunnaki was as much a diminutive, curvy knockout in stilettos as the original actress had been at age twenty-nine; an exact replica, complete with the seductive, smoky voice.

'You saw me on the Sydney street this afternoon!' She huffed. 'Can't you take a hint? Or has just a few days of third density living – and sleeping – *mostly sleeping* – already addled your puny human mind!?'

The Gugino clone turned to Harding.

'Hello Harding.'

'You are far too young to be Carla Gugino.'

'It's me Harding.'

'I know it's you, Xylata.'

She looked around haughtily. 'Where are your friends?' Xylata shrugged. 'I thought you would be celebrating!'

'You're all here.' Thys held up her hands. 'Yay!'

Xylata and Harding exchanged the same look; they knew her extremely well.

'Well! You're coming with me right this instant. There's a new war starting on the Earth plane and we're going to need a lot more than just *love* to get out of it this time, Amethyst Pyne!'

CHAPTER 83

'A *new* war?' Thys was aghast.

Xylata waved one hand dismissively as she ran the fingers of her other hand over the base of a ruined balustrade; the bottom of a once glorious spiral staircase that now led to nowhere.

'Well… the same as the old war, probably!'

It was covered in mud, and she flicked it away.

'This place is a disgrace!' She hissed.

Thys had the feeling she was not just joking about its condition.

'*You're* Xylata?' Tarni was aghast.

Xylata ignored her. 'I had to get to you, Thys Pyne, before you vanished as well.'

'What do you mean?'

Her eyes narrowed.

She was hiding something, wary now.

'I mean – on your holiday circuit; to the places you go where nobody knows.'

'The…?'

The expression sounded exceedingly strange, although she and Heather had often used it.

She… Xylata… and Heather?

'Before you vanish through your *wardrobe* again,' Xylata complained. 'The way you *always* do when you come back… when you've *had enough*…' Xylata pouted suddenly, and looked almost look hurt. 'And never tell anyone…'

Thys huffed. 'I have to have my own space, Xylata. I have to be able to leave and be somewhere nobody knows.'

'The places you go where nobody knows! I know, I know! I have those places too!' Xylata snapped airily at Thys. 'We're not supposed to, but the higher up the ranks you get, the more you'll find it happening, and now I don't have to answer to any of those other petty male-driven clans…'

She huffed and swiped her hand, grandly.

'Never mind. The new concern is because of that *thing*. Suddenly everybody wants an escape hatch, a bolt hole, a cabin in the woods. Off the grid, the humans are saying, as they hoard their tinned food and bullets.'

'What *thing*?' Harding asked.

'That thing that's coming? That everyone knows is coming; the big event?'

'You really think it's coming?' Thys asked.

Xylata grinned. 'Oh, I think it's coming. Everyone senses it. Look on your television and internet; the end of the world is even nigher than it was on that ridiculous December Twenty Twelve stunt the mass-media pulled – or were steered to pull.'

'The Mayan Calendar?' Harding asked. 'There's something like that every ten-to-fifteen years or so; it keeps consumers anxious.'

'Yes. But this one in particular was particularly wasteful.'

Tarni kept staring. 'The Xylata who is leading her clan, the female dominated Ymira Clan, against her race, to help humanity rid the astral of the Anunnaki? The Queen Elizabeth clone I saw dying that afternoon in –'

'Please don't say Paramatta…!' Thys sighed, staring at Tarni, who was still staring at Xylata. 'I am so sick of Para-bloody-matta!'

But Xylata continued to ignore her.

'That was obscene. The mass media! Deluded into warping a beneficent harmonic convergence, meant to spiritually enlighten a small percentage of the population, so that they would be able to teach others, into a massive *fear and anxiety campaign* where half the population were expecting *Armageddon*!'

Tarni's mouth fell open. 'I know!' she exclaimed. 'Oceans of negative energy were channeled like pole shift tidal waves into the astral!'

At that, Xylata seemed fractionally to acknowledge her

presence. 'We have done well, Thys Pyne; but this planet is becoming more and more dysfunctional – and you mark my words, this all has something to do with whatever's making a commotion on Saturn! I don't understand the Draco Clan, or the Cheneks for that matter. It doesn't make sense to waste humanity like this. Who brought the witch, by the way?'

'Saturn?' Thys aired. 'Belle mentioned something… about the moons, Pandora and Prometheus – wait a minute; the *witch*?'

Tarni took a step back.

'She's a witch,' Xylata shrugged. 'She's got second-density magical auras and Inner Earth… dust and dirt and pollen and seeds; fragments and insectual buzzing, dancing all over her. Is she with you?'

Thys looked from Tarni, who was completely stunned, to Xylata, who was completely smug, and back again.

'Ye – yes!' Thys announced. 'She is!' She turned to Tarni. 'Aren't you?'

Tarni shook her head, switched off her torch, and folded her arms.

'What part of '*Yelina sent me to help you*' do you people never understand?'

Then she spoke to Thys very formally, very clipped again, as though their relationship really had been drop-kicked right back to the first time they'd met.

'Do you not remember what happened to us; when we were together? Those creatures? The Blood Moon?'

Thys began to feel flushed.

'To-geth-errrr…?' Xylata purred.

Harding cleared his throat. 'Apparently…'

Tarni snapped. 'That is not what I am referring to; you are deliberately taking the wrong information from my inference. And, if you do not mind…!' Tarni shot a look at Xylata. '…this is not time, nor the place, to discuss who I am, or what I am, or what I am capable of doing! Nor is it appropriate to discuss whatever relationship I may or may not have had with Amy! – I mean, Thys!'

There was silence as her words echoed distantly down the ruined hallway, as her attitude set in.

'You're really a witch now?' Thys asked quietly, but intensely.

'Yes,' Tarni growled. 'As it happens. After *what happened.*'

'Good,' Xylata nodded. 'Now we all know, relatively, who we all are. And perhaps she can help us with the graffiti?'

'The – ?'

Thys looked around, shining her flashlight on what remained of the walls. The inside front wall of the house was almost totally intact, and almost completely visible, up through the shattered ceiling, to all four damaged floors. Over what structure remained, as high as they could see, someone had drawn a seemingly endless series of magical signs and occult symbols.

'Enochian magic...' Tarni uttered. 'Essentially neutral, but used this way... very dark. Too dark.'

'What is that, exactly?' Harding growled. 'This Enochian...?'

'It's complicated. Construction spells... old as Orion... from the time of the Gods, capital G, Gods, and the Watchers, but... brought to third density by darkness...'

'What do you mean – *too dark?*' Thys demanded.

Tarni didn't look at her as she responded. 'Too dark to be standing around at dawn telling whoever's listening exactly who we are and what we're doing here. Harding, take the rear. I'll lead us out.'

She flicked her torch quickly away from the occult graffiti.

Thys was still looking.

'Don't look at it too long; it's designed to scare you.'

'It's on the surface of some of the dark astral temples...'

'The what?' Tarni snapped.

Thys turned to her. 'We really didn't know each other as well as we thought, did we?'

Tarni scowled. 'This is not the time or place. But since you brought it up; this is most likely a similar crew to the people, the creatures, we saw on the beach that night.' Tarni turned and looked at her now; looked at her dead-on, and furious. 'You do remember that night, Amy?'

Thys didn't respond.

It had been like a slap in the face, a real one, with passion.

Tarni turned to Harding. 'Thys and I came across these people once before. Years ago. But I have since dedicated my life to finding out who they are and what they want.'

'And?' Harding asked.

'Enochian magic is rooted in the Earth, in the primal forces of nature. It involves the psychic and vibrational manipulation of Inner Earth energies, through third and higher density symbols; Yelina used a form of it, in cooperation with Gaia, the living spirit of the planet, it to demolish this place and create the Inner Earth tunnel at the back of the house. But what's been done here since...'

'Is that where you've been...?' Thys heard herself ask.

'There is a positive Earth magic residue here,' Tarni proceeded, ignoring Thys. 'But because the house was already so poisoned by the Beigeman, others have come here since and exploited it for...'

Tarni paused, dry-mouthed, and gulped, loudly.

'...I *really* think we should leave. We should not have come here. We have almost certainly been lured into a trap.'

They heard a sound near the door. All their flashlights flicked to the ruined cavity.

Five people stood there, blocking their exit.

'I can't see them,' Thys uttered.

They had three military grade flashlight beams on whoever it was.

'Why can't I see them?'

'Because they exist...' Tarni sounded frightened now. '...in near total spiritual darkness.'

A voice spoke from behind them, and they spun about again.

'All of you leave. Now. The Pyne girl stays. Take that as your one and final warning.'

It was a man, a man with a rough French accent. Harding's

flashlight went out. There were two sharp, unmistakable clicks as he let them know he was armed and prepped.

Thys knew; that would be *his* only warning.

Her torch was directly on the man, but he was clothed in a dark brown monk's cassock, with a giant cowl that covered his entire face and neck.

'They are prepared to die for me...'

The Monk spoke clearly as he waved his long, draping sleeve to his left.

'...as are they.'

Five more black shadows stepped out of one of the ruined internal doorways.

'And they.'

Again, to his right, five more.

'And, naturally, they.'

Dirt and dust fell from above; they all shone their torches up through the remains of the upwardly-shattered ceiling to see that standing upon the edges of whatever stable parts of the upper floors remained, upon the broken extensions of the jagged beams and splintered floor boards, were dozens more of the shadow figures, balanced and leaning down, staring silently.

'We only want Amethyst Pyne,' the Monk reaffirmed. 'You others, leave, now, and you will be spared.'

'You're...' Thys began, as a distant but furious recognition began to set in.

She and Xylata had started to back into each other, slowly and carefully at first, with the floor creaking beneath them, but faster and more urgently as they grew closer.

'...he's the Skype call, correct...?' Xylata muttered. '...from –'

'...*fucking Paramatta*. Yes.'

'I thought so...' Xylata sighed, angrily. '...fucking Paramatta.'

Thys saw that Harding was noticing, subtly, that the dust in the air was not necessarily settling; she trusted that he would understand, and act accordingly.

The Monk sighed deeply; then he gave an order in a tone of

resigned malevolence.

'Take the girl, kill the others; drink their blood.'

Harding stepped closer to Tarni, but halted when he saw that she was standing with her palms open and had begun to utter an urgent melody under her breath, in the back of her throat.

From behind the Monk, from the tunnel of the abyss, a woman's voice cried out.

'Idiot! They're stronger than you!'

'No!' The French Monk was grossly offended. 'That is not possible!'

'The Creole Aboriginal has gone away and secretly trained in Earth magic!' The woman was furious, but in control. 'Take the daughter! *Take her now!*'

'Now!' Thys cried out.

Immediately, the ring of telekinetic concentration that she and Xylata had been holding back sprang to life. All the dust, dirt, pebbles, rocks, nuts, stones, nails, wood, sticks, branches and vines that had gathered on the floor in all the years of ruin, including much of the weather-worn floor boards, shot up around them in a terrible psychokinetic hurricane, within the eye of which they stood, back-to-back.

Thys was angry, but at the same time elated.

She and Xylata had performed this maneuver many times in the astral, although rarely if ever in third density. But this was her friend, her backup, her partner. They hadn't even needed to communicate telepathically to know that the telekinetic hurricane, The Eye, was the move they required here.

'Tarni!' Thys shouted. 'If you're doing...!'

Thys heard as Tarni kept uttering. She had raised both her hands now, outstretched in the air before her. Some of the dark figures moved forward, but fear had taken them, and they could not bring themselves to attack. Tarni's arms were tense as bamboo as her mutterings became clearer, a strange but beautiful language with crisp syllables, poetic yet intimidating, almost tuneful but not quite songs. Her long fingers were stretched out before her so that the tendons in her wrists and along the backs of her hands stood out like cyborg piston rods.

Then the five black shadows behind her at the entrance leaped as one, hissing and snarling, their eyes suddenly lighting up in the darkness; a fiery, hellish red. Then they dropped with the sound of five shots; Harding had her back. Five more immediately replaced them in the doorway, but it was too late.

Tarni's upstretched hands closed into tight fists, like knotted balls, and with a savage, grasping motion she pulled her arms back down to her sides; a wild, primitive, elaborate snatch. All of the foliage on the wrecked floors above them flew down; the limp, hanging vines were suddenly erect and sliced the darkness toward her, as though shot from harpoons. All the internally growing branches of the surrounding trees seemed to have been wrenched toward her as well, and the entire ruined mansion trembled. What remained of the ceiling and floors above fell in, and with those remains, all the black minions who had been perching up there, screaming as they toppled, some falling two or three stories to their deaths, some breaking limbs or smashing themselves useless or immobile, all of the others incapacitated and in pain.

'Down!' Xylata cried out.

Tarni was falling unconscious to the floor anyway as Harding caught her, then covered her with his body. The spinning hurricane of debris that surrounded Thys and Xylata blew out, like a shrapnel explosion, spraying the collected ammunition in an outward and upward directions simultaneously.

The sound was momentarily deafening, as the mansion screamed, finally, its long death rattle.

None of them stuck around to see what happened next.

Thys and Xylata were out of the house, Harding in their wake and Tarni in his arms, before the first of the larger debris had hit the floor. Then, as Tarni came to, she was immediately alert and running at Harding's side, toward the dilapidated fountain.

'I can't gap!' Thys cried out.

Xylata skidded to a halt at the fountain, her Paris Green dress spinning like a Flamenco dancer as she snarled back up at the wobbling frame of the mansion.

'Damn black Enochian – *swear words!*'

'No!' Tarni shouted, as the mansion began to creak, as the sound of huge pieces of splintering wood vibrated out at them, as though the mad, tortured, dying creation was somehow spitting its last hate-filled splinters of bile at them. 'It can't be! It can't effect astral gaps!'

'Jesus women!' Harding exclaimed from the top of the drive. 'Don't just stand there watching it fall on you! Run!'

They bolted as one down the sharp decline, as rubble and girders crashed down and rolled and clanked, propelled toward them out of the ruin with the pained, screeching, crunching sound of total collapse, driving them on, steeply down, crashing behind them until Harding turned mid-run and, still sliding backwards down the drive like an ice skater coming to rest, gazed upward.

'Look out – to the sides!'

They were halfway down the drive now as a huge chunk of stone; something from the original front wall, rolled between them with fierce momentum, sailing and bouncing like a crashed comet with a tail full of foul-smelling dust.

They watched it crash into the bushes where the drive curved below to their right, then Harding started up again, barking:

'Come on!'

'I recognized that voice, damn it!' Thys was furious, walking now but stomping ahead.

'We both tried to gap!' Xylata aired. 'To no avail!'

Thys knew how Xylata was feeling. She was feeling the same way; she'd gapped so many times in her life, and occasionally something had blocked her, but rarely had it been in such dire circumstances, nor had she been so outraged.

'That was a fucking trap!' Thys cried out.

Tarni, walking slightly behind her, stared daggers at the back of her head.

'Who was that?' Xylata demanded. 'Who are they? That Frenchman – and the woman behind him? We must find out! That is the second time they have turned up to cause trouble!'

'Whoever it was...' Tarni grumbled, '...they were black sorcerers, using wraiths and the dark Enochian magic – and *she* was in charge!'

'I can't place her...'! Thys hissed. 'It was the same when I was ambushed by DeVora's cabal! That woman, I know her from somewhere, but I *can't* – ' Her teeth were clenched as she talked. 'I was too *freaked* to *read her...*'

Thys' furious stomping finally got her to the bottom of the driveway; and then she was actually standing on Mulholland Drive. She had never done this before, always meant to but never had. She had wanted to make something special out of it, but now it was all rather mundane and unromantic; just another hillside street, with the bins out, rusty letterboxes and weeds along the asphalt.

They all walked onwards, up the road's slight incline, until Xylata huffed.

'There was a psychic shield. I sensed it. Enochian maybe?' She looked to Tarni for confirmation. 'That spear thing again, from the 'P' place? I am not familiar with second density, not in reality, not this strong. It seems very strong; very primal, very elemental, very physical and real. I do not mind saying that I do not like it! At all!'

'Yes.'

It was all Tarni said in response.

She had been holding herself together extremely well, but she was now visibly shaking. She was still staring at the back of Thys' long blonde locks, which were bouncing madly as she strode onward, and apparently still blasting the skull beneath.

Finally, Thys spun about.

'Who reported that there was activity there?' Thys demanded. 'Why did you contact Harding?'

They all stopped.

'I knew it!' Tarni snapped. 'I already told you! Contrelle told me, but the report could have come from anywhere!'

'I don't understand!' Xylata looked back and forth between them, up and down Mulholland. 'You seem angrier at each other than you are with her evil counterparts for luring us into a trap!'

There was an awkward silence.

Again, a coyote howled, somewhere near.

'Thank you,' Tarni sighed.

'For what?'

Tarni didn't tell her, although it was readily apparent to Thys, who now felt ashamed. How could she possibly have thought that Tarni, of all people…

They all started walking again.

'I think…' Tarni resumed, seeming much calmer. '…Contrelle said it was just a regular police report. She sends them through to me. Usually it's just a teenage dare thing; the Hines Hell House, Reclamation House, Death Orgy Mansion, whatever they're calling it now, and I call Harding to see if he's in town. Either way, it's usually dealt with very easily. But recently these dark clowns have emerged, and then a few weeks ago, the spell-runes and Enochian glyphs on the walls. There was a documentary crew here last week, filming without permission, but by the time I got here… I thought getting Harding to come here would be a good excuse to find out what you knew about the place. I have been looking for you Amy, these past few days. But I honestly didn't know you were here with Harding. I'm sorry for dragging you into it.'

For some reason, Thys was suddenly furious again.

But Harding cut her clean.

'Wait.' Harding seemed stunned. 'They didn't have permission? They had papers. They – came to the house, they used your name! I was unable to contact you, but Mirabelle said you had cleared it through Mitch!'

Tarni was shocked. 'No! I would never have allowed anything like that!'

'Jesus!' Harding seemed to swell to one third larger, as his whole body tensed with anger. 'Who *are* these fuckers!'

'I keep trying to tell you!' Tarni guffawed. 'They are black sorcerers!'

Xylata shook her head, and finally paused to take off her heels.

'I know... nothing of... such things. That's better! Only the tale Thys Pyne has told me, of her friend Yelina.'

Thys looked back at Tarni.

She remained furious.

'We should get Yelina here,' Thys demanded, deliberately engaging Tarni's wrath. 'Can you contact her?'

'No!' Tarni stared up the street at Thys, her startling golden eyes flashing with anger. 'That was my real purpose in coming here, if you must know. I thought there would perhaps be progression here. I needed to confirm that something is very wrong; I thought having Harding as backup would be sensible.'

Harding grunted; he couldn't argue with that.

'Amy; Thys. Nobody has seen Yelina for days! Usually she comes and goes, from Everett to her family, at least once every day, without fail, even for just a few minutes, for either sunrise salutes or sunset gratitudes – most days both. But it's been three days! That's never happened before. Never in thirty; forty years, they say!'

'Yelina?' Thys was shocked.

'We are worried that she had been – hurt somehow!'

'*Hurt?*' Thys was puzzled. 'How do you *hurt* an Earth Goddess?'

'With –'

Tarni spread her arms, her biceps tight, staring wide-eyed, as though Thys were a complete idiot.

' – dark – Enochian – magic – *Einstein*! That's why I was trying to contact you all! I was worried! I didn't know how much you knew; how much danger you were in!'

'*What?*'

'Move faster!' Harding started up again. 'They will come after us once they realise where we are! It is only a few minutes further from here and up the drive, another ten houses down. *Then* we can debrief!'

Thys suddenly turned on Tarni. 'Where did you go! Hey? Where have you been all this time? Not one call!'

'I called – I called and called, I called for – *you* never replied to any of *my* calls!'

'That – !' Thys cried out, stopping still as Tarni walked on past her. ' – is *manifestly untrue!*'

Xylata scampered past them, and caught up to Harding.

'What am I missing here?'

Harding muttered to Xylata. 'I am told some girls experiment in college?'

'Yes, I have heard the same.'

'Well, I think they went to college.'

'Oh…' Xylata uttered. 'I was teasing before. They really…?'

Harding nodding sagely.

Xylata threw her hands into the air, as though uncovering a mystic revelation.

'*Holy vaginas!*'

Her cry echoed across the valley.

'*Save us from ourselves!*'

After that, none of them spoke for the rest of the way back.

CHAPTER 84

'And what department is that?'

Tarni smiled, again somewhat wicked, but now thoroughly suggestive.

'What department is it we're on, up here? On the seventh floor?'

Thys swigged her beer back.

Seven floors down, the tide was coming in and the sound of the waves breaking lightly against the shore was becoming slightly louder. Sometimes the repetitive, crashing water blended into the background.

Not tonight.

Tarni seemed to pick up on her thought.

'The waves….'

Thys smiled, almost serenely.

Tarni smiled back. 'The cove has a shelf. In winter, when the weather's rough, it's a secret surf destination for the Sirians. Orions too, I think. Agents on sabbatical. I hear the waves can be… amazing.'

'Are you gay?' Thys blurted out.

Tarni scoffed, seeming tremendously confident.

'No! And even if I was, I don't even know if I would necessarily use that word to describe myself…' She laughed. 'But then, nor would I want to be one of those people who posed, all pretentious either, like; *I don't want to be labeled.*'

'Bi, then?' Thys smiled, nervously.

Tarni laughed; then she looked at Thys very curiously.

'I don't know… I've never…'

Tarni shrugged.

The same way she always seemed to shrug.

Just; confidently open.

'Truthfully, I've never been sexually attracted to a woman before. I can't believe I said that in the elevator when I left last time. I've never been so bold, with anyone. Usually, I like to let the guy make the first move, so I know he's thought about it. I mean; I don't even think of you as being a woman, not like that. But I don't think of myself as that anymore either. Not since…'

'Since what?'

'Since we met. Probably, when you vanished, in the car park, and after all that went down, I realised that I didn't want you to go. Or since, this time, when I realised that I didn't have a professional excuse to see you anymore. And, that felt bad.'

Thys swigged her beer again. It was malty and bitter but with some kind of sharp tang. It had taken her three swigs to acquire the taste.

Tarni jolted, frustrated. 'I just want to…'

Thys' heart skipped a beat. Jesus; *what* did she want to…?

'Just want to what?' Thys heard herself ask.

'Just…' Tarni took the five steps toward her that closed the gap between them. They were face to face now, intimately close, with no concession to personal boundaries, and no lingering pretense as to what it was they were approaching. Tarni raised her hand and brushed Thys' hair back over her shoulder with the back of her hand.

'…touch your hair.'

She whispered, throaty and nervous.

'Like that.'

Thys put her beer on the bench without looking behind her and tipped over her Eve cradle. She did not have to push her neck forward, or tilt her head much to the side to initiate the kiss; her lips touched Tarni's and pressed against them, and felt tiny, and overwhelmed. Tarni's mouth opened but Thys' mouth just closed over her top lip, and pulled it with her own lips, then moved down and snatched quickly to do the same with her bottom lip, which felt huge, and was flushing. She pecked up and down and across, until Tarni opened her mouth and engulfed her whole mouth, with the full passionate suction of a forceful, anxious, desperate French kiss.

Then their hands were on each other's hips, and the kiss kept going.

A track started playing on the apartment sound system; knocking the Eve over had somehow activated it, and Kylie Minogue's *Confide In Me* started. The song was decades old now but Thys really liked it, thought it always sounded fresh and timeless. She made no effort to cancel it.

Thys knew how to make out.

She had discovered sex later than a lot of women, then embraced it with equal measures of calculation and recklessness.

She had stood with her legs braced apart, grinding into Nathan Juror's thigh for hours as they'd kissed and pressed and fumbled over their clothes; she'd done that on a couch, she'd done that on a bed, and then, finally, when she'd turned sixteen, she'd been just about to do it when her mother had moved them to London.

But this was okay, she told the part of herself that did not know if she should be doing this, that it was wrong somehow; that was all it was, just the grind. Just the making out. Innocent, essentially.

Saxe, then Jade (and she still hated that) had become fully sexually active almost immediately upon hearing her first British accent, but Thys had been extremely cautious and it hadn't been until she had found like-minded boys in The Pan, like DJ, that she had found her groove. Then, about a year later, discovering and exploring the astral plane had made her understand that there were many different ways, and means, and reasons to have sex, and even different kinds of orgasms, and that had allowed her initially to explore, and embrace her recklessness, but then with her duty to her father, and Pan, and the future of the Pandorans to consider, she had radically withdrawn to reconsider her ways.

She had looked for love, but as the demands of her role in the astral had become more time consuming, and extreme, she had found no time for romance. Only biology, only the usefulness of orgasm, even over the pleasure; searching for bliss was just a side-benefit. She had ventured into astral voyeurism, backed off, then reembraced her own body in contact with others and had, just recently, initiated two male lovers into orbit, with another in the wings, finding herself finally, efficiently and satisfactorily in control of her own sexual being. Now she was breathing another woman's breath. Another girl's breath.

They stopped kissing and were panting, their faces close together and open mouthed.

'What's happening?'

Thys heard herself ask, pressing her left temple against this other woman's, other girl's right cheek.

'What's *happening*?'

There was a pain in her chest; she felt like crying. Tears started forming in her eyes and she squeezed them shut, but that just guided the tears down her cheeks, so she kissed Tarni again, ferociously, crying.

'Are you oka – ?'

'Don't stop…!'

Pleading right into her mouth.

They kept kissing, and Tarni seemed to understand now that something new was happening, something urgent was emerging, and she moved closer to Thys, with greater force, holding tighter and pressing harder. Thys began to make crooning sounds, Tarni soothing sounds; Tarni pushed the yellow shoulder straps to the side and Thys fumbled behind Tarni's neck with a knot of material and then their dresses both fell to the slate, simultaneously. Thys didn't look, didn't want to see Tarni naked, didn't know what that would mean if she found it exciting. Didn't know what any of this meant.

She started to feel guilty.

She started to feel wrong.

This was un-natural.

CHAPTER 85

'You must never..'

She remembered the old woman telling her, and the other children.

'...*ever* let anyone touch you down there, ever; it is unclean, and un-natural and wrong! Never let boys do anything, and never let girls do anything; if you are a boy, and you let another boy touch you down there, that is a great sin, and it is The Devil who is making you do that! You must never give in to sin! Never give in to sin – or you walk the path of The Devil – to Hell itself!'

Deep, this was buried so deep...

'But if you are a girl, and you let another girl touch you down there...? Then; there is an especially bad place in Hell, waiting for harlots of that sort of wickedness; both boys and girls but especially girls, because boys are brutes and closer to the animals! They can't help themselves – ! But girls are pure and closer to grace!'

The programming; so early...

'So if they descend to that kind of sordid wickedness – *lustful wickedness* – with boys, but especially with *other girls,* then the angels *weep* and the sucking funnel of Hell *gapes open*! Weeping, and gaping! Like an open wound – with teeth! – that festers and never heals! Never, never, never let anyone touch you down there! But girls – never, ever, ever let another girl! Or it will be eternal doom – and Hellfire – with the Devil – poking, poking, *poking,* red hot *pokers* down there, *down there* – for eternity! *Poking down there!* Forever! *Forever!'*

Thys was panting now; the feeling in her guts, the knot in her stomach was so tight. Panting into Tarni's open lips, enormous and swollen, her own lips brushing against the top row of her glistening white teeth, her mouth closing over her cheek, then her jaw, down her neck to the top curve of her tightly-muscled shoulder, feeling them; squeezing her eyes closed, pressing her body in close.

'…God…' Thys uttered, guttural. '…God…'

Then a young woman's face, behind the old woman.

Grimacing uncontrollably, horrified, wanting the children to know; she was horrified, she didn't want this for them, she didn't *believe* this.

The younger woman had spoken to them, before the elder, and warned them.

'…we've spoken about his, and I don't think it's necessary; but the minister says… he says it should be taught…'

She was emotional, barely conflicted; she knew this was about as wrong as it could get.

'…and I don't think you'll understand it; I don't think you're ready…'

Amethyst remembered sitting with the other girls and looking up, and not really understanding, but *somehow* understanding.

'They'll understand soon enough!' The Crone had stated. 'They'll understand Temptation!'

The Devil.

They had been lectured about The Devil and Sin and Temptation at Sunday School… the younger teacher had fought, with the elder and the minister, to be progressive, that this should not be taught, not like this; Thys understood that now, but – how could little Amethyst have understood it?

She gasped as she remembered; she had been… five, six years old?

At six years old, The Church, and The Crone; the old Sunday School teacher, had put this in her head. Fear of sex, of intimacy, of pleasure, of orgasm…

Just for starters!

And it had stayed there.

But: who had put it there?

Who had put it there, in the Church, in the system to be spat out in the first place?

In: The First Place!

To be psychologically weaponized; to keep people apart?

To spiritually rape the little children?

Who had done this?

Why?

Here, now with Tarni…

How could this be wrong?

Why should she feel guilty?

She had been in the astral, seen it often enough; the act itself, the energy, the erotic energy, the reality of it and the fantasy, the desire… and yet when faced with it here, in the realm of the mind, there was a program that still, after all she had seen and been through, was installed in her brain, installed at a time when everything imprinted permanently, as a child, before seven, when tracks were embedded forever and played on loops without anyone knowing, so constantly you didn't hear them anymore, not as an adult. They became just part of the subconscious background; the ebb and flow of the waves on the beach, blending onto everyday reality; the white noise at the start of the universe, her personal universe, her personal white noise; reminding her, always, unconsciously…

Christ, they were fear programs; The Devil was a fear program.

Hell was a fear program.

God was a fear program.

She knew this, had always known this, but now she was experiencing it.

Now it was a reality she was facing.

Janine had sent them on autopilot, out of tradition, but Mitch had pulled them out.

Too late.

The true horror; the program system, the control matrix, was on autopilot too.

But who?

Who?

Confide In Me ended with Kylie's high, wailing pitch.

The damn thing was going to play *Better The Devil You Know*, she just knew it; it was going to run through the complete Kylie best of – but no, *Confide In Me* started again.

It would repeat until one of them stopped it.

Neither of them was going to stop it.

Thys remained standing.

She felt as her bra was undone, then Tarni was pushing her underwear down; then Tarni was crying out as Thys had one hand on the back of her head and the other on the small of her back, and was kissing and sucking at her neck like a vampire. Thys felt her knickers drop to her ankles, and pushed Tarni's down too, her hand moving evenly along the crack of her buttocks, pushing the material and sliding under, feeling the back of her vulva; wet flesh, and Tarni flinching then laughing; shortly, deeply. Thys shivered as Tarni pushed her panties down now, and as her thin, long fingers moved with a facing, open-palm down her belly, over her neatly, newly-trimmed pubes and down again, a switch was flipped; their chests were pushing together and they could feel each other's nipples pressing on each other's breasts; they were communicating mostly wordlessly now, through groans and throaty expulsions, the occasional *yuh* or *uh-huh*; then they each parted their legs and were dancing, forcing, thrusting, intertwined, and she understood, finally, physically, how it worked, how it would work and had worked, always, for women; the grind, the wet sticky grind, the involuntary swelling and natural puckering and liquid suction that washed away the old lady crone in a flood, in waves, screaming as she drowned, melting, melting, onto the floor and going to water.

CHAPTER 86

Thys, Xylata and Tarni were exhausted when they reached the top of the driveway where Harding, in order to let them all in, had to guide them past the many and varied security systems he had activated upon leaving The Fork, and remotely once there.

The top of the drive, the courtyard, the front door and vestibule; then the entrance parlor, then the fully three-dimensional motion sensors beyond; all of which required both verbal and retinal scan deactivation, but for most of which he also had to remember complex passwords.

'I need a master-command kill-switch.'

'You think?'

Thys was too tired now to make it sound sarcastic.

'I need a drink.'

Tarni looked at Xylata; *oh yeah.*

When they could finally walk freely about The Fork, they were all grumpy and impatient, so he directed the two still-simmering humans, and one still-slightly-puzzled Anunnaki, through the front door, up the stairs to the second floor, through the lounge area, and directly to the bar, which Thys called "The Sphinx".

Tarni's eyes darted around the room.

'Should we be so close to the other house? Won't they come after us?'

'I assure you,' Harding spoke quite gruffly, 'that all of the many and varied levels of security you just saw have been firmly sealed behind us. There are a great many supernatural, magical, alien-tech, and multi-dimensional levels of security in operation also.'

'Okay. If you say. Can I have my drink now please?'

'This Enochian magic, you say? It is possibly similar to the symbols used by the Orion-level demonic entity that held Oliver

Hines prisoner?'

Thys stared at him as she walked across the room.

'What?' Harding shrugged his huge shoulders helplessly.

'I just hardly ever hear you talk like this. It's weird.'

'That actually happened?' Tarni asked. 'I'd heard...' She frowned. 'Yelina doesn't like to talk about it; nobody does. You mean that's – all actually true? All of it?'

Nobody answered.

Harding continued to watch Thys as she sat and folded her arms over the bar, then slumped forward and let her head fall into them. He had seen Thys like this before, a few times, as had Xylata, and opted immediately for distraction, in an effort to calm her down more readily. He threw the remote control from the bar to Xylata, who immediately raised it and activated the massive television on the other side of the room. Harding then turned to the alcohol rack and proceeded to pour her favorite neat spirit, which was the same as her father's had been; Southern Comfort on the rocks.

Thys, in turn, had immediately recognized the plot and the tactics and resented being handled as such, especially by both of them, her two closest friends, clearly in agreement that she required handling, and in such precise collusion to make it happen.

'I know what you're doing!' Thys called out, into her arms, and the bar. 'Do not turn the volume up!'

'Your father told me that in times of impending crisis we should always watch the scrolls.' Harding slid the father-daughter favourite closer to her head. 'It's what they want in your subconscious, he said. While your conscious mind is entertained by action, color, eyes and hair, and lips and chins and teeth, they slip the programing in under the cleavage and neckties. Given that we know this and are immune, maybe we'll find something out, eh?'

'Harding,' Thys snapped, glaring up at him through bitter eyes. 'I've watched the news since I got back, I've surfed the net;

believe me, I did the crap out of that. My own profile aside, it all looked the same to me. The same as it ever was!'

Xylata walked slowly to the bar, but watched the screen tensely.

'Thys Pyne, you know what it's like for people like us; if we dip in and out of popular culture and relevant media, it tells us exactly what we need to know. And while it might seem sometimes like more of the same, over and over, it's also different every time; the focus of it all; where the various clans of my people want you to place your anxiety for this cycle; what fears they want energized this time round. Every time your race goes through one of its cycles –'

'That you created!'

'That you seem designed to respond to!'

'That you designed!'

'Not me personally!'

'Girls!' Harding growled. 'I don't want to have to send you to you rooms!'

Thys huffed, but she sat up with a resigned pout, turned around on her bar stool and watched the news briefly. Much to her chagrin, something immediately, intuitively leaped out at her.

'Phoodco – fucking; again! Will that DeVora woman never fucking rest?' Thys frowned. 'That's their third major story in under two days. This is not good. What's happening? How the fuck did anyone let them become that big in the first place…?!'

'That big?' Tarni uttered, moving to the bar. 'Anything Harding, please.'

Thys stared at her as though her proximity, after their childish fight, was highly improper. Then Tarni turned to Thys and engaged her directly.

'Everyone is wondering that. But while everyone was watching and protesting Monsanto, all Monsanto's minor rivals ganged up, swallowed each other and glommed together to become the major competition. Now they're the biggest agricultural biotech company on the planet. Last night they announced they're trying to merge with Physcore, the company who have the best chance at finally creating gene patents…'

'Gene patents?'

Thys turned to Xylata.

'Who the fuck is Physcore? Isn't that Chenek? Who owns that down here?'

'Nobody knows,' Xylata sneered, still watching the scrolls. 'The public face are all shills and patsies.'

'It's totally demented,' Tarni spat. 'My people are very concerned. That's why I'm trying to find Yelina. Privately, Physcore are bragging that they've almost altered human genes sufficiently enough so that they can be claimed as original work, and patented. Owned. This is much worse than Regene, worse than Oliver Hines ever was. It's going through the courts again now; we think they'll get it through this time.'

Thys put her hand over her mouth.

'Xylata; is that where all those visons of chimeras are coming from in the astral? And alien hybrids? Could this be Crossbreed? Bloodroot? Even Whitehole? Because they've all been experimenting with this, all this time?'

Tarni sighed, angrily. 'That's what I've been doing for the past three years, Amy. Trying to stop this Physcore merge. But they're too big, way too big now. We need something else, something – I don't know. Monumental, to hold them back now.'

'And this is happening at the same time as we are attacked by crazy occult junkies, your father and Heather are out of contact in the middle of the desert, and Yelina has gone missing?' Harding scowled. 'Those ruins came down like a house of cards, and my security system is the best on the planet. Still, we should move out of Los Angeles until we know who they are; there seemed to be a lot of them. Xylata, are you sure you didn't recognize anyone? The Monk? The voice of That Woman? Are you sure none of this Enochian business has anything to do with your people?'

Xylata was staring worriedly at Thys now, who was staring blankly at Tarni, who was trying to ignore Thys. Still, Harding tried.

'Tarni; is there something to counter this Enochian foolishness? And Amy – you said you *definitely* recognized That Woman's voice? Surely we can piece some clues together here?'

Xylata continued to ignore Harding, but made her own attempt at reaching Thys. 'Thys Pyne, you don't remember much of what we did in the astral, do you?'

Thys turned from Tarni and shrugged. 'To be honest, no. That's what I've been trying to tell everyone!'

Xylata huffed, more than a little annoyed now, and Thys let off again.

'It's not like I haven't been worried about it! But Heather said she knew what was going on! And she'd tell me when she got back! But now the satellites are down… and why couldn't we gap?! I don't like this, Xylata! There's too much going on!'

Thys turned back to Tarni, and the daggers in her eyes returned as Xylata nodded her Gugino head to herself. 'I have seen this before. Don't worry, it will come back to you. We have seen these things coming, and more. We will have taken steps… and we will have hatched a plan. Is that not what Heather Everett inferred?'

'Wait. You mean…?'

'The truth is, I do not remember the plan either. Not since I returned here, the same night you did. I was hoping you would. But for now we must wait. It will come back to us. We must see what we will see.'

Thys looked into her friend's eyes. For a second, Xylata flicked her reptilian irises at her.

◊ *I am not lying to hide this from your ex-lover* ◊

☾ *…I know… I'm sorry… my heart…* ☽

Xylata smiled, a little sadly, a little sympathetically. It was very rare; she was doing her best to placate her confused and frustrated human friend.

'We have done well, you and I, Thys Pyne, I know this much. The Sea of Humanity is clear and enormous and free. The Amethyst Palace is giant and labyrinthine, and *stable*.'

'I remember that. I remember Sea and the Palace. But the last few nights… I'm running about in there, in my dreams, like I don't know the place. Like it wasn't me who… designed it, I guess! And I *still wish* they wouldn't call it that.'

Xylata seemed to take a small amount of joy in the fact that Thys did not relish her position of the Christopher Columbus of the astral dimensions.

'But they do, Thys Pyne. It is a great honor for you. And what we're doing with it may be holding back this *thing* that's coming. Perhaps even those – Monsters, and Psycho Corps. But listen now; Harding is right, we must move from this place and figure out why a coven of witches wants us dead, and you captive.'

Tarni sighed as she accepted a drink from Harding, a straight vodka. 'Please don't call them witches; I might be a witch; they are not witches; they are… zombie psychos!' She sipped. 'Thank you Mister Harding, perfect.'

'Just Harding.'

Thys ignored them.

'So, where do we go that's safe? Back to the Palace?'

'You truly don't remember the plan at all?'

It was Thys's turn to scowl at Xylata.

'I told you. I've tried to remember, but it's like the way clairvoyance works here. Or rather, it doesn't. You have to try too hard, and the trying gets in the way. Not like 'potency' in the astral, where it just comes, where it's part of the Pleiadean fluidity of things. The longer you spend in third density, the less real fourth seems, and vice versa.'

Xylata nodded and shrugged at Thys, again as sympathetically as an Anunnaki could. 'Yes, yes, I am experiencing that same thing. And the trouble we are having, with the gaps…'

'You talked about that, at that awful apartment block…' Tarni told them. 'The Cook-staff and The Spear. You mentioned that before. But I got the impression that those things, those totems, were only blocking a room, right. But; the whole astral can't be blocked? Can it? Not like satellites can block wi-fi?'

Thys and Xylata looked at each other.

'I mean...' Tarni looked to Harding. 'Can it?'

'We'll try again,' Xylata offered. 'Shortly. It can't last!'

Tarni shook her head.

Xylata took up. 'I suspect we have discussed whatever plan we have many times, Thys Pyne. If Heather is supposed to remind us, perhaps she is a failsafe, perhaps she is the catalyst. We will soon find out, and laugh that we were here, discussing it as though it were something new and mysterious.'

Thys frowned at her; she clearly wasn't buying it.

'Such things as dreams are made of...' Thys uttered darkly.

'It will be alright, Thys Pyne. All will be well. Humanity will learn all this in due course, and change it for themselves; this amnesia does not happen elsewhere, on other worlds, with we Anunnaki. Only here, in the human colonized realm. I suspect that is the cause of it, but like all else that is a negative result of our dominant presence here, changing it will take time. Real time, hard time.'

'I know, I know,' Thys nodded testily. 'You know – I know we have done well. And I know that our victories in the astral must be reflected here on Earth, in third density, somehow. Right? But I've never really ever taken the time to examine that; not more than a look at the TV news, anyway. All I come back for are birthdays and weddings, and Christmas; and everything, always, seems the same. More of the same, and more, and more.'

Xylata grumbled. 'Yes, I know. I must admit, I haven't either. But I am sure, it will manifest. We will see it! The changes we have wrought; they must, soon, appear here! Maybe we should take a tour, one day, the two of us, after all this is over. Inspect what we have wrought, even if the wroughtings are only small for now. We should go out, and look. Examine?'

'It's true then?' Tarni nodded to herself. 'You really are still working together?'

Thys nodded. 'We always were – even when you and I were –'

She stopped herself abruptly, then snatched up her drink.

Xylata huffed. 'I may not clearly recall our plan, but I do

know this. Whenever you cross to the astral it's like the whole of the Anunnaki Earth Colony goes to Def Con One. For a time that was a good thing; we were able to use it, reverse the fear humans had for the Anunnaki, so that for once, all Anunnaki feared one human. But still, it is like we are powering up an ultimate weapon, a weapon of mass destruction, every time you arrive.' Xylata leaned forward now, and spoke somewhat more urgently. 'You said it yourself, Thys Pyne. We must let the human dreamers find the Palace without your powerful presence there to frighten them off. Let all the Anunnaki clans get used to the Palace being there; you're not just Columbus, you're also; kind of; the Anunnaki Gandhi as well.'

'What?'

Xylata seemed surprised. 'What?'

'What did you just say?'

'I just –'

'Did you just say; Anunnaki Gandhi?'

'Yes.'

Tarni raised an eyebrow. 'I wonder if that has *ever* been said before…?'

'It has. Anunnaki Gandhi. You said it, Thys Pyne. Toward the end. It is your stupid human joke!'

'I remember!' Thys slapped her forehead. 'Anunnaki Gandhi! Heather sent me a text – it said: Anunnaki Gandhi! We *did* agree upon this! That's some kind of… code word, isn't it? We need time for all the victories to stabilize, and crystallize! Yes!'

'Maybe…' Xylata seemed momentarily puzzled. 'Maybe it is a good thing that you and I cannot access the astral for a time? Maybe it is part of the plan?'

'You believe that?' Thys asked, highly doubtful.

'Have we not…?' Xylata smiled wickedly as she thought slowly. '…have we not hatched some spectacularly mad plans in our mutual history? And have they not, almost always, worked?'

'I don't know, Xylata – I don't remember!'

'Was there not some kind of – Siren… *something*?'

'I – don't – remember, Xylata! I don't remember if we had a plan, if we had others that worked, or others that didn't!'

'Then we must assume that we did have them, and they did work! And that... so will this one! Correct?'

Thys threw down her Southern Comfort in one gulp, turned back to the bar and collapsed her face back into her arms, along with a muffled cry.

'Uuh – muuh – guuuuuhd!'

'Good,' Harding bellowed.

He had been listening to every word, and been slowly tensing, but that seemed to have settled things for him.

'Now; may we please get on with the business of finding out *who just tried to kill us all?*'

'*When* did you try and contact me!?' Thys looked up again, and demanded again of Tarni. 'You say you called and called – I never got *one message*! I called you – again and again!'

'Jesus,' Harding sighed.

'Oh, sure! Sure you did!' Tarni snarled. 'I went to train – the hardest time of my life – I needed you – and you froze me out! I called and called, I came over and you weren't there; Harding said he didn't know where you were, your father said you were in Africa, but Heather said you were in China!'

'She *did*? They *did*?'

'Of course I tried to contact you, Amy! We were friends!'

Thys was obstinate, childish in the face of what the war had, apparently, cost her. She huffed, and spoke with childish vitriol.

'Well apparently there were plenty more friends where I came from!'

'No! How could you think that!' Tarni was outright shouting now. '*There wasn't anyone else, Amy! Nobody else for months; a year, even!*'

'What?!'

'We were having an affair; you were the only one! The only person in the world – *and you fucking hung me out to dry!*'

CHAPTER 87

Thys woke feeling weird.

But, waking and feeling weird wasn't unusual for her.

The air in the bedroom was hot, and humid; the windows she had opened late last night to allow the cool of the night breezes through had not been closed during the heat of the day. Now there was not a breeze to be felt.

She listened.

The air over the cove was as still as it had ever been; she could hear insects and a few birds, waves lapping on the shore and fish plonking. She guessed by the position of the sun, low in the western sky, that she had slept through most of the day with the windows open. The entire apartment would be roasting hot.

Accordingly, she was naked, spread out long on her giant bed, with no top sheets. The mattress sheet beneath her had become pulled out, and had twisted beneath her, and was damp with her sweat. She could see the top sheet on the floor, beside the bed.

None of this, however, was unusual for a summer night on the seventh floor.

Certainly though, what was usual, if not unprecedented for her was that Tarni lay beside her, also spread long, and naked, and also wet with her own glistening perspiration.

Thys blinked, and stared at Tarni again.

Yes.

Yes, she really was there.

It really had happened.

She remembered no dreams, although she was sure she would have had some. She did remember hearing the kookaburras, in the morning chorus, as the sun had started rising. Pillow talk, as the two of them had lain side by side, coming down from the massive rush they had provided each other; and very little after that.

Thys had awoken on her back, but Tarni was sleeping face down, with her head turned away, her dark brown hair splayed out, all over the pillow, like a black squid. But her hand was backwardly outstretched, and rested on Thys' stomach, with her fingertips just above her pubis mons. When Thys realised this she felt an immediate sexual change and shivered, but then Tarni rolled over and her hand slid away. Now, on her back, Tarni lay flat with one hand at her side, the other resting flat on her own stomach.

Thys rolled gently onto her side, careful not to wake her.

She stared at and examined Tarni's body in disbelief, that she should awaken beside something so spectacularly and aesthetically pleasing to her, and noticed things about her. She noticed that the sides of her huge lips and wide mouth, which were parted invitingly as she breathed smoothly but lightly, ended right above the sharply defined nadir of her cheek bones, and that this was one of the things, the angles, that made her so beautiful. Her eyelashes were abnormally long, but her ears were tiny. Her hair, as long as her own when un-bunned, seemed natural. The tight mounds of her small breasts, rising and falling, hardly went to her sides, and the muscles in her arms were pronounced even when she slept. She had a thin appendix scar which was as white as her teeth. Her public hair was fine and short and tightly curled. Her vulva, which last night Thys had practically studied, charted and navigated over the edge of the world, was on the exterior a much darker brown than the rest of her pretty much all-over light mocha pigment; the closest match was the natural darkness under her eyes, and her nipples, which reminded Thys of the buttons of cooking chocolate she had found so bitterly delicious as a child. But last night, Thys now recalled, once the smooth, dark lips had been parted, and had flushed, she had found an almost shocking-pink skin within; hidden now to all but her memory as she lay there, her heartbeat increasing, as her new lover's body seemed to glisten, if not actually glow, in the morning sun. As Thys recalled the pressure of Tarni's trembling thighs against her cheeks, her face a slobbering, bittersweet mess, Tarni's eyes opened, and she looked over.

Black, and liquid-gold streaks.

Tarni hummed to herself, lightly, innocently, obviously pleased, if not delighted to have awoken where she had. Thys watched as she rubbed the sleep out of her eyes and rolled onto her side as well, facing her, her head propped up on her elbow. They smiled at each other. She had never seen Tarni smile so broadly; it seemed to take up fully two fifths of her face.

'I have a big smile in the morning, don't I?'

Her eyes flashed.

'You have a big smile, regardless of when. I've just never really seen you use it.'

Tarni reached over and gently put a hand on the raised curve of Thys's hip, then ran it back and forth.

'Your skin is so pale; actually pink and white. I've never really seen skin like that up close.'

Thys didn't know what to say.

'Is this okay?' Tarni asked, her hand moving up, under her rib.

Thys leaned over and kissed her.

The kiss lasted until the light had almost gone on a hot, clear, sun-drenched day, and into the bathroom, and under the shower, and paused for enough time so they could collect themselves, and order food, then resumed as they took the elevator down to the lobby, wearing the same dresses they had removed from each other's bodies last night, then paused again as they found themselves bang on time for the pizza delivery.

The kiss hovered, secretly, as they giggled and told Zeke, girlishly, that they were going skinny dipping, and long enough for Zeke to assure them that with their permission he would turn off the security cameras, but that nobody would get past him.

Almost as soon as they were through the lobby and out of the back double-doors, the kiss resumed as they stood on the lawn a few minutes, then broke again as Thys took Tarni's hand and somehow, without even thinking, ran with her, without incident and without accident, under the lemon scented gum and down the complicated, rocky path to the secret inlet beach, squealing and giggling like girls all the way, until they ran down the last stretch of dirt path onto the glowing white sand below.

They left the pizza and the Coke and the garlic bread in the bushes by the shore and stripped off their dresses and ran again, straight across the sand, leaping over the low waves and splashing straight into the sea.

They embraced in the water, which was warm on the surface but cooler beneath, and were kissing again as they staggered down, deeper and further out, with the salt of the seawater strong on their tongues and in their mouths, lapping against them as they began to feel a stronger, less playful desire for a more passionate connection rise from their loins and into their hearts once again; not as anxious as last night, but urgent and eager all the same.

They could each feel the rocks and the seaweed between their toes, the water bobbing under their arms, with each having raised one arm to the back of the other's head, with the other arm wrapped around the other's back. Their feet found purchase in the sand, and they held still as they each intertwined their legs and pressed themselves into each other, moving their hips, tightening their embrace. The water still lapped at their shoulders as they kept kissing and kissing, as each felt the other's labia part as they widened their stance and began to slide against each other, and press harder; and there was the groove, the mutual rhythm. Each felt the other tighten and relax against the other's thigh, squeeze and push, and tighten and shudder, until Thys felt herself call out, her open mouth crying into Tarni's open mouth. Her knees gave out as Tarni's knees came involuntarily up, wrapping around her back, and there was nothing left to support them as Thys fell backwards and they were submerged, Tarni shaking, her head buried into Thys's breast, pulsing and pulsing as Thys floated down and felt the sand on her back, her own body only just calming; allowing it, descending, then pushing gently, with Tarni in her arms, back up to the surface.

They gasped and released, breathing heavily, their hearts still pounding as they came splashing back up together and kissed again. They had drifted out a little more now, with the soft pull of the underwater tides, and once they had righted themselves had found that while they could still hold each other's forearms, it was now more for balance as the water lapped just under their chins.

They stared at each other a while, over the water between them.

They laughed playfully, but also with surprise at how powerful the experience had been; shocking in a way that they had both just lost-it to that extreme. They heard the kookaburras again, having their last laugh, as the final glow of the sunset finally vanished.

Then abruptly, they both stopped laughing.

A crow called.

Thys felt a familiar nausea in her gut.

Tarni's face squirmed as well.

'Seriously?' Thys demanded, of no-one in particular.

'You too?' Tarni asked, wincing.

'Mine's not due – at least another few days.'

'Mine neither – a week.'

In the darkness Thys saw the glistening of her menstrual blood reach the top of the water before her.

'Jesus,' Thys groaned.

'You mean Mary,' Tarni sighed.

'But – how? Why would we…? And in synch like this?'

The crow called out again.

Rah! Rah!

Suddenly Thys saw an intense orange light strike from behind the top of the cliff at the back of the cove, beaming like a halo over the rocky amphitheater wall, striking the line of tall eucalyptus gums into stark silhouettes.

Tarni first saw the fiery light in Thys' widening eyes, then turned as well.

'What is that – a bushfire?' Tarni panted.

She backed away involuntarily and bumped into Thys; her hands came up and Thys found herself embracing Tarni from behind as her buttocks rested neatly into her lap, and Tarni floated, still, accepting the embrace.

The light grew more intense, slowly revealing over the course of a few awestruck minutes the crest of an enormous harvest moon; orange as the fruit, and as wide as the cove itself.

A Blood Moon.

As it continued to rise, the orange flare lit the pier, making the old wood look like new copper, making the sand of the beach look apricot, and the water look like fiery steel and chrome. As the Blood Moon continued to reveal itself; (herself, many would say) they saw her surface in magnificently, almost impossibly magnified detail.

'Nobody really knows for sure what does that...' Tarni whispered. '...there are theories; it's one of those things.'

She turned sideways and gently kissed Thys, rubbing her buttocks up and down. There was crimson in the water, along with the fire, as they faced each other again, realising that something, maybe something sacred, something even divine, was happening, and again they mutually sensed and delighted in the passionate energies that the event seemed to provide; they courted and celebrated those energies, eroticizing them and made them work through their bodies, with the touch of their lips, the pulse of their hearts, and the stroking penetration of their fingertips.

'Mary, Mary, Mary...' Tarni gasped, her head upturned, as Thys made her come again, a little time later; she was beginning to understand now, how to make it happen, what she liked, how to control it. It was coming very easily to her, how to...

Control *her*...?

Thys dismissed the thought; lovers sometimes took turns in controlling each other, it was part of it, all lovers knew that. Yet she was already picking up on what did it for her, already across the moves, already enjoying the fact that she knew… she could read her, in her heart, and loins, and mind, in a non-invasive way. She was realising that, as the power was accepted, that Tarni was allowing it; allowing her, accepting the manipulation in return for the –

'Mary, Mother…'

As she came again.

'…mother, mother*fucker*…'

She cringed and squeezed her legs so tight around Thys that she almost lost balance again in the sand, trembling with an open mouth, then sighing, almost chuckling as she embraced Thys again.

'Who *are you*?' Thys was panting, feeling the energy as well. 'You *know*. You know, *don't you*?'

Tarni's eyes seemed distant, but connected to her.

'Amy, I think we're activating…'

'We're activating… what?'

'Us.' Tarni released her arms from around Thys' neck. 'Our union, and –'

'Really? You and me? Are… doing this?'

'I know these energies. I didn't know you did too.'

'I don't know that I…'

Tarni seemed high now, happy. 'But I suppose, this is a special place. Yelina said that not just anyone could stay here; and hardly anyone could actually sign a contract, without force.'

'I didn't force anyone!'

'I know; that's the point.' Tarni kissed her again. 'I think she chose you to guard this place, and you have chosen me. And now, we're sort of staking our claim on it, in the mystic… primal…'

Tarni rubbed her lips against her, almost teasing.

'…sacred feminine sense…'

Thys sensed it and became suddenly, extremely turned on.

They were about to kiss again, when Thys saw something over Tarni's shoulder.

'Look.'

Tarni looked back to shore.

There was a line of people, standing there, at the edge of the bushes, along the shore.

Watching.

CHAPTER 88

'What do you mean…?' Thys demanded, her arms still folded over Harding's bar, almost softly. 'I hung you out to dry?'

Thys was starting to remember more now, and she could see that Tarni was remembering as well. It was not that she had forgotten what had happened, not in the same way that she had forgotten what seemed like her last bunch of time in the astral, and whatever half-assed plan they had concocted.

In fact, Thys had privately reminisced over her weekend with Tarni, quite often since.

It was just that; she had not done that, laid back and recalled it, not vividly, in some time.

Thys frowned, frustrated.

'…I went back to the war – the astral – I tried to tell you…'

The spark of angry golden fire was returning to Tarni's eyes as she stared across the bar at her. Four years, Thys thought.

If they had stayed together… what might have passed between them in that time?

With *that* passion between them?

Then: wait; what *had* passed between them, that had intercepted their communiqués?

Thys looked to her, starting to see.

But Tarni just gave her daggers, and wouldn't respond.

If they had gone on, would she still be seeing her three men; the same three…?

Jesus Christ, the same three she had been seeing (and thinking about starting to see) back then?

But – they were okay.

They were important, too.

But who had stopped her, her and Tarni, from being…?

'What's happened here?' Thys demanded, of no-one in particular. 'And for fuck's sake – why!?'

Xylata remained exasperated. 'Thys Pyne; you must snap out of this! Witch woman; you as well! Be like your human Gandhi Man, Thys Pyne! Keep karma!'

'Seriously?' Tarni turned to her, frowning deeply. 'Gandhi Man?'

Harding laughed, despite himself.

Xylata continued. 'You have to keep being like him, Thys Pyne, like the other leaders who have successfully seen off occupation by a dominant force. You must remember that this is a war of spirit, not of flesh. True, some of our enemies have been dispersed, and some killed, as they would be in one of your flesh wars; like those idiot witches we just faced. And remember, Anunnaki who are killed on this insane world, reincarnate on this insane world, back into the pain and madness of the Earth Karma Forge that they helped to maintain; disgraced, shamed and shocked, and forced to make a radical reassessment of what they believed to be their status, or reality. This may, or will, surely, bring change to my people. But you must now exhibit pause, or grace, to show them that things have changed, and allow them room to accommodate change, to realise that things will never be the same, and allow them time to process this.'

'To process; not to assess?' Thys asked worriedly. 'Not to re-assess?'

'Or regroup?' Harding chimed in.

'No,' Xylata seemed adamant. 'The things you have done, we have done, cannot be reversed. I may not remember them clearly, but I know that as clearly as I know that we have achieved a truce. This will not be undone – not by the Draco, not by any of the Anunnaki clans. Certainly not the Cheneks or the Pshola or the Xyntyx. You are the Anunnaki Gandhi; Heather knows, and will remind us!'

Xylata turned to Harding, as though he were the only other sane member of the quartet.

'But this attack tonight; I agree with you Harding; it is very suspicious. We must all remember that there was once a terrible power in that place. Those witches may be drawing power somehow from the trapped Orion Agents.' Xylata growled. 'They might even have been trying to release them, if they're stupid enough, which judging by their exhibition tonight, I would assume that they are.'

Thys responded. 'Xylata, maybe it's the Orion Agents, or the Orion Renegades themselves who are doing this? Out for revenge? Could they be in league somehow with these witches? Controlling them? The Renegades tried to stop Pan, and the Pandora Sequence itself; you think they just gave up?'

Tarni was watching them all, listening carefully as Thys proceeded.

'Dad was really concerned about this; just after the Quake, for about a year. He kind of got over it, but he was onto something. Uncle Bo talked him down, but I could tell; he was concerned as well. That the Satanic Thing did what it did, opened the permanent portals through the astral planes, deliberately; either by design, or just to cause chaos. Maybe... this is the start?'

'The start of what?' Tarni demanded.

'Fucking Enochian-zombies and Mad Monks! Shutting down the wi-fi; shutting down access to the astral plane! Satanic Shenanigans! Who fucking knows!? Chaos; pure and simple!'

Harding frowned and turned to Thys.

'But, surely things stabilized here? Your father and Heather petitioned the Elohim, and, by all accounts, they stepped in and prevented the earthquake from killing the entire population of Los Angeles? The Renegades lost, and chaos was prevented. Is that not what happened? Haven't they shared that story over enough wine, enough times with us?'

'In a way, everybody won,' Xylata nodded. 'At least, they got what they wanted. The Orion Renegades can handle change in small orderly increments, so long as the balance is restored... they got their stability. And from what I understand, the Elohim simply – moved everybody out of harm's way, en masse, during the quake.'

'What you're talking about; that's what the legends say...' Tarni whispered, almost to herself.

'Legends!' Harding scoffed. 'We were all there – well, most of us, for most of it. I was betrayed by my friends, transported through time, blown up, faced up to Satan with Byford and his men, and watched a garden destroy a mansion. But I met Gabrielle Fenwick, so, it all evened out.' He remembered something else important. 'Her Pan friends shot me in the head, though...' He nodded at Thys. ' – on a boat!'

Thys made a face at him...but that; it made her remember something. Something she had not really thought for a long time, since...

'Satan again?' Tarni enquired edgily.

Harding shrugged. 'You think that's the connection with these witches?'

Tarni shook it off, as though he's just handed her a live slug from the garden.

'I *really* wish you would all stop calling them *witches*,' Tarni snapped. 'Those creatures are earth demons, or earth devils, *at best...*'

'Earth demons?' Xylata asked. 'There are such things?'

'There are,' Thys confirmed quietly.

Tarni was trying to focus. '...maybe they are being driven by some kind of djinn creatures, but they are essentially neutral. And... not in a pack like this. Unless...? No. No; these are the drak earth spirits; possessing drug-addled fools with no capacity for hope remaining, who have burned out their lives through their self-abuse. They seek out the hopeless; the tragic people who have burned all their bridges, lost as self-worth, with near-dead, cul-de-sac souls; these people do not take much persuasion to surrender their bodies voluntarily.' She sneered, looking up again at the others, one by one. 'The things that *possess* them however, are old and malevolent; but they are also foolish and grasping, and – *stupid*. But they have been here forever and they cannot be killed, and they are relentless.'

'I remember,' Thys uttered.

'You do not remember,' Tarni spoke clearly and bitterly, leaning toward her slowly, '*anything*.'

Xylata hummed awkwardly.

'Wicca child, how do we fight them?'

'Those people we faced tonight…' Tarni began. She sighed. '…I've heard them called wraiths. You just have to keep repelling them. The people they possess are better off dead and cast back into the reincarnation cycle. But the things that possess them; like most things, when you destroy their form on one plane, they revert to another, or back to source. These things go back down deep into the Inner Earth. You repel them, they have to work their way back. It takes time.'

'How many are there?'

'Legion. Isn't that what the Bible says? Enough so they'll never run out. And I would never turn my back on them, even if they are now buried under the rubble of a ruined mansion. I was – angry when I spoke before, but the people who use Enochian magic for evil recruit the lowly, the ruined and despairing, those who have truly abandoned all hope; often junkies near death, or homeless people with severe, irreversible emotional disorders, all kinds of broken people who have slipped through the cracks and have no advocates remaining. Many of them are people who should already be…'

Thys could tell she didn't like to say this.

'…should have been allowed to pass, but are holding on, through hate or addiction or pure will, even base genetic strength. And these practitioners of evil find them and offer them – a last chance. Nothing about it is good, in any sense of the word. But what it becomes is a "Living Hell"…'

Thys flinched, Tarni noticed.

'…worse than the one they were already in.'

'Jesus…' Harding uttered.

'They become possessed by the malevolent energies of the Inner Earth, and the creatures of malevolence that live here, on this planet, deep below in second density, who have never been human but are always trying to get up here and possess us, to feel and experience again, in the basest, crudest fashions… there are many different manifestations of these creatures; there are types of djinn who are playful, or tricksters, or who are wise and helpful; but those pitiless ones, those that possess these hopeless wraiths are the lowliest; the grunts, you might say. Just barely intelligent malevolence, mean spirits distilled and personified. Some say that the old, Biblical Demons are the personification of the higher Inner Earth forces; the more evolved second density creatures of darkness, and they can control them; as we would train a pack of attack dogs. Some say the old, Abrahamic names; like Beelzebub and Azazel… are one and the same, all referencing different aspects of one being. But others say; there are many of them still, major demons controlling different legions of creatures; these low things and others, other creatures... to whatever purpose their wills may turn.'

Tarni turned to Thys.

She looked sad, but proud.

'But we've met them before, haven't we Amy? It was our last meeting that inspired my quest; and I haven't stopped looking since.'

CHAPTER 89

Surprisingly, Tarni walked forward in the water, staring defiantly at the people on the shore. She pushed her long, black, curly wet hair back from her face as Thys watched her shoulder blades break the surface of the glistening ocean cove, as the water rippled down the skin of her back, making her entire form shine with a chrome-like ferocity in the harvest moonlight.

Then she stopped, the water lapping at her hips, and turned back at Thys with a puzzled expression. Her mouth was dead straight, her high forehead in a deep frown, her black nipples erect, with her chest puffed-out and her shoulders back and tense in an undeniably aggressive stance.

'Are they ghosts?' Thys demanded.

Tarni turned back.

Thys stayed where she was; she was not as comfortable in her skin, not with strangers, and certainly not with… well, if they weren't ghosts, they were doing a good impression.

'Or; some kind of shadow beings maybe…?'

'The blood…' Tarni uttered. '…we're being set up… we're being used…'

'Used? For what?'

Tarni turned back to her. 'My grandmother is very old. Older than anyone. My mother told me…' Then she turned to the shore again, thinking. Thys moved a little closer toward her; the water and the night air remained warm, but she still felt weird about exposing herself. Tarni seemed to sense this and walked backwards to her, and the two of them backed off a little more, again standing together with the ocean up to their shoulders, modesty preserved.

She felt Tarni reach out and they held hands beneath the

surface.

'I know Yelina's not normal,' Tarni uttered. 'You father and Heather come and go, without… they don't travel. They don't leave a trace. Neither do you. I know it's called gapping. I know there's a network of lime-green names; I'm the one who set it up; I'm on your side of things, but I'm new. I think that's why Yelina sent me to your father, to find you. So we could find this out together. Do you know what those people are?'

Thys was suddenly feeling quite helpless; as though she had been conspired against on several levels. 'No. But instinctively, I think you're right about our… families. Although… I think they'd be surprised to learn that we… hit it off this well.'

Tarni hummed. It was a laugh of sorts, albeit grim.

'The Moon…'

They looked up; the illusion had ended and the harvest moon was normal sized, in brilliant relief before the Milky Way.

'…and the blood. This is magic. What do they want?'

'I've seen magic,' Thys confessed. 'Very strong magic. And I live half my time in the astral plane. This isn't anything I can't deal wi –'

A grey fin broke the surface of the water about six feet in front of them.

'The blood,' Thys gasped. 'Take my hand.'

Tarni looked at her. 'I have.'

'There is no need to flee.'

They spun about.

The feminine tones were well-modulated, and neutral; if veering toward condescension.

'Your blood-magic was foolish, but I arrived here in time. These hunters respond to me.'

Indeed, there was a woman in the water behind them, but for some reason they couldn't see who she was. Only her head and shoulders were above the water, as though mirroring them, and her wet skin seemed to reflect the moonlight, making her features impossible to discern.

'Why would you even consider it…? Here?'

'We're just friends,' Thys spluttered.

'Are we?' Tarni asked, surprised.

'I – sex friends,' she quickly corrected.

'What does that even mean?' Tarni guffawed.

'Not that,' the woman interjected. 'The blood-sex-magic. In a place like this…?'

Thys began. 'We didn't…'

'We were lured here…' Tarni complained.

'She is the lure.' The newcomer nodded at Thys. 'Like a Siren. Surely you can see that?'

The woman was coming into greater focus now; she seemed young, yet spoke with great confidence.

A shark fin broke the surface behind her, arced and then re-submerged; Thys wasn't sure if it was the same shark, but it had definitely not been a dolphin. She was starting to feel frightened. Under the water, Tarni squeezed her hand as she realised that she had involuntarily squeezed Tarni's hand very tight.

The woman in the water before them glided forward, maybe half a foot.

'She is human, but she is from the higher plane you call astral; I know almost nothing of this. But you, you are human but you are from… where I am from. Are you not? Perhaps I know your tribe? Your blood is Inner Earth; deeper even than mine. Who are you? Why do you come here to do blood-sex-magic? Answer truthfully and I will do my best to ensure that you remain living.'

Thys stared, and tried to fit – whatever the woman was – into her frame of reference, so that she could determine whether or not to trust her; the shark fin almost instantly arced up, breaking the surface between them this time, as though to distract her and prevent this. She felt the strong flow of water that the shark had created in its wake; it billowed right into her hips, into her loins.

'I do not know what you are…' The woman stared at Thys. 'Is it possible that…?' She turned suddenly at stared out at the back of the cove, in front of Thys's tower. There were now figures standing there as well; along the beach, along the pier, and on the sand beneath it, at the edge of the water.

Immediately to their left, across the water, the seventh floor of the Sirianapartments lit up; all of the rooms at once.

The sea woman submerged, then re-emerged on the other side of them, so fast Thys would have not thought it possible.

She was staring up at the apartment.

'Now we have higher planes descending…?'

It sounded like a confounding nuisance.

There was a rumbling and the water shook; Thys saw the shark's dorsal fin momentarily surface as it shot away, out toward open sea, then two more, answering her question, the question she had not wanted to ask, as to their number. The whole bay was vibrating; on the beach, the people, now behind them, were on their knees. Those on and around the pier were resisting, trying to stay on their feet, but wobbling and falling and looking ridiculous.

'Is it an earthquake?' Tarni demanded, releasing Thys's hand as they both anxiously tied to tread water.

'Sirians…!' Thys informed her.

As they watched, the light from the sixth-floor apartment seemed to extend beyond the building itself, stretching out in crystalline planes, as though outwardly replicating the floor space within the apartment in the sky around it.

'That's…' Tarni gasped.

'Yeah…' Thys grumbled. 'It might look amazing…'

'But…?'

'But wait and see.'

They kept watching as three figures stepped out, into thin air, walking on the light plane, and stared down. They were dressed in tight robes of as many variants of pale blue as Thys had ever seen; then they fanned out, evenly spaced along the edge of the light plane as another Sirian, a woman, came out and stared down as well. The three others moved in a little more closely around her, flanking her respectfully, perhaps ever cautiously.

The water woman stopped looking at the spectacle and turned

to Thys.

'You own this bay in third density? Who are you?'

'I do, I suppose, in a way; my father owns a… corporation called Cleverco…'

'No, Thys, your own company own this, remember? You lease it to yourself, it's not Cleverco.'

'Oh! I never really…'

'Third density had strange ways, but not respecting them brings consequences; this bay was embraced within a dark – corporation?'

'Olivera?'

'Yes. But by the ritual you have performed you have claimed it as a place of loving emotion and residence, or privacy and performance. If this is not your intent, you should leave now.'

'Leave?'

'And never return. If this has been a mistake, then that may be the only way the wraith coven will allow you to leave. Is your clan name; Cleverco?'

'No…' Thys was shaking now. 'It's Pyne. My name is Amethyst Pyne, and this is… this my lover, Tarni Lavé.'

Tarni's fingers released her hand and her fingertips traced affectionately up the inside of her lower arm, then back down to re-grasp her hand.

Thys nodded to the pier. 'I think those people, the ones who are not wraiths, are Anunnaki, possessing human bodies. Are you familiar with them?'

The water woman did not look pleased. 'I understand your meaning. But I do not understand how to fight astral beings. Only those of my plane, and humans.'

'Are you a mermaid?'

'No.' She sounded very definite.

'Okay.'

'Can you help us get out of this?' Tarni asked.

'Out of the water? But; you must not leave the water.'

'No; out of this… mess?'

'You do not want to extricate yourself from this mess, as you call it.'

'We don't?'

'No.'

'Umm. What do we want then?'

'You want to go deeper into it.'

Thys understood. 'Claim my cove. My home?'

'Yes; that building with the shining ones from the higher planes of light; it is not a building, as yours is. It is not designed for living, for occupation. It is an observation post. Like one of your lighthouses, but for alien species, of – less density? It has also changed – corporations, recently. The fifth and sixth dimensionals, and those above; they use it, to watch you.'

'The Pleiadeans too?'

'Never at the same time however. There seems to be an uneasy truce. This whole bay is in flux, and there are other dimensional entities who do not wish it to change. They would fight anyone who comes here; to do so.'

'I understand,' Thys nodded.

'I think I do…' Tarni agreed.

'But what about you?' Thys asked.

'We would prefer a change of human influence over the area. I hold some influence, but… I understand you could not consult us if you did not know we existed… but, some time to prepare, for a challenge of this level, would have been advised.'

'Sorry.'

'You really did not intend?'

'No – well, maybe later, but – no.'

'Then why did you leave the windows of your home open while you sexed? That is a well known claim ritual; combined with the blood?'

It was starting to get frustrating. 'Yelina must have known.'

'Who?' The woman asked.

'Yelina.'

'That is the human name for – ' She looked at Yelina's block.

Thys and Tarni glanced too; in the moonlight, it looked like a massive stone monolith, standing before a series of cave-apartments that had been carved into the face of the cliff behind it... all around to the very back of the cove.

'She's...' Tarni just stared at the structure. '...my – great, great, great grandmother. *Is that really there?*'

Thys looked away from the caves, to Tarni, aghast. 'Yelina's really your *great* – what grandmother?'

'Great, great, several times, but yeah. My actual grandmother – she's as old as the hills.'

'Literally!'

Thys and Tarni gasped. A pulse had run through the water, exciting their nerves and invigorating their bodies.

'I apologize,' the not-mermaid stated calmly.

'Don't...' Tarni purred, smiling a little.

'I am calling allies.'

She raised her hands to the surface of the water. They too were silvery, almost like mercury, and somehow disguised in the moonlight.

'You are Thys and you are Tarni. I am Seysh.'

Through the shimmering disguise, they could see she had irises of a deep, rich violet.

Seysh's hands remained flat, just above the surface crests of the undulating water. Thys wasn't sure; it was almost as though she were royalty, in that, if she had been wearing rings, Thys might have felt compelled to bob over and kiss them. She stared into the deep-violet eyes; even in the astral, she hadn't seen anything quite like this.

She was new to her.

This ocean woman, Seysh, was somehow... *all* new to her.

Then she realised, as Tarni did; it was a handshake offer.

She was being friendly.

They each took her hand and, with Thys and Tarni's hands still linked beneath, for a moment the three of them became a triad, linked within the fluidity of the cove.

Seysh smiled.

'This is good. Now, here.'

Her hands went underwater and they seemed to go to her waist. Then she raised them again and there was a loose, glistening-silver belt in each hand; an offering.

'Place these around your hips; they are called shiftrielles. I will not hold you to the bargain that they represent within our culture; wear them as garments.'

Thys was beginning to understand; she knew this at least from the astral, and her father had stated it many times; but she had not experienced much of it in her actual 'home density'. It was; when someone was awakened, or enlightened, or became in some other manner embroiled within other densities and dimensions, symbols and symbolic actions became incredibly important.

A cigar was never just a cigar.

And a silver belt was never just a silver belt.

Thys accepted, and lowered the belt toward her waist. Just as she was realising that the silver garment was a closed loop, it seemed to slip through her fingers, and settle softly but tightly about her waist, all of its own accord. Then she was covered, wrist to ankle, up to her neck, with a thin layer, like a wetsuit, that seemed to be the general color of her skin.

It had just happened; simply manifested.

It felt amazing, indeed, just like a second skin; a 'second density' skin maybe?

'Come, now – advance. We must show them you have aligned with me.'

Seysh turned and glided toward the shore; Thys and Tarni walked behind her until Seysh finally stood and placed her hands on her hips. As Thys came up behind her, she saw that Tarni had experienced the same; the color of her wetsuit seemed, like the one Thys wore, to be some kind of blend of all the subtle differences of pigment, from all over her body, evening out to become one startlingly aesthetic tone that enhanced almost every aspect of her physiognomy.

They stood just behind Seysh; she was a clear foot shorter than both of them, but still shimmering in the mercurial moonlight, so they could not get a clear fix on her.

Both of them had the silver belts still, resting easily over their hips.

'This is as I was worried about.'

'What?'

Seysh flicked her violet eyes back at Thys.

'They're not backing off.' She glanced at the dock. 'Your reptiles remain standing ground also.' She looked up at the Sirians, still observing like Roman rulers, staring down at the gladiatorial pits.

'They want a fight.'

'I'm accustomed to fighting in the astral. I've been leading a campaign against the Anunnaki there for nearly two years.'

Tarni stared at her. 'You *really have?*'

Thys gave her a sharp nod. 'Those wankers on the pier probably see this as a chance to take me out; here, in third density. Usually that would be against the rules, it would mean death for them regardless. But seeing that me and Tarni seem to have been used... or let's say *deployed* here, and have inadvertently initiated a second density blood ritual... I think it's pretty much open season somehow.'

'I am afraid that this seems is correct,' Seysh sighed. 'This is the flux I spoke of. What you have done is not unlike... I know the images, I have seen people do it, on this beach as a matter of fact, but... the words escape me.'

Tarni growled, grim.

'It's like we've taken a Ouija board to a cemetery and told the ghosts we're moving in. Then fucked all night in a crypt for good measure.'

Thys gasped. 'Bloody hell, Tarni!'

'That is not what I was thinking; but I sense she is correct, at least within the sense of boldness, within the imagery, if not quite the extent of the profanity.' She gave Thys a look to suggest that, even in the dire circumstances before them, Tarni had perhaps been a tad over-dramatic. 'But regardless, we must see to it that this ritual ends well, in your favour, and mine. This is a place of peace; strong third density peacemakers should reside here, and that has not been so, for too long.'

They sensed disruption from above; there were four women now. Two were tall and slender, in the pale blue robes, while the other two were average height and curvy, with robes still pale blue, but with sapphire accessories. Three more men had also joined the women; dressed in pale tangerine, they all seemed to be arguing. One of the curvy women broke off, away from the shouting, and stared down directly at them, as though apologetic.

Sirians were highly telepathic, Thys recalled.

《 *Do it* 》 she heard from above 《 *do what you are going to do – now!* 》

For whatever reason, this Sirian seemed to favor them.

〖 *Daughter!* 〗

Even as others decidedly did not.

Most of the others began shouting at her again...

...*the daughter...*

...and she was recalled into the verbal melee, which only seemed to accentuate as she returned.

Returned to: ?

Oh Goddess it was her! And they were all watching... from one of those timespace installation windows... from The Inter –

《 *Mi – !* 》

A terrible popping crack shattered everything.

Something so ordinarily horrifying had happened, that it was, in fact, when contrasted against the almost magical, metaphysical otherness that surrounded them, quite extraordinary.

Somebody had fired a gun.

Thys felt, then heard the bullet whistle past her ear.

Paramatta.

She didn't know which direction it had come from; the shot had echoed around the cove so thoroughly. Then another, then another, making everyone jolt each time. Even the Intersection balcony seemed to flash and fizzle for just a quick second.

'Fuck!' Tarni cried out. 'That went straight – !'

Seysh grasped a handful of water and threw it toward the pier.

The water skipped across the surface of the cove, becoming something solid along the way, then decapitated a man standing at the end of the pier. He and his gun, and his head, all fell separately into water and sunk.

'Screw this,' Thys spat.

She stared up at the moon, still looming, still bright and larger than life. It was an excellent channel for astral energies and she immediately called some down, angrily demanding that a portal open instantly. She hadn't realised that her command of the fourth dimensional energies had become so strong until exactly that moment; the water in the cove seemed to rise suddenly above their heads, then several feet higher. It was a strange, thick kind of fog, a misty ether that Thys had commanded into being, to extend up from the water and –

'Are you doing this?' Tarni demanded.

Opal glittered down from the Sirian tower; they seemed outraged but Thys did not care, she simply summoned and directed it. Commanding all that power, Thys thrust her hands into the third density water, then grit her teeth and, bracing her arms, thrust them out again, toward the pier. An inordinate, disproportionate amount of water splashed up and arose before her as she completed the gesture, then she did it again, and then a third time. As the water rose, the fog seemed to envelope it, slamming down and condensing, lifting it and pushing the water in, toward the pier, until it had become three huge tsunami waves, so high and wide that they could not see past them.

There was screaming from the peer, the kind associated with terror and flight, but instantly there was heat from the beach; three of the people there were advancing, already ankle-deep into the cove, and breathing dragon-like fire, projected in long streams from their mouths, jetting out at them across the ocean.

'Drop!' Seysh cried out.

Thys plunged down, holding her breath as the air above glowed white-orange, and the ocean around seemed to instantly heat, and increase, already at a too-hot bath level when the fire vanished. She pushed herself backwards and resurfaced, seeing Tarni do exactly the same, then they plunged under again as more fire spat out from the demonic human flamethrower.

Thys got the sense of Seysh kicking off, towards the now-steadily approaching fire-demons, then she was out of breath and up again, spluttering, aware perhaps that one of her golden locks had been singed, and coughing sea water.

Her eyes stung from the salt and sand but she saw that Tarni was okay, and still beside her in the water. She also saw ahead as Seysh glided at the three men like a stingray, swirling in the water beneath them as they fell, shrieking, one by one, cut off at the ankles and bleeding out in agony. The ocean around them filled with blood, then Seysh was on her feet, glistening mercury, and shouting back at them.

'Run! To the shore!'

Then she dispatched the wraiths, one by one, with a long silver dagger, made of some kind of metallic ice, impaling it methodically through the tops of each of their skulls.

Thys and Tarni began to trudge through the sand, into the blood that was washing back toward them, vaguely aware that the three tsunami waves had hit the shore to their left, and were pounding into the trees and foliage along the shoreline.

'I won't be able to hold them!'

They knew Seysh was not talking about the demonic agents, but what was fast approaching in the water behind them.

The sound of crashing of waves on the pier snapped at Thys; reminded her of her abilities, still not second nature in third density. She grabbed Tarni around the waist and summoned down what remained of the foggy astral ether, still lingering in the air around them, commanding it psychically to impact the water before them. The wave of energy slammed down and parted the remaining distance to the shore with a giant, pounding splash, throwing up sand and seaweed and rocks, but also curtailing the path, they were horrified to see, of a shark, perhaps the same shark that Seysh had protected them from not a few minutes ago, that had just circled about with open jaws to savage them. The shark was flung into the air and crashed back down on its back, flailing, then vanished, flicking itself over and darting out into the water as the two women staggered onto the shore, past its vanishing tail fin, with Seysh standing before the remaining ten-or-so demonically possessed assailants, all with red eyes and snarling yellow teeth.

Thys was disgusted and appalled and pitied them; they were clearly veteran meth-heads, addicts far too long gone, who had sold their souls, the remainder of what would have been their sad and wasted lives, for… what?

Power?

Was this power?

They were empty and possessed. Just vessels. Was it just another video game, more television, the ultimate virtual reality to go out on? Drug free but still burning out on killing and maiming; and – well, pure evil?

Her pity did not last long as they attacked, the first man coming at her with fierce, hateful abandon, but falling as Seysh sliced him down with her ice-metal sword. Thys remembered then, to her horror, that although she had been trained to shoot, years ago now, she still had no idea how to actually guide her body through face-to-face combat, and fight outside of the astral.

She backed off, startled by the realisation, and tried to reummon astral energy; opal or dreama, or anything, but through the panic, something she had become totally unaccustomed toward over the past years, she forgot how, and lost the instinct entirely.

Tarni danced forward on the sand and smacked one woman in the face, biff-bang, like a boxer, and Thys saw instantly that she had been trained.

Of course, she thought, *the muscles in her arms!*

Then she proceeded to kick box her way across the beach, taking out two, then three and four of the demon people, as Seysh slayed another two. Another spat fire at Tarni but she ducked and rolled in the sand, and the flames passed her completely; after which, the ice sword slammed through the thing's open mouth. The others turned as some insane collective courage simultaneously broke within them, and they fled, with just a few of their number remaining, down the beach, into the trees and were gone.

Thys spun about; the sharks were devouring the corpses of the three that Seysh had hobbled, the water frothing and erupting in a feeding frenzy that for some awful reason excited her more than appalled her. She had never seen anything like it, nothing so utterly primal and real.

'You okay?' Tarni demanded, her face covered in sweat, the strange wetsuit glistening.

Seysh, displaying surprising strength, was taking the corpses of her four victims along the beach and throwing them into the frenzy as more sharks arrived; there had to be a dozen or more now. Then there were more flapping, savage sharks, and body parts, than there was water.

Thys couldn't stop watching.

'Thus perish interlopers...' Seysh remarked, then, if she read her correctly, gave a kind of wry huff and looked back at Thys, almost candidly. '...something my sister would say.'

One of the four meth-heads Tarni had knocked out awoke and screamed, and kept screaming.

'Go!' Tarni shouted.

She got up and ran, then another got up and groggily followed her with a trail of blood. Two remained there, unconscious.

Thys looked up to the Intersection balcony.

The Sirians stared down.

There were just two men and the two taller, slender women remaining. She had no idea what their expressions were and made no effort to perceive, nor receive their thoughts.

Had it been Misha?

Had Misha's daughter been chastised, or had Misha's father spoken in the scalding tone?

Regardless, whoever she was; the shorter, curvier one who had warned her, been her ally, was gone.

'You will allow these two their lives?' Seysh asked Tarni.

'Let them wake on the beach and remember; their kind will think twice about returning.'

Thys looked back at her. She was surprised at how she'd said it, as though responding naturally to Seysh in her stilted, pseudo-Middle Earth manner. It was kind of a turn-on, to hear her speak like that, after the fighting skills she'd just displayed.

Thys turned back and raised a middle digit to the Sirians.

'This beach is mine!'

The lights went out.

The Sirians were gone, just like that.

'Mine, you fucking *watchers*!'

She turned back and saw that Tarni and Seysh were staring at her; there was so much adrenalin in the air, she couldn't tell what the hell they were thinking.

Seysh nodded to herself.

She walked forward and stood directly in front of Thys, shimmering mercury with deep violet eyes, and slipped the shiftrielle from her. Thys stood naked on the beach and didn't care. Then she went to Tarni and did the same. She held the two silver belts up before her and nodded, then turned toward the water, apparently ready to leave without another word.

Then Seysh turned back.

Beneath her shimmering cloak, they both thought they detected a strange, satisfied smile.

'No. Keep these, you have earned them. But do not go about in them; not in your world; they must be reserved for battle, and for battle only.'

Seysh went down on one knee and placed the shiftrielles in the sand before her, then backed away, with her head down. The silver mercury covered her hair, which was very long; down to her waist. Her hair, perhaps purple-grey, draped almost to the sand as she walked backwards from them in a low bow to the edge of the surf, leaving a kind of hair-trail in the sand.

As Thys and Tarni watched, she seemed to become shadow against the water, then she stood and touched her own shiftrielle, and she was there, without camouflage too. They could not quite make her out through, until she moved to bow, lightly, revealing from afar, shadowy distance, less than a second of total-knockout humanoid beauty.

Then the ocean around her frothed, and she wasn't there anymore.

The cove seemed still.

The feeding frenzy was over, the water from the mini-tsunami had retreated, and their new comrade had vanished as quickly as she had appeared.

The only sign that anything had disturbed Thys' home was the debris, not as much as she would have thought, that her mini-tsunami had dragged back from inland. Even the pier was still standing, and for that she was very pleased.

Tarni walked up the beach a little, to the shrubs that signaled the start of the land. She bent down and reached for something, and raised a roll of silver foil.

'The food's still here!'

'Thank the Goddess!' Thys uttered. 'I'm fucking famished.'

CHAPTER 90

'Very well, Skinny Not-Witch Called Tarni Lavé. You and Thys Pyne have met these creatures before; but these creatures are new to me. The Inner Earth is alien to me, and to my kind. But given that, Thys Pyne, I have a relevant confession to make.'

'Oh, Jesus, Xylata. What is it this time?'

'I do remember some things, from before deciding to come here to find you. When we departed the astral, you asked that I allow you time alone, and that I did not disturb you for at least a week. Even if the war resumed. Do you remember also?'

'I think I do, actually.'

'Well, I broke that agreement, because in truth, I was aware of what our Wild Wicked Don't Call Me A Witch companion here had already stated, and I was coming to tell you. Nobody has heard from Bo Everett for days.'

Tarni was horrified. 'You mean – Bo Everett is *really* missing?!'

Thys sat bolt upright against the bar.

'Wait – what? Bo *and* Yelina are missing – and the satellites are going down, *and* this attack – *and* the gaps not working!?'

Xylata spoke slowly, and softer now. 'I am afraid so. For the past few days, nobody has been able to tell if the *Lady Ann* is even still there, above The Harbour. For months now it has been stationary there; now, some say, it is gone.'

'That's right, that's where it's been,' Thys confirmed, 'whenever I've visited.'

Harding nodded. 'I don't like this at all…'

'Join the fucking club!' Tarni cried out.

'Bo Everett is an extremely cunning and resourceful man,' Harding offered. 'In a good way, I mean; maybe he's finally mastered the flight controls? Maybe he has done something to it; trapped it in between dimensions so we can't see it, something of that nature?'

Xylata considered it. 'Those Pleiadeans, the original commanders of *Lady Ann*, were not forthcoming with the knowledge Bo Everett required. Once they'd handed their broken ship over and departed, they were of no help to him. They are a serene and artistic people, but they do not appreciate impurity. Maybe they just took their ship back?'

'I know what you are saying…' Harding had added an unpleasant edge to his deep timbre. 'Maybe the landlords didn't like the renovations? And from what I understand, they were never too pleased that this Satan-Thing passed through it, on his way to claim Mitch's sanity.'

'You keep saying that,' Tarni snapped again, shivering. 'But do you really mean it?'

'Yes…' Harding growled. 'At least – I believe I do.'

Tarni scowled. 'Satan is not those things we met tonight; he is not those wraiths, nor the Inner Earth devils and demons who control them, nor the Primal Personifications who control them. The Beigeman, as we call him, is a disembodied entity of immense power who lives – almost outside of time and space. Out beyond the Orion Sphere, past The Void; where we are unable to comprehend. He is true despair, true hopelessness. And it is not wise to speak of him lightly. If at all.'

Harding stared at her darkly.

'I know this, child. The thing I saved Mitch Pyne from was very different to the things we saw tonight; and different again from the being that called itself Lucifer, that was hiding inside Vance McLeod. I am aware that we all have to avoid cultural training, especially when experience tells us differently. So, I know that the thing that was inside Vance was Lucifer – a being who has lived so long that he is like a god, or an angel – like the Elohim or the Orions.'

'Or Yelina,' Tarni snapped.

'But this – Satan-Thing – that is something else, and I do not, ever again, wish to be within its proximity, so long as I exist, or even beyond that – in any form. Am I making myself clear?'

Tarni was staring at him, curiously, but more respectfully now. 'Yes. Yes you are. I'm sorry.'

'Indeed.' Xylata nodded. 'Lucifer is Nephilim; their shared history is long. Nobody really knows what the Nephilim want any more. Some are worse than others, but none of them can be trusted; they are Supreme Tricksters, at best.'

Harding handed Xylata a tall glass of warm beer.

'Thank you. I am liking you more and more, old action man.' Xylata sipped. 'That drink is disgusting.' She placed the beer back down on the bar.

'I thought you cold blooded reptiles liked it warm?' Harding shrugged. 'It is an acquired taste, I suppose.'

'Yes. Acquired by slaves and the worker classes.'

Harding grimaced. 'I think that's a bit harsh –'

She ignored him, but saw that once again Thys and Tarni had exchanged a meaningful glance.

Finally she could stand it no longer.

'Really? Does everything have some kind of hidden significance to you two!?'

'What!?' Thys protested.

'I – ' Tarni started, but couldn't find any words.

Xylata picked the beer up from the bar again.

'Interesting aftertaste.'

She looked back and forth again, from Thys to Tarni; they were deliberately not looking at each other, but each had tiny, secret smiles.

'Interesting aftertaste? Good Goddess! I do not want to know!'

Xylata took her beer and walked across the room, clearly trying to concentrate. She took a long swig. Then she looked at the glass, curiously.

'Or maybe I do?' Xylata considered. 'Who is that man? They let him on television sometimes, just to make sure he looks crazy. He knows a lot about the creation of evil in third density, and how these stories inter-relate. You see him on panels with Derek Nurding sometimes; they're very different, they hate each other, but they both despise The Church.'

'Zaq Qwerty?' Thys asked.

'Yes. That's him.' Xylata assessed her slyly. 'You know him, don't you?'

Thys leaned back, feigning ignorance. 'No, not really; he's offering money if someone can prove I'm actually alive and not an imposter!'

Xylata did not believe her.

'He rings a bell with me. He knows a lot about the differences between things like devils and demons and The Devil, and Lucifer, and Satan; this so-called Beigeman; and how they, and their existence, have been employed to control your race, and the creation of evil.'

'You said, the creation of evil?' Harding frowned uneasily. 'I thought your race created that?'

Xylata laughed. 'No, Harding; we have merely corralled you, blocked your access to the other dimension and densities, narrowed the frequency of your psychic vibrations…'

'Oh,' Harding spread his mighty arms. 'Is that all?'

Her sly look returned as she walked back toward the bar.

'…but we merely exploit your natural capacity for evil, and your responses to your own nature, and the nature of the other beings on this planet. We did not create them, nor any of this that is already within you.'

She placed her empty glass before him.

'I will have another disgusting drink please.'

'How do we know, Field Marshal Xylata…?' Harding responded, taking an unrefrigerated beer bottle from under the bar, and dispensing the amber contents into her glass as he leaned in, not at all intimidated. '…that what you did, did not cause us to be more evil than we would have been?'

'You would have to ask Miris about that,' Xylata leaned in to match him, 'and he is long gone.'

'Miris?' Tarni asked.

Thys sighed. 'Dad told me about him; Miris was the Scientific Executor of the First Anunnaki Earth Mission; he was the one who genetically modified humanity. His diary is encoded within some of our DNA. In a way, that discovery is what got Pan… well, starcophagized.'

'Yes,' Xylata hissed. 'And even so, Miris' true secrets, the actual transcribed diary, all remain the property of Oliver Hines, and nobody has seen him for… it must be years, plural, now. Hines showed me enough to know what he was saying was true, but what Miris' true intent was, or truly how it was achieved, or what was *to be* achieved, remains a secret, or to be seen. Certainly, it goes way beyond the initial task of creating a limited third-density slave race; and the creation of a Karma Forge – that is believed to be an accident. However, I am sure that Physcore, and maybe even Rio DeVora, and her monstrous Phoodco empire, have the same information by now, and are assessing it as we speak.'

'But…' Tarni gulped. '…is this really all interconnected? With Yelina and Everett disappearing?'

It was as though the fact had only just sunk in, and she still could not quite believe she was talking to a genuine Anunnaki.

'I mean, how come you don't know? Aren't *you* thousands of years old? Like the Nephilim? Like Yelina? Weren't you…?'

Xylata raised a Spock-like Gugino eyebrow. '…here when Miris was? No, I was hatched here, but much later. Four thousand years after his time.'

Harding seemed genuinely impressed by that. 'Not to be indelicate, but doesn't that make you…?'

'Two thousand years old, or thereabouts. It's difficult to truly quantify my third density age. In the astral, as we are fond of constantly pointing out, time works differently. But my first mission was to observe the destruction of the so-called Druidic Pagans. To monitor the ongoing war between Yahweh and Sophia.'

'Between God and the Earth?' Tarni asked, incredulous. 'Is

that what you mean?'

Xylata had become distant as she spoke, her Gugino vocals very husky.

'It was a baptism of fire,' she whispered. 'And a desecration.' She shook her head sadly, not a little disturbed by her memories. 'We should not speak of such things. It is the witnessing of such actions that allows a young Anunnaki to de-spiritualize a race, to see them as less-than-essence, so that we allow ourselves to exploit them without mercy. It was this kind of processing, this kind of de-humanizing, that allowed me to go on from there to exploit the Crusades, and the Inquisition.'

'*The* Inquisition?' Thys gulped. 'I've never heard you talk about that...?'

'Hundreds of years of war and nothing else,' Xylata smirked. 'Sometimes I think your shorter reincarnation cycles are more merciful. To forget, even just for a while...'

She looked at Thys and flashed her reptilian irises once again.

These were the ones Thys was accustomed to; strangely enough, she realised. She wondered what had triggered such an emotional response; to reveal her true self like that, in third density, was akin to choking up.

'To answer your question, Tarni Lavé, these forces...' Xylata uttered, '...no matter what we each believe, individually, or as a culture, are interconnected.'

She looked to Tarni; Tarni nodded, once, stiff.

Xylata proceeded. 'If they are on the rise, in any shape or form... then the fact of their presence must be included in any theory we devise henceforth... to do with the disappearance of Bo Everett, and Yelina...' Xylata nodded to herself. '...and the fact that we have been attacked tonight.'

Tarni narrowed her eyes, and stared at Xylata, perhaps for the first time feeling almost equal, and not intimidated.

'These Dark Orion beings; if they truly possessed Oliver Hines, as the rumors have it...?'

'Yes...?'

'What if they are working together? If the dark forces they exploit – as you suggest – do overlap within the dimensions; what if second density Demons, seventh density Nephilim, and the Orion Renegades; Norions and the new O'Renegades who were formed at the 'P' Place; and the Great Dark Force of the void beyond, the Beigeman, the Shadow of Stars, have somehow aligned through their interconnectedness?'

'This what I am saying!' Thys insisted. 'What Dad was worried about!' That the greatest of those seventh, eighth density forced, or higher, could, feasibly, oversee all this! All they needed was a reason to look here; all they needed was...'

Harding grumbled. '...the Pandora Sequence.'

Xylata nodded. 'Perhaps. If they could control Oliver Hines... maybe there is another they have power over now? Perhaps these mad power brokers and despoilers of the environment, of Gaia; perhaps the mad-woman DeVora, or Styger?'

'Maybe they are the mysterious owners of this Physcore thing?' Thys uttered, almost speaking aloud. Then she looked at the others, all at once. 'Fucking hell; *what if they are?*'

'Or what if they have somehow gotten to Yelina?' Xylata's eyes widened. 'Maybe they now desire to control Bo Everett as well?'

'Nobody controls him,' Tarni spoke quickly, as though the truth of what she'd suggested were biting back, unpalatable. 'Yelina loves him because his mind is unique. He cannot be possessed! Those Black Enochians may do what they do in the name of... the name of... the Beigeman...'

'Why do you call him that?' Thys asked.

Tarni shrugged and seemed incredibly uncomfortable. She was speaking to Thys again, suddenly, as though nothing had passed between them. Like it had been back at the mansion ruins, pretending that they had never been lovers.

'It's a bit like those villains in story books; you can't speak their names. Their names have power. Inevitably, they kind of realise that they are giving the name power by not speaking it, but in this story – in reality, and especially in the denser realms, the name *truly does* have power, and should not be spoken casually. But when we refer to him, we call him Beigeman.'

'Why Beigeman?' Thys asked, incredulous.

'Well, if you 'say tan', you're almost saying 'beige'. So it became…'

'Beigeman,' Xylata smirked, but not without begrudging respect. 'The ultimate in dullness. Reflect it back. I like that.' She nodded, smiling, looking strangely satisfied.

Tarni shook her head, and went to say something.

'Go on…' Thys encouraged, gently. 'Everything is on the table.'

Tarni took a breath. She shuddered a little.

'It's true.'

She looked at Thys.

'Yelina debriefed me after Paramatta; but I hadn't seen anything. But Contrelle saw it all.' She looked at Xylata. 'You saw it all.' She turned to Harding. 'You and she, and Mendoza, pulled her out of an unstable vortex to the Inner Earth.'

Thys heard herself shout, before she could stop herself.

'I don't want to talk about this…!'

Tarni seemed shocked, but the spike only encouraged her.

'I'm sorry, Amy; Thys, I'm sorry *Thys*. But – we need to know what happened at Paramatta; it might be –'

'*I mean it!*' Thys snapped.

'But it's the one thing we don't – you said everything was on the table!'

Harding whispered, urgently. 'Leave it, Miss Lavé! How many more wounds do you need to open for her today?'

Thys met his eyes; she was so grateful for his protection in that moment, but also, for making her realise. Now it was all happening, she had no right to keep it from them.

She hissed something nasty under her breath, but rolled up her sleeves; the black coat and the burnt-orange hoodie, revealing the dagger-shaped tattoo.

'This body art is my timeline. I took it from Gordian's time map. It was just tech. Amazing, but, in the end, breakable. So, I broke it, tore it out, took it and kept it. I was helped, helped by one of those Orions who manifested, but I don't know where they went. But... I know where Gordian went.'

'Gordian?' Harding, Tarni and Xylata all spoke his name at once.

Thys stared down at the beautiful art along her arm; sword-like, but also like a strange Celtic Cross; and again, a crystalline, diamond kite. There were designs, perhaps a kind of alchemic symbology, perhaps a kind of sacred geometry, weaved into several symbols, down and across, weaving out and back like vines. But also, looking deeper into it, circuity like veins; fibres intertwined around and through it... it started to spark. Gold and bronze, silver and copper.

She couldn't look any more, so she looked away.

Then it was just a gorgeous tattoo.

'Can I tell you another time?'

'Yes...' Tarni affirmed, gently. 'I'm sorry.'

Harding was silent, but exchanged a look of concern with Xylata.

'We know...' Tarni began again, slumping a little with a sad, resigned sigh. '...that some of the so-called O'Renegades worship this Dark One, this *Beigeman*. They say that the O'Renegades were formed, on that day, around Gordian. Before he... vanished.'

Thys said nothing.

Xylata spoke. 'Others, here and elsewhere, from every plane, worship the Nephilim, or Lucifer, but in reality – this *Beigeman* entity has no real interest in any of them... only...'

Xylata trailed off, puzzled, but clearly working something out in her mind.

'...yes... maybe...?'.

'What?' Thys looked up.

'Maybe what your father did, Thys Pyne...' Xylata spoke very thoughtfully, with more than a trace of concern for where her own thoughts were leading. '...has ignited his interest in this world again. And – well, maybe he, the Beigeman, will indeed use the O'Renegades now. Maybe, for a time, he will answer the dark prayers of these Black Enochians? Certainly, the Orion Renegades despise change, and insist upon order; and what we have done is to instigate change. Major change. I have done almost nothing other than that, from the moment I met your father and possessed poor Saph. If they can somehow…'

'I see where you are going,' Harding mumbled, as though he too were considering the options.

Thys looked over to Xylata.

'This was basically Dad's theory; his fear, anyway. If he is somehow reaching out – and answering the call, from the void… the Sirians, even the Pleiadeans… the Anunnaki; they must all have access to Enochian magic – or their race's equivalent?'

'Our people are…' Tarni offered, her voice choking up a little. '…as I said; deeply concerned.'

Thys looked at her. Her voice was empty of anxiety or resentment now. Suddenly she gave up, and her heart went out.

'Where did you go, Tarni? What happened? You clearly know a lot more than when we were together at Omega?'

Tarni sighed and shrugged.

'You know where I went… I told you… and I tried… I tried to explain – but you never replied, never answered.' There were tears now, rolling down her cheeks. 'You never answered…'

CHAPTER 91

Thys and Tarni each ate a slice of pizza, naked on the beach with their shiftrielles on the sand before them, then greedily chomped down another piece on their way back to the apartment.

Zeke was asleep, missing a live Big Brother double eviction, and they let him sleep and ate some more on their way up, with their clothes and their new silver belts in their hands.

Then Thys levitated a couch chair for each of them across the slate and out onto the balcony, and they sat and devoured the rest of the food like animals, with the night just getting hotter.

Once between chomps, Tarni had shouted suddenly;

'We kicked some girl power ass!'

And Thys had responded;

'Fuck yeah! We own this fucken cove!'

They swigged down the Coke, swapping the bottle between them, then they both got up to get some left over beer from the fridge.

'Who *was* she?' Tarni had asked, opening the door and passing a bottle back. 'Seysh?'

'I know!' Thys exclaimed, accepting and cracking the top. 'She was awesome!'

'I wish she was still here!' Tarni smiled, cracking hers too.

'No you don't,' Thys smiled back, and kissed her full on the mouth.

Then she pulled back, mid-kiss, and swigged again.

Tarni swigged too.

Then they stared at each other, still high on adrenalin, as though each was daring the other to begin, working up to it, swigging their beers with devilish grins, standing cool, in front of the light of the open fridge.

CHAPTER 92

Their third session was fueled with adrenalin and the excitement of victory, of having staked a claim for the forces of good, and having driven away the forces of evil. Thys had experienced and encouraged nights of sex, powered by such emotions before, but with men, none of whom had any idea why she had been so vigorous, so pleased with herself, so adventurous on those particular nights as opposed to any of the others. Those men had reciprocated regardless, and thanked their lucky stars.

This time, both Thys and her partner were aware; they were both high with it, and the fact that they proceeded quite aggressively this time, athletically if not outright primal, was more to do than either would have admitted with a feeling that they deserved it. It was a reward, as they both saw it, each without verbally informing the other, but physically reinforcing that reward for hours on end. The charge of their combined flesh, the base energy that savaged them, deep and earthy and severe, drove each of them in turns, at first less gently than before, then gradually harsher and more urgent, to see where one could steer the other, to encourage greater response, more surprising and then even more shocking reactions, and in turn to inspire more, and more, and furthermore. Their sex encompassed nothing that either had felt before, and blasted the boundaries that either woman had previously assumed themselves to have had, whether coyly, consciously, or reserved for some potential future act of daring, or abandon; it blew them out of their respective comfort zones with the kind of expulsive blast they had all seen, a dozen times on film, as the planet explodes and the brilliant ring of fiery cosmic plasma energy bursts across the endless void of space.

They had opened every window, wide.

CHAPTER 93

Thys woke, and Tarni wasn't there.

Again, the bed sheets were damp, with the classic Sydney beaches humidity having settled throughout the cove to stifle everything, and stay for months. Thys rolled out of bed, her muscles sore all over; arms, legs, lower back, neck; and realised that the fitted elastic had come completely undone on three sides, so that she had actually been sleeping directly on the mattress.

She felt taller, and thinner as she stood, like there was less of her. Her nipples were sore, a little, as were her lips, and her loins felt numb. Her jaw was sore and her tongue felt strangely like she had been smoking, but her whole body felt more alert, fitter somehow, as though she had become more attuned to herself.

'Tarni!'

She expected that she had gone for supplies.

There was no food in the apartment.

She hated air-conditioning so she left the windows open and decided to acclimatize.

It was Monday… or was it Tuesday?

Maybe Tarni had just slept in and rushed to work?

Jesus, how was she going to tell her father?

She knew she had things to do, business to attend do, but it was the first time since their affair had begun that she had been alone in the apartment without Tarni. She decided to wait, and remember the night.

She remembered that she had tasted nice.

She remembered telling her.

An acquired taste, but…

Something like ginger, and turmeric, and honey.

CHAPTER 94

'Yelina called me,' Tarni shrugged.

They were beginning to calm down, starting to see a shape behind what had happened, a strange silhouette.

'Yelina?'

'She said she needed me. I wanted to stay with you – believe me I did, but I had never been so honored by my family, to be called. Required. I went. I sent you a text, on the way to the city. I know I did; I almost crashed the car on a bend, sending it. I put my phone down and promised myself not to pick it up until I got to Cleverco.'

'Cleverco?'

'Yelina said, meet me at the penthouse. There's never anyone in it, so if someone needs an alibi, or a quick meet, they can say they were there.'

'Oh…' Thys hadn't known that.

She was forgetting that Tarni must have been privy to machinations and subterfuge planned and executed by her father and Heather and Yelina and Bo that she… simply had no idea about.

She just outright wasn't here often enough.

'Amy…'

Thys blanched. She didn't know why. Tarni noticed and took it the wrong way.

'Thys, then. I remember, because I couldn't wait to get there, because…' She looked at Xylata, then Harding. They were clearly uncomfortable. '…we should talk about this privately.'

'Yes,' said Harding, with unmistakable compassion, but also no small measure of suggested propriety. 'I believe that you should.'

Thys and Tarni looked away from each other.

Xylata sighed. 'All things must evolve. Maybe you and Thys Pyne were close once, closer than you are now.' Thys looked up, surprised. 'Things here, on this world, at last, must change, and evolve. That must be accepted and processed by all; humans, Anunnaki, all the dimensional beings who have had a hand in creating this situation, whether by direct intervention or by remaining neutral, or aloof and indifferent. And that goes for the malevolent forces as well. We have no choice but to face them.'

She turned to Harding.

'And so, we shall see what we shall see. I'm sure Bo Everett and Yelina will turn up somewhere. This notion of an evil alliance; the Beigeman and the Renegades, the Inner Demons of this planet… then to extrapolate that into the alliance of evil, of all races? It cannot be. It is fear talking, between us this evening. Adrenalin and imagination. Everett will turn up; alive and grinning and shaking hands and kissing babies, donating to charity and having earthy sex all night with Yelina on their *Lady Ann*. He will run for President, and we will walk the West Wing, all in a row, around and around in circles, making clever, witty banter.'

Thys and Tarni looked at each other; it was an honest look, free of ghosts.

Neither believed Xylata.

'Still…' Harding grumbled. 'We must go to ground, until we know more. I know you all have your places, as I have mine; we must consider…'

'You're serious?' Thys sat up. 'Go to ground? Hide?'

'Because, on the reverse side, if someone – whoever, has taken out Bo Everett…?'

'*Taken out?*'

'You must understand, Miss Lavé – Tarni?' Harding nodded, frowning. 'That I am processing aloud, and quickly, but…'

Harding looked back at Xylata. They had met several times, when Xylata had come to the house with Thys; they were friends by now, surely, by an definition; but Thys had never seem them so well aligned.

She backed him up.

'Harding is right. As I tried to say, I heard we were unable to contact *Lady Ann*, discovered that it had vanished from all maps, all dimensions, checked immediately with my sources and came directly to see you, to warn you. You are important, Thys Pyne. I have spent nine years trying to tell you that. We cannot afford to lose you. None of us would survive. Just because you are not as well known here as you are in my culture…'

'Thank you, Xy. I appreciate your concern.'

Xylata squirmed.

Thys had only used the abbreviation a few times during their slow-developing professional-military relationship, not to mention their even more cautiously evolved private friendship, but they both recognized it now as a candid sign of genuine affection. Xylata however did not deal well with subtle emotions; she quite literally barely knew she had any.

'I know we have spoken of this before Thys, but it is remarkable how that initial campaign, or… adventure…? Whatever it was, when we all met, all those long five years ago… how it seemed to at once bond us all, and yet set us apart. You too, tree trunk.'

'Yes. Agreed.'

'Almost instantly upon our meeting, I became an outcast, a rebel leader, as did you. Harding, you ceased to be an active mercenary. All of us, who came into contact with the vortex that surrounded your father, at that time, seem to be connected, while at the same time to exist outside of their normal cultures. And now it seems that you, Tarni Lavé, met Thys Pyne, had an experience of rarified intensity, and were then summoned to train with Yelina in the ways of the Inner Earth. I further admit that have since even watched all of Gabrielle Fenwick's movies, and even posed as a film producer in order to meet her. Since the Pandora incident, her performances have improved, as have her script choices.'

Thys scoffed. 'Even acting with Krimson Azureus?'

'America's sweetheart and Australia's pride…' Harding shook

his head. 'Why do you hate her so?'

Thys ignored his jibe, however friendly. 'Should we warn Gabs? It seems like we should be concerned for anyone who had any involvement, right? That's a lot of people; even the captain of Everett's boat… what was his name again?'

'Mason.'

'Wait…' Thys held her hand up. Something about that tickled her brain. 'That's right. His name was Mason. But that boat… I'm spiking on…' Thys frowned. 'We spent time on it, we were all nearly killed on it… I rode it into the astral and… now it's our mobile base. I never got her name. Uncle Bo almost told me once. Years ago now. He said it was important…' Thys checked Xylata. 'What is she was called?'

'Boats are 'she's' here?' Xylata enquired, curiously. 'And; why would you suddenly care…?'

'Do you know?' Thys asked Harding, sitting up straighter.

'No,' Harding shrugged. 'Is this really a spike-instinct moment?'

'I think so…' Despite herself, Thys found herself immediately pondering this some more. 'Yes… I was going to name her… but then I remembered, it's bad luck to rename a boat. And I never got around to asking Uncle Bo again. I mean, I rode her, then she vanished, then after she went to the void with Dad, she came back…'

'Yes,' Xylata agreed testily. 'We just called it 'The Boat'. Sometimes, 'The Human Boat'. We did not know it needed a name…'

'But you gave *me a name*. "Thys!" You named me that.'

'Yes. But, you are a person.'

'I slept down there in the cabin for the first few weeks, after you came to call me back…' She narrowed her eyes, intensely attempting recall. '…and we made plans – there was a conference room. For a while it was like… home. Just a little cruiser, compared to all the Anunnaki craft… but the name. Bo said; the name was important…'

Tarni slid off her bar stool and walked across the room.

Thys watched, then Tarni turned suddenly and looked at Thys; it was enquiring, emotional. Thys knew what it was; she wanted her to know – she wasn't like that.

She hadn't just… run.

Thys looked away, feeling guilty.

Xylata looked back and forth, quite demonstrably, but continued to ignore it.

'Amy…'

Harding was staring at Thys, intense and earnest.

Here it comes, she thought.

'I have never asked you this. But I ask that you do not consider it a breach of trust. Do you have the Pandora Sequence?'

Thys looked to them, one by one. Two of the six people she *actually* trusted most in the world, along with her father and Heather and Bo Everett and… yes, Yelina.

And Tarni; the one she wanted to trust, more than ever.

'Are you worried? That if Dad's missing as well…?'

'Yes, partly. Did your father entrust it to your safe keeping?'

'I have it. I'm sure he kept a little back. But I have it. The original six elements. They are hidden. Like Uncle Pan did first off; in parts.'

Harding sighed.

'That is good. It could not be in safer hands. I know he wanted you to select other candidates… and you have taken great care in thinking it through. Perhaps too much. If the situation is dire, there may not be enough of you, enough of us…'

Thys gulped.

She looked at Tarni.

Could she?

She had thought it once.

Been *certain* of it once.

Xylata seemed to intercept her thoughts. 'But you must not activate any further Pandorans now. We do not know who to trust, who may have been compromised already, in a worst-case scenario, that is.'

Harding began pacing. 'But if the others, Mitch and Heather, were on the Pleiadean ship when it went down…?'

Tarni was aghast. 'Taken out? Went down? We don't know –'

'It's possible…' Harding stated definitely. 'And it must be taken into account.'

Thys became tense. 'Tarni's right, Harding. Someone's taken out Bo? His ship went down?'

'It's the way I think, girl. It's how I've managed to survive this long. If Bo, Yelina, Pan, Saph – and forgive me, Mitch and Heather do not return, then – you, and Trudy and Vance, are all that remain.'

'Don't forget Suzie.'

'I have not; the scroll on the television behind you just reported that she has cancelled her concert tour; I told you we should pay attention to the scrolls.'

Thys didn't even look.

'Pan was on that ship too?' asked Tarni, clearly fearful now.

'He's right…' Thys uttered. 'But – if they were gone – *actually gone* – we'd feel it, surely? If something had…'

She swallowed.

'… *taken out*… Dad, or Heather – I would know… surely?'

'Yes,' Xylata nodded, sharply. 'I believe you would, if they were dead, not just as a fellow Pandoran, but as a devoted offspring. But let's not… as far as we know, Pan is still trapped in the starcophagus…' Xylata shrugged hopefully. Then she sighed. 'If – if the ship is gone, then maybe that survived?'

'Survived…?' Thys was stunned. But she understood. This was 'worse-case'. 'I always thought he just would appear again. Like Suzie Saturn. In the astral. To make his presence felt. But he never did…'

She shook her head slowly, sadly.

'He said it would take him a while, but… I just don't think anyone thought it would be this long. If only he could just go to the void, like Suzy did… reset his incarnation through space-time.'

Xylata was becoming frustrated now. 'Didn't we see him though? Once or twice?'

'Did we?'

'That once… in the Palace, before the third campaign?'

They thought for second.

'I have a vague memory…' Thys uttered. 'I suppose, of seeing him in the *silverbluemoonroom*, under the stairs?'

Xylata frowned. 'I don't know what that is.'

Thys thought about it; tried to gap there.

She had never had such a push-back.

Just nothing; nowhere to go.

No options at all.

Xylata saw the look on Thys's face, knew the disappointment.

They had both been trying.

'How can this…?'

There was a sudden commotion. A shuffling; something heavy, it sounded like, moving down the hall toward them.

For a moment, Thys had forgotten about Heff; then he trundled in. The giant black dog, the size of a small bear with red eyes (not glowing mind, but - properly red) had a human hand in his mouth, which he proceeded to chomp, something like an alligator, as the fingers wobbled about. There were a couple of huge crunches and the hand was gone.

Everyone had frozen, except Harding.

'I thought it would be okay. I saw him sneaking out of your room. I assume he's yours…?'

'Everyone, this is Heff. Heff eats ninja assassins. Rio DeVora was kind enough to send him some. He'll be helping with security from now on.'

Heff plopped down on the floor and started to lick his bottom.

Before Xylata or Tarni could properly react, Thys' felt something; felt her eyebrows shoot up in surprise as she did.

'I have something. Guys; I have a way! The *silverbluemoonroom*; it's a back door. A secret! But if we go, we go now!'

CHAPTER 95

Thys simply opened the door to the corridor that led out of the second-floor lounge bar and revealed to them a lunar landscape.

'That's The Moon!'

'It's not the actual, "The Moon", Witch Tarni.' Xylata rolled her eyes. 'Or we would all be dead.'

Tarni nodded nervously. 'I think I got that. When we all didn't die.'

Xylata walked first through the door, into the astral landscape. It was as though she were just standing in the next room.

'This is the lowest level of the true astral pathway from Earth; the lobby to the astral proper, and to the Terrastral Territories as well.' She looked at Thys. 'We walked here once. While I healed.'

'Walked a lot...' Thys nodded, and smiled. 'Talked some, too.'

Xylata looked out, distant. '...so many questions.'

Thys stepped out beside her, paused, then walked ahead a bit.

They both left footprints.

'I think the *silverbluemoonroom* was the first thing I built of my own. Susie told me how to make a bedroom here. A proper bedroom. I... don't think I can tell you where it is, even if I wanted to. But the door I need to find, in order to get back there, I think it's out here somewhere, on the Lunar Stargate. I use for special reasons. When I was thinking of the *silverbluemoonroom*; I could sense it; it was still here. It's still active somehow.'

'Indeed,' Xylata approved. 'A lasting, solid connection.'

'I'm holding it in my mind somehow; but I don't know how long for.'

'Come on then, humans.'

Tarni and Harding stepped through.

They now stood as one before the other side of the door,

exactly as it would have been, had they been in the corridor; just the frame and the door, and Harding's lounge bar beyond.

Thys turned. Heff waited anxiously.

'Come though Heff. I's okay, boy.'

Heff went to move forward, but stopped and sat again, juggling himself on his paws. It was bizarre to see such a huge creature so nervous.

'Come, dog!' Harding barked.

Heff barked back. 'Ruh!'

'Heff! Come on!' Thys insisted.

Heff gave a little whimper as something in him gave way and he trotted reluctantly through. As he did, it was as though he had moved through a cascade of white paint. Walking quickly up to Thys, Heff was no longer solid black but bright white, with deep, red ears to match his red eyes. Thys was astonished, but reached out and patted him under his chin.

'Polar Heff now, not grizzly Heff!'

Heff's pythonesque tail wagged; the end-tuft of that was red now too.

Harding walked up to them as the door closed; just the door restored wooden door, as it would have been in The Fork.

'He does not obey me.'

Thys smiled. 'Heff?'

Heff looked right at her, ready and obedient and adoring.

Thys held up a fist. 'Me.' She held up another fist. 'You.'

Heff made a little whimper and licked out, over her joined fists, right up the middle of her face with an enormous bright-red tongue.

'Hah!' Thys squeezed her eyes shut. 'Okay!' She opened them again. Heff was still staring at her, very happy. She shook her two fists, still tight together, then turned and beat them against Harding's chest.

'Harding!'

Heff looked from her, to Harding, then back into to her eyes.

Then he turned his giant head back to Harding and licked his face as well.

'Ruh!'

'He is a good boy…!' Harding wiped his mouth and nose and chin with the back of his jacket sleeve. '…he does not need to be told twice!'

Thys looked around the "astralunar surface" for Xylata, to bond her to her creature as well. Just as before, the landscape before her looked exactly like the surface of Earth's moon as she'd seen in pictures, in famous photographs, and she was here as though she were on an ordinary beach.

Xylata and Tarni had walked ahead to a rise.

They were standing at the top, looking down.

Thys walked up to them, Harding at her side.

'I do not believe I have ever been into the astral before…' Harding uttered. '…it feels almost normal.'

They reached the top of the rise.

The Moon was a little more crowded now, it seemed.

'You were saying…?' Thys smiled.

All around the plain below, there were people.

The people were dotted here and there in the middle and far distance. They were standing around several rows of apparently free-standing doorframes, of all shapes and sizes, some with open doors, some closed, and a held ajar by rocks.

Each doorframe was spaced a few meters apart, so as to be easily spotted and readily accessed, but otherwise they were in no particular pattern, type, or style; not that Thys could immediately discern anyway.

'Is this normal?' Harding asked, as though the knew the answer.

Thys grumbled. 'Even for here; not in the slightest.'

The craters had changed, as well.

As with the general view, the craters here looked a lot like the ones she had seen in famous photos and videos, but now, here in the astral, not only were impact circles more evenly spaced, like the doors, but they also…

...all seemed to all have holes in the middle of them.

Like drains, but also, almost... Thys frowned; almost a bit sphincter-like when you really looked at them. Many and varied random items were levitating all around the lower atmosphere. Some were popping up, seemingly expelled from the holes in the craters with a puff; some were simply rolling out, like an excretion.

Regardless of what speed they appeared though, the objects were simply floating up and around, drifting about the generral vicintiy as though in zero-gravity (even though, conversely, Thys and her companions were walking around as though they were on Earth) and just... hanging about in the air around them.

As they walked down the hill toward the closest doorframe, another materialized beside it; these were side-to side, like a hotel corridor, but other rows, not far off, were stacked like dominoes.

As Thys approached, she saw a transparent, pop-up toaster float past her; then a pink teddy bear with an eye-patch; an Old West handgun covered in rust; and a bright-blue, battery-operated dildo, still whirring. Floating about to one side of the new door; a nineties game console covered in anime stickers; a glistening wood axe, brand new; an original hardback copy of *Catch-22*, flapping like a dove, displaying hand-written annotations on every other page, and on every alternate page, colour-coded post-it notes; and a tube of hemorrhoid cream covered in melted white-chocolate; to the other side; a rare bottle of vintage cabernet sauvignon with 'Drink Before Divorce' written on the label in black sharpie; and a cracked Faberge egg with a diamond ring, jingling around inside, right in front of her; and a silver slinky, intertwined with a plus-sized red bikini top, just over her head.

Also contributing to this debris were the people and the doors. There seemed to be, like the doors themselves, people of all shapes and sizes, from all times and walks of life, traversing the lunar doorways, emerging and exiting through the doors like mass-participants in some kind of black-and-white movie farce. Every time they did, more astral debris entered the lunar landscape with them, but every time someone departed, some of it (proportionately less, if the ever increasing depth of it was anything to go by) got sucked down into their wake and drifted back with them. Still, the remaining, gathering debris did not float off into space; it just floated around, above the surface and in the air, the highest floating object no more than a few feet above the tallest dreamer, like soap bubbles that never popped.

'These are our people,' Xylata observed. '…although many do not know it.'

'No…' Thys watched as they all came and went, none the wiser. '…they're still asleep, still dreaming.'

Xylata shook her head. 'This place will be pandemonium before long. Professional dreamers, creatives, meta-psychics, astral travelers and channelers, and all the rest; they have nowhere to go, no access to the higher astral plains. Not even the lower astral plains, to have a good nightmare! No dimension at all. This is not good!'

Already, even as they observed, more doors were appearing over the horizon, and the collective sounds of them opening and closing had begun to accrue, to the point of an approaching hailstorm, just one suburb away.

Xylata spoke to Thys under her breath as her eyes scanned the lower astral lunar surface. Thys knew; she was looking for someone, anyone she might know, who might be useful. In fact, she was doing the same thing herself, hoping to spark upon someone on instinct.

'Heather must return soon and tell us how to set things right. This will effect human dreaming; humans who cannot dream go insane. From what you've said, we have obviously consulted with her extensively… maybe we have provided her with a solution should this – *astral block,* which is clearly causing our astral amnesia – ever occurs as it has.'

'Like, maybe we knew this was going to happen?' Thys shrugged.

'Or that was a possibility; if things went terribly wrong.'

'It's not normally like this, is it?' Tarni asked, bewildered. 'I've never traveled through the astral before.'

'There are usually a dozen people here at most,' Xylata hummed, 'every few seconds, one leaves and another goes; so fast that nobody ever remembers this landscape is here; even when it is here… which most of the time, it isn't.'

Thys looked about. She could see at least two hundred people now, and probably a thousand doors. The chaos, whatever it was, was definitely approaching.

Then she was struck with a thought.

She didn't like it.

'You are thinking heavily,' Xylata told her. 'I can feel it.'

'If Pan has been here; in the astral, trying to get through…' Thys pondered. 'When we remember, I wonder what that will mean? Maybe he was trying to tell us something? Maybe he needs us to… I mean, I know it's harsh, but I sometimes thought…?'

'I know what you thought; that it would be wiser just to take him to the void, and throw him and his starcophagus in. We've all thought that at one time or another. It would either reincarnate him or re-set his timeline. But that is incredibly dangerous. Suzy Saturn only did that to save your father from what Vance McLeod had become, from being a possession vehicle for Lucifer. By all accounts she performed an act of great bravery and self-sacrifice, and was unaware that it would restore her true timeline. But now Vance McLeod thinks he's a movie star and he has two sets of memories, although he denies the most unlikely one.'

'Maybe Pan doesn't want to put himself through that?' Tarni offered.

'Mayhap,' Xylata frowned. 'Resetting a major incarnation like Pan's – it could have devastating effects, both personally, and for third density space-time as a whole. It could reverse the Pandora Sequence and destroy Los Angeles; end the human race. Again.'

'Again?' Tarni asked.

Xylata ignored her.

'Regardless, Pan doesn't seem like he's anywhere near as whole, or restored enough to contemplate anything but his coma.'

'But...' Thys gulped, watching the chaos before her increase, 'what if this is the result of...'

Something landed on the sand behind them with a soft thud and they spun about as a growling voice, that vibrated as cool incarnate, but was resolutely feminine, spoke to them with an easy familiarity.

'...what if he's already done it? And what if this is what happened, when he did...?'

Standing behind them was Suzie Saturn.

'*Oh my God it's...*'

'We know who it is, Witch Lavé...' Xylata uttered, sideways at her.

Suzie beamed a radiant but uneasy rock star smile at Thys and Xylata.

'Do you guys know how many concerts I've had to cancel since I returned to the physical plane?' Then she turned. 'Heya Harding! Branching out, are ya, y'old oak?'

Harding reached down and took her hand, raised it to his lips and pecked it with a kiss.

'Suzie Saturn... I have met many rock stars since I put down roots in Los Angeles, and you still remain...'

She cocked her head, waiting for it.

'...the one who looks most like an ex-stripper.'

She snatched her hand away and laughed, heartily.

'You star-fucking psycho!'

Her boisterous laugher echoed across the lunar surface until her smile faded, and she turned back to Thys and Xylata.

Tarni just kept staring.

'Your friend here might be star struck...' Suzie smiled warmly at Tarni.

Tarni tried to talk, but only succeeded in making a weird snorting sound that thoroughly embarrassed her and rendered her speechless.

'But have you noticed there's a lot less to be struck by?' Suzie's eyes flicked briefly up. 'They're being blocked out, one by one.'

'I have all your music,' Tarni uttered, as though she couldn't help herself. 'Even Yelina likes it.'

'And I like Yelina – and I don't like the fact that she and everyone else I like are pulling up sticks and making with the vanishing act. I'm starting to feel like I might be next!'

'I think we all are…' Xylata grimaced.

'Like I said, I had to cancel a god-damned concert tonight, and my whole tour for the foreseeable future – because I couldn't remember any of my god-damn songs! And not just the lyrics – the actual fuckin' songs!'

Thys and Xylata exchanged glances.

'Do you remember talking to us about any of this?' Thys asked.

'Sure – and Heather. Maybe even young Mitchell. But I don't remember diddly squat about any of it… and I've been fully conscious in the astral longer than any human alive! However – I am damn sure that whatever it was, this thing we all – *had in mind* – out of our minds, probably; was big, and it was about to kick off! *Big time.*'

Again, Thys and Xylata exchanged worried glances.

'Oh yeah,' Suzie nodded angrily, 'you better exchange worried glances! Because the dark side of the moon is getting darker, and the shadow is growing taller, and longer, and wider; and before long, it will be total darkness, and the world will be night, and full of dark, dark lunatics, prowling an infinite god-damn witching hour!'

Even Harding shivered.

'Jesus, Suzie…' Thys wrapped her arms around herself.

A small box filled with silver bullets floated past, emptying into the air and swirling out into a spiral. Then the bullets jingled like a wind chime as they collided with a large gold crucifix on a wooden stand, scattering off in all directions.

'Being on the astral plane normally vents all that shit…' Suzie grimaced. 'I know; I stand on stage in front of thousands of people every night; I channel their frustrations and send it all up to your Palace… then at night, I go and hang there and listen, and write songs and make music as a salve… to try and make it better – but what if me, and all the other poets and presenters, and bards and bastards, and minstrels and motherfuckers, and the whole hell-of-a band up in rock'n'roll heaven stopped doin' that…? All at once? Like; now? That's gonna have an impact, believe me. And sooner that you think, sweet tarts.'

Xylata looked around angrily. 'This astral block is good for no-one. Even the higher density beings will find it difficult to come and go; as it stands, it is most likely that wherever you are right now, is where you stay. Until we find a solution, anyone who was in third density is stuck there. Anyone dreaming in the astral may have woken; but the connection will not have been properly dissipated.'

'What will that do?' Tarni demanded.

'Speculation is pointless. Being here is pointless.'

'Well; Trudy was here,' Suzie offered. 'Looking for you all.'

'Thank God,' Thys sighed.

'She went again; but look, I'm stuck here – my body's been sleeping down there almost twelve fricken hours; I haven't slept that long since I smoked weed! It seems the stronger you are here, and the longer you stay, the harder it is to get away now. You guys had best skidoo, before you get stuck here too.'

Xylata turned to Thys. 'That settles it. The places you go, where nobody knows?'

'Yes?'

'Go. They are genuinely secure, I have tried to follow you on numerous occasions and failed utterly.'

'Again, Xylata?'

'You know that I will always try to protect you!'

She sighed, and Thys sighed too.

'I know…! But, still!'

'…and remember what I told you last time? That, if I, Xylata, have tried to follow you, and failed…?'

'Oh. I see.' Thys frowned. 'Still! Trust!'

'Security, Thys Pyne, trumps trust every time. I am going to break the gap-jumping protocols Mitch initiated; they must be secured. Suzie, I can get you out; will you come with me and try to find Mitch and Heather, and Trudy Pankhurst?'

'If you can get me off this fucking rock, I'll do anything you say.'

'Good. Thys, Harding – Tarni Lavé?'

Tarni understood, and nodded.

'Yes, yes I'm with you.'

Xylata smiled, a serious but grateful smile. 'If there's anything wrong you will hear from me. If there's something really, very wrong, I will let you know covertly somehow. We will need a code word.'

'Okay. Lonely Goddess. That's the code.'

Xylata smiled broadly. 'And you *will* go to ground?'

The memory of this morning, and seeing her on George Street triggered another realisation.

'I have something I need to do. It should only take an hour. Then I'll go, I promise.'

'That may be all the time you have before this place closes in on itself and we have a bottleneck of too many doorways. Before the next sunset, maybe after the next sunrise… who knows what dreams will come back to Earth? What insanity this will bring?'

'True fear and loathing…' Suzie uttered. 'All around us; chaos and madness.'

She snatched an old CD from the air before her, and opened the cover. The contents immediately launched away, spinning off somewhere else like a Frisbee.

Xylata narrowed her eyes. 'But that may work to our advantage…'

'How's that, lizard tits?'

'So long as this… secret *silverbluemoonroom* doorway? Contained only in your mind, Thys Pyne?'

'I think that's what's happening…' She did not sound exactly supremely confident.

'Should that continue to operate, it will be too chaotic soon for anyone to trace anything, or anyone coming and going; like you, Def Con Amethyst. If we are the only ones who can come and go, it will certainly be an advantage in solving this dilemma and bringing to account those responsible.'

'Okay...' Thys was started to sound worried now.

'Try not to...' Xylata sighed.

Thys knew; reassurance was not her strongest gift.

'...when this is all over, you will be back helping your father and his sweet mammary monkey-girl, running Cleverco, and reaping the rewards of what we have done in the astral. Trust me, Thys Pyne.'

Tarni looked around, very worried. 'That looks ominous.' A fight was starting over who went through one door first.

It looked as though it was between Benjamin Franklin and Stephen King.

Xylata grinned. 'That looks like an opportunity.' She turned back to Thys and stared at her, and for a second Thys saw her vertical reptilian irises flash out at her again; this time surrounded by an astral emerald green.

'What?' Thys asked.

'You trust me. I could be setting you up for all sorts of nightmarish things, but you trust me.'

'Yes.'

There was not a trace of doubt in her voice; it was fact. Somehow, in that moment, she had, at least partially, answered her question to Harding.

This Thys was the kind of person she was.

Xylata seemed furious for a second. Then she squared her Paris Green shoulders.

'Until we meet again, Field Marshall Pyne.'

She gave Thys her clan salute, then turned and took Suzie Saturn's hand, and dragged her toward Franklin and King.

Suzie flung the empty CD at Thys.

'Every now and then,' Suzie called back, disapproving, 'I find one of these…'

She didn't meet Thys' eyes.

'Next time we meet, we need to talk more!'

Thys stared down at the CD in her hand. The cover was for the first, and self-titled album by an artist, the memory of whom should no longer exist, let alone have any physical trace of her having existed, for a short astral period, as one of the best-selling pop singers on Earth.

Tarni looked over her shoulder.

'Mistress?'

Thys took the paper sleeve out of the plastic cover and placed it securely in her pocket, then threw the plastic square spinning into the air. Suzie had already reached the door with Xylata.

'Suzie's one of the great singer-songwriters of her generation; when the Anunnaki tried to wipe her out of existence, they replaced her with an ordinary production line pop singer, and our world was a lesser place…'

'Mistress?'

'I only just remember her; I'm one of the few people who can.'

'But surely…' Harding frowned. 'If the job was done right, there should be nothing left of Mistress? Nothing, as in; *nothing*.'

Thys watched Xylata do her thing.

'Learned men and scholars! Look who it is! It is the world-famous rock star Suzie Saturn, and I am the beautiful Black Irish cult actress Carla Gugino!'

The two men stopped fighting and stared at them dumbfounded, even as they passed right by them, walked through the door and closed it behind them.

'I have never met an Anunnaki before tonight,' Tarni aired. 'She was not what I was expecting.'

Thys looked wistfully at the closed door for a second, then she examined the crazed lunar landscape.

'If only they were all like that.'

Behind them, Harding harrumphed. 'This Mistress material bothers me. I do not like completed missions to be incomplete.

Maybe, my girl, we all remember things we shouldn't, in our unconscious? Or maybe, that exists, purely as an 'after thought' because you are here?'

Thys tried to hide her surprise at his reasonable diagnosis. 'Sure, I suppose. But, look; I'll talk to Suzie. I'm sure she has a theory. We can sort it later.'

Harding nodded. 'Then; are you sure you want to do this, girl? Hide? Do your routine? Your circuit? Your world tour? Your vanishing act?'

'Harding, I know you don't like it. Neither does –'

Her eyes flicked sideways at Tarni.

Harding raised an eyebrow at her, as though to suggest, 'careful what you wish for'.

' – neither do a few other people, who don't think I can handle myself without Xylata. But I can, and I have, and I will. I'll do what I have to them go through the wardrobe; I'll clock in after twelve hours, say, thirteen from now. Okay? By that time Dad and Heather and Xylata and Suzie will have contacted you and we can all sort this out together.'

Tarni nodded to herself. 'I will report back to Yelina's family. They will want to know what is happening.'

Something bright purple flashed past Harding's feet, and through the door behind him. Then another, bright green. By the time he saw the bright orange one, Harding realised they were cats, and by then, a bright blue one had run between his legs.

He stared at Thys, paralyzed.

'This is not happening.'

Harding, Thys recalled, was not a cat person.

'Take her where she needs to go and come straight back!'

Then he turned and went back down the rise, to the door through which they had arrived, back into his mansion.

The door slammed involuntarily behind him.

Heff was a little further up the rise, watching the crater below like a father watches his litter. Thys and Tarni stared down as well, not wanting to look at each other, alone for the first time since...

'You are returning to Sydney?' Tarni asked.

'I'll drop you off, then go back to Harding's, pick him up, then go back to...'

'Omega Cove.'

'Yes.'

'Can you gap me from here to the Cleverco penthouse? I'll wait for news there.'

Thys couldn't help herself. She still couldn't look Tarni in the eye, but she reached out her hand. Tarni took it. Her skin had changed. Her hand wasn't as soft as it had been. A warped old wooden cottage door appeared where Harding's had vanished, and a handsome man with a handlebar moustache and black top hat, dressed in a florescent, canary-yellow mankini walked through, ignoring them.

Beyond looked neutral.

'Fingers crossed,' Thys breathed.

CHAPTER 96

The Cleverco penthouse was two floors high, with a rooftop pool and helipad.

Thys and Tarni entered via the gap into the lower floor, a luxurious open-plan entertainment area that essentially covered the entire floor. Heff followed, sniffing the whole way.

The penthouse consisted of nine distinct areas in a checkered pattern, with each square bordered, albeit loosely, by transparent support columns. Heff, returned to his grizzly form, started making his rounds, sniffing each pillar in turn.

Only three other architectural obstructions blocked the spectacular three-sixty view; two sets of thin-railed open staircases, ascending from each side of the central square lounge area, and an elevator cage that was presently parked, with the transparent cage sitting still beneath the western-side stairs.

The southern arc offered the tops of other office blocks in the CBD, but one did not have to step too far north from the center of the penthouse to begin seeing down, into Sydney Harbour and Circular Quay, The Bridge, The Opera House, and far across the north shore. It was always stunning, even with the rain and the storm clouds.

They had arrived in early evening; magic hour, where the apricot and pink half-light of the setting sun reflected on the steel and glass and made the southern arc of the city look completely cyber-enchanted.

Lightning struck in the distance, against the swirling backdrop, a mass of grays and whites of every shade and smear.

'That's not fair…' Tarni uttered, releasing her hand.

Thys knew what she meant; it almost felt like a set up, it was almost too Hollywood-romantic.

Thys squared herself. 'Stay here, when I have news, I'll come and get you.'

'Really?'

'I'll come directly here when I get back from hiding. Twelve hours, give or –'

'What I was going to say before was that I remember sending that text, because I nearly swerved off the road, sending it, then I put the phone down and I knew, I knew, that by the time I got here, to meet Yelina, here, three and a half years ago, that I would have a message from you. And I was so excited to see what it was. I waited all the way, until I got into that elevator, to check. And there was nothing. I remember my heart sinking, irrationally; you were still asleep. But being separated from you, it hurt. I texted you again, and again, and tried to call and tell you... Yelina was aware that my ancestral genes, that my natural abilities had awakened. She wanted me with her, and so I had to tell you that I would be gone for...'

Tarni's bottom lip was trembling.

'...I think she did put us together, deliberately, so it would happen, so you would progress as well, but I don't think even she knew that we had the connection we did...'

Thys gulped audibly.

'I cried, but I could not see you, I could not come. I thought you must have been offended, or hurt as well, maybe even angry. When I returned, weeks later, you were gone. I had remained celibate all that time, I could not... imagine another. You were everything.'

'I –'

'Then I began to think that you had used me, to secure the cove, and I became angry, and bitter. Other things, Yelina things, happened. I could not think of what to say to you. I was irrational; but I wanted for you to contact me, because I had sent the text, and you had not replied. And that is the version of you I have held onto until now. That you were pretending; that the aspect of you that I loved was fake. That you are cold and mercenary.

Nobody would tell me where you were, but I was stupid. I see that now; I didn't tell them. They were protecting you, lying to me, ever so slightly, not knowing that I knew that they had to be, because I knew that you were so much more than what the world saw. They didn't know what had passed between us, and that I had a right to know. I should have said to them; we are lovers and she will want me to know where she is. She will want me there. She will *want me.*'

They were both crying; tears streaming down their cheeks.

Thys couldn't speak.

This was an onslaught, an attack. It was a soliloquy, a rhetoric to which she had no defense, no response, nothing adequate or rehearsed that meant anything anymore, because there was nothing to answer for. She had prepared her own version of this speech, in bed, grinding her teeth, and had done so for probably a year after she had been abandoned.

Abandoned.

Yes; they had both been abandoned.

Falsely, unintentionally, but somehow, Thys was starting to realise, not without malice. Someone had done this, purposefully. It had been a premeditated uprooting of what had been growing between them, just as it had sprouted.

Thys sniffed and Tarni jolted; as though, even though she had been staring at her the whole time with her golden, fiery eyes, and their pitiless blackhole pits, she had truly seen her, and not the memories of her absence, for the first time since they had returned.

And then she knew what Thys was thinking.

Tarni sighed, her heart shaking. 'I know. I knew when I saw you at that awful, ruined house. You looked as hurt as I felt; to see each other again. I'm sorry; I… couldn't help but play this out. It's been on my mind for so long.'

There was silence a few seconds.

'Who would do this?' Thys gasped, quietly; incredulous. 'Are there Inner Earth… I don't know? Elders? Who would forbid it, come between us?'

Tarni shook her head. 'Maybe, but I could not detect anything of that nature. And they would – tell me! They would not do this, they would explain; not this way, with intent… to *hurt*.'

There was a terrible twist in Thys' stomach.

All that year, the first year of the war, she had stayed in the astral, thinking that Tarni had abandoned her, returning to the apartment maybe once every couple of months, avoiding her friends and family, believing that Tarni had changed her mind; that she was one of those people, more sophisticated than her, who could move from one lover to another without attachment.

And so now, she still had three lovers, whom she could only consider in terms of function.

'I have some friends, now, here, who have made a terrible mistake; not exactly like we did, but there are similarities. I don't have many friends, but I should warm them, and… can you wait here until I get back?'

Tarni stared at her; there was strong desire in the look.

She walked forward and raised her hand.

With the back of her slender fingers, she brushed Thys' long blonde hair back over her shoulder.

Someone else in the penthouse cleared their throat.

Tarni spun about.

Mirabelle Contrelle stood halfway down the stairs.

'Oh sorry! I didn't mean to – is that you, Thys?'

Thys cleared her throat, somehow finding composure.

'Belle?'

Thys and Tarni exchanged conspiratorial glances.

Mirabelle padded down the transparent, open steps in bare feet, wearing only a large tee that went down to her knees. The tee was white, with a black, electric-blue and bright-violet print of the poster for the movie *Silent Lucidity* down it. She crossed to the kitchen area, to the side of the bar behind them. The tee was basically a poster of Krimson Azureus, and the last thing Thys felt she needed at that point was that precious, pretentious face staring out at her.

'You still hate her, huh?' Tarni uttered, low and intimate.

Mirabelle cleared her throat. 'Sorry Tarn, I didn't know you still used the place. My pin worked on the elevator, figured whoever was here didn't mind sharing. Fucking place is big enough, eh?'

She was right, Thys thought. It was four, five times as big as her own luxury apartment.

'We… just needed somewhere to talk. Sorry, I didn't check.'

'Mitch back yet?' She took out some orange juice and gulped it out of the carton as they watched, then gasped. 'Sorry. Figured Heatherette wasn't returning either, so I went out last night. Standard procedure.' She sniffed the juice. 'Is this okay?' Then she looked around. 'Smells like the zoo in here!'

Thys had not seen Mirabelle Contrelle in person since Paramatta, although she had spoken to her many times. Once again, she immediately liked her; they would have made a good trio, and in a way, she supposed they still did; Heather's trusted PA, her father's trusted PA, and – well, the third; the reason they needed to be trusted.

Mirabelle had a catlike grace as she slunk about, hungover in her giant tee with her nipples poking up where Krimson's eyes were, but her sleekness seemed totally natural and honest. She had retained that sort of wild-child persona from before; just the kind of girl with whom Heather would have torn shreds out of the next available city with, on a daily basis, way back when. But thinking on that; she hadn't remembered Mirabelle to be so young, given that she had apparently been Heather's partner in crime, literally. If Thys had to guess she'd say that she and Mirabelle were all around the same age, too; mid-twenties. But Heather was… what now? Thirty-seven? Eight?

'You're taller than I remember,' Mirabelle smiled, putting the orange juice back in the fridge. Her hair remained bleach-blonde, in a ruffled pageboy cut; she had a lot of hair and it held the look well. The nose ring and the smeared black eyeliner made her look cute and playful as opposed to what remained, in this day and age, of their independent cache.

'Belle...' Tarni sighed, as though she were used to this, but wasn't prepared to put up with it today. '...we need the room, okay...?'

'It's okay,' Thys shrugged. 'It's nice to see you again; put a real face to the name, as opposed to a memory.'

'Not that I need to do that,' Mirabelle smiled.

Thys was stunned by that; it was like she'd flashed her boobs, or passed a sexy note, that only she could see. But it was just a smile, just a casual smile.

Thys was puzzled; what the hell?

She tried to take it in as Mirabelle turned and moved back to the stairs. She had the face that might have comfortably belonged to either a French actress, or a French porn star; elfin-pixie, with a pert nose and a small mouth, but full lips and high cheekbones, with penetrating, almost ethereal blue eyes behind long, lazy, beguiling eyelids. And her dark, thinly accented eyebrows made her shock of pageboy blonde even sexier.

Then the notion hit Thys like a slap in the face.

She's a bit like me, Thys thought, *without Pandora.*

Mirabelle noticed her noticing.

Thys saw that she was well accustomed to that.

'You used to party with Heather?' Thys smiled. 'How did she keep up?'

'You know,' Mirabelle smiled, 'I never knew. I thought she was a bit older than me, but it wasn't until she got it together with your old man that I found out it was, like a decade or something. You'd never have known; she outlasted me almost every time!' She shrugged. 'But she was always a one man gal – go figure!' Mirabelle laughed as she made her way back to the stairs, flicking her gaze up to the bedrooms. 'More for the rest of us!'

Then she scampered away and was gone.

Tarni stared at her as she vanished, then turned to Thys and shrugged.

'That's her line, and it never ends. She's let me down massively as many times as she's totally saved my arse.'

'You don't trust her?'

'I trust her; within those parameters.'

'I should go,' Thys sighed. 'Xylata was genuinely worried. She almost ordered me.'

Tarni looked at her, her eyes almost fully black and filled with deep concern.

'We're not going to get it back again, are we?'

Thys couldn't tell if she was hurt, or just sad, or simply clarifying.

And she had, for the most part, all this time, held firm to her boycott of reading her friends.

'There's something even psychics don't take into account very often. Certainly science and medicine don't seem to register it as much as they should. And that is that emotion is a physical thing. Strong emotions… they release chemicals into the body that make us feel, and the stronger that feeling is, the longer we feel it. Eventually, we come down, but if we go over things enough times in our minds, our minds don't know the difference, and it's like reliving that event, or that emotion, over and over. Our brains do it naturally; relive things over and over, as a way of comprehending things, analyzing things that shocked or surprised or changed us, things that impacted, and mattered, so we can fully understand them, and perhaps be prepared if they happen again.'

Thys shrugged.

'They're very glitchy, someone told me once.'

Tarni was silent.

'It's a theory, anyway. But eventually the events, the shocks, the thrills, the delights, whatever, they become hardwired; they become a concrete reality, so far as our memories are concerned, and we view those events through a reality tunnel of our own making; on our own terms, through our own lens. We don't like this person, or we love that person, because we remember and keep reinforcing the things that created those emotions in the first place. It becomes part of us, something emotional, and physical. And if we're right, those people keep reinforcing it themselves, right back at us. But…'

'I understand.'

'Do you?'

'I'm the same. I was angry with you for abandoning me for so long – I think I'm still angry with you. And now I know you didn't, I'm just non-specifically angry with you. Even though, seeing you again, I still –'

Thys held her breath.

'I still want to be with you,' Tarni offered. 'I want you – around.'

Thys let her breath go.

'I will be. But let's see if it comes back. When I get back.'

'Okay.'

'Okay.'

There was a pause that was not awkward, but not comfortable.

It was just – there.

Thys looked around. 'I wonder if I need a door?'

CHAPTER 97

After a flash of *silverblue* and a room made of moonlight, Thys found her way back to the Lunar Terminal, where the dreamers were trying to organize a system, but in the meantime seemed not to realise that many doors were remaining open, or vacant.

She and Heff had edged their way past the cast of her favorite eighties sitcom (exactly as they had looked back then, but all wearing checkered flannelette pajamas) and simply gone through one. She had more experience knowing where she was in the astral, as opposed to simply dreaming, she assumed.

They gapped straight back to The Fork, where Harding was back behind the bar, musing.

'Clever girl that one,' he stated.

'Which one?'

Harding smiled.

'Tarni is in the penthouse suite at Cleverco Castle with Mirabelle. Safest place to be right now. Hiding in plain sight, keeping an eye open. I'll gap in tomorrow when I get back, and we can all meet there when Dad and Heather are here again.'

'I feel bad about joking, at the mansion. I did not know it was real between you. I did not realise you were hurt, that you still felt it.'

Thys nodded, her expression making it clear there were no hard feelings. 'Harding; someone deliberately kept us apart. Deliberately stopped us communicating at a vital time. I may have lost something very precious, very valuable.'

'I am sorry.'

'I want to find out who did that, and fuck them up.'

'Very well. I can help you with that if you so desire. And I can advise you one way or another, when the time comes. Like many things, vengeance is nine tenths anticipation, but unlike many, nine times out of ten the results are nine tenths disappointing.'

'What about the other tenth?'

'You will know that, when the time comes. Whether you are the sort of person who gets pleasure from revenge. Should I be expecting a guest to watch over at the apartment? Will you try again with her?'

Thys looked over to Heff.

'How many ninjas do you think he'll need? Per day?'

'He is a dog. But he is the size of a bear. I'd say, we have some googling, and some calculations, to do.'

Thys nodded. 'I mean, he ate, like, six ninjas this morning, though?'

'He doesn't seem hungry. Maybe we wait for him to tell us?'

Thys looked up, out of the room, toward her Paw.

'I never thought…'

Harding watched her, then spoke. 'Some people are never honest with themselves. You don't like boys or girls, you like a certain kind of person. And you never know if a person is that kind of person before it's too late. Because by then, you like them.'

'How the hell do you know that?'

'Because I know someone else, exactly like that.' Harding threw back the last of his drink and walked out from behind the bar. 'We have not been to the Omega Cove for some time. Drop me there, then go. I will be okay. The women there are not so familiar to me, and I am not so familiar to them. All being well, I am looking forward to this.'

That seemed to snap her out of it and she rolled her eyes.

'Clint and Arnie, huh?'

'And Mel. For Australia, they say I have some Mel in me. Not the crazy part though.'

'Really?'

'The good crazy… maybe.'

'I'd stick to Bryan Brown if I were you.'

'Hmmm. If you say so.'

CHAPTER 98

The doorman's chime went off.

'Intercom,' Thys told the house.

It was Zeke. It was always Zeke.

She liked that, liked Zeke.

'There's a young lady down here to see you, Miss. She says you know her, but she won't tell me her name. She says she's been in your apartment before.'

Thys' heart skipped a beat.

'Do you think she's telling the truth?'

'I…? Ummm; she does seem familiar, Miss Pyne.'

Thys assessed the security monitor. She couldn't see anyone there; she was using some kind of obfuscation.

'Send her up.'

Thys waited.

What the hell would she say to her after all this time? Six months? That she had now slept with that third man, whom she felt she was torturing? And that it had ended in disaster, when he had realised that he wasn't the only one? Just as she always had known it would? Tell her that?

Why did people do these things?

But... also, that he'd made something spectacular? Because of her; because of them? Something that would stand the test of time, she was sure! And, surely, withstand the temporary, shrill frequency of the critics and haters... ssomething that, *somehow*, would be more important than… anything?

Also; that he had given her an idea?

An idea so bold, and radical, as to win the war once and for all? To free Earth? That she dare not share with anyone?

And that, all of that might not have happened if she *had* come back to her, and they *had* kept fucking, woman to woman?

Or... should she tell her that she wanted to pick up?

That she had never met another woman she wanted to taste?

And had thought that she never would, never could; and yet would turn her back on all three of her men, in an instant, if only she would just tell her…?

And where had she been and how dare she and where had she fucking well been and *how fucking dare she*?

The elevator dinged.

Thys stood in the empty space; the vestibule.

It had been a humid night, their last night together. The middle of one of the hottest, most humid summers on record.

Now it was the middle of winter.

Thys had been wearing a sports bra and a tee, with a long jumper, with her knickers and track pants and full length uggs. She quickly took the uggs off, and the tracks pants, and then, very quickly, the bra; she wanted to look sexy, available, and then, possibly, not be.

The doors opened.

A woman stood there. She stood with her hands behind her back, wearing a lavender karategi, tied with a dark violet belt. Her features were serene, and plainly gorgeous. But she was about a foot shorter than Tarni had been. She was, essentially, an utterly different physical specimen in almost every human regard.

'Xylata…?' Thys assumed, somewhat shocked and doing her best not to sound massively disappointed. 'Are you supposed to be Seyfried or Johansson or… what?'

The woman smiled, as though to say;

…no.

Thys thought; she has the most amazing hair.

It was a light lavender violet that seemed almost natural, with interwoven light blonde; thick and long and lustrous and falling about the shoulders of the white robe, draped down over her back and bosom like a glorious fur; long, very long, and naturally voluminous and high-crowned. She looked Northern European,

Scandinavian or Nordic; or… that particular kind of…?

Now she realised it wasn't Tarni, and the idea of Tarni was fading…

Beauty.

She was beautiful in another way entirely.

It was sinking in.

She'd seen this beauty before, bowing at a distance, then rising and vanishing.

'Hello, Amethyst Pyne. I've entered your home the correct way – ? The formal entrance? I mean no disrespect. I am aware of your emotional hurt. I feel it empathically, as does the whole of the cove, and I would wish it to be resolved for you. We like Tarni. Tarni is funny, and good, and brave.'

'Yes…'

The woman shrugged, beguilingly, and smiled. It wasn't quite a shy smile; just a smile that was a tad awkward, from someone who was behaving an edge more forward than was usually within their comfort zone.

'I know you haven't really ever seen me out of the water, or in third density. But – this is what I look like in third density. I overheard your giant, Harding, saying that you should know how to fight properly in third density, when you told him what happened. It was painfully apparent, that night, that you do not know how. The Pan have not trained you well in the ways of men. And also…'

She seemed more thoughtful now, almost pitiful, but not in a nasty way; it was empathic, real. She felt for her.

'…I personally do not like to feel your loneliness. So I am here to train you. To take your mind off the things that are hurting you. If this is inappropriate, I will go. But, I have been around a while on this planet now, and I know the subtle vibration of a woman who needs company. Who needs… a new friend?'

Thys gulped.

Bright-violet eyes.

'Seysh?'

THE PANDORA INHERITANCE

PART (..)

HEATHER REDUX

CHAPTER 99

When they arrived, they were surprised to see that there was a wide, barge-like construction in the middle of the desert, as though the remnant of some long-lost, ancient riverland society, ages ago abandoned to the long drought.

It was sitting flat, however, and bordered with a veranda and a café-style landing. There were glass doors and windows all around, and inside there was bar and seating. The whole thing was beautiful, as though it had been designed to be in that very place, since the dawn of time, yet its architecture was ultra-modern and sleek.

Mitch and Heather said nothing as they arrived and were greeted by one of several waiters who offered them each their favorite beverages; Heather a locally brewed root beer from her childhood neighborhood, Mitch the same, but a ginger beer.

The drinks were still in the bottle, as they preferred, but chilled.

Slowly the other guests began to arrive atop the rise, until the pressure upon the waiters to deliver drinks was practically an attack; still, the staff managed with aplomb and before long, seventy-odd people had realised that they had a stunning and rarified view of the Simpson Desert from every angle, on a spectacularly beautiful day.

'Did you think there'd be a bar way out here?' Heather asked finally, swigging her root beer as she stared out at the desert through the wide windows.

'Well, it is a tourist destination… isn't it?'

'Mitch, I googled this place before we left; people take days to four-wheel drive out here just for the hell of it. It can't be reached for half the year because of flooding, a hundred kilometers away, or something. People have to bring like a month's worth of gas –

I mean *petrol*, and water, and come in *teams*. It's beautiful, but it really, truly is the middle of out-back-nowhere. There isn't a hotel for light years. They – I mean – we – must have built this place purpose-specific. And I mean; just for the press launch.'

'But –' Mitch looked around. 'It's so *well appointed…*'

'…must have cost us a *mint.*'

'Well, we did as much for that third Eve launch, the one in the rainforest… I mean, we do own a multi-billion dollar –'

'Mitch – *what's that?*'

She could see something, just over the horizon. They were standing perpendicular to another, much longer undulating sand dune, but on the rise above it, something was shimmering; something huge and silver-gray.

And it seemed to be growing; if not actually coming toward them.

Behind them, near the bar, Frieda Humphries seemed to have noticed the fact that they had noticed, and cleared her throat.

'Ladies and gentlemen, I'm going to keep this very short. Welcome! We are honored to have our Executive CEOs and, well, let's say it, *bosses*, so far as most of us are concerned, here with us today. And for those who know them as I do, we're pleased also to call them *friends.*'

There was light, polite applause.

Many false smiles, but some genuine ones too.

And that's about as much as you can hope for, Heather had long ago decided.

Frieda made some elaborate moves across her Eve tablet, which rested securely in the crook of her arm, and suddenly the glass around them twinkled like fairy dust and simply fell away like sand, and was gone.

'Bloody hell!' Mitch gasped. He turned to Frieda.

Frieda was a tall, slender woman with dark brown hair who, Heather was sure, had undergone Regene treatment so as to more resemble Frida Lyngstad, in her days as a singer with ABBA. She was attractive, no doubt, and had carried the resemblance, no doubt, to the maximum legal limits, right up to the edge of copyright law and physiognomic license. Heather was pleased about that; Mitch in particular had worked long and hard, alongside Oliver Hines of all people, who through their work together had done more to redeem himself than anyone would ever have thought possible, to ensure that Regene's cosmetics range could not go too far. Frieda was beautiful, had her own face, everyone knew what she was going for, and that she'd gotten there.

Everybody won.

But right now she looked more beautiful, more herself, more proud and elated and glowing, than she ever had.

She smiled at Mitch and he reexamined where the glass had been.

What had happened had been like a like a special effect; like a computer-generated animation.

But it had been real.

'So…?' Heather mused, half to Mitch and half to herself, half excited and half concerned. 'This was a computer hologram or something?'

'Or…something.'

'No, wait, I touched it, I remember, I…'

They were now standing on an empty platform; the entire structure had glistered away.

'…I touched the glass over there, before. It was real. It was solid.'

'I know,' Mitch responded quietly.

There were whisperings and mutterings as they all adjusted to the sudden direct sunlight, the sudden heat, the sudden… well, everything.

'Ladies and gentlemen. We have done it.'

Mutterings, whisperings, even fear.

'Nano-technology,' Mitch nodded to himself, speaking loudly.

'Indeed,' Frieda smiled. 'Please, keep your eye on the horizon.'

All eyes turned; nobody noticed that a large canopy was

erecting around them, out of nothing, to once again keep the sun at bay.

Gradually, slowly but very surely, an enormous structure was rising out of the desert, now way above the curve of the dune. Layer upon layer, again like a digital effect, a massive building was emerging. A path began to rise and flow toward them; a Yellow Brick Road appearing spontaneously out of nothing.

'Please!' Frieda gestured broadly to Mitch and Heather.

They stepped from the platform, directly onto the yellow bricks, and walked. They were solid, Mitch saw; they might even have been actual gold.

'They're gold,' Shandi said, coming up behind them. 'Solid gold pavers…'

'You sure?'

'Trust me, I know.'

'Then this really is *the* game changer…' Mitch uttered. 'Nothing can ever be the same after this…'

'What's happening?' Shandi asked.

'This is like science fiction, surely Mitch?' Heather demanded. 'I know what it is, but… nano technology is a permanent ten-year horizon. It was never supposed to…'

'Never supposed to what?" Shandi asked as the neared the top of the rise.

Mitch spoke softly, with concern. 'Nano technology is a game changing science. It involves creating machines so small, that they can alter atomic structure. It's the genuine Philosopher's Stone. Desert into water, water into wine. Lead into gold, gold, back into sand again…'

Heather started to feel quite panicky then. 'There have been… limited applications for years, but… nobody has ever cracked…'

'So you mean – they've created this gold path – out of sand?' Shandi was, quite rightly, astonished. 'By creating machines that… turn sand molecules into *gold molecules?*'

Mitch stopped and looked at Shandi.

'That's exactly what I mean!'

Frieda was behind them, and caught up.

Heather frowned at her.

'Is this real? It's not an illusion?'

'This is a Cleverco breakthrough. Exclusive. It happened after the merge; two major companies developing on their own, suddenly mashed together. The mash became a mesh, and out of that…'

'I see.'

'Everyone here has top Cleverco security clearance. That's why you don't really know any of them. It's strictly "need to know". That's why we couldn't tell you until now. Everyone here knows who you are, of course. Many of these people are the research physicists and programmers who developed the –'

Suddenly Frieda was looking over Mitch's shoulder, and past Heather; not to the shimmering silver-gray leviathan that was still emerging in the desert, but to something else. Mitch turned to look as well. There was something hovering up in the air. Then another, then another. Mitch was staring up, and took a few more steps up the golden path.

'Not merkabas…' Heather heard Mitch utter. 'Not anything I've ever…'

There was someone, some thing, new to the party.

Heather watched as Mitch shielded his eyes and stared up.

'What the…?'

Then Heather was suddenly aware of something else; another person standing beside her who hadn't been there a few seconds before.

A man whose face Heather could not immediately get a fix upon.

Frieda looked back from Mitch, and the things in the sky.

'It's not supposed to do that…' Frieda uttered, deeply concerned.

She sounded almost afraid.

'Do what?' Shandi asked, staring at the man-shaped blob.

'The nanos; they're programmed not to appear in human

form. It's never happened bef – '

'Heather Pyne.'

The sand-man spoke. It was statement, not a question. Perhaps a form of address. He was only a rough approximation of the human form; humanoid at best, like a tremendous effort by a child on the beach to build a sandcastle that looked like a real man.

And yet, he had spoken.

'Yes. It's Everett actually. I kept…'

'You are here – we are sorry.'

'Who – what are you?'

'We tried to send word but – we are sorry.'

The desert began to rumble.

'Oh no,' Heather uttered. She looked to the sand man. 'Are you in league with the Sirians? Have we pissed them off?'

'No. This cannot be helped. It cannot be stopped. It is very ancient, and we are very new. We are so sorry.'

The desert around them began to erupt.

The structure had emerged, fully completed, over the horizon.

But Heather wasn't watching that; she had seen that before.

It was the things erupting out of the desert that had taken her attention.

With fear.

With the sheer, ludicrous terror of them.

'What – !?' she exclaimed. 'Mitch!'

Mitch was still a number of steps away, up ahead. He turned back and stared at her down the gold path with horrified confusion in his eyes.

'I can't gap!'

'Neither can I!'

Heather turned to the sand-man. 'Do something!'

'We cannot – we do not know – how?'

Heather was desperate.

All around, people were screaming.

'My company created you! This is an order! All previous orders are countermanded! Whatever you can do – do it!'

The sand-man seemed sad.

'We need to kill you, Heather Pyne. We are very sorry.'

Heather looked down the gold path, at Mitch, and their eyes met.

'Oh well…'

She called out, her voice shaking, tears in her eyes, knowing she would never reach him in time, to hold him one last time.

She smiled at him; her world-famous smile, just for him.

He smiled back, as he called out in response.

'Fun while it –'

Then together they realised.

'Amy's Plan!'

And then the screams carried across the sand, and evaporated into nothingness.

THE PANDORA INHERITANCE

EPILOGUE

UN/SAFE

CHAPTER 100

She was going to leave.

To hide along her tour of The Places Where Nobody Knows.

Gap to Tutto's, then on to Craterfall...

She was going to take Heff back to the grotto there.

Where she had first heard him, where he had first seen her again, sniffed her, but been too afraid of completely crossing over.

She wanted to see him take a bath and have a swim.

And then on they would go.

The full tour; the whole day.

She really was.

But there was something that was bugging her.

A thought, from earlier in the day...

A memory; a spike.

They arrived in the vestibule.

She knelt before him and made the fists over her heart again., then she put both palms down on the tiles, still looking him in the eyes.

'Home.'

He licked her face.

'Ruh.'

'Come with me.'

Thys made her way from the vestibule into the master bedroom, past the Californian King, unmade from the last time she had slept in it, months ago, and went directly into the walk-in.

Heff was sniffing everything along the way, but did not pause.

The walk-in was basically a long corridor between the master bed and bathroom, with sliding doors that opened to built-in wardrobe space on either side, leading up to head-height set of drawers, facing out at the end. She didn't turn the light on, but went to directly the end and turned, offering Heff an upright, open palm, like 'stop'. He did, and sat, taking up the whole entrance, staring down the thin, dark, wardrobe corridor at her.

She made a fist.

Guard.

He stiffened, and sat still, his ears spiked up.

Thys opened the middle drawer and reached to the back, where her nible fingers flicked a tiny latch. As she removed her hand, the drawers slid away to the right, into end of the wardrobe.

And there it was; at the back, in the wall.

The safe.

Well; one of the safes.

She could not recall if Tarni had insisted that this be the dummy, or the real one.

But, in the end, Thys figured, if you had two safes, you had two safes, and that was that.

There was an electronic password, which triggered the old-school, left-right-left tumbler lock.

She typed in the password.

FizzyLollyWater2014.

The tumbler was released.

She turned it once to the left; once to the right, and once to the left again.

Special numbers.

It clicked.

Just then, her Eve went off.

It hadn't, almost all day, because of all the blocks.

But it was from Qwerty.

Sent three hours ago; but just coming through now.

Curious.

It was a link.

To her Wikipedia page.

She opened it.

Amethyst Pyne

From Wikipedia, the free encyclopedia

Amethyst Pyne was the eldest daughter of <u>Mitchell Pyne</u> and <u>Janine Norway</u> and was the primary heiress to the so-called <u>Cleverco fortune</u> until her suicide elevated her sister <u>Jade Pyne</u> to primary inheritor. It is believed that Pyne's death, ruled as self-inflicted by the New South Wales Coroner's Office, was a reaction to the untimely deaths of both her father <u>Mitchell Pyne</u> and his second wife, <u>Heather Everett</u>, in a helicopter accident in outback Australia several days before, along with the recent untimely deaths of several close family friends.

Personal Life

Amethyst Pyne was a notorious <u>recluse</u>,[1] falsely creating several fake <u>charitable foundations</u> to disguise her chronic agoraphobia, and subsequent chronic bipolar depression, until revelations after her death revealed that she had lived primarily in a private apartment on Sydney's upper-north shore for most of her prolonged absences from society at large [2].

Because so little is known about her life, and reclusive nature, there remain to this day many <u>internet conspiracy theories</u>, most of which dispute the suicide ruling and claim that Pyne was murdered. Theories as to why and how remain numerous and highly varied, and are ultimately interconnected with other conspiracy theories involving the tragic series of other deaths that surrounded her at the time, known colloquially as <u>The Cleverco Curse</u>, and preceded her own.

Main article: <u>Amethyst Pyne Conspiracy Theories</u>

CHAPTER 101

'Jesus, Mary...'
She gulped.
Her gut twisted.
Her hands were shaking.
She could not imagine seeing anything more startling.
Until she realised that the door to the safe had swung open.
There inside was the stolen amethyst Arcana.

THERE ENDS

The Pandorans
Book Three
"The Omega Sequence"

Next in the series is:

The Pandorans
Book Four
"The Pandora Arcana"

For further exciting titles in this series visit...

www.GalexyTales.com

THE PANDORANS:

Book One: The Pandora Sequence
Book Two: The Pandora Inheritance
Book Three: The Omega Sequence
Book Four: The Pandora Arcana
Book Five: The Sirens Sequence
Book Six: The Daughters of Pandora
Book Seven: The Lucifer Sequence

(return to the front of the book for other titles,

and keep searching

"Galexy Tales" and "Pandorans"

at amazon.com!)

ACKNOWLEDGEMENTS

MANY, MANY THANKS TO:

Melissa Sheldrick, and Romana
Stan & Gennie James
Lily McDonnell, Gretel Newman-Sugrue
Pat McNamara, Gary Turner
Travis Pollard, Adam Dutkiewicz
Kay Leanne, Julie Dinsdale and Michael Aspden
Chris & Ange Collings, Adam Vale
Greg C. Grace

Gallifrey Stands!

Alex James,
March 20209

ABOUT THE AUTHOR

Alex James is a writer who lives in and is inspired by Adelaide, South Australia.

Alex studied European History, Classical Mythology, Film Studies and Screenwriting under the Communications and Liberal Studies banners at the University of South Australia.

Between 1992 and 2005 he wrote many, many, many outlines, treatments, concept documents, bibles, pilots and screenplays, for just about every active Australian production company there was.

From 2008-2014 he was an in-house writer for Angel-Phoenix Media, who published his first two e-book novels, *The Pandora Sequence* and *Venus AI*, both of which were launched at the 2013 San Diego Comic-Con.

Alex's most recent works are ongoing epic novel sagas which include *The Saga of The Urban Sorcerers*, *Amazon Seven*, *Dark Streets*, *The Chronicles of The Terraguard*, and *The Pandorans*.

He publishes via his own independent imprint, Galexy Tales.

"If not you...then who?"

9 780994 461896